RETURN TO VALETTO

RETURN
· TO ·
VALETTO

DOMINIC SMITH

FARRAR, STRAUS AND GIROUX   NEW YORK

Farrar, Straus and Giroux
120 Broadway, New York 10271

Printed in the United States of America
First edition, 2023

Library of Congress Cataloging-in-Publication Data
Names: Smith, Dominic, 1971– author.
Title: Return to Valetto / Dominic Smith.
Description: First edition. | New York : Farrar, Straus and Giroux,
    2023.
Identifiers: LCCN 2023001269 | ISBN 9780374607685 (hardcover)
Subjects: LCGFT: Novels.
Classification: LCC PS3619.M5815 R48 2023 | DDC 813/.6—dc23/
    eng/20230123
LC record available at https://lccn.loc.gov/2023001269

Designed by Abby Kagan

Our books may be purchased in bulk for promotional, educational, or business
use. Please contact your local bookseller or the Macmillan Corporate and
Premium Sales Department at 1-800-221-7945, extension 5442, or by email at
MacmillanSpecialMarkets@macmillan.com.

www.fsgbooks.com
www.twitter.com/fsgbooks • www.facebook.com/fsgbooks

1   3   5   7   9   10   8   6   4   2

This project is supported in part by the National Endowment for the Arts.

PART ONE

The Saint's Staircase hangs down from the cliffs of Valetto, spiraling into thin air. It's all that remains of the house in Umbria where a disciple of St. Francis of Assisi lived until 1695, when a massive earthquake cleaved a third of the town into the canyons below. Because Valetto sits on a pedestal of volcanic rock—an island jutting up from the valley floor—the spiral staircase appears to float, a twist of wrought iron eerily suspended between the chestnut groves below and the twelfth-century church spire above.

Over the centuries, as Valetto has dwindled from a town of three thousand to just ten full-time residents, including my mother's family, the staircase has become a favorite spot for reckless tourists and ruminating locals. Some have claimed otherworldly vistas from the stairs: apparitions of the medieval saint or visitations from the dead. As a boy, when I visited the town during the summers, I'd get up early to see the fog rolling up the riverine mouth of the valley, and climb down onto the bottom lip of the stairwell so I could stand sheathed inside a cloud for fifteen minutes, watching my hands slowly disappear at the railing.

But then one morning, as I descended, my throat thickened with dread as an enormous figure loomed toward me through the haze. And that feeling returned over the years. It came for me on suspension bridges and high rooftops, in an elevator stuck between floors, and in the waiting rooms of hospitals. I'd find myself descending through that fog, halfway down the stairs and filling with dread before I reminded myself that it was all a trick of light and perspective, that it wasn't real. So many times, I told myself that figure must have been simply a shaft of early sunlight glinting down the aperture of the narrow valley, projecting and refracting my silhouette into a cloud of vapor. Still, I avoided the stairwell until one harrowing November night nearly four decades later.

φ

I specialize in abandonment. This had always been my quip at academic conferences and faculty gatherings, but it wasn't until I published a book about vanishing Italian towns and villages that people realized how serious I was. *Famous for Dying: A Social History of Abandoned Italy* was well reviewed in the journals and sparked a series of invitations from universities in Rome, Milan, and Turin. And so, after a two-year absence, I found myself preparing to return to Italy for six months in the autumn of 2011.

Between conference panels and guest lectures, I intended to revisit some of the places where I'd done my research over the course of many summers. From Craco in the south, to the hillsides of Umbria and northern Piedmont, I'd walked along empty cobblestone streets and overgrown trails, taking photographs and interviewing current and former residents, including my aunts and my grandmother. Sometimes there was a single holdout, like the hermit in Abruzzo who'd lived in a deconsecrated church for twenty-five years, and sometimes there were a few families left, or no one at all. And although the towns and villages all had their own abandonment stories—landslides, earthquakes, the ravages of time and urbanization—there was always somebody who dreamed of a comeback, a return. That hope, however naïve, is perhaps what drew me to these desolate places to begin with: the heroic idea of going up against history.

On my college campus in Michigan, my "desolation book project" was celebrated as its own comeback of sorts. I'd lost my wife and mother within a four-year span, and so it was said I'd written an important social history from the crucible of my own grief. Just before I flew to Rome, the dean of liberal arts, a *Beowulf* specialist who spoke some Italian, hosted a small going-away party for me and gave a toast that ended with *in bocca al lupo!*, into the mouth of the wolf! Technically, this means good luck in Italian, but leaving his mouth it took on an Anglo-Saxon menace—violent and foreboding—as if he were rallying me into the carnivorous maw of the future, as if he knew that something was waiting to swallow me whole.

That swallowing began with an email from my aunt Iris the night before my flight. My mother had died a year earlier and left me the stone cottage behind her family's medieval villa in Umbria. For six months, Valetto and the cottage would be my home, just as it had been during my childhood summers. Iris lived in the villa with her sisters, Violet and Rose, all of them elderly and widowed, and my ninety-nine-year-old grandmother. The email's subject line read *Una Occupante Abusiva*, and it took me a moment to port the phrase into English and realize it meant a squatter. A female squatter, to be precise. In her winding, academic Italian—Iris was a retired sociology professor—she explained that a middle-aged woman, a northerner, had recently shown up at the villa with some correspondence from Aldo Serafino, my maternal grandfather, and taken up residence in my mother's cottage.

During World War II, Aldo had sympathized with the partisans—an umbrella group of Italians resisting the fascists and occupying Germans—but he went into hiding in the spring of 1944 and was never heard from again. My grandmother had attempted to find him during and after the war but eventually she gave up. The woman from the north asserted that her family had been promised the stone cottage at the back of the villa in exchange for the assistance they'd afforded Aldo, who'd joined the resistance movement in Piedmont. She intended, nearly three-quarters of a century later, to take up her family's rightful claim.

φ

After spending a weekend in Rome with my daughter, Susan, I took the train to Orvieto, where Milo Scorza, the villa's handyman, was scheduled to pick me up. Susan was completing a Ph.D. in England and had to get back for a conference, but she would return later in the month for my grandmother's hundredth birthday. And so I found myself alone in my second-class car, looking out the window and occasionally paging through Luigi Barzini's *The Italians*, a neglected classic that chronicled the nation's quirks and obsessions. It was a book I hadn't read since I was a teenager, when I was first trying to demystify my mother and her Umbrian family.

Normally, on Italian trains, I'm invisible because I resemble a vacationing Anglo-Italian librarian in a pair of scuffed Swiss alpine boots, or a semi-retired bureaucrat who makes bird feeders on the weekends. Kindly, bookish, a vaguely Roman nose. But this was November 2, *il giorno dei Morti*, when Italians head out to ancestral villages and gravesites to pay their respects to the dead, and so my lack of flowers drew accusatory stares from passengers cradling white and gold chrysanthemums. I pretended not to notice, glancing between my book and the landscape out the window.

The woman sitting across from me—seventies, wool skirt, silk headscarf—kept looking up from her knitting at the Polaroid I was using as a bookmark. Taken the day before, the photo showed an Italian man, dressed as a gladiator, standing between Susan and me in front of the Colosseum. He was holding a plastic sword to my throat, grinning into the camera, while Susan's head was thrown back in laughter. I had the glassy, hangdog expression of a fish that has just been plucked from a lake.

I could see that the woman was assembling a bread-crumb trail of clues: the unmarried left hand, the photograph with the blonde in her twenties, the scuffed boots and my lack of flowers. I knew from my grandmother and my aunts that older Italian women were capable of deductions that bordered on the omniscient, that in a few lacerating eye-strikes they could infer your marital status, your religion and intestinal health, whether you slept through the night. And I felt sure that I was being regarded by this woman as a shambling drifter without morals or respect for the dead. To set her mind at ease, I looked up from my book and into her Old Testament face. *Mia figlia*, I said, my daughter. For good measure, I told her in Italian that I was a widower, that it had taken me the better part of five years to remove my wedding band, that Susan was getting her Ph.D. in economics at Oxford, and that I was very proud of her. This information passed through her like a muscle relaxant as she returned to knitting a tiny mauve sock.

Out the window, Orvieto came into view like some floating colossus from an ocean liner—rising a thousand feet above the plains of Umbria, its stone walls and rooftops resting on a plateau of volcanic rock. *Italy is seismic*, I'd written in my book, *an ancient rider forever shifting in her saddle*. So much of what I'd seen during my research, moving from one dwindling or emptied-out place to another, could be traced to seismology, to the honeycombing of rock and clay beneath a Bronze Age or medieval settlement. *Italians have been paying homage to their geological overlords since the beginning*. But somehow Orvieto stood intact and preserved, presiding over Umbria from its lofty perch. Less than an hour away, my mother's ancestral town had been sliding into the valley for more than three centuries.

φ

At the train station, I waited for Milo Scorza. This was the new part of Orvieto, at the base of the ancient butte, where squat apartment buildings were painted pea green and salmon pink. There were metal shutters above the windows and rusting balconies full of desiccated plants. A few old men were sitting in plastic chairs, smoking and watching the trains glint across the plains. Foreigners often want Italians to live under leafy pergolas and terra-cotta roofs, to live on rocky outcrops that overlook the shocking azure of the Mediterranean, but plenty of them live in concrete monstrosities of the post-Mussolini era, in buildings that were made quickly and cheaply in the upswing of Italy's recovery after the war. And it's not uncommon to see these drab apartment blocks within a quarter mile of an ornate Gothic cathedral or Romanesque church.

Across the street, the funicular—half school bus, half gondola—made its narrow-gauged ascent up the steep hillside into a tunnel of trees, ferrying people to the ancient city above. As I stood waiting, a memory overwhelmed me—a flash of standing behind the sunlit windows of the funicular one drowsy summer afternoon, between Clare and Susan, Susan still a girl, holding their hands as I watched the plains dim away. I could remember feeling Clare's silver bracelet against the back of my thumb, the sensation somehow threaded through with the flickering light of ascending through the trees.

A car horn jolted me back to the street and I heard Milo Scorza bellowing my full name—*Hugh Fisher! Hugh Fisher!*—as if we hadn't known each other for decades. Milo bundled out of his iridescent-turquoise Fiat 500, a car he'd owned since the late 1970s and whose engine he'd replaced twice. Still spry in his seventies, he left his door open and the engine running, coming toward me in his pressed jeans and an unbuttoned, postman-blue shop coat. There was a single grease pencil in his breast pocket and a leather cell phone holster on his braided belt. Even when you saw Milo buying flowers or picking up the widows' prescriptions, you got the sense that just moments before he'd been operating a bench lathe or hoisting an engine block into position. We shook hands and he wedged my suitcase into the Fiat's cramped trunk, amid coils of rope, handsaws, and wrenches.

And then we were driving out toward Valetto in early

November sunshine. The blacktop curled between straw-colored fields, the farmhouses shuttered and set back amid stone pines and woodpiles, the church spires and bell towers of small towns flip-booking through the bare-limbed trees along the roadway. The Fiat gave out little adenoidal shunting noises whenever we climbed a hill, and Milo patted the side of his door with tender encouragement. There was no rearview mirror, but a laminated portrait of the Madonna had been glued to the sun-bleached dash for our navigation and protection. The radio was low, alternating between static, vintage romantic hits, and soccer scores. Milo's right hand made frequent sorties between the gearbox and the tuning dial. Mysteriously, the higher gears produced more static, and therefore, above fifty kilometers an hour, the radio required vigilant recalibration.

We talked about the weather, villa repairs, the widows' ailments. By which I mean I listened to a synopsis of wind, rising damp, and arthritis. Milo still sported the same mustache I remembered from my childhood visits—a big swooping throwback to nineteenth-century lumbermen and prospectors. Now speckled gray and white, it curled down to enclose his small, thin-lipped mouth parenthetically. This had always made sense to me, since Milo spoke in asides. He predicted weather or noted local scandal with a sense that he was briefly deviating from a main thread—*by the way, tomorrow, rain is coming*, or, *in fact, confidentially, the mayor's wife had a miscarriage and now suffers from fits of public crying*—but the main idea never presented itself.

Milo had been working for my mother's family since the age of eleven. His parents had been employed by the Serafinos in the 1930s, the mother to keep house and the father to apply the sort of mending, patching, jury-rigging, and unpermitted repairs that a centuries-old villa requires on a regular basis. Somewhere before the end of middle school, and after Aldo Serafino fled, Milo was apprenticed to his father as a *tuttofare*. Although a tuttofare is understood in Italy to be a general maid or handyman, the literal translation of *everything-doer* was closer to Milo's job description: plumber, carpenter, electrician, bricklayer, messenger, forager, digger of pet graves, catcher of rats, woodcutter, driver, grocery shopper, bearer of restorative soups. My aunt Rose also called upon him to occasionally disconnect the intercom system that ran between the widows' apartments, when the glacial silences between Iris and Violet erupted into a plague of staticky insults.

When we made it to the neighboring town of Bevona, less than a mile from Valetto, we started to see signs that read "This way to the town that is dying." These signs, organized by the mayor and the Umbrian office of tourism, never ceased to infuriate Milo on his trips into town for supplies. As we drove along the narrow, cobbled streets, Milo honking into the kinked, blind approaches, he pointed out the window and scoffed, "Ah yes, look at us, we're still dying after all this time!"

Milo sped along the walled-in streets, honking and waving to pedestrians he knew, gesturing profanities to shopkeepers smoking under their awnings. He left the Fiat idling—*she does not like to reignite*—and dashed into a few stores to buy wall putty, toilet paper, apples, and bresaola while I waited. And then we were headed down the final hill toward the footbridge that leads into Valetto. Halfway down, before the valley came into view, Milo said, "In actual fact, Hugh Fisher, you have been ravaged by your losses. A wife and a mother extinguished—" He ran a thumb and forefinger along the bowed perimeter of his mustache. "You must swim on a tide of great sadness and I am very sorry for it."

The shoelaces of my Swiss boots, I noticed, were frayed at the ends. I remembered the word *aglet* to describe those little terminal sheaths that prevent fraying. Could you replace the aglet without replacing the entire lace? I heard myself gathering a response through a breath, my face out the window. "*Mille grazie*, Milo," I said, leveling out my voice. "*Molto gentile.*"

I had known Milo for nearly forty years and yet we mostly spoke like neighbors or distant relatives. Outside the embrace of politics, local intrigue, weather, and family, we had little to say to each other. But as I heard my cordial tone mingle with the creeping static of the radio, I thought I sounded like I'd just thanked a kind stranger for museum directions. *A thousand thanks. That's very nice of you.* I wanted, suddenly, to forge some new intimacy with Milo. In Italian, I asked him how his wife, Donata, and sons were, ashamed that I couldn't remember the sons' names. He answered me in his Italianized English. The older son had a commodious *statale* job in Rome and the younger one was a tractor *meccanico*. His wife still cooked and cleaned for the Serafino widows, but she suffered from *la gotta* and general nervousness and she spent one night a week with her sister a few towns over. "*Vuole che vada in pensione*," he said. "She wants me to retire, but from what? This has never been work to me."

Milo's sense of service and ceremony for the changing of lightbulbs, the building of fires, and the digging of pet graves had always baffled me. I remembered him from my childhood summers, climbing a ladder or hauling wood in his pressed jeans and shop coat, a sense of fraternal good cheer as he hummed a radio love song, a sprig of rosemary or holly in his lapel during the holidays. His affability suggested that meticulous pleasures were to be had in handsaws and wrenches, that holding a nail between your humming lips was a privilege, and I realized now that I'd never quite believed any of it was real. I'd spent years trying to uncover Milo's deeper unhappiness, trying to debunk his cheerful industry. As we descended the hill, it seemed impossibly cynical and mean-spirited of me.

"Do you think the woman in the cottage is *bonafide*?" I asked him.

"*Bonafide*," Milo said, "or *malafide*, yes, that is the question." He drummed his callused fingertips on the steering wheel. "We will let the inquiries run their courses."

"Is there going to be a royal commission?"

His forehead and eyebrows suggested it was not out of the question. "Your auntie Iris is very complete."

As we rounded the bend and descended from the plateau, he gestured toward Valetto, at his unlikely birthplace barnacled to a spur of rock in the middle of a valley of canyons. From a distance, the town is a faint, medieval silhouette atop a pinnacle, set against the haze of distant hill towns, their fields and slopes and church spires arranged around the edges of a blue bowl. But then, as you get closer, the colors come into relief—the pale umber walls, the surrounding moonscape of chalk-white canyons and escarpments, the fringe of chestnut and olive groves at the base of its cliffs. Still closer, it becomes a diorama of windows and terra-cotta roof tiles. In my mind, the twelfth-century campanile of the church—towering high above the other rooflines—has always resembled an obelisk of some ancient civilization, a primitive, tapering monument to fickle and vengeful gods. The skyline is beautiful but also desolate and otherworldly. It comes at you by degrees, as you descend the hill, and then suddenly you're a diver coming upon the hulk of some ravaged galleon at the bottom of the sea.

φ

Milo parked the Fiat near the long concrete-and-steel footbridge that connects one side of the valley to the mesa that supports the town. Wide enough for four people to walk abreast, the bridge rests on a series of reinforced piers that rise twenty feet from a rocky escarpment, the valley floor and the river a few hundred feet farther below. I helped Milo load his supplies and my luggage onto the custom rear mount of his moped and told him that I would walk across. Only Valettini can use mopeds and ATVs to cross the footbridge, and I watched as he gunned up its incline toward the main entrance, an enormous Etruscan archway. Three tourists— older women with alpine trekking poles—stood at the railing to let him pass. Valetto attracts a few intrepid, offbeat visitors, especially in the cooler months. People weary of basilicas and museums, who want to wander through a nearly empty hill town in anoraks with telescopic lenses around their necks. There hasn't been a shop or restaurant in the town since 1971, the year of a sizable earthquake and the year my grandmother closed the restaurant she'd opened after the war to provide for her four daughters. The few tourists who come stay for an hour. They eat sandwiches and apples from their knapsacks, take pictures of the stray cats and the spiral staircase that ends in dead air, and then leave forever.

As I crossed the footbridge, I could see crumbling flakes of clay around the fluted rim of the town, where enormous pillars of earth and ashen rock had cleaved away like icebergs from a melting glacier. In settling Valetto, the Etruscans tried to elevate themselves above the malarial swamp of the river valley, but they chose a column of tufa, a shifting tower of hardened, volcanic ash, on which to build their town. I climbed the final steps, passed through the Etruscan archway, and cut across the piazza. The three tourists were photographing building façades backed by air, their roomless interiors held in place by invisible struts. It was easy to imagine people sleeping and eating in these phantom rooms for centuries, or see them standing on the intact balconies that brought to mind opera boxes with an excellent view of oblivion.

So much of Valetto is negative space, I thought as I walked along, the conjuring of imaginary forms, but then you turn a corner and see the curled Cs of a dozen sleeping cats in the piazza, the clay-potted geraniums on the edges of stone stairs, the winter rooftop gardens, or the old man in a leather apron walking to the church every hour to ring the bronze bells, and you feel certain that this town of ten will be here forever.

I passed into the narrow alleyways behind the main square, where my grandmother's defunct restaurant and a series of empty stone houses rose from slabs of basaltina. On my boyhood visits, I was forbidden from entering the abandoned restaurant and shuttered houses, but, as with the Saint's Staircase, the allure was too hard to resist. Some of the buildings had been abandoned after the '71 earthquake, their rooms and furnishings frozen in time, and some had been packed up and left vacant years before or later, when their owners emigrated to another town or country. I spent countless afternoons wandering through these spaces, look-ing for clues about the lives that had once animated them.

In one house, it looked as if the inhabitants had fled in the middle of dinner. The table set with tarnished silverware, china plates stippled with blue-green mold, a vase of ossified flowers. In another house, the living room ceiling had col-lapsed, the floor strewn with broken terra-cotta roof tiles, but in the bedrooms there were clothes still hanging in the wardrobes and sheets on the beds, the fabrics filigreed by moths. And there were tins of food in the kitchen, towels and a bar of soap and a razor in the bathroom, a shoebox in a linen closet filled with photographs and children's school certifi-cates for good conduct. In my grandmother's restaurant, which she'd opened in 1947 and named Il Ritorno, The Re-turn, a rafter had fallen into the dining room, and the caned chairs were tumbled about, but the tablecloths were still on the tables, along with a few tattered menus and dusty green wine bottles. All these rooms had a damp mineral smell that made me light-headed and that I have always associated with the sorrows of the past.

To some extent, I became a historian within those mildew-blotched walls, on those secret afternoons when I inventoried what remained of those who had fled. In the restaurant, I studied the tattered menus, imagined what people had been eating when the tremor shook the town, who had ordered the *donzelline aromatiche*, the little damsels with herbs, right as the windows began to rattle, and I went into the kitchen to count plates, saucepans, and silverware, because a precise tally of the past seemed important. I never quite understood why no one had cleaned up the ruins or rescued what was still intact, but I've since seen the same thing in dozens of abandoned places—a barrage of objects people left behind, a monument to the day and the hour when everything changed.

φ

I felt a wave of fondness when I caught my first glimpse of the villa at the very back of the town. I hadn't seen it in two years and it looked exactly as I remembered—presiding over the terraced hillside of pruned gardens and umbrella pines, the pale ravines dropping away to the valley floor below. With my eyes, I followed the footpath that led down to the tangled olive and chestnut groves and then back up again to the house. It has never been the classical Italian villa of coffee-table books. There are no porticoed courtyards or turrets or loggias. Instead, Villa Serafino is a cobbled-together, brick-and-stone bulwark designed to keep marauders from the river valley at bay. A beleaguered, slightly charming fortress against the world.

The ground floor is set with wide archways, now bricked over, where animals once wintered in their pens, and there's a series of deeply recessed windows that resemble tiny grottos. The second and third floors, where adjacent rooms were converted into the aunts' apartments, are blue-shuttered, iron-balconied, and gray-stuccoed. The stone cottage sits at the edge of the terraced gardens, less than fifty feet from the ravine, and the caretaker's house—little more than a woodshed with a terra-cotta roof—stands all by itself in a clearing at the back of the property. Milo and Donata raised two sons in this tiny house.

On my approach that November afternoon, I almost laughed aloud when I saw a flutter of white pillowcases and hand towels from Violet's rusting iron balcony on the top floor, a longtime source of tension with Iris, one floor below, who routinely told her that only peasants still hung their laundry out to dry on balconies. There was, after all, a laundry room on the ground floor and a clothesline out back. From the five consecutive summers I spent at the villa until I was thirteen, during the implosion of my parents' marriage, I remembered that Violet liked to flaunt her drying petticoats and underwear from the balcony whenever she could, her brassieres flapping like carnival pennants, and it was surely to infuriate Iris, the sociologist who'd taught at universities in Rome and Milan.

From the top of the stone passageway, I could also see the rooftop terrace where Rose, the diplomat and go-between of the Serafino sisters, spent many of her summer afternoons in the 1970s, listening to opera from a small transistor radio and reading fashion magazines under a beach umbrella. There was always a tall glass of Aperol spritz beside her, an orange wedge floating on top, the glass full of ice and beading with condensation. She would routinely call me up there and have me read passages aloud from Italian *Vogue*. I could remember her enjoying my narration of Milanese or Florentine scandal, the ice cubes gently hitting her teeth when she laughed into her glass.

As I continued down the stairs, my boyhood trips to Valetto floating all about me, I felt briefly certain that I could find my way back to something meaningful here. This was where I'd spent years, one summer at a time, working on my well-regarded book, the one project that anchored me during my grief. In Rome, just moments before Susan had paid ten euros to have that ridiculous Polaroid taken in front of the Colosseum, she'd asked me whether I ever planned to be happy again, and I'd pretended to tie my frayed shoelaces so that I could avoid the look in her eyes. Susan has her mother's thin nose and high cheekbones, but nothing of Clare's knowing in the eyes. Susan's are two flecks of pale blue mica in a slab of granite, and they have been unwavering for as long as I can remember. She waited for me to stop crouching on the senatorial platform that overlooks the excavated arena, and when I'd straightened, she said, "She wouldn't have wanted this for you."

"How do you know what your mother wanted?"

There was an edge to my voice that surprised both of us.

"We talked about all kinds of things near the end."

"She was loaded on morphine."

"She told me that I shouldn't let you wallow. That your people are wallowers."

"That does sound like her."

"I mean, Dad, I get the book about dying towns, but you going to live with the widows for six months"—she looked down into the arena—"well, it just feels like you're drifting into the past instead of the future."

"I'm a historian," I told her. "The past is my profession."

At the time, Susan was doing research that focused on economic decision-making under ambiguity, and I saw her study me through a haze of professionalized skepticism. When she continued to say nothing, I admitted, very reasonably and quietly, that I was sure she had a point and that I would work on being happier. I would embrace the future with both hands. To prove it, I briefly took both hands out of my pockets.

But now, descending the stairs, it was the past that burned clear and bright, not the future. I saw myself as a boy of twelve, riding Milo's rusting old Bianchi bicycle across the footbridge and into town with a knapsack full of books and a sketchpad, stopping to play chess with old men in the piazza. Milo's sons and my Italian cousins all played together, but my Italian was slow and Latinate, and theirs was full of jousting, rapid-fire dialect. More and more, I spent time alone, or with the old men, who did most of the talking. I saw myself on the Saint's Staircase, or climbing to the top of the eight-hundred-year-old bell tower, writing poems about wanderers with the lunar valley spread out before me. Stepping off that final stone ledge, I couldn't help feeling some tenderness toward this previous person I'd inhabited.

I continued along the tilled garden beds, the rose, asparagus, and fennel plots that Milo tended with seasonal devotion. From a distance of about fifty feet, I saw a tall, broadshouldered woman standing at the front door of the cottage with her back to me. Behind her, on the flagstone patio, a paper grocery sack rested on the wrought iron table. This was the spot where my mother used to sit during her visits, reading Agatha Christie novels and drinking strong negronis under the wisteria and bougainvillea. The woman had a Tesla coil of brunette hair, and she was wearing olive-colored corduroys and a black angora sweater. When she turned, I saw her face in profile—she was somewhere in her forties, wearing a pair of red-framed eyeglasses, the kind I imagined in Milanese advertising agencies, all geometry and burnished metal. I saw that she was trying to unlock the front door of the cottage. Apart from a few families who store goods and supplies in abandoned houses, no one in Valetto has locked a door in five hundred years. I felt myself flush with annoyance.

Then the door opened and I caught a glimpse of the cottage kitchen before she grabbed her grocery sack, went inside, and closed the door behind her. I stood for a moment longer and thought about how this cottage, perched above a stony, eroded valley, was my only tangible connection to my mother now that she was gone. Hazel Serafino, like her older sisters, Violet, Rose, and Iris, had been named optimistically after a flower, though unlike her sisters' springtime namesakes, hers was an enigmatic winter bloomer, the female flowers appearing like tiny red starbursts on the still-bare branches. In life, she was withdrawn and prone to brooding silences in darkening rooms. Exiled by an unhappy marriage in the American Midwest, she had kept her dominion over the cottage through sporadic visits but had never bothered to fully furnish or decorate it. Where the villa ran to rococo excess, the cottage was Spartan, equipped like a budget holiday rental. You were lucky to find a working can opener and a sharp knife in the kitchen drawers. A single, generic painting hung in the living room (Rome skyline at dusk). Apart from a bookshelf full of thousand-piece puzzles, board games, and detective novels, there were few signs that anyone had ever whiled away an afternoon within its walls. The cottage, like my mother, was a cipher.

2

The villa was no longer set up to accommodate house-guests. The spare bedrooms had all been annexed by the widows' apartments, or given over to clutter. The cavernous, frescoed dining room had been losing a decades-long battle with rising damp and mildew. So when Rose insisted we all share a meal that first night, Donata stood in her flower-print pinafore and directed us down to the taverna—an Etruscan trench, carved into the tufa and bedrock below the villa. Over time, it had become a cellar for storing wine and the taxidermal kills of our forebears. The head of an ibex, cryptic and antlered, presided over the stone mantel. A petrified lynx prowled from one corner.

"That lynx was shot in Sardinia by our great-grandfather," said Violet. As eldest sister, she always sat at the head of the table. "They were thought extinct, the lynxes, for a century, then a farmer found one trotting along the roadside."

I sat at the other end of the table, dressed in a suitcase-rumpled blazer and tie. The widows were all wearing evening dresses, and when they shifted in their chairs I could smell the pungent chemistry of mothballs and dry cleaning.

In the long silences before Donata brought out the antipasti, we sipped our prosecco and watched Milo tend the fireplace. He wore a pair of asbestos gloves, his shop-coat sleeves rolled up, so that he could reach into the blue-white mouth of the flames to rearrange a piece of burning wood.

"The chestnut smokes too much," said Violet to Milo's hunched back.

He spoke quietly into the flames: "Only some of the blend is chestnut, Signora. Mostly oak."

Violet seemed satisfied with this answer and gave me a little nod to show it. In her cerulean-blue dress, with a lavender shawl and diamond-teardrop necklace, she looked as if she might be headed for the opera, but I suspected she'd spent the afternoon watching Italian pro wrestling on television. She'd become an avid fan in her old age, and you'd sometimes hear her jeering at some *fottuto imbecille barbaro* from inside her apartment. She also watched boxing and horse racing or, when she needed to relax, British professional dart or snooker tournaments. Of all the sisters, she was the one who'd inherited her mother's pale, freckled skin, and she seemed to take pride in looking the least Italian. My mother had been dark-haired and olive-skinned—a resurgence of Umbrian blood.

Donata wielded the charcuterie board, her gout giving her a slight hobble, serving each of us in turn. In the subterranean light, the smokelike grain of the wooden board, the hunks of bread, and the thin, curling ribbons of meat—capocollo, mortadella, bresaola, culatello—all reminded me of a Dutch still life.

"A toast to our dear nephew," said Violet, raising her prosecco.

Iris and Rose took up their glasses and I did the same.

Violet said, "We hope your stay with us, Hugh, will be

very fruitful. I know you will soon be restored to the cottage that our father gifted to your mother, the lastborn of the Serafino sisters, and that she, God rest her soul, gifted to you. You are always welcome here."

"At least until we all slide into the valley," added Iris.

Violet closed her eyes for a second, willing her sister from her mental landscape. When she came blinking back to the room, she said, "Here's to Hugh's sabbatical in Umbria. *Salute!*"

"*Salute!*" said Iris.

Rose raised her glass, blew a lipsticked kiss at me, and drank. She had a raffish smile that revealed small teeth and that bowed her blue-penciled eyebrows. Years of reading *Vogue* had rescued her from the broach-and-pearl severity that many Italian widows wield. Instead, she wore an opal necklace and an ivory dress with a cherry-blossom print and kimono sleeves. It was hard to believe that she was the most religious of the sisters, the one who made an annual pilgrimage to a basilica in a remote mountain town in southeastern Umbria, where she paid homage to Santa Rita, the patron saint of lost causes and heartbroken women. Rose was the only sister without children, and it haunted her. I suspect it was part of why she'd beckoned me up to the rooftop terrace during those sunny afternoons in the 1970s. She'd returned to the villa in her forties after escaping a childless, abusive marriage that ended only when her alcoholic husband died of a stroke at dinner one night. In the rooms that would become her apartment, I remember seeing the pictures of all the children she'd sponsored over the years in Africa and Latin America. *I miei figli del mondo*, she called them, my children of the world.

Violet said, "Now, I let Nonna know that you arrived.

Perhaps you can visit her tomorrow. She does better in the mornings, after she has her fennel tea and soft-boiled egg. Nina and Sofia are the girls who come to help with her. One of them will be there."

"I'd like that," I said.

"Naturally, we're not telling her about the intruder from the north. It will only upset her. So not a word," said Violet.

"Of course," I said.

Violet said, "She deserves to turn one hundred in peace. We are planning a big party for her and we've invited some of the old residents. Many of them have not come back to the town since they left, decades ago."

Iris had emailed me about the birthday party but had made it sound like a small family gathering. "Susan is coming for the celebration," I said, "but I didn't realize it was going to be a big party. Is it a surprise?"

"Oh, no," said Violet. "There is no surprise. Mother was put in charge of the guest list. She started writing invitations six months ago."

I tried to imagine the villa hosting a large gathering without a working dining room. I pictured Donata hobbling between rooms with platters of food. Making sure Donata and Milo could hear me, I asked in Italian, "How many people do you think will come?"

"Who knows?" Violet said, returning to English. "We will make a tally before too long."

Milo wouldn't meet my eyes. Standing beside the Sardinian lynx, Donata said, "Unless you bring in caterers, it has to be a small gathering. Otherwise, it will send me to my grave."

Violet gave no indication that anyone had spoken. She said, "Hugh, I was standing out on my balcony when you arrived and I noticed you watching the squatter over at the cottage. Did you meet her?"

"No, not yet."

"Her name is Elisa Tomassi," said Iris.

Violet draped a piece of mortadella over a hunk of bread. "She can call herself whatever she likes."

"The family lawyer, Orlando Fiorani, advises us to treat her hospitably until we can investigate her claims," said Iris. "My old colleague, a retired criminologist, is arriving in a few days from Milan to help us. Rest assured, he will get to the bottom of it all."

"Ah, yes," said Violet to her mortadella, leaning into the grudge she'd had with Iris since they were girls, "the old colleague from Milan riding in on a white Vespa."

To her dinner plate, Iris said, "Rinaldo Fumigalli, you will find, is unparalleled. A true gentleman and an expert in his field. Believe me, he wouldn't be caught dead on a Vespa. He drives a Moroccan-blue Alfa with kidskin motoring gloves."

This sounded pretentious, even to my academic ear, and I knew Violet would rush to the net. "Perhaps," Violet said to me confidentially, "you should tell your aunt to marry this fop. Though she should probably ask for a physician's exam first."

Iris had married a series of tall, barrel-chested type A Italians with chestnut hair and enormous wristwatches and vulnerable internal organs. Two died of heart attacks, the third of liver cirrhosis, all before the age of sixty-five.

Violet continued: "The husbands die on her like large-breed dogs. At a certain point, it's a problem of the choosing, not just the pedigree."

"At least," said Iris, turning to me, "I didn't marry the first fertilizer salesman to wander across the footbridge."

This clearly stung Violet, but she took a sip of prosecco and let a brief silence take hold. I knew from my mother that Violet and Rose had both married young, settling on industrious older men from nearby towns to help the Serafino household stay afloat after Aldo disappeared. There was a photograph in my grandmother's apartment of an eighteen-year-old Violet sitting sidesaddle on a donkey, being led across the footbridge by her new husband, a stout, curly-headed man in his thirties. In the photo, Violet has a carpet-bag slung over one shoulder and she's staring out from under an enormous sun hat with the expression of someone carrying out a penance.

Rose—wedged like Switzerland between two warring nations—told Donata to go ahead and bring out the *primo* course whenever she was ready. Milo removed his asbestos gloves, his fire snapping in the hearth, and followed after her. Rose turned to me, arched those blue-penciled eyebrows, and asked how Susan was getting on at Oxford.

"She likes it," I said. "She's found her little tribe of friends. A brilliant Miltonist in the making, a Rhodes scholar who wants to cure cancer . . . She lives in a college called Lady Margaret Hall, which has some beautiful gardens."

"Reclaiming her British roots," said Violet. "Before Australia, our mother's family tree branches back to East Anglia on the paternal side."

"Norwich, in fact," added Iris.

"Remind me what she is studying," said Rose.

"Economics," I said. "She's currently studying how people make decisions when faced with ambiguity."

"How marvelous," said Violet. "Whatever does it mean?"

"She studies the relationship between reward and risk in economic decision-making, especially as it varies by age and culture and gender."

They all looked at me, nodding politely but without interest. Donata arrived with little bowls of risotto topped with shavings of truffle and Parmigiano-Reggiano, and I nudged the conversation elsewhere. "What was this room used for when you were all growing up?"

Iris craned up at the barrel-vaulted ceiling, chewing into a memory. "Before the war, it was used just for storing wines and cheeses. Mother didn't like the taxidermy, so she banished all the dead animals down here. Your grandfather wanted them in the billiard room upstairs, because he thought that's where aristocrats would have kept them. They were terrifying to us as children. I used to come down here to feed the lynx so that he wouldn't rip my throat out in the night."

"Then," said Rose, "this is where the children slept during the war, starting in February of 1943. I remember because it was my birthday month and we had a little party down here."

"You all slept down here?" I asked.

"No, no," said Violet, running the tines of her fork through the steaming risotto, "the refugee children."

I looked at Rose, waiting for an explanation.

She said, "The children who came to us from Turin and Milan. Mother had to make an extra birthday cake to feed them all. She had to make it with chestnut flour because of the rationing."

"And if we are to believe Elisa Tomassi," said Iris, "her mother was one of those children."

My mother had been eight in 1943, so surely this family

lore should have filtered down to me from her, or from my aunts or grandmother during my interviews in Valetto for my book. They would have known that refugee children sleeping in the villa's cave-like cellar when the Allies began bombing Italian cities near the end of World War II might have been of interest to a professional historian. I felt the need to downplay my shock at this revelation because I knew my incredulity would stifle the flow of information. If you wanted to get something out of a Serafino sister, including my own mother, you had to appeal to her British sense of indirection and pretend you were already in the know, that you were merely asking for confirmation. And so I met the glaucous-yellow gaze of the lynx and imagined that I was trying to coax a wild animal into a clearing. Then I tried to imitate a reasonable person eating a bowl of risotto. "Remind me," I said, "how long did the children stay?"

Violet turned to Rose. "More than a year, if I'm not mistaken, even after Father left in the spring of '44. Is that right?"

"Yes," said Rose. "They brought the children from the north in two cars and drove through the night. They carried the younger ones across the footbridge, a few at a time. Ten of them, mostly girls, brought inside while they were still sleeping."

"How old were they?" I asked.

"Mostly four and five," said Rose. "The oldest girl was seven when they arrived."

"The big one was Elisa Tomassi's mother," said Iris. "Again, allegedly."

Rose continued: "They arrived with a nurse, who told us many of their houses had been leveled in the bombing raids up north. I remember coming down here and seeing our mother bathing them with a warm washcloth. She sang to them, fed them soup, but they still cried a lot."

"The crying was terrible," said Violet.

"Yes," said Iris, "human emotion is a terrible thing, especially among war orphans."

"Remind your sister," Violet told Rose, "that they weren't all orphans. She might not remember since her nose was always in a book. Some of them had parents working in the factories and warehouses up north, but their mothers wanted them as far away from the bombing as possible. They sent letters and we would read them aloud to the little ones."

I heard our silverware dinning against the china plates, amplified under the barreled ceiling. I saw the four of us sitting twenty feet below ground, chambered in the volcanic rock of the town's pedestal. Family histories are porous, I thought, and full of seismic gaps. Without any emotion, I said, "And they stayed down here so no one would see them?"

Now Iris took control, leaning into her years at the lectern. "You will remember that there were a quarter of a million Germans in this country during the lead-up to Mussolini's fall. We all thought the American flying fortresses were going to drop bombs wherever they pleased. So the children were hidden away, kept secret, in case word got out to the fascist militias or the Germans. We didn't want to be punished as Allied sympathizers."

"Also," said Rose, "a lot of these children had been sleeping in tunnels up north, below the city streets, so Mother thought it would be a good idea to give them a sense of security. Sometimes, she would lead them out into the gardens at night, if the moon was full, and I remember seeing them standing at the edge of the terraces, lined up like little birds planning a flight over the river valley, their blankets draped around their shoulders like wings . . ."

In a faraway voice, Rose said, "I wonder what happened to them all."

"I remember tiny Nicoletta," Violet said between mouthfuls, "the deaf mute with the terrible fainting spells . . . I don't remember much about the other girls."

"I remember Alessia very well," said Rose. "She was our mother's little kitchen helper and we were all jealous of her. She stayed on after the others left."

"No, no, I can't quite picture her," said Violet.

"She lived with us for at least two years," said Rose. "She and your mother, Hugh, were the best of friends. Inseparable."

"They were?" I'd never known my mother to have a close friendship, so the thought of her befriending this refugee girl from the north was touching.

Violet took the last bite of her risotto and set her fork against the rim of her bowl. "There must be cheerier topics." She dabbed at her mouth with her napkin, careful of her lipstick. "Hugh, are you ready for Donata's famous *cinghiale*?"

It was wild boar hunting season, when the cinghiali gorged themselves on truffles and teams of dogs and men pursued them through the Umbrian countryside. I had eaten Donata's wild boar many times over the years; it was marinated in red wine and herbs overnight and then stewed with tomatoes, lard, olive oil, and spices. I said that I was indeed ready for the wild boar, but for the rest of the meal my mind went to this omission from my family's history, to these children bundled through the night. Then I thought about the Etruscans settling this seismically doomed hilltop to get

away from malaria, pictured them digging this trench, perhaps as a burial site, not knowing that it would become a
hiding place for war refugees a few thousand years later. We
want history to be a unified narrative, a causal, linear plot
that cantilevers across the centuries, but I've always pictured
it like the filigree of a wrought iron gate, our unaccountable
lives twisting and swooping against a few vertical lines.

3

My grandmother hadn't left the first floor of the villa for at least a decade. Occasionally, she used a walker or a wheelchair to make a sortie down to the library, which had been Aldo's study before the war, and where she had been in a decades-long battle with clutter and alphabetization. Otherwise, she remained in her apartment, her meals delivered on a tray. Donata brought her soups and pastas from the main kitchen, but Nina and Sofia, her teenage caregivers, smuggled in bottles of Coca-Cola and grappa, as well as jars of Marmite and tins of French pâté that a grocer across the bridge imported especially for her. She ignored Donata's warnings about plaque, diabetes, high blood pressure, and cholesterol, spreading pieces of toast with Marmite in the mornings to go along with her fennel tea and soft-boiled egg, and with goose livers in the afternoons, when she took a demitasse of grappa and sat by the window where she kept a pair of caged budgerigars, Marconi and Tesla.

The morning after my dinner with the aunts, I came to my grandmother's door bearing nougat. I'd bought it in the

Rome airport because it was one of her old favorites, but as Nina ushered me inside and I smelled Ida's looming century—a drowsy blend of talc, fennel, and musk—I wondered if she still had the dental horsepower to navigate the sticky candy. *La nonna* is napping, Nina said, but she will wake soon. She directed me to an upholstered bench at the foot of an empty canopied bed. Despite the chirping budgies, my grandmother sat dozing in her mottled leather recliner, a copy of Auguste Escoffier's *Memories of My Life* open on her lap, her slippered feet up on a Moroccan ottoman, a horsehair blanket around her shoulders. Her mouth arched open as she slept, the white-spun halo of her hair pressed into the headrest, her breathing slow and pneumatic.

On the mantel, there were silver-framed photographs of the living and the dead. Violet, Rose, and Iris on their wedding days (my mother had eloped in Greece, so her photo showed her pregnant with me and already married). In the center, occupying the largest frame, was Aldo Serafino—mid-thirties, mustached, grinning from a parapet in high summer. There was also a Christmas portrait of me, Clare, and Susan in our holiday finest, all in green and red, taken a decade earlier, when Susan was beginning to burrow into her adolescence and Clare had taken up jogging and given up sugar, so that she looked aggressively healthy under the studio lights of a Michigan mall photographer, the backdrop of alpine evergreens draped in snow like a scene from a ski resort brochure. We all looked happy, aglow, oblivious.

Ida's bedroom was full of nineteenth-century novels, cookbooks, and the memoirs of famous chefs. In one corner, on a Victorian Bible stand, was the family cookbook started by her Venetian grandmother, handed down from mother to eldest daughter. Each generation added her own recipes, admonishments, and anecdotes. I got up from the bench and went to study *I Zanetti a Tavola, The Zanetti Book of the Table.* Going against Italian tradition, my grandmother had given up her maiden name of Zanetti and become Ida Serafino upon her marriage to Aldo at seventeen. She'd come to Europe from Australia as a general maid and helper to a governess in 1927 then met and married an Italian engineer and heir to a crumbling villa. I gently turned the vellum-like pages. There were headings that covered hygiene, table settings, and recipes for children, convalescents, and those with a weak stomach. In the margins of recipes were small corrections, notations, and the names of people, presumably dinner guests, who'd been served the meal before, since it was bad form to serve your visitors the same thing twice.

I remembered looking at this book as a boy and feeling as if our entire complicated Anglo-Italian history were contained in its pages, the exiles and returns, the dislocations of the heart and palate. Ida would encourage me to read it, so long as I didn't take it from the stand, and when I was finished with a few dozen pages she'd offer me a Coke to reward my gastronomic time travel. The cookbook had been taken aboard the *India* in 1880, an ill-fated voyage to New Guinea with hundreds of Italians who'd paid for their passage, all of them scammed by a French nobleman, the Marquis de Rays, who promised a new and bountiful life in Port Breton at a time when Italy was plagued by poverty. After near starvation and bouts of malaria, the voyage survivors arrived on a barren, hostile island in the South Pacific—Port Breton was a con man's mirage—and were eventually rescued and taken to Sydney, my great-grandmother among them. She married an Australian butcher a few years later. On a page dated August 1881, after the ordeal of New

Guinea, my great-grandmother wrote, *I recommend the habit of eating everything to avoid becoming a burden to your family.*

When my grandmother woke, I came over to her chair and kissed both her cheeks. She smiled up at me, her eyes the lucent blue-green of sea glass. "Do you want a Coca-Cola?"

"No, thank you. I brought you some nougat. You used to like that." I placed the box on the small table beside her recliner and returned to the bench.

"Are Clare and Susan with you?" she asked.

Nina looked over from her laundry folding to see me scratch the side of my face. I stared at the budgies flashing yellow and green in their suspended cage by the window.

I said, "Clare passed away six years ago."

"Oh, I'm so sorry," she said, looking at me kindly. "My memory isn't what it used to be. I can remember the old days but not this morning or recent history. Remind me, how did she die?"

"Cancer. They found it very late."

"I hope I wrote to console you."

"You did. It was very kind. Thank you."

"Your mother liked Clare a great deal."

"She did?"

"Oh, yes, I'm sure of it. How old is Susan now?"

"Twenty-three," I said.

"Don't tell fibs."

"It's true."

"Impossible. And what does this grown woman do?"

"She's at Oxford, getting a Ph.D. in economics."

"Good for her. Wonderful. Will you be staying long?"

"A six-month sabbatical. I'm giving a few guest lectures and presenting at some conferences. And I plan to do some new research."

"The cottage should be nice and quiet for you."

I nodded. She moved one hand shakily across the cover of the Escoffier book, her fingernails pink and ridged, her knucklebones raised and white. "In that cookbook you were studying there is a recipe for homesick Italians, a soup created by my grandmother. It calls for lean, milk-fed veal, untrimmed prosciutto, butter, cream, and a dash of nutmeg. She ground nutmeg into everything."

"What is the soup called?"

"Zuppa del Paradiso."

"Lovely."

"The exiled Italians took their villages with them in their pots and pans."

Already knowing the answer, I asked, "Did you make recipes from the family cookbook in your restaurant?"

"Oh, yes, and when I made improvements I jotted them down in the margins."

"Do you miss cooking?"

"Never." She puckered, shot out a breath. "What I miss is tasting and smelling food. I don't recommend living a day over eighty-five. Everything after that is like reading a novel you never liked for the second time."

Ida held the box of nougat in Nina's direction and the girl left her laundry to oblige. I wanted to broach the subject of Aldo's disappearance without violating Violet's injunction against mentioning our visitor from the north. As my grandmother nibbled at the edges of a nougat cube, I said, "Remind me how many people lived in Valetto right before the earthquake in 1971?"

"A little less than one hundred."

"What about during the war, when the Germans started to arrive?"

"Over three hundred, if I had to guess."

So many of the vanishing towns I'd visited had experienced a mass exodus after the war. The Italian economic miracle of the 1950s drew people to the cities in waves, but I've often wondered if their complicity with two fascist regimes also sent millions looking for a fresh start. There was a hill town in Calabria where the entire population of a thousand left on a single day in May 1945, within a week of the final surrender and many years after the most recent landslide or earthquake.

Ida said, "By the time the Germans came over the bridge, there were partisans scattered throughout the woods and the valley. Factory workers, peasants, men who'd deserted the Italian army."

I tried to sound indifferent: "You had refugee children living here in the villa during that time, if I remember correctly? From up north?"

"Of course we did. They were all over the place, at farms in Tuscany and in little villages across Umbria. I was very active with the Red Cross. I wanted us to do our part."

"It must have been difficult. All those extra mouths to feed."

"We had to hide our olive oil and hams and cheeses from the fascists and the Germans, buried them in tins and jars in the ground."

"Do you remember the children?"

"Of course."

"The aunts mentioned an older girl. Alessia something?"

Ida thinned her lips, her eyes drifting to the faded gold dust jacket of her book—Auguste Escoffier, mustached, chin on hand, looking pensive from inside an oval daguerreotype. "Alessia was like another daughter to me."

"How so?"

"She stayed on after the war, until things settled down up north. I taught her how to cook and how to forage for mushrooms, and sometimes we went down into the valley, into the orchards and olive groves. She loved all the old recipes and stories. During the war, she helped me with the younger ones and then worked in the restaurant kitchen with me. After she left and went back up north, she never answered my letters. I often thought of her . . ."

"Do you remember anything else from that time?"

"What time?"

"The year that Aldo left, 1944."

She tightened the horsehair blanket around her shoulders. "It was terrible. People kept stealing our chickens, so we had to build a coop on the rooftop terrace. At night, we'd all huddle in the cellar and listen to the BBC, which was illegal, waiting for the bombs to drop. In summer, when the moon was full, I took the girls and the refugee children blackberrying, trying to keep them in peace as long as possible. The winter was bone chilling and we didn't have enough food or shoes or blankets. There was dynamite hidden in gardens all over town. I really don't know how we survived it all."

"My mother never really talked about that time."

Ida looked down at her hands. "*Dimenticare a volte è una benedizione.*" Forgetting is sometimes a blessing.

"And there was no sign of Aldo after the war?"

"I spent years looking for him, making phone calls and writing letters to the Red Cross and the missing-persons bureau. Eventually, I came to the conclusion that he was either dead, or that he didn't want to be found. Either way, I was furious with him for leaving us." She blinked back the suggestion of tears, slightly annoyed by this sudden upwelling.

Nina snapped a towel in the air to fold it and said it was time for the signora's fennel tea. I wondered if she would be giving a full report of my visit to Signora Violet. Changing the subject, Ida said, "Come see me again. It's almost my birthday. I'm turning one thousand."

"A hundred is no small feat," I said. "I hear there's going to be a big party."

"Who knows if half these people are still alive . . ."

I kissed her on the cheek as she returned to Escoffier's life in gastronomy.

4

Since the cottage was occupied, I moved into Iris's spare bedroom. Over two decades, beginning in the 1970s, Milo and a local crew had renovated the villa to create the widows' apartments, as each adult daughter returned home. They joined adjacent rooms and plumbed out a bathroom and a kitchenette for each sister, but only Iris's apartment had a guest room. They also installed the *sistema citofonico*, the intercom system, to connect the far-flung apartments—Ida on the ground floor, Iris on the second floor, and Rose and Violet in two different wings of the top floor.

Like the rest of the villa, Iris's guest room ran toward the baroque. A four-poster bed with a tasseled canopy, a mausoleum-like wardrobe, flocked wallpaper with peacocks and citrus trees. It felt like a room where a forgotten composer might have written his final symphony. My mother had never indulged such excesses at the cottage, and I allowed myself to walk through its Spartan rooms in my mind, picking along the trail of my boyhood hobbies—the categorized rocks and minerals, the dog-eared paperbacks, the notebooks of sentimental poetry. The undecorated cottage was my mother's stern rebuke of the villa's suffocating interiors, and I longed to be back inside its bare walls.

While I drafted an upcoming guest lecture on the social history of abandonment—how a fourteenth-century idea of relinquishing control became our modern sense of renunciation or desertion—Iris worked on her forensic investigations. Since retiring as a professor of sociology and losing her final husband two decades earlier, she had volunteered as an archivist for a nonprofit internet project that gathered data on unsolved crimes. She plotted statistics and fed them to a computer scientist in Rome, and to a retired detective in San Francisco, and together they used an algorithm to look for patterns in thousands of unprosecuted kidnappings, missing-persons cases, and killings. Her apartment was strewn with the entrails of her work—newspaper clippings, maps, FBI and Interpol reports, census printouts. In the living room, an ancient Macintosh emitted its pale blue digital light from a sewing table.

And so we worked on our separate projects during the mornings—me on abandoned places and her on missing persons and unsolved murders—and we would meet every now and then in the kitchenette for a shot of stovetop espresso. Then, around noon, she would make us both a prosciutto sandwich with provolone and a bowl of arugula drizzled with balsamic vinegar. One lunchtime, sitting in her embroidered silk blouse, she told me about her spreadsheet that correlated strangulations in upstate New York from a decade earlier with recent murders in southern Italy, with a string of women's bodies being found in vacant houses in Naples. "I think it's the same man," she said, setting her sandwich down on her plate to give the arugula her full attention. "An American."

"How do you know the murderer is a he?"

"Statistically, it's almost always a man."

"And now he's here?"

"Let's say he spent some time in prison, probably for another crime. When he gets out, he wants to go somewhere to reinvent himself, to ply his trade. Italy is the perfect place for a lustful murderer coming out of retirement. So many places to hide and so many beautiful young women."

I'd walked through dozens of deserted and dwindling places in Italy, including remote settlements in Abruzzo where it might take the locals a year to realize someone had moved into an empty house up in the mountains. Iris went on to speak about serial killers the way a botanist might talk about rare orchids or parsley ferns, her scientific curiosity sounding vaguely enthralled. "There are four categories of killers, each based on motivation. Visionaries, missionaries, hedonists, and the ones doing it for power or control over another person, usually a woman."

"Which one is Naples?"

"A hedonist from snout to tail. Nothing thrills him more than chasing a woman through an empty house."

Iris took an enthusiastic bite of her sandwich, and I imagined her continuing this off-color obsession well into her nineties. Had the retired detective in San Francisco ever Skyped with her? Had he seen her homespun version of a forensic investigation, the corkboard with red yarn connecting pins on a map? Iris Serafino was no more qualified to track serial killers as a retired sociologist than I was as a social historian. But then I thought of her training in statistics and data collection, her endless hours of devotion to the cause. Perhaps, I thought, even with her yellowing computer and her red-yarn vectors, she is a ferocious detective.

"Why do you do it?" I asked.

"What could be more fun than hunting men down when they think they've gotten away with something?"

I thought of her three dead husbands, all Italian captains of industry with full heads of hair and weak hearts or livers. Maybe she was drawn to the overachievers among murderers the same way she was drawn to accomplished suitors, to men who loved nothing more than the adrenal seductions of risk and reward. The idea that she was hunting down the socio-pathic proxies of her dead husbands unsettled me so much that I told her I wasn't feeling well and went to lie down. After a nap, I returned to my guest lecture and a volley of texts from Susan:

> thx again for Rome!

> fwiw, I think about her every single day and it still kills me . . .

> But her shoes are still in your closet, her candle making stuff and LPs still in the basement . . .

> Have you thought about going back to that therapist/life coach?

I looked at my phone, tried to push out a breath by imagining my rib cage inflating like a balloon, the one useful thing Evelyn Woodrow, licensed grief counselor and life coach, had taught me. I'd started seeing Evelyn about two years after Clare's death, when her Saab was still in the driveway, its doors locked and its tires long deflated. I'd been aware of my own vanishing for a while; in the middle of my wintertime lectures on the Russian Revolution, I'd catch a glimpse of my reflection in the classroom windows, snow-spun and whirling, and feel myself emptying out one word at a time. So when I booked a session with Evelyn it was to prevent myself from dissolving completely. She also took my insurance and her office was on the way home from the college.

One winter dusk I sat in the parking lot of a strip mall on hard times, fifteen minutes early for my first session. Evelyn's office stood next to a twenty-four-hour laundromat that did a thriving trade—the customers hauling their clothes between washers and dryers under surgical-grade lighting, pushing wire baskets on wheels, the metal poles gliding above the fixed rows of plastic seating like IV drip poles. I almost didn't go in; I could have sat there watching this chrome-lit fraternity for hours.

Evelyn had taken over the lease from a bankrupt chiropractor, whose therapeutic equipment had been repossessed or now lay in state under ocean-themed fabrics. She told me about the previous tenant during our first session, as she pulled the Japanese paper partition behind her so that we wouldn't have to look at the chiropractic museum. The consultation room had her certificates and diplomas on the walls, all of them from far-flung universities and colleges that carry geography in their names, the southwesterns and central valleys. And I could hear and feel the laundromat next door, the ambient hum and the heat of the dryers. I was determined to give Evelyn a chance, despite the furnishings that suggested a corporate liquidation sale. But as I sat on the imitation-leather couch, I wondered how this person could have anything to teach me about rising back to life's shining surfaces.

And whenever she asked me about my grief, or how happy Clare and I had been together, I found myself distracted by her candles. They were the kind you buy in the cleaning aisle of the grocery store, the ones that extend promises of Tahitian vanilla or the northern woods but in fact deliver something aggressively cosmetic and artificial, the progeny of engineered pinesap and Chanel No. 5. Clare, a longtime scented-soy-wax-candle maker, would have been horrified.

The candles, combined with the general shabbiness of Evelyn's office, made me sad, not for my own losses, but for the way I imagined her struggles leading to this particular strip mall. If I had to guess, I would say that her particular unhappiness commingled with the scent of artificial sea foam to block my own healing. She asked the right questions, assumed the right poses of concern, but I couldn't help feeling that I was in the presence of a kindly impostor, someone who has learned the mannerisms and words, but not the inner life of a role.

I texted Susan back:

> The therapist just wasn't a good fit for
> me. I love you!

φ

I saw Elisa Tomassi one more time before Rinaldo Fumigalli arrived from Milan. I was out walking the widows' dogs with Milo, his longtime habit at dusk. Violet owned a British bull-dog named Rocky IV, Iris a white spitz named Volpino, and Rose a spaniel named Chester. Milo walked the dogs along the same loop each evening—out to the Etruscan archway, back through the piazza toward the villa, past the shuttered houses and the restaurant. He let the dogs piss against lamp-posts and slabs of basaltina, reclaiming their territory from the stray cats and the few tourists who might have wandered across the footbridge.

We came upon Elisa Tomassi sitting on a stone bench in the piazza with Lorenzo Conti, Valetto's resident bell ringer. She was hunched in a black down parka with a fur-fringed hood and smoking a cigarette while Lorenzo, dressed in a black fedora and wool coat turned up at the collar, pulled on his pipe, their exhalations floating up toward the campanile of the church. Milo was telling me about the problem of an old cistern below the villa that was slowly leaking into the rock below the foundation, which was itself a detour from a discussion of the markup on spare auto parts, when we bustled into the piazza with the dogs, just twenty yards from where the two smokers sat talking in the early dusk.

Perhaps it was because I'd spent too many hours cooped up with Iris and her forensic conjectures that my first thought, upon seeing Elisa Tomassi and Lorenzo Conti together, was that they had, in fact, conspired together to steal the stone cottage from me and the widows, that this was just a stepping-stone to infiltrating the villa itself, and that the entire town was next. Perhaps they were going to force the remaining full-timers out and sell this teetering medieval monument to a hotel developer, which would explain Elisa Tomassi's futuristic eyewear, I thought, because obviously she routinely pitched deals to rooms of Milanese hoteliers and financiers. In Abruzzo, I'd stayed in a once-abandoned medieval town that had been restored and converted into an *albergo diffuso*, a hotel where the guest rooms were distributed across a collection of centuries-old houses. Maybe Elisa Tomassi had a similar vision for Valetto. All this came to me as the dogs pulled on their leashes and scampered toward Lorenzo, who always smelled of olives and pork fat.

"*Buonasera*," said Lorenzo, dipping his fingertips so that all three dogs could lick them.

"*Buonasera*," said Milo.

Elisa Tomassi said, "*Buonasera*," lifting her cigarette to one side, away from the dogs. In Italian, she said, "You must be Hugh Fisher, the nephew from America. Your aunty Iris mentioned you'd be arriving." Her accent carried the zees for esses of the north and it sounded less like she was from Milan or Turin than from somewhere up near the border with Switzerland and Austria. She had a spray of freckles across the high bridge of her nose, a long, graceful neck below a volume of graying brunette hair. She flicked her cigarette with her thumb and smiled up at us.

"Yes, Hugh Fisher," I said awkwardly. My mother had kept her maiden name, true to Italian tradition, and I had taken my father's last name. "And this is Milo Scorza."

"Milo and I met briefly when I arrived," she said, nodding politely at Milo. "As you may have heard, I am Elisa Tomassi. The one from Milano, but my family originally comes from the Ossola Valley."

I felt gratified to have pegged her accent. "Almost in Switzerland," I said.

"Very good," she said.

We all nodded politely, the dogs snuffling at our feet.

"*Bella notte*," I said. In fact, it was a cold dusk layered with fog.

Elisa lifted her chin and brought her light brown eyes up at me under the fur fringe of her hood. I was standing close enough to see that there were tiny flecks of gold and copper in her irises. They gave her gaze a slightly startled, leonine quality. In the uncomfortable silence that followed, I wondered if she'd been accused of staring her whole life, and I found myself thinking of predatory birds and exploding stars as I stood there speculating about what causes that kind of pigmentation in the human eyeball. She cinched her coat collar closer to her throat. On her left wrist, just below her sleeve, I noticed a small tattoo of the Greek letter phi—φ— the symbol, I seemed to recall, for the golden ratio, though I couldn't quite recall the mathematics behind it. Was she a scientist, a mathematician? She took another languorous draw on her cigarette and glanced at me with a bemused smile. She could tell, I think, that I was desperate to know what she and Lorenzo had just been talking about.

"What time does the last bell ring, signore?" Milo asked Lorenzo, as if he didn't know.

"Always at ten," said Lorenzo. "So we can all get our beauty sleeps."

All over Italy, mechanized bell ringing had become the norm, tolling every quarter hour, synchronized to internet atomic clocks and standard mean time, but Valetto, or at least Lorenzo, had refused to let that convenience take hold. Maybe in a town with such a precarious relationship to time and geology you wanted to pull the ropes yourself, climb the ladder in the dark with a headlamp and announce your continued existence in a valley of drifting clay and crumbling rock.

"*Come stanno le sorelle?*" Lorenzo asked how the sisters were.

"Alive and well," said Milo.

"*E l'antica madre?*"

"Ida is formidable as ever."

"Give them all my fondest regards," said Lorenzo, pulling on his pipe.

We all said good evening again before Milo guided the

dogs away from the square. Because it felt a little like we were being dismissed, I asked Milo when we returned to Via della Porta, the narrow main street that doglegs toward the villa and the valley below, whether he got along with Lorenzo. The street had once connected Valetto to Etruscan towns along a major trade route.

"In actual fact, he was in love with Donata," Milo said, "a lifetime ago. He even proposed, but she refused him. Lorenzo never married or loved another woman. Today, he is married to his bells and the olives he gathers from the valley."

Here was a new strand for my conspiracy theory: in helping to wrest the cottage and villa from the widows, a jilted Lorenzo was also settling an old score with Milo and Donata. Across the valley, I could see the moon rising through an envelope of fog above the *calanchi* escarpments. I gestured to it and Milo hummed in appreciation. I'd been thinking about the wartime refugee children ever since my dinner with the aunts and my conversation with my grandmother, and I wanted to ask Milo about them. At the dinner, he'd left the fireplace in the taverna by the time the topic came up. By my reckoning, he'd been seven the year the children came, a year younger than my mother, and not yet apprenticed to his father as a *tuttofare*. On his dusk walks with the dogs, he always seemed expansive, like you could ask him about love, ruin, or the nuances of building a French drain, and he'd give you the unmitigated truth. So I asked him, "Do you remember much about the year my grandfather left?"

"Some things. My father didn't like me under his feet at the villa and I was still in school."

"The aunts and my grandmother told me that there were refugee children from up north, who came to live at the villa in 1943."

"This is correct. I remember helping my father make a special metal grate in the cellar so that they wouldn't burn themselves on the fireplace."

The dogs all stopped to piss, one after the other, by the remains of a medieval butcher shop.

"Is it just a coincidence that Aldo went into hiding after the children came? Or did the Germans or the fascists find out that the family was hiding the children?"

"He was hiding more than just refugee children."

"What do you mean?"

"It will be dark soon, but if you're game for *una passeggiata*, I will show you."

Milo led me along the kinked, narrow roadway and around the terraced gardens of the villa. The cobblestones petered out and we were descending on a footpath of packed tufa and smoothed clay, hugging close to the cliffs that formed the town's pedestal. During my summers in Valetto, I'd routinely come down here to play in the Etruscan caves dug into the sides of the cliffs, or I'd go deeper into the woods and the valley, where the old orchards and chestnut groves were choked with weeds along the branches of the silty river.

The dogs scampered up an embankment and fell into single file as we got close to one of the caves, the mouth of which had been closed off with iron bars and chicken wire. We stood peering into the dark and I could make out the remains of donkey stalls and a series of dovecotes dug into the earthen walls. Off to one side, there was a wooden altar with framed portraits of saints hanging above it. Over the centuries, the cave had been used to shelter animals, roost pigeons, and serve as a chapel for peasants, only to be sealed off in recent years with chicken wire to discourage vandals.

"Aldo hid two British soldiers for several months in here.

They were prisoners of war who'd escaped from Laterina. They'd been on the run for weeks, sleeping in barns and out in the fields. My father used to bring them meals and sometimes I would follow after him. Both men were from Manchester and their accents made me laugh. They called me *little mate* and their food *scran*."

The dogs sniffed through the metal bars.

"What about the rest of the town? Didn't Aldo worry that someone would inform on him?"

"So then, yes, we always suspected someone in the town did inform on the Serafinos, because not long after the refugees and the prisoners arrived, Aldo received a letter from the fascist militia requesting him to make a gift of a motorcar for their activities in the south. I always thought it was Silvio Ruffo who told the *fascisti*. He was the local pharmacist and a known party member. After the war, they eventually forced him out of Valetto, but to this day his grandson still runs the farmacia."

I remembered Silvio Ruffo as one of the old men playing chess in the square during my boyhood visits. He came up from Rome on summer weekends to visit his son's family, who lived above the pharmacy in the neighboring town of Bevona. The Serafinos had been collecting their prescriptions in this pharmacy for generations, and I'd always been given a free packet of chewing gum or a caramel whenever I went in there as a boy. I couldn't picture Silvio Ruffo's face, but I recalled that he fed the stray cats from his pockets between chess moves and that he smoked a cigar. And he beat me every time, letting me take white to go first, but routinely opening with the Sicilian Defense—a dash for control over the center of the board.

"What did Aldo do when he got the letter from the fascist militia?" I asked.

"Do you remember the ruined automobile at the bottom of the valley? You and my boys would go down there to play in it sometimes."

"I remember it."

It was a black hulk cankered with rust, its grille slanting in front of a stripped engine, its steering wheel, shredded seats, and gear stick still intact. The names of Milo's sons suddenly came to me—Nico and Antonio—and I remembered that we'd made imaginary road trips in that car my first summer, across African deserts and through South American jungles, before I'd felt the pull of my solitary, bookish nature and the chess games with the old men in the piazza. By then, my father had left us to "find himself" in New York City.

Milo said, "It was Aldo's pride and happiness, a four-door Lancia Ardea, the same kind they used in Rome as taxis during the war. Rather than give it to the fascists, he took it to the top of the hill on the other side of the footbridge and pushed it down into the valley . . . Aldo took me and my father for a drive in it one night when he first bought it, and I remember the steering wheel was on the right side and it had a little dipper switch on the floor for the headlights. It must have crushed his spirits to send that beautiful black angel off the cliff tops . . ."

I could hear the longing in Milo's voice and I suspected it was for the Lancia, not Aldo Serafino. To ruin a machine in its prime, even in the name of patriotic resistance, was a form of sacrilege for someone like Milo.

5

Rinaldo Fumigalli rode into Valetto on the back of Milo's moped, a burgundy attaché case under one arm. When he stepped down in front of the villa, his cognac-brown oxfords crunching on the gravel, he peered out at the valley, craned up at the villa façade in the mild November sunshine, and I saw a slight deflation work into his shoulders, as if he'd expected something grander from Iris's emails and telephone calls. I waited with Iris on the front steps before she bustled toward this manicured, willowy figure in a great flurry of apologies for his long journey south and gratitude that he would come all this way. They kissed on both cheeks and he called her *mia cara professoressa*.

Everything on Rinaldo's person was a thing of refinement—from the Borsalino hat with the grosgrain band to the white alligator-skin watchband to the delicate Ben Franklin wire-frames perched on his big, aquiline nose—but the colors and patterns of his clothes made him look more like a stately piece of furniture than a retired criminologist turned Milanese private detective. I'd never seen so many shades of moth, taupe, or tan on a human being, and all of it had a weave, a texture. Iris introduced me to Rinaldo and I came down the steps to shake his slender, cool hand.

A few moments later, Rinaldo's opposite arrived in the form of Orlando Fiorani, the Serafinos' local lawyer. He came on foot in a shapeless black gabardine suit, a bulging, scuffed leather satchel under one arm, eating a cornetto out of a grease-blotted paper bag. He trotted up the stairs, wiped his crumby hand down one pant leg, and shook hands with each of us. Clearly embarrassed by his disheveled, parochial appearance, Iris introduced Orlando by saying his law firm had been with the family for nearly half a century. Then she whisked us up the stairs and inside the entrance hall, where Donata took Rinaldo's hat and overcoat and put out her hand for Orlando's crumpled cornetto bag. She gestured toward the formal dining room, which had been freshly scrubbed, bleached, and arranged as if for a court-martial in some far-flung pocket of the colonies.

On the enormous walnut table in the middle of the room, there was a silver tray with a carafe of water and four glass tumblers. Lemon wedges floated in the throat of the carafe, and a little paper cone covered its mouth, presumably to keep out plaster dust from the pockmarked fresco above. Three high-backed chairs were arranged along one side of the table and then, ten feet from the opposite edge, a single chair with a brass ashtray on a stand next to it. But the real centerpiece was an outdated speakerphone and hulking fax machine at one end of the table, each attached to thirty feet of wiring, as if whatever was about to unfold would entail telexes and conference calls with the 1990s.

The legal basis of this meeting was unclear to me. An informal discussion before arbitration? A review of the correspondence? But then I heard Iris refer to me as *il quere-lante*, the plaintiff, even though I hadn't brought any case or complaint against Elisa Tomassi, and she said that the complainant, *la denunciante*, the northerner, was due to arrive in fifteen minutes with the documents for review. Rose and Violet stepped into the dining room wrapped in their housecoats, their dogs trotting and wheezing behind them. They sat along the wall, and since I wasn't comfortable with my role as *il querelante*, I went to join them.

Rinaldo took the middle of the three chairs and rested his attaché case on the table. He lifted the paper cone on the carafe and poured himself a glass of water, careful not to unload a lemon wedge, and took a few meditative sips. Orlando and Iris sat on either side, watching him drink, unwilling to approach the water tray, as if hydration were a matter of etiquette or rank.

Rinaldo said, "Since we have a little time at our disposal, perhaps we should review what my firm has ascertained in the course of our due diligence. I have asked my secretary to stand by in case we need additional documents from the files."

I pictured Rinaldo's secretary: a venerable Milanese stenographer in cashmere and pearls.

"I also have some documents written in Aldo Serafino's hand," offered up Orlando, running a finger along the bulging mouth of his leather satchel. "Including his holographic will"—he seemed particularly proud of the word *holographic*— "dated before his departure in 1944. As it happens, my own father witnessed his signature."

Rinaldo ignored Orlando and turned to Iris. "Signora, does my plan meet with your approval?"

Iris gave an approving nod and folded her arms. Rinaldo

opened his attaché case and produced some loose-leaf pages written in loping fountain-pen cursive.

"*Allora*, Elisa Tomassi was born in 1964 and is originally from the Ossola Valley, from a tiny village of chimney sweeps and woodcutters up in the Alps. She moved to Milan when she was eighteen to attend university on a scholarship, but she dropped out to enroll in culinary school and become a chef. In Milan, she and her husband owned and ran a restaurant for more than fifteen years, an establishment that was highly regarded and won several prestigious culinary awards."

I hadn't noticed a wedding ring on Elisa Tomassi's hand and I wondered if the marriage was still intact. And she was a chef, not a mathematician or an ad executive or architect, and surely her culinary calling must have come from her mother, Alessia, who in turn had been taught to cook by my grandmother. There was something satisfying about making this connection, and I pictured a young girl standing beside Ida in the villa's wartime kitchen.

"Signora Tomassi owns an apartment in Milan, in the Isola district, and she now lets a room and sometimes the entire apartment to tourists on Airbnb, and this enterprise enjoys a 4.2-star rating among its former guests . . ."

I wondered if Rinaldo was going to read us a few online reviews of the apartment.

"This is the apartment where she lived with her husband, teenage son, and university-aged daughter until the restaurant burned down and there was a subsequent divorce. I gather there was no insurance." The word *subsequent* seemed to imply causality, as if the fire had also devastated the marriage. "These events transpired a few years ago. The son went to live in London with his father and the daughter stayed behind with the mother in the apartment."

Even as a historian, I have always been unnerved by the brute facts of other people's lives. But it's not empathy that causes me to linger on the torments and hardships in the archive or during interviews, it's the galvanizing fear that these things could happen to me. As I listened, I knew Rinaldo wanted to establish Elisa Tomassi's motivation for wanting the cottage, but all I could think about was the award-winning restaurant burning to the ground, or the son going off to live with his father in England. Even a few years after Clare died, I would call Susan several times a week in her college dorm on some logistical premise, but mostly to make sure she was still alive and breathing in the world. Now, I found myself taking my phone out of my pocket to text Susan that I loved her and was proud of her, my go-to whenever I felt "the fog on the staircase," the phrase I'd used in my few therapy sessions to describe this vague and recurring sense of dread.

Rinaldo continued thumbing through his notes while I looked at the screen of my phone, waiting for Susan's reply, for proof of life and love. Elisa's grandparents, Rinaldo said, were active in the partisan resistance after the 1943 armistice, an umbrella group of antifascists who pushed for liberation after the Italian government surrendered to the Allies and the Germans took control of the central and northern regions. The grandparents were living in Milan during the first part of the war before returning to the Ossola Valley after the bombings and the armistice. Her grandfather Giulio Parigi was involved in the short-lived Republic of Ossola.

"A *republic*?" scoffed Violet from the sidelines.

"*Sì, signora*," said Rinaldo, enjoying some banter with his courtroom gallery. "They even had their own flag and official recognition from the Swiss. It lasted less than a month, be-

fore the Germans sent reinforcements and crushed everything. It was their last hurrah." Rinaldo flipped through
some pages. "It is alleged that Aldo Serafino was given protection in a *baita*, a mountain hut, owned by Giulio Parigi
and his wife, Carmela. They sheltered him after he was re-
nounced as a partisan in the resistance during the German
counteroffensive. These details, we are told, are contained in
letters, as is the promise of the stone cottage upon Aldo's
death."

Violet gripped the edge of her seat, the way she did during
a televised pro-wrestling match. "Are we to suppose that our
father traveled all the way up there, practically to Switzerland, during wartime?"

"Didn't he leave on horseback? I think I remember that,"
said Rose.

"And where have these supposed letters been all this
time?" asked Violet. "Our father writes letters to some alpine
peasants and promises a cottage that's five hundred miles
away?" She waved a dismissive hand in the air.

From the back of the dining room, Elisa Tomassi's voice
called through the slatted sunshine: "Signora, there is only
one letter, and it was written to your mother, but never sent.
It was composed during Aldo Serafino's last days, when my
grandmother was caring for him."

She must have been standing there for some time, listening to us assemble the outline of her life. Her bootheels
rapped staccato against the terra-cotta tiles as she crossed
the room, a slim cardboard box held close to her chest. As
she approached the walnut table, she said good morning to
everybody and Rinaldo gestured to the high-backed chair
with the ashtray beside it. She sat down, her back straight,
her knees together, and rested the box in her lap. From the

pocket of her plum velvet dress, she took out a pair of white cotton gloves, the kind I'd worn a thousand times in reading rooms and archives. She opened the lid of the box and placed the gloves on top of some handwritten pages in plastic sleeves. "If you wish to remove the pages from their plastic sleeves, then please use these cotton gloves to protect the old paper. It's quite brittle."

Rinaldo removed his wire-frame glasses and held them at an angle, one earpiece pressed against his lower lip. "Before we examine the documents," he said, "perhaps you would be willing to answer a few questions, Signora Tomassi?"

"As many as you like."

Apparently oblivious to the digital age, Rinaldo lifted a black-and-chrome Dictaphone from his attaché case. He pressed record, watched the miniature cassette begin to spindle, and aimed it out toward the complainant. "How did this letter come into your possession?"

"I discovered it in my grandparents' house, after my grandmother died."

"Both grandparents are deceased?"

"Yes. My grandfather was killed by the Germans for harboring partisans in the autumn of 1944, but my grandmother lived until she was in her eighties. She died in 1988, but I only found the letter in her attic just a few years ago among some other documents. We still own my grandparents' house in a small village northeast of Domodossola."

"It seems she's got a taste for real estate all around Italy," announced Violet.

"Signora, please," said Rinaldo.

Elisa Tomassi addressed the side of the room. "I cannot change the past, or the wishes of the dead."

Rinaldo asked, "In what way were your grandparents involved in the resistance?"

"They took supplies up into the mountains for the partisans by mule. My grandfather was a chimney sweep, woodcutter, and carpenter, and he knew the Alps very well. My grandmother was also a coordinator for the *staffette*."

"*Cosa significa?*" asked Orlando.

"The staffettas were women who worked in the resistance. They helped smuggle weapons and resistance newspapers or acted as messengers. My grandparents ran their operation out of the Society for the Noble Burial of Cadavers, a charity they had started for burying the war dead. They hid weapons and supplies inside the coffins."

"*Che coraggio,*" said Rinaldo. "And how did they meet Aldo Serafino?"

"The partisans recruited Aldo to work in the Ossola Valley because he was an engineer and had already been sympathetic to the cause."

"Because he took in refugees like your mother?" asked Iris.

"*Sì,*" said Elisa. "That was how my grandparents knew about Aldo."

"Please continue," said Rinaldo.

"They needed someone who could live a double life up there in the towns, completely unknown, and then go out into the mountains at night to radio with the British and Americans, to organize the air drops. My grandparents were his cover. They employed him as a coffin maker during the winters, when it was too cold to be in the mountains. But then—" Elisa swallowed, adjusted her glasses, tucked some curls behind her ears. "Aldo's real identity was revealed after he was denounced as a partisan during the German counter-offensive. He had to disappear into the Alps. My grandmother talked about him on her deathbed, but only referred to him as the engineer, *l'ingegnere*, his nickname in the resistance. It wasn't until I found the letter that I realized who he was. My mother, who had never spoken about these events, confirmed that it was Aldo Serafino, the father from the villa where she'd stayed in Umbria."

"And what about your mother now?" asked Rinaldo, looking down at his notes. "Why isn't she here claiming the cottage on behalf of your family?"

"She is unwell," said Elisa, straightening the empty fingers of a white cotton glove.

Rinaldo poured himself some more water and took a few sips. Susan finally texted me back—a kissy-face emoji—and it echoed through the room with pinging, submarine glee. I apologized, turned my phone to silent, crossed my legs.

Rinaldo said, "Thank you for being so forthcoming, Signora Tomassi. Could we now review the documents?"

"Of course," said Elisa, standing up and bringing the box and gloves to the table.

Violet folded her arms and said, "My mother still has some of my father's old letters and documents in the library, so we can compare the handwriting. This little hoax will be revealed as a forgery very handily."

"Naturally," said Orlando, finally composed, now pouring himself some water into a tumbler, "there is the matter of whether such a letter has been witnessed and how it stands against Aldo Serafino's *holographic* will, which, as I said earlier, I happen to have in my possession here . . ."

Rinaldo put his two palms together, prayer-like, at the tip of his hawkish nose. "Perhaps we can ask Signora Tomassi to give us an adjournment while we review the letter. Shall we reconvene this afternoon? Is four too late? I want to make sure we have plenty of time."

Elisa, who was still standing at the edge of the table, said that would be fine and turned toward the back of the dining room. When she was almost to the entrance hall, she stopped to address us again. "My grandparents were poor and mostly forgotten after they died. But they were heroes of the Italian people and they saved your father's life. As you will see in the letter, the cottage was a debt of gratitude from your family to mine, when my grandmother had lost almost everything she had in the world. I know the right and moral thing will prevail."

Violet leaned down to rub her dog's stomach as he stretched into a ribbon of sunlight. "Rocky feels unwell . . . *mal di stomaco*. I will go and find some of the handwriting. Otherwise, you can call me on the intercom when this foolishness is over." She stood up and walked from the room, the dog ambling and grunting behind her.

August 21, 1947

My darling Ida,

A man is a frail thing. Not much more than a wire, a
spring. He can be unraveled by silence, poison, fever,
ink . . . My long silence will always be unforgivable, but
I will attempt to explain the fracturing of time that has
led me here, to this mountainside and this letter. I write
to you from a tiny village up in the Vigezzo Valley, a
stone's throw from Switzerland, shocked to be alive two
years after the war has ended, but also humiliated to be
dying of an infection the doctors seem unable to treat.
Where to begin the unraveling of this wire?

By some miracle of God, I managed to get through
the German line in the spring of 1944. I rode north only
at night, through the woods and plains, stopping at
small farms where the salt of the earth fed me and kept
me abreast of soldier movements and road blockades. I
also received messages from the partisans who'd enlisted

my help in the mountains. A man of my age and background was of no use for the actual fighting, so they put me in charge of radio equipment and transmissions.

Between March and October I lived up in the mountains with former waiters, barbers, shopkeepers, and factory workers, all of them with rifles and code names. We slept in stone shepherd huts, up in the log rafters nestled in piles of hay and dried ferns. In the winter, we came down to the villages and towns to work incognito. I went by Ennio and made coffins.

Because I was the lifeline to the airwaves and the Allies, I was kept out of harm's way. So my injury didn't happen on some night raid of a German barracks or an expedition to blow up a bridge. In fact, it happened one afternoon while I was communing with honeybees.

I had discovered that I could hide spare radio equipment inside the alpine hive boxes and that the bees would happily go about their business. This particular afternoon I was forced to use a little smoke to clear out some of the hive and I suspect it drew the attention of a fascist or German sniper. These lone wolves sometimes roamed the mountains looking for partisan hideouts like furriers looking for pelts. As I crouched over the hive with a smoking branch of spruce, I heard the shot and fell to the ground. There was a starburst of blood against the wooden hive box, and on my left thigh, but the bees were unperturbed as I waited for certain death. I had a small pistol in my rucksack but I'd stupidly hung my gear on a branch of a tree while I worked. So I waited for the next bullet out of the sniper's chamber, while the honeybees murmured and swarmed.

Eventually, when the gunfire came, it was from my alpine brothers who'd come to investigate the single shot. They fired their rifles into the treetops, but we never found the sniper. Instead, we managed to announce our presence all throughout the hills, and so we spent the next eight hours on the move, a former barber and waiter hauling me out on an improvised stretcher of vine poles and saplings. They smuggled a Swiss veterinarian up into the hills to remove the slug from my thigh and patch my wound. If there is a hero in this story, it's the man who sewed me up with the equanimity he offered to livestock. This partisan war was full of bravery, but it did not erupt from my veins. I fled Valetto because I'd rapped the iron-knuckled grip of the local fascists and German officials, and I'd ended up in the north more as a man on the run than a man roused by his own conscience. This is something you should know.

Rinaldo Fumigalli paced under the fresco while he read the first section of the letter aloud to us. He held the papers between white-gloved fingers, leaning into the meticulous vowels of his Milanese accent. At first, his voice sounded far off, abstracted, but by the time he got to Aldo's description of being shot in the leg, a note of tenderness crept in. I listened from the side of the room, wedged between Rose and her sleeping dog. Rose had been thirteen the year that her father left. She clutched my arm the whole time, whispering *è lui*, *è lui*, it's him. Over at the long walnut table, Iris didn't betray any emotion, but she took detailed notes in her notebook. Orlando Fiorani shuffled papers during the reading

and jotted down—judging by the little shakes of his head—
objections and inconsistencies. Rinaldo reached for the second half of the letter and began to pace again.

August 25, 1947

At night, when I am wakeful between feverish dreams
and regrets, I can smell Lago Maggiore, even though it's
thirty kilometers down through the sunless wooded
hills above Cannobio. We sometimes ventured into
these murky warrens during the war . . . hiding weapons
or planning attacks . . . and I see it now as a labyrinth of
switchbacks and stone bridges before the big blue eye
of the lake. I see myself swimming out to Isola Bella . . .
I once canoed past the island under the cover of night, on
a four-day journey to Switzerland to pick up a suitcase
of grenades and radio equipment. I remember the
peacocks calling to each other from different sides of the
island with shrieks of indignation . . . I can still hear
that sound. Or perhaps it's a calling from the other
side . . .

Before I sign this letter, I must acknowledge a debt
of gratitude. It begins with Giulio Parigi, the father of
our dear Alessia. He grew up in this very house and
village, and until the war made his living as a chimney
sweep, woodcutter, and coffin maker. Although he was
a partisan, he never thought of himself as a communist
or altruist. He simply believed in the freedom to decide
his own affairs, those of his mind and heart included.

In the winter of '43 he was living with his wife,
Carmela, and his two children in Milan. After the big

air raid in February, the couple decided to send their children to relative safety—Alessia to us in Umbria and her older brother to a Red Cross family in Switzerland. Then they returned to the Ossola Valley, where they'd both grown up, and started the Society for the Noble Burial of Cadavers to help bury the war dead with dignity, but also to hide ammunition, messages, and food destined for the resistance fighters up in the mountains.

When the Ossola Republic was formed, Giulio delivered one of the many newspapers that flourished during this brief flame of independence. He drove a truck around the hills, handing out newspapers and firewood to villagers, but his route also made him widely known and a target once the fascists rallied. After thousands of German-Italian troops marched into Domodossola in October of 1944, a brief and bloody battle followed and then the republic was dissolved, sending most of the town's residents into Switzerland as refugees. By some act of supernatural courage, Giulio and Carmela stayed behind to tend to their mission.

Initially, it was my name, not Giulio's, that surfaced on the lips of informants during the German counteroffensive. Carmela had already nursed me back to health after my gunshot wound and now Giulio hid me in a mountain hut that had been in his family for generations. My alpine brothers had all been killed in the line of duty, or during the fascist backlash.

One night, Carmela came to me with the news that Giulio had been shot as a traitor for aiding the resistance movement and that his body had been left hanging in the Piazza del Mercato in Domodossola. I've

never seen a woman so broken—her husband shot and
hanged, her children far away. She was distraught at the
idea of Giulio's body not being given a proper burial, but
it was impossible to move into the town undetected. She
wept all night, up in the hay and dried ferns, her face
pressed into a wool coat to stifle the sound.

I could tell you of our nights up in the mountains
together, of how we fled into Switzerland and were
interrogated at the border as potential spies, how we
spent a week looking for Carmela's son . . . We clung to
each other the way sailors do in a shipwreck. I did and
do love Carmela, the woman at my bedside. Alessia,
who returned from you a few months ago by train, is
now the supreme cook of the household. She barely
speaks, but she brings me delicate broths that carry the
aromas of your kitchen. These broths fill me with
nostalgia and shame for my silence. You must believe
me when I say I have missed you all profoundly each
and every day.

The villages and towns here are in a bad way. The
Germans sacked and looted the houses and shops and
now the people struggle to get by. Carmela's children
will almost certainly be forced to look elsewhere
for work, even Alessia, not yet eleven. With your
permission, Ida, I would like to bequeath to this family
our stone cottage. I know that might seem like a whim
of a feverish man who's been gone too long from his
own family, but I have thought long and hard about it.
Valetto is a sanctuary compared to this valley, and I can
imagine Carmela and her children beginning again
down there. The son might help with household repairs
and tending the property, while Alessia might be

employed in one of the local kitchens, perhaps even ours. It's possible that I am underestimating the changes that have occurred in our shifting valley, but I know that this family's chances of survival up here are slim. I owe my life to them, Ida, and it is my dying wish that I give them some tangible refuge in the world that I am about to flee.

With my deepest love and affection,
Aldo Vito Serafino

The coil heaters ticked away, burning up the afternoon's plaster dust. None of us spoke for a full minute. Despite Rinaldo's pacing, I'd sat transfixed during the reading of the letter, as if my grandfather were speaking directly from the afterlife. I wondered if the stone cottage had, in fact, rightfully belonged to Elisa Tomassi's family for decades and that we were the ones occupying it under false pretenses.

Rinaldo slid the papers back into their plastic sleeves and rested them on the table. He turned, cotton gloves still on, hands butterflying white behind his back in contemplation. Orlando Fiorani looked down at his notes before taking up the plastic sleeves. After a pause, he addressed Rinaldo's back: "With regard to several matters: first, there is no witness to the signature, nullifying the effect of this as a testamentary document, and, second, Italian law requires that a *testamento olografo* be written by a person of sound mind, a condition that runs counter to the suggestion of sepsis and fever in the letter . . . There is also the *fatto brutto* that the letter was never sent." Quite pleased with himself, Orlando folded his gabardine arms.

When Rinaldo responded to the lawyer, he did so by

addressing Iris. "These are valid legal points, *Professoressa*, and no doubt this letter could be contested in a court of law through such a lens. Before we proceed along those lines, however, I think it would be prudent to have an expert graphologist review the letter and compare it against Aldo Serafino's known handwriting. If there is no match, then we can drop the matter at once."

It occurred to me that Rinaldo was on a retainer with Iris, that he had no interest in wrapping things up quickly or passing the baton off to a probate court, where he had no authority.

"How long will all of that take?" asked Iris.

"Assuming Signora Violet can find some of Aldo's handwriting, we will fax and overnight it, along with a copy of the letter, to my secretary in Milan. We should hear back within a day or two. She can arrange to have a graphologist we've used before on standby. Does that meet with Serafino approval?"

"That sounds like it's for the best," said Iris.

"Very well," said Rose into her handkerchief, "but I can tell you that those are the words of our father, plain as day."

"Let's not rush to conclusions," said Iris.

After a pause, I said, "We asked Signora Tomassi to come back here at four. Should we let her know that we need another day or two to evaluate the letter?"

Rinaldo picked up the plastic-sleeved pages. "It would be very kind if you could let her know. I must begin preparing the dispatch at once."

"Would you mind?" asked Iris.

"Of course not," I said.

And with that, I became an envoy of Rinaldo Fumigalli's *tribunale*.

φ

There was no answer when I knocked on the door of the cottage, so I walked around the back in case Elisa Tomassi was sitting out on the terrace. I found her with a wool blanket across her legs, smoking a cigarette in a wicker chair, watching the sun pink up the chalky calanchi ravines. On an ironwork table next to her, there was an uncorked bottle of wine and half a glass of red, and a Penguin paperback of Agatha Christie's *The Body in the Library*, its cover banded in ivory and bottle green. I recognized it as one of my mother's books right away, from the shelf of thrillers and crime novels and puzzles in the living room, and I felt myself prickle with annoyance. Here was a stranger disturbing the scant evidence of my mother's presence in this house and on this earth. Then, an image from the letter flashed into my mind—Elisa Tomassi's grandfather shot and hanged in the piazza of Domodossola, a town I'd visited—and I did my best to sound polite and friendly as I stepped onto the terrace. "Apologies, Signora Tomassi, I tried knocking."

She turned, shifted in her chair. "Please, call me Elisa. Is it time for *la deliberazione*?"

"There's been a delay. Rinaldo would like to have the handwriting analyzed in Milan, but we should hear back in the next day or two."

She stubbed out her cigarette into a cracked floral saucer from the kitchen. "At home, I'd given up completely. Now I'm smoking like a schoolgirl. Or is it a chimney?"

"Probably both," I said.

She picked up her wineglass, cradled the bottom in her

palm. "Would you like some wine? Or is that fraternizing with the enemy?"

I tried not to appear wary, but I could feel myself averting my eyes and looking out over the valley. Would my aunts notice if I didn't return directly to the villa? Would accepting a glass of wine divulge my stance on the letter? When I said nothing, Elisa got up, draped the blanket around her shoulders, and said she would fetch another glass. I sat down in the other chair and wondered how many sunsets I'd seen from this terrace with my mother, or with Clare and Susan. This was always the designated afternoon spot for lounging in good weather, because it got the late sun and frequent moonrises over the distant hills.

Elisa returned, handed me a stubby trattoria glass, and poured some wine into it. It was a point of pride with my mother that no two glasses in the cottage matched. Elisa sat back down with her blanket, a pair of Ugg boots halfway up her calves.

"The chiminea works if you need to build a fire out here," I said.

"Yes, I should do that. I need to get some more firewood."

On the edge of the terrace, there was a line of clay pots, mostly filled with neglected herbs—leggy rosemary and spindly, browning thyme—but there was also a single agave plant that dappled pale green and blue-gray in the late-afternoon light. Beyond the lichened stone ledge, there were topiaries of indiscernible shapes, a quince tree, and a stand of cypress, before the darkening lunar void itself. Clare used to call our gatherings out here existential happy hours because of that view, and I could remember, as a boy, that I used to imagine sleepwalking right off the side of those cliffs and falling through time itself.

"What did you make of the letter?" Elisa asked after a sip of wine.

I studied the tessellations of flagstone. "I don't think I can say just yet."

"Shrewd," she said softly.

"My aunts want to be sure. We all do."

"Naturally."

She swayed the tiny ocean of wine in her glass, rippling it under a sconce. "But didn't you have some reaction to hearing your grandfather's voice? Let's assume for a second that this is really his deathbed letter to your grandmother. What then? I promise I won't take your response as legally binding."

"As a historian—"

"Excuse me, sorry, but what about as a human person? As just a man?"

I stretched my legs out and crossed them at the calf to regain composure. "History *is* personal for me. So it's hard to separate it from who I am. This place is in my blood . . . but listening to the letter felt like I was hearing my grandfather for the first time . . . Up until now, he has always been the methodical, mustached engineer in framed photographs, or the man behind the ornate bookplates in the library and the poetic taxidermy plaques. The lynx down in the taverna is called *emperor of the dark forest*, engraved onto the brass plate as if it's the real Latin name. Now, I feel like I know why. When I heard the letter, it was as if he was standing in a doorway. Suddenly, he seemed knowable." I took a slow sip of my wine and then, to taper things off, I added, "I mean, as much as anyone is knowable. Anyway, that's what I thought of the letter."

"That was quite honest. *Grazie*."

"What happened to your grandfather was a horrible, horrible tragedy."

"We have carried it all these years, I think. They ran the image of him hanging and mutilated in the square in the newspaper, recorded for all time. The letter tells some of his story but it also repays a debt. I think you see that."

"My aunts' lawyer seems to think the letter may not hold up as part of a last will and testament."

"There is the legal question," Elisa said, "and there is also the moral question. If it turns out to be his handwriting, which I know it is, then why would your family go against his wishes?"

I let the question hang in the air. Dusk was hardening against the tree-studded hills and down in the blue-shadowed gorges choked with chaparral. It was possible that I'd inherited a cottage that was not my mother's to give, but regardless of what I thought—or might come to think—I didn't see my aunts rallying around the final wishes of a father who'd left behind a wife and four daughters in wartime. As the German and Italian fascists retreated north, they blew up the Valetto footbridge, and the Serafino women found themselves marooned in a crumbling town without prospects. As soon as they were of a remotely marriageable age, Violet and then Rose left home to marry industrious older men, and according to my mother, these were loveless, economic alliances. My mother was too young for a swift, strategic marriage, and Iris was determined to save herself for a life as an academic, so they stayed on at the villa, working nights and weekends in Ida's restaurant after the bridge was rebuilt.

But Aldo's absence had still left its mark on them. Iris never dated until she went to university in Rome, and then she promptly had an affair with her married philosophy professor. And I was sure it was partly because of my mother's experience of growing up fatherless that she mistrusted the idea that men would ever stick around. When my own father, an American photographer she'd met in Greece in the late 1950s, left her—and me—to go live in New York City in 1976, she told me *we always knew we would end up alone together* and proceeded to dress like a widow and speak of him in the past tense to our midwestern neighbors.

Weary of my silence, Elisa Tomassi said, "Your aunt Iris, when we first spoke on the telephone, said you were coming here on a sabbatical. Are you a professor?"

She didn't seem like someone who asked polite questions or made small talk, so I wondered if this conversational shift was a tactic. But then she leaned forward in her chair and said, "Tell me, what do you teach?" and I realized she was genuinely curious.

"History," I said, "at a small college in Michigan. I'm in Italy for six months to do some guest lectures and research."

"What is your research area?"

"Lately, I study the social history of abandonment. I published a book a few years back about Italy's ghost towns and villages."

"Towns like Valetto?"

"Yes, exactly."

She smiled into her wineglass. "Excuse me for saying, but it sounds like a very depressing topic."

"I actually find these sorts of places inspiring."

She pushed a strand of hair behind one ear, held my eye until I looked away. "*How* could that be possible?"

I imagined that she ruffled Milanese feathers with that cauterizing, leonine stare and the abruptness of her questions, but there was such genuine wonder in her voice that it was impossible to dismiss, as if she were asking how planets or electricity were made. I suddenly found myself wanting to make her understand my fascination with towns and villages on the wrong side of history. I brought my gaze back from the valley and said, "Most of these places have a story about an earthquake that decimated the town overnight, or the generations of young people who left for jobs, but then there's always someone, a mayor or amateur historian, who wants to bring the town back to life. There's a town up in the Alps where the deaths outstrip the births by four to one every year, and it's offering houses for a few hundred euros if the owners will fix them up and live in them. And they'll give ten thousand euros to any family that has a baby in the town and stays. My favorite scheme is the village up in a sunless northern valley that installed an enormous mirror on the opposite mountainside to direct sunlight down into the town square in the middle of winter."

"That sounds very Italian," Elisa said, laughing softly. "And does someone rent you a deck chair and blanket and newspaper down in the sunny square?"

"No, but the mirror has kept people from leaving the town every winter. I love those stories. Italians talk all the time about art and beauty and history, but only a few of them are really willing to keep their ancestral villages alive."

"I'm not sure I agree," she said flatly. "I think most Italians want to save their own history, but they're also drowning in it. It's all they've ever known. Maybe we don't think it can be taken away."

"That seems possible," I said quietly.

As an American with an Anglo-Italian mother, I knew better than to pick a fight with a native Italian on some matter of cultural belief. I'd been cornered by Italian historians and sociologists at conferences before and knew that there were certain arguments I could never win. We sat through a silence, watching a seam of light fade within a cloud. I could feel the wine warming my chest as the air came up from the river, cooling the backs of my hands. The dusk smelled of clay and flint. Determined not to circle back to the cottage dispute or Italian history, I asked Elisa how old her children were.

"Marcella is twenty and Matteo is seventeen. Yours?"

"My daughter is almost twenty-four. Susan."

"Where is she?"

"She's getting a Ph.D. at Oxford in economics. She did a semester abroad in England during undergrad and she got the British bug."

"A terrible disease. My ex-husband was Scottish." She nudged her glasses back onto the bridge of her nose. "Well, I suppose he still is."

I wasn't sure how to respond, so I said, "I just spent a few days with Susan in Rome."

"Very nice. My daughter is running our Airbnb in Milan and hopefully still going to her classes. I will call her tonight to check in."

She tightened the blanket across her legs, crossed her arms. I wondered if she was afraid that the conversation would turn to her son in England, to his reasons for leaving with his father. In my grief, I'd discovered a gift for reading avoidance in other people's body language, so I set her at ease by asking about becoming a chef.

"I hated cooking at first. When I was young, my mother was always trying to teach me about food and get me into the kitchen. Then, when I went to university, I was supposed to study art history. I got a part-time job as a kitchen hand in Milan because my scholarship wasn't enough for three meals a day. I washed the dishes and sliced charcuterie and plated salads and I watched everything the chef did, a big Milanese oaf with tattoos and knife scars on his arms who never spoke to me. One winter night, the chef was in a car accident and the owner was going to close the restaurant. I asked him if he would let me cook. The whole night, it was like my mother was standing there in the kitchen, telling me what to do, guiding my hands. It went so well that I never went back to the university."

"How did your parents take it?"

"My father had moved away for a job by then, but he wrote that I was making a terrible mistake. My mother, on the other hand, was very happy. A year later I went to culinary school." Elisa drained her glass and set it on the table beside her. "My mother learned her passion for food and the old Italian ways of cooking from your grandmother. She used to tell me stories about foraging at night for mushrooms and about a hundred-fifty-year-old pear tree that grew down here in the valley. The Fiorentina pear was the best thing she'd ever eaten. These were the fairy tales of my childhood."

"Is the tree still there?"

"I haven't found it yet, but I am determined. The valley still has some old-world fruit and nut trees, varieties that have been largely forgotten."

"I spent a lot of time playing down there as a boy. I didn't realize there was anything special in those overgrown orchards."

We sat silently for a moment watching the sunset. I thought about the way personal histories intersect, across bloodlines and decades, the way she grew up hearing about a mythic pear tree in Umbria, a place she'd never visited, while I'd climbed a thousand trees in that very valley, oblivious to the living heirlooms around me. We were strangers with shared history, sitting in the falling dark on a terrace suspended on the side of a mesa, but somehow also suspended in time. It occurred to me that neither of us ever got to meet our Italian grandfathers.

I asked, "Are both your parents still alive?"

"Not my father, but my mother is alive."

"You said earlier she's unwell."

"Yes, that's right. She has been unwell for some time. What about your father? Is he still alive?"

I set my glass down on the table. "He died when I was a teenager," I said. "He took his own life." The phrasing had always struck me as odd but I remembered that was the way my mother told me, six months after she'd gotten word of her ex-husband's suicide. She'd said it as if he'd taken something that didn't belong to him and as if it had happened just that morning. *Your father has gone and taken his own life.* Years later, I connected with my father's parents only to find out that they'd called to tell my mother the news as soon as it had happened, that we'd been invited to a memorial service in Brooklyn.

"That's so sad," Elisa said. "I'm very sorry that happened to you."

The easy tenderness and concern of her comment caught me off guard. I cleared my throat and looked off into the gardens. I couldn't remember the last time I'd divulged something about myself to anyone besides Susan or Clare, let alone to someone I barely knew and who, if things unfolded a certain way, might take away one of the few anchors I had left in the world. I could have just told her that my father was no longer alive. When she stood and drifted over to the edge of the terrace, I wondered, gratefully, if it was to give me a moment to recover myself. The blanket around her shoulders reminded me of Rose's description of the refugee children standing at the edge of the terraces like little birds about to fly over the valley, their blankets draped around their shoulders like wings. I wondered if her mother had stood in that very spot.

Taking the last sip of my wine, I said, "You can always smell the river at dusk." When she didn't respond immediately, I assumed things had shifted uncomfortably between us and, in a preemptive strike, set my glass back on the table. "Well, I suppose I'd better head back to the villa. My aunts will be getting anxious about dinner." In fact, they'd probably all be eating alone in their apartments and at least one of them would be checking the clock every now and again to measure how long I'd been down here.

"Thank you for the conversation," she said, turning with a smile I couldn't quite decipher. "I'll wait to hear about the handwriting."

I got up to leave. "Yes, apologies again for the delay." As I walked across the terrace, I noticed through the French doors that the cottage was settling into darkness, and I had to fight the urge to go inside and switch on the lamps my mother had bought at an estate sale twenty years earlier.

After the writing samples had been sent off to Milan, Iris and Rinaldo went to dinner at a restaurant in Bevona, catching up on old times, while Rose and Violet kept to their apartments. In the main kitchen, Donata had made some minestra soup with local sausage and kale from the garden, and I offered to take some to my grandmother and aunts. My grandmother was already asleep, the birdcage covered, so I left the soup with Sofia. Next, I brought soup to Violet, who answered her door in a nightdress, her dyed reddish hair in rollers, Rocky IV barking at her heels, a pro-wrestling crowd howling for revenge in the background. She told Rocky to "go roll it up" on his bed and he did.

"Thank you," she said in the doorway, "but I'm not feeling well and have no appetite. I thought a grudge match between a Roman *barbaro* and a horse-thieving *stronzo* from Calabria would lift my spirits, but no luck."

"Can I get you anything else? Aspirin or Hospasol?" During my boyhood visits, Milo had often deputized me to run errands for my aunts, and I remembered Hospasol was Violet's antacid of choice.

"Very kind, but I think I'll just go to bed before long. *Buonanotte*," she said, gently closing her door.

Of all my elderly aunts, Violet was the one I understood the least. Unless I was caught in the cross fire between her and Iris, she was invariably polite and welcoming, but she could also be standoffish. Even when my mother stayed at the cottage, or when I came with Susan or Clare, she'd never once stopped in for a cup of tea or coffee, or to say hello. She mostly kept to her apartment, and I'd often suspected that the burden of being the eldest, of marrying so young to keep the family afloat, had left her embittered. And where Rose had transformed her youthful unhappy marriage and subsequent widowhood into a calling for charity and religion, Violet didn't seem to have hobbies or interests beyond watching professional wrestling, boxing, darts, and snooker on television. She doted on her British bulldog, Rocky IV, whose suffix was a reminder of the short-snouted, wheezy Rockies who'd come before and her devotion to this genetically doomed breed. Over the decades, Milo was forever taking the Rockies to the vet in Bevona and delivering prescriptions to her apartment. Maybe, I thought, turning back down the hallway with the soup tray, these overbred dogs with their ear infections and droopy, bloodshot eyes made her feel needed and gave her a sense of purpose.

When Rose opened the door to her apartment at the other end of the third-floor hallway, she looked at the two bowls of soup on the tray and said, "Sharing a meal with my favorite nephew is just the thing to cheer me up." I'd been hoping to work on my lecture while Iris was out of her apartment for the evening, but I let Rose keep the impression that dining with her had been my plan all along.

The inside of her apartment was just like I remembered it.

The couch and lounge chairs wrapped in plastic, the terrace through the French doors occupied by dozing stray cats. When it came to neutering and spaying the town's feral cat population, Valetto hadn't made any progress since its medieval prime. During the day, a dozen cats slept and lounged in the piazza or on the steps of the church, inadvertently posing for tourist snapshots, but at night they either crossed the footbridge into Bevona, where the food scraps were better in the alleyways behind the restaurants, or they sauntered back toward the villa, scampering up the vined pergolas and ramparts to settle on Rose's mildewed terrace.

The living room was a shrine to Rose's rescuing instincts. Every surface sheathed in plastic or doilied against spills and marks, decades of Italian *Vogue* protected in cardboard magazine files, the walls crowded with framed portraits of her sponsored children from Africa, South America, and Asia, all of them with earnest or exuberant smiles. Ever since the big earthquake of 1971, she'd been sending "a nominal amount" per child each month to an international relief agency in Bologna. She'd never taken down a portrait and by now there were twenty-five or so children looking gratefully out from her walls, even though some of them were, by now, closer to retirement than college. As we sat on the polymer-wrapped couch with the tray of soup, I conjured two scenarios: either Rose stopped sending her monthly installments for a better life after each child aged out of the program, or she continued to send it directly to them and now there was a fifty-year-old Nigerian surveyor who, inexplicably and happily, got a money order from Italy once a month, just enough to cover his cigarettes.

The terrace doors were open, despite the cool weather, and we watched the cats preening and sleeping. Craning up at the wall of faces behind the couch, I asked Rose if any of the children she'd sponsored had come to visit her.

"*Solo uno.*"

"Which one?"

She pointed up at the middle row with her soupspoon. "That happy fat grinner on the end."

"I'm not sure that's the best way to refer to him."

"*Perché?*"

"Fat might be considered insulting by some people."

"What about happy? Is this word still safe?"

"Yes."

She swallowed some soup. "*Allora*, the happy one came to visit me some years ago. His name is Duc, which means *passione* in Vietnamese."

"How was that?"

"He was studying in America on a scholarship and he was in Rome for study abroad. He asked me if I wanted to donate to his kick-starting program."

"Kickstarter."

"Yes, that was it. He was making a film or writing a book or something. I told him he should study business and get me a return on my investment."

I laughed, a little uneasily.

Rose said, "He never wrote letters to me again after that."

In the hallway, I could make out a portrait of Saint Rita, the Augustinian nun and widow of the fifteenth century, patroness of abused wives, loners, and impossible causes, whose life had obsessed Rose since her twenties. Despite a bleeding forehead and a cloud of white bees swarming around her in the portrait, Rita smiled cryptically across the centuries, radiating filaments of gold-and-rose light. I pictured my aunt on her annual pilgrimage to the basilica in southeastern

Umbria, on her knees, rosary in hand, praying before the ossified nun's body that slumbered for eternity in a glass-domed reliquary. This was the same woman—my aunt, not the champion of the underdog—who loved magazine scandal and *Vogue* fashion shoots but who was also known to introduce herself at family gatherings as *la sorella sterila con cui è facile andare d'accordo*, the barren sister who is easy to get along with.

After a while, I asked Rose what she thought of the letter.

She contemplated the space above her soup bowl. "I think it is a truthful letter, but it made me very sad. We have spent our whole lives wondering what happened to him and suddenly he is dying right in front of our ears in the dining room."

"Do you think Iris and Violet will allow Elisa to take over the cottage?"

"Never in one million years. Violet because she is stubborn and never admits when she's wrong, and Iris because she has convinced herself that this is the crime of the century. Rinaldo Fumigalli could tell her that Elisa Tomassi's family, all of them forgers and petty criminals, has been plotting this takeover for fifty years and she'd believe it. But who in their right mind wants a stone cottage at the edge of a town plagued by earthquakes and stray cats and a population of ten people, most of them above the age of seventy years?"

"It's hard to imagine."

"What will she even do with a *casetta nell'oblio*?" A cottage in oblivion. "No, only blood can do this to a woman like Elisa Tomassi, only the curse and blessing of an Italian family."

I thought of Luigi Barzini writing about the Italian family, where, he said, you could always turn for consolation, help, advice, provisions, loans, weapons, allies, and accomplices. There was something primal and unconditional about Italian familial love, but also something brutal and ponderous, a beautifully made millstone around your neck. Elisa Tomassi, it occurred to me, was here to collect a debt, to balance the historical ledger by honoring her grandparents' legacy, but she'd also run aground in Milan, I sensed, and had come here to find solace, reclaim some space to think or start over.

"I can try talking to Iris about the cottage," I said. "Maybe she will listen to reason."

"To be honest, I am worried about her facilities."

"Her faculties?"

"Yes, her brain box. I have flip-flopped between English and Italian for so long that both are crispy around the edges."

"Why are you worried about her brain?"

"She has traces of the forgetting, the beginning of *le demenza*. Only a little, but perhaps it's spreading into the bedrock."

"You think so?"

"*Certo*. Sometimes she calls her dog the name of her last husband, and I've seen her eating butter like it was pecorino. One time, I dropped off a lasagna to her apartment and I went to warm it up in the oven and what do you think I found in there?"

I waited.

"A pair of shoes."

"Maybe she'd been drying them and forgot to get them out."

"They were not her shoes. I think they belonged to one of

the dead husbands, Federico, who was very tall with feet like an albatross."

That seemed to exhaust the topic for Rose. She set her soup bowl on a side-table doily and crossed to an old RCA Victor. Adjusting the dial to find a classical station, she turned up the volume to release a sonic cloud of Rossini out toward the sleeping or preening cats on the terrace.

φ

Back in Iris's apartment, I looked for signs of her unfolding dementia. I went through the kitchen cupboards, opened the oven and refrigerator, tried to find a paperback novel in the icebox or a pile of unopened bills wedged into her wooden recipe box. My mother had died with her faculties intact, after a lifelong battle with asthma and a brief encounter with pneumonia, so I didn't exactly know what I was looking for. Would there be a series of Post-it notes with family members' misspelled names scrawled on them? Would I find handwritten instructions for operating toasters and bank accounts, a set of CliffsNotes for everyday living?

When I sat down at Iris's whirring computer and moved the mouse, I was surprised to see the geometric screen saver dissolve without a password to a desktop clogged with files and minimized browser windows. Then again, who else had come into her apartment in the last decade? As I started to sift through my aunt's desktop, I remembered that I'd invaded Susan's privacy during her early adolescence by "previewing" her diary for signs of depression. After a few pages, I'd instantly regretted it, finding nothing but to-do lists and disparaging remarks about my dinnertime banter and the burdens of being an only child. I was braced for that same feeling of regret now—even as I clicked open folders and files—that betraying my aunt's trust outweighed the possibility of uncovering signs of her dementia.

There were spreadsheets and documents for each of her missing-person and serial-killer cases, including "l'assassino di Napoli," but then I maximized one of her internet browser windows and found myself staring directly into her university email account, which she'd kept in retirement. There were several recently returned emails marked *nonexistent email address*, all of them addressed to HaroldMcNeil@sfgov .org, and they carried details of Iris's recent findings and speculations. When I googled the name, I found an obituary for Harry McNeil, a retired detective from the San Francisco Police Department who had continued to volunteer for the force but who'd died a year earlier. I thought briefly about leaving the obituary open for Iris to see, but that seemed unnecessarily cruel. I would find the right time to ask her about the project, to probe what she knew and understood, but I couldn't get the idea out of my head that she'd been emailing a digital ghost for over a year.

When I heard laughter drifting up the stairs, I reduced the browser windows and went to the door. I opened it a crack, peering through the balustrade and down into the gaudy rose-marble stairwell that is the villa's ancient femoral artery. I could hear Iris's lilting voice coming up through the sconce-lit space, followed by Rinaldo's elongated vowels. They were talking about a former colleague from the Catholic university where they'd both taught, a buffoon from the school of mathematics who fancied himself a monastic, who went barefoot and refused to use electricity and burned candles in his office and smelled of onions.

As I waited for them to come into view through the

aperture of the cracked doorway, I saw a flash of my boyhood espionage at the villa. I routinely spied on my aunts and grandmother, so maybe I was continuing the habit when I'd opened Susan's diary decades later, fooling myself into believing it was a necessary transgression instead of voyeurism. But what I remembered from my childhood—both in America and in Italy—was the need to become invisible. In Michigan, I was an only child living in Ypsilanti, reading Jack London or Mark Twain in a canvas tent in the backyard to get away from my parents rampaging at each other like Vikings, while in Umbria, my aunts avoided touchy subjects and deflected my questions about family intrigue, so if I wanted to know why one of them was crying, I had to move through the villa in my tennis socks and hold glass tumblers against walls.

I came out onto the landing to greet Iris and Rinaldo as they climbed the stairs. Iris called up through the dim stairwell. "*Mi dispiace*, Hugh, did we wake you?"

"No, no. I just finished a lovely dinner with Aunt Rose."

They arrived on the landing, Rinaldo holding some papers, Iris's hand on his elbow. She unclasped his arm and kissed me on both cheeks, the smell of vermouth and truffles on her breath. Smiling, she said, "The graphologist reached Rinaldo on his mobile telephone while we were at dinner, just as we were looking at the photocopy of the letter. He has reason to believe there are discrepancies in some of the letter formations and angles. Isn't that wonderful news?"

Rinaldo gave a slight but providential nod to the photocopied letter in his hand.

"Aldo was dying and suffering from a fever when he wrote the letter," I said. "I imagine that might have affected some of his letter formations."

Rinaldo fingered the edges of the paper. "Whether we

contest the letter as a legally binding last will and testament, or we argue the authorship, it appears Miss Tomassi does not have a strong footing. She has one foot in the mud, as my father used to say."

"I think we all know the letter is real," I said. "So we should focus on coming to some arrangement with her."

"Real," said Rinaldo, "in my experience, is a *nozione porosa.*"

Iris stage-whispered: "Miss Tomassi studies Aldo's handwriting, interviews her mother, who remembers some details of the villa from when she was a girl . . . and then they concoct a plan for property theft."

I wanted to tell my aunt that she'd spent too many hours on the forensic dark web, or that she might need a CAT scan sooner rather than later. But there was still a part of me that hoped the cottage was unencumbered, that her police-procedural fantasy was true.

Rinaldo said, "Of course, this is entirely a matter for your family to decide, and I will leave you both to it. I will return in the morning at ten for our conference call with the graphologist."

Rinaldo kissed Iris on both cheeks and descended the stairs. On a whim, I called after him, "Would you mind, Signor Fumigalli, if I took another look at the letter? Just until the morning. That's a photocopy, isn't it?"

Rinaldo stopped on the landing and craned up. "As you wish," he said, holding the letter into the ether of the stairwell. It was clear I would have to come down to collect it.

When I came into Iris's apartment with the letter, she was standing in front of her roused computer screen. I set the letter down and said, "I hope you don't mind, my laptop was having some issues."

"Of course," she said, a little curtly.

"Can I make you some tea?"

She brightened. My grandmother and aunts were the only people I knew in Italy to always have tea in their cupboards. "With a splash of milk and one teaspoon of sugar," she said, sitting down at her computer. "I am in the mood to correlate. Vermouth makes me want to find needles in haystacks, bodies in sewers . . ."

I went into the kitchen, put the kettle on, and stuck my head back in the doorway. "How are things going with Naples? Do you hear much back from the retired detective in San Francisco?"

"He's dead," she said without looking up.

"Oh, I didn't realize. I'm sorry."

"It happens."

Testing the waters, I said, "I thought you said you were still in touch with him . . ."

"Well, I still email him, just to clarify my thinking. Not surprisingly, he doesn't email me back. The dead are fickle that way."

I watched Iris in profile, her face in the transfixing digital pall.

She said, "I was hoping someone else would take over the archive project and my emails would be forwarded to his successor. So far, that is not the case. I am now looking for a teenage girl from Slovenia who went missing last year in Venice."

The kettle whistled and I went to make the tea, Earl Grey for Iris and chamomile for me. Clare always hated chamomile tea, said it tasted like twigs and grass clippings, but I've always found it soothing, a tea that suggests convalescence and therefore reminds you of the wild luck of being alive and healthy. I brought Iris a steaming cup on a saucer and set it down beside the computer. I took my teacup and sat on the gondola couch on the other side of the room, blowing across the rim of the cup. I watched Iris clicking at the keyboard and tried to intuit her mood.

"She was last seen at a hostel. This girl from Slovenia."

"I'm not sure we should contest the letter. The claim seems legitimate."

Iris continued to type. "Her name was Lana Horvat."

"Did you hear what I said about the letter?"

"Yes, and I'm ignoring it."

Iris peered into her browser as if through a fogged windowpane. "Why wouldn't we contest the letter? We have evidence of inconsistencies in the graphology."

"I can't see how it would be possible to fake such a letter."

"Everything can be faked," she said matter-of-factly. "Paintings, letters, orgasms." She'd always enjoyed these little conversational detonations. I remembered that in Milan, Iris had taught a course on the history of sexual attitudes in Italy, no small feat at a Catholic university in the 1970s.

"How would she know so much about your father?"

"Maybe he left a journal behind at the grandparents' house up in the Alps. She finds the journal, copies the handwriting and the style of his prose, and makes her demands."

"I thought you said it wasn't his prose style."

"It's a bad imitation of his prose style."

I sipped my tea. "If my mother was within her rights to leave the cottage to me, then maybe I could come to an arrangement with Elisa Tomassi."

Iris finally looked over at me. "What sort of an arrangement?"

"I don't want to sign the house over to her—"

"Excellent, because, in fact, the villa estate is indivisible, by the ancient property laws of Valetto, and also by my father's will. The land and the separate dwellings can never be partitioned or sold separately."

"Yes, I know, but Elisa Tomassi could become my tenant for part of the year. Out of respect for Aldo Serafino's final wishes, we could let her stay here, rent free, for nine months of the year. She would pay only for upkeep and utilities. But she would need to leave during the summers, which is when I'd like to come back each year. The way I used to when I was a boy."

"Have you heard of squatter's rights?"

"She's not a squatter if she signs a lease."

Iris let her eyes go to the gravitational center of the room—the corkboard that connected photographs and handwritten notes with red yarn. She said, "We are being manipulated by unseen forces."

"Most of the time the cottage is empty anyway."

"We are running out of money. My late husbands are still financing us from the grave, all four of us. I had plans to turn the cottage into an Airbnb when you are not here."

"Who would clean it between stays? Donata can barely walk without wincing."

"A touch of *la gotta*."

"She and Milo both need to retire. They're old now."

"They are in the puberty of old age."

"Regardless, there's no one to run an Airbnb. And besides, who would book it? Come stay in a town of ten people, with a colony of feral cats, on a tower of shifting volcanic rock!"

"You're being melodramatic. The *terremoti* always come from the sides, never the front and back. This villa has been sitting here since before Shakespeare was born. It's not going anywhere."

I wanted to remind my aunt that just a few nights before, she'd side-mouthed to Violet that all of Valetto could fall into the valley at any moment. Instead, I said, "Just sleep on it. I'm asking for us to use common sense and do the decent thing. A lease for part of the year is a good middle ground. Don't we all owe it to Aldo's memory, to respect his final wishes?"

Her eyes went cold. "In fact, we owe the dead very little. They could care less. Especially my father, who apparently abandoned his family after the war instead of dying a partisan hero. He's living up there until the summer of 1947 while we sell off the cows and pigs and marry off two daughters to scrape by . . . your grandmother slaving away in a restaurant . . . Why does that man get to decide the fate of a place and a family he left behind? We are the ones who've lived here for the past sixty years . . . and we will be the ones to decide." Getting up, Iris said, "I must go to bed. Lana Horvat will have to stay lost another night."

As Iris headed for her bedroom, I stayed on the couch and used my phone to email Orlando Fiorani to ask about my rights as the inheritor of the cottage, albeit on an estate that could not be divided. Then, I took the photocopied letter down to the first-floor library that had been my grandfather's study before the war. I turned on some lamps and picked my way toward the hulking desk that had been handmade for a Serafino forebear and that was now covered in decades of *National Geographic*s, cookbooks, and family photo albums. On the floor, stacked into open file boxes were the entrails of seventy-five years of memorabilia—birthday cards, photo albums, children's artwork, pale-blue aerograms postmarked in faraway places.

Among the brittle papers and foxed photographs, there appeared to be no organizing principle but exasperation itself. Spread around the desk on the floor, I found the places where my grandmother had auditioned papers for culling, each pile topped with a note that read *non tenere* in blue pencil, *don't keep*—old utility bills, the monthly account statements from the grocer and butcher—but even this tentative approach had run aground. Was this where my fascination for documented history came from? From a family so afraid of earthly erasure that they couldn't discard the transcript of ordering two pounds of prosciutto on June 15, 1988?

I recalled my first archive trip in grad school, a week in a university basement that contained, in no particular order, a lock of Byron's hair, a first quarto of *Hamlet*, and a fountain pen that had belonged to Teddy Roosevelt. There was also a small piece of notepaper entitled *lunch today*, dated August 1940 and handwritten in Winston Churchill's prime-ministerial cursive. To this day, I can recall that it read: "1 tin consommé soup, 1 wedge Gruyère cheese, ½ lb. cold chicken, 2 slices buttered toast." Was it a request, to be handed to the Downing Street head chef, or a record of what he'd eaten that day? Regardless, it was this list that held my rapt attention, as if I'd just discovered the note in Winston Churchill's coat pocket, the man's cravings one month before the bombing of London would begin. I have always loved the window dressings on a street that is about to be looted, the ragtag proofs of our daily existence. I recalled now, looking across the sea of paper, that in Michigan, in the back left corner of the walk-in closet in my bedroom, I'd kept a shoebox of Clare's dry-cleaning receipts.

I drifted over to a bank of metal filing cabinets, their

drawers unlabeled. I found wills belonging to dead husbands, tax documents and bank statements dating back to the 1950s, a fading comet trail of my aunts' and grandmother's finances across time. I couldn't find more than a few scraps of Aldo's handwriting—on receipts and memos—and wondered what Violet had found for the graphologist to compare with the deathbed letter. An entire filing cabinet was devoted to the business of my grandmother's restaurant, each year's expenses and revenues chronicled in tattered manila folders, all of it stopping in the middle of 1971.

At the back of one drawer, at the very bottom of a cabinet, I found a few files that had belonged to Aldo Serafino's engineering firm. He'd kept an office in Bevona, and I assumed most of the related records had gone with the business liquidation. One folder contained what appeared to be annual newsletters, written at Christmastime, sent from Aldo to his clients and prospects, to farmers and businessmen and architects who'd sought his counsel on the structural integrity of bridges, houses, and factories. All of the newsletters were typed, so there was no chance of comparing the handwriting, but I took a few of them over to the leather chair behind the desk and cleared some space to read.

Esteemed friends and clients,

Now that the iron-knuckled grip of winter is around our throats, it's worth remembering that we have much to be thankful for across this valley. Time with family during Christmas, the aromas of roasting chestnuts, your grandmother's favorite recipes, and, naturally, the trusses, beams, and roof tiles above your heads. With so many venerable old dwellings in our area, you can never be too careful with roofing and cladding, the wearing-and-tearing of the centuries . . .

Another newsletter included the following:

One of my clients, a farmer with substantial grain and porcine interests, has the supernatural courage of a saint. He has been wintering his pigs in a brick-and-stone barn that leans like the tower in Pisa. One day, as we all know, gravity arrives on your doorstep like a hungry, uninvited dinner guest. *Catastrofe!* My firm is here to help you avoid unwanted dinner guests.

The villa had hosted its own share of uninvited dinner guests over the decades. I flipped between the newsletters and the photocopied letter from Rinaldo, trying to find consistencies in prose styles, in the phrasing and diction. I am no linguist, but I have read thousands of historical documents, and to my mind these were written by the same hand, in a tone that was at once wry, playful, and a touch poetic. And there were two particular phrases, used in both sets of writings, that seemed personal and idiosyncratic: *iron-knuckled grip* and *supernatural courage*. These seemed to be part of Aldo Serafino's voice, his unique way of expressing himself on the page. I underlined the phrases and took the newsletters back to the apartment, where Iris had turned out all the lights, forcing me to find my way in the dark.

· 8 ·

Rinaldo arrived the next morning alone and on foot, attaché case under one arm, a trench coat belted against the November rain and bluster. Iris greeted him on the stone stairs, unfolding an umbrella as he came toward her. He was unlike any of the men she'd married. The dead husbands had all been barrel-chested, big-knuckled, quick to anger. Rinaldo's slender hands were the color of almonds, and he gave off a watchmaker's precision and patience. When he came into the entrance hall, where Rose and Violet had also gathered with their dogs, he said, "As your sister may have suggested, signori, our man in Milan has found some *incongruenze* in the handwriting."

Our Man in Milan was now my least favorite Graham Greene novel.

He removed his trench coat to reveal a black turtleneck sweater under a blazer of herringbone tweed.

Violet shot out an audible sigh of vindication. "Tell us more about these *incongruenze*."

"We will hear all about it from the graphologist," said Rinaldo.

I checked my phone and saw that my email from the previous night had just received a reply from the family lawyer. "Is Orlando Fiorani coming?" I asked, opening the email.

"He has other commitments," said Rinaldo.

This seemed implausible. Orlando's law firm barely had enough business to hire a part-time receptionist. Most of the time, Orlando's disgruntled wife answered the law office phone. His email was a noncommittal blend of Italian, English, and legalese, but the upshot was that as long as I didn't intend to sell the cottage I could do with it as I pleased.

As Rinaldo gestured for us all to go into the dining room, a figure moved outside through the fog and drizzle—Elisa Tomassi, walking briskly toward the villa under a red umbrella.

"Where on earth does she think she's going?" asked Violet.

Rinaldo stepped to the front entranceway. When she arrived on the stone steps and came within ten feet, he called out cheerily, "Good day to you, Signora Tomassi, what a pity about the rain!"

Elisa stopped a few steps from the top, blinking under her umbrella in a buttoned-up green raincoat. "*Buongiorno*."

"Can I be of service?" asked Rinaldo.

"I saw you arrive just now and wondered if there'd been any news?"

"News about what?"

"The letter. I was told it was being sent to a handwriting expert for examination."

"Ah, yes," said Rinaldo. "Well, in fact, we are about to learn of his findings. We are due on a conference call with Milan any minute. We will report back in due course. Your patience is appreciated. *Molto gentile*."

"There are inconsistencies," called Violet from the rear.

Rinaldo waved one hand behind his back, as if to quiet a dog or small child.

Elisa looked out from under the rim of her umbrella to see us all gathered in the entrance hall. "I see. Well, would you mind if I listened in? After all, surely the family has nothing to hide. This way, I will hear it directly from the horse's mouth, no matter the outcome."

Rinaldo bristled, but before he could say anything, Violet spoke again, this time with a step toward the door. "This family has nothing to hide," she said. "*Né ora né mai.*" Now or ever.

Rinaldo glanced back at Iris for air cover. But before she could respond, I said, "I think it's fine if Signora Tomassi wants to listen in."

Rinaldo folded his arms and Elisa climbed the final few steps. As she came into the entranceway, she brushed past Rinaldo's tweed elbow, whispered *scusami*, and proceeded to drip rainwater onto his burnished oxblood shoes.

φ

In the dining room, Milo had lit a fire in the hearth, and the mahogany table, still set up with the speakerphone and fax machine, smelled of furniture polish. We all sat, the widows on one side of the table with their dogs curled at their feet, me and Elisa opposite, Rinaldo at the head, the original letter laid out before him in its plastic sleeves. When Rinaldo dialed the number in Milan, a woman picked up—"*Pronto!*"

"*Buongiorno*, signora, I am looking for Professor Francesco Costa, is he there?"

"This is his wife. Just one moment."

We heard Mrs. Costa walking across a stone or tile floor in heels, a cordless phone apparently clutched to her chest or shoulder, the sound of her footsteps magnified. She began calling out to Francesco as she moved through a cavernous-sounding house. Rinaldo didn't move his eyes from the phone, but I saw a faint ripple against his clenched jawline. His man in Milan had dropped the ball. Eventually, Francesco Costa, expert witness and veteran graphologist, took up the phone.

"I thought we were speaking this afternoon," he said through a quivery breath.

"I have you on speakerphone, Professor. Nice to hear your voice," said Rinaldo.

"Likewise!"

"The Serafino sisters are gathered with me, as well as their nephew from America, Hugh Fisher. We also have Signora Elisa Tomassi, the one who brought these documents into the light."

"I see. Good morning, everyone!"

Elisa pulled the coil of her hair back into a ponytail and took out a small notebook and pen from her purse. She flipped open to a blank page.

Rinaldo said, "*Cominciamo*. When we spoke last evening, you indicated that your handwriting analysis of the materials we sent you revealed some inconsistencies between known samples and the supposed letter. Could you elaborate?"

"The first thing I want to say is that Aldo Serafino had quite distinctive handwriting, which makes my job a little bit easier. His hand revealed a quick mind and steady powers of decision-making. We see this in the shape of his *m*'s and *n*'s, which are almost buckled, hump-shaped. His dots above the *i*'s are quite beautiful and pronounced, like full stops, firmly planted and round. I would almost call them voluptuous *i*-dots." We could hear him smiling into his own turn of phrase. "There is a general rightward slant to his writing, which suggests that he was an expressive man, open to the world of emotion, and that he was also future-looking."

"Yes, that sounds like him," said Rose.

"Now, when I compared the letter with the other samples, I noticed that the dots above the *i*'s in the letter are quite weak and the slant is considerably less."

"Excuse me, Professor Costa, this is Elisa Tomassi speaking. May I ask a question?"

We all turned to look at her, but she didn't budge her eyes from the speakerphone.

"*Certo.*"

"Can handwriting change over the course of a person's life?"

An ocean of long-distance static.

"Yes, it can happen. If someone develops Alzheimer's or a psychiatric condition, we can see a marked change in the shape of the letters. We also see variable pressure in people with high blood pressure, for example."

Elisa jotted something in her notebook. "*Allora*, would it be possible that those changes you described could have been due to an illness? If the writer, say, was very weak from a fever?"

In the long pause that followed, I could detect the graphologist's years of experience on the witness stand. Whatever he might say next could have a major bearing on the outcome of the dispute. "Handwriting *can* change due to illness, yes, but one would expect to see the overall pattern preserved. If some of the *i*-dots were weak because of illness that would be one thing, but there is also the rightward slant to consider."

Rinaldo shifted in his chair, rousing Rocky IV below the table into a single bark.

"I think the dog agrees with me," said the speakerphone.

Rinaldo laughed uneasily into his pressed palms. "We would expect the overall pattern to be preserved. This is what I'm hearing . . ."

Elisa grazed her bottom lip with her front teeth and nodded almost imperceptibly. No doubt she sensed some informal arrangement had been reached between Fumigalli and Costa, the kind of fraternal understanding Italian men love to forge. Clare would have advised her to seek out her own graphologist; in fact, any lawyer would have told her to dispense with the charade of informal negotiations with the Serafino family. Unless the letter, although genuine, didn't carry weight as a legal testamentary document and she knew it. I suddenly wondered if she'd already sought legal advice before coming down here to play her hand. I could hear her breathing and turning pages in her notebook beside me, stalling for time, and I imagined everything that was ticking over in her mind. More than anything, she wanted to collect this debt in the name of her grandfather, who'd been strung up in an alpine town square after saving a Serafino, and she wanted to find a new thread to pull on after her own life had burned to the ground up north. But now she'd been cornered by something she suspected but couldn't name—a meeting between old friends in a Milanese backroom tavern, a handshake sealed with grappa and cigar smoke. I watched this realization take the wind out of her sails.

When I leaned toward the speakerphone, it was not to

renounce my claim to the cottage. I still imagined Elisa Tomassi could become my part-time tenant and that I could
force the widows to come to some arrangement with her. But
I also couldn't watch her being pinned in place by some Milanese collusion between a bureaucrat of handwriting and a
retired criminologist who looked like he was dressed to go
grouse hunting. "Professor, this is Hugh Fisher. What if the
writer had suffered through years of stress, had seen friends
killed and knew real hunger and hardship? Could that
trauma, not to mention the fact of his dying days, change the
overall pattern?"

From across the table, Violet looked at me, clenched her
fists in the air, and shouted, "A traitor to his own flesh and
blood!"

It was the sort of insult she hurled at pro wrestlers on
television, and I half expected to be called the son of a crip-
pled donkey or a drunk and stupid Calabrian horse thief
next. But Violet said nothing more and looked away in dis-
gust, while everyone else looked at the tabletop or the floor,
except for Elisa, who was staring directly at me.

After a long, stunned silence, from inside the tiny, crackling universe of the speakerphone, Professor Costa said, "Under those circumstances, as you describe them, it is possible
that the personality changes and the handwriting along with
it. It is rare but possible. I once examined the letters of a pris-
oner of war who had been tortured for many years. If you
compared them to his journals before the war, you would
think they'd been written by two different people. Again,
this is a very rare thing."

I said, "So, it sounds like the handwriting analysis is
inconclusive at best." When Costa said nothing, I continued:
"I should also point out that I found some Christmas news-

letters from my grandfather's engineering firm in his old study, from before the war. There were several phrases that were consistent with the letter. For example, he used the phrases *iron-knuckled grip* and *supernatural courage* in both places. Don't you think that's an unlikely coincidence if we are talking about two different writers?"

Elisa closed the notebook and began drumming her fingertips against its cover.

"That is beyond my area of expertise," said Costa. "I am strictly a specialist in handwriting analysis, not the voicing of the words themselves."

I said, "But you agree, if illness and mental distress are at play, that the handwriting analysis of the letter formations is inconclusive?" I wasn't entirely sure why I was pressing the point, but I remembered how happy it made Clare when I mustered the wherewithal to call the city or the phone company when they'd made a mistake. For years, she'd coached me on the delicate balance between wielding logic and voicing grievance.

"I suppose I would have to agree," said Costa, "though it could be argued that the least radical interpretation is the one that should sway rational minds."

He was stepping beyond his own competencies, and we could all hear it in his voice.

"And what is the least radical interpretation?" asked Elisa, rallying.

"That the writer did not become a different person."

Rinaldo said, "Even if he did become a different person up there, even if he did go mad up in the mountains, then that just further proves the point that he was not in his fit mind to make a decision like this at the end of his life. Anything he might have written can be ignored on that basis."

The fireplace whirred and popped, and a windowpane rattled from some drafty alcove of the first floor. Violet pressed the bones in her arthritic hands, wincing slightly, while Iris worried a gold necklace with her fingertips, both of them refusing to acknowledge the two plaintiffs who'd somehow formed an alliance on the other side of the table. Rose gazed out the windows at the November drizzle. Eventually, Rinaldo thanked the professor for his time and ended the call.

At first, Elisa spoke to her closed notebook, her voice indignant. "I could bring you all Aldo Serafino, deliver him back from the dead, have him stand here and swear on a stack of Bibles that he wrote this letter, that my grandparents saved his life, that my mother brought him soup in his final hours, and you would still dismiss it as a conspiracy. Most of the year, the cottage lies empty, but you still won't honor his memory and his dying wish." She looked at the aunts, one by one, saving Rinaldo for last. "This is the most spiteful and ungrateful family I have ever encountered. Your Serafino ancestors are turning in their graves with shame."

Violet had lost her temper once, and now she held her anger tightly. She leaned back in her chair, her eyes and voice going cold. "I've had about all I can take of this woman. You show up in a town you have never laid eyes on with a letter that you probably concocted, but even if not, you have assumed the memory of our father is something we hold sacred. From what I can tell, he shacked up with your grandmother and abandoned his family after the war. We owe him precisely nothing. Do you hear me? Not a goddamn Hail Mary or an Our Father! So even if the letter is real, it changes nothing."

"I'd like to say something," I said.

"No," said Violet. "You've said enough. This is a matter for the Serafinos."

"The cottage was left to me by my mother, so the decision is mine to make. I've thought of an arrangement where we can keep the cottage in the family but Elisa can occupy it most of the year as a tenant. There will be no rent, of course."

Elisa said, "How can I be a tenant in something that rightfully belongs to me?"

This rankled me, especially after I'd gone out of my way to challenge the graphologist on her behalf. I folded my arms, felt the room pull away on the tide of Violet's anger as she pushed her chair back.

Violet said, "My nephew seems to think he has the right to decide the fate of a house that sits on our ancestral land. The custodians of this place are the ones who live here, not tourists and vacationers and part-time Italians, not American academics, not the dead father, and certainly not a stranger from up north. We will decide. If I make one call to the local carabinieri, men we've all known since they were in short pants, you will be removed. No questions asked."

Rinaldo snugged the cap of his fountain pen into place. In a hushed tone, he said, "All things considered, I don't believe you have legal recourse to stay in the cottage any longer, Signora Tomassi."

"I agree," said Iris, speaking for the first time in half an hour.

"Bravo!" said Violet.

Rinaldo said, "You will have until the morning to vacate the premises."

To get away from the long, unbearable silence, Rose leaned under the table to rub on Chester. Then, from behind us, we all heard the sound of my grandmother being wheeled into the dining room. Nina pushed her under the fresco, Ida's head cocked to one side, her rheumy eyes blinking from inside the halo of her finely spun white hair. "We heard a terrible commotion."

"Mother," said Iris, "what are you doing out here? You'll catch pneumonia."

"It seems reasonable that I would want to know what's occurring in my own house." She sat parked right under the crystal-and-bronze chandelier, shielding her eyes for a better view. "What's going on?"

I watched Elisa get up and move across the room. When she was six feet away from Ida's wheelchair, she curled her hands together like a child for an elocution lesson. "My name is Elisa Tomassi and I am the daughter of Alessia Parigi. My mother stayed here during and after the war. I came here with a letter from your late husband that promised my family the stone cottage behind the villa in return for saving his life. Your daughters have denied my claim."

My grandmother let this revelation wash over her, squinting through the aura of chandelier light. She reached for a pair of glasses and put them on to sharpen her view of this emissary of the past. "When was this letter written?"

"August of 1947, just days before he died."

We all watched as Ida nodded almost imperceptibly and puckered her lower lip in consideration. She hadn't known her husband's fate for more than sixty years and now it arrived like a telegram, with a month and a year, delivered by a stranger. For a long time, she said nothing, looking down at her hands, then she brought herself back to the present and asked plaintively, "Where is the letter?"

"Over on the table," said Elisa.

Ida looked at the mahogany table, then back at Elisa. "I see," she said quietly. "And you are Alessia's daughter?"

"That's right."

Ida extended one frail hand and Elisa stepped a few feet forward.

"I am honored to meet you," said Elisa, touching only Ida's fingertips.

Ida took control of the wheelchair from Nina and backed away from the brightly lit center of the room. Over one shoulder, she said, "Signora Tomassi, would you like to have some fennel tea in my apartment? And would it be possible to bring the letter? I'd like to see it up close."

Elisa came back to the table and took up the letter with the casualness of a waitress collecting a menu. She kept her eyes down, careful not to provoke the widows. And we were all silently gripped as she returned to the safety of her wheelchaired rescuer, by the way she strode across the terra-cotta in her bootheels, passing under the fresco of shepherds delivering their flocks from an onslaught of weather.

PART TWO

9

Elisa Tomassi didn't emerge from my grandmother's rooms until evening. By that time, my aunts had returned to their apartments, Rinaldo had fled to his hotel, and I'd spent a few hours drinking wine and grappa with Milo in his workshop behind the villa. He hadn't been in the dining room during the conference call with the graphologist, or when Ida appeared, but his prediction was that I was now officially dead to both Iris and Violet, *ufficialmente morto*, and he suggested that I sleep in his sons' childhood bedroom or seek political asylum with my aunt Rose. If there is a blood feud, he said, *una bega familiare*, you will want Rose as your protector and ally. I couldn't tell if he was joking, but it came to me that the English had borrowed the word *vendetta* from the Italians during the nineteenth century, during the Victorian golden age of cyanide and strychnine poisonings.

Gently drunk, I walked through the Umbrian night into the empty piazza, then out along the corrugated edges of the town, the wind and rain siphoning up from the valley. From a distance, I could see the Saint's Staircase spiraling down into the blue-gray void and I thought about Italians' refusal to demolish the past. There was no reason to keep the stairs perilously attached to the side of the cliffs other than to evoke a house where a saint lived more than three hundred years ago. In my book, I'd written that Italians walk through their own histories every day, passing the ravages and triumphs of bygone days. There are streets and hillsides where Roman and Etruscan ruins butt up against papal and nationalist monuments. And in dozens of empty towns and villages, the new settlement was made a short distance away, in plain sight of the original devastation or abandonment. Walk away and don't look back was the least Italian idea I could imagine. In fact, looking back seemed to be the main point of leaving something behind.

I wandered back through the piazza and tried to imagine my grandmother's reaction to the letter. Was there peace or anger in knowing where Aldo had ended up? Was it mitigated by the fact that she'd lived more than half her life without knowing his fate? It occurred to me that, unlike stone monuments and ruins, family histories live and die on a tide of paper and memory, and they can vanish or return without warning. All this turned over in my mind as I walked back in the rain toward the villa gardens. From the top of the terraced hillside, I noticed that the lights were on over at the cottage and I saw a silhouette shifting behind the gossamer curtains in the kitchen. I descended the stone steps and walked over to the front patio, but then I lost my nerve and stood for a long time in the halo of the porch light.

Elisa Tomassi peered at me through the kitchen window and opened the door. "You frightened me," she said, standing in the doorway in a sweatshirt and jeans, pulling the untamable comet of her hair into a ponytail.

"I was trying to talk myself out of knocking."

"You're drenched. Would you like to come in to warm up?"

"It's getting late. I'm sorry for disturbing you."

"I'm not going to hold this door open forever. Come in."

I stepped into the kitchen, took off my wet jacket. She fetched me a towel from the bathroom and we both saw, in the same moment, that it was monogrammed with my mother's initials—*H.S.* There were half a dozen of these monogrammed towels at the cottage, a long-ago gift from my grandmother to encourage better décor and more frequent visits.

"I was going to make something to eat," Elisa said. "Are you hungry?"

"I could eat something, thank you."

I dried my hair and face and she hung the towel back in the bathroom. I sat on one of the high stools at the orange-tiled countertop. When she came back, Elisa moved with ease around the cramped galley kitchen as she cooked, as if it weren't furnished like a holiday rental with a two-burner gas stove, a tiny oven, and a dorm-room refrigerator. The drawers and cupboards, once desolate with tins of expired soup and battered, cheap utensils, now contained her hand-forged German knives, her glass jars of spices, the coffee beans from a roaster in Milan, and the antique glass measuring cups that might have been in her family for generations. On the stovetop, there was a coppered omelet pan and a vintage espresso maker of aviation-grade aluminum. The fact that she'd brought all these things here, even though the outcome of her claim on the cottage was uncertain, struck me as brazen, but then I imagined that these were the things that gave her comfort, that as a trained chef it pained her to cleave garlic with a blunt, plastic-handled knife. Perhaps she always traveled with her knives and pans and vintage measuring cups.

She poured me some red wine, sautéed some porcini mushrooms in olive oil, mixing them with garlic, onion, and fresh herbs.

"You should know that the *funghi* were gathered illegally," she said proudly.

"How so?"

"These days, you're supposed to have a permit to go mushrooming. It's to deter over-collecting and amateurs from picking a deadly variety. In theory, you can take your basket of mushrooms to a local doctor or pharmacist and they will confirm that you're not about to kill yourself or your loved ones."

"Sounds like my life is in your hands," I said.

"*Naturalmente.* If it's a consolation, my mother taught me how to forage when I was a young girl. So you are quite safe in these hands." She spooned the sautéed mushrooms into a ceramic dish of polenta, grated some pecorino on top, and put it into the oven.

I said, "According to my grandmother, you should only ever stir polenta clockwise."

"She is correct. Unless you want wolves and demons on your doorstep. This should be ready soon. We can go sit by the fire."

I was happy to see that nothing had changed in the living room. The massive chestnut beams and the white plaster walls, the stone floor covered in threadbare kilim rugs, in faded golds and blues, the smell of wood and cinders, these were all exactly like I'd remembered them. The walls were still bare except for the generic cityscape of Rome, and the bookshelves were still lined with puzzles and paperbacks arranged in no particular order. There was an impressive fire burning in the hearth.

"Did Milo bring you some wood?"

"I gathered it myself down in the valley," she said. "Along with the mushrooms."

I pictured her bounding up the steep chalky ravine with firewood and a basket of mushrooms looped on one elbow. There was something of the sturdy alpine north about Elisa Tomassi, a suggestion that despite her sleek metallic eyewear and her years in Milan she still moved through the world as the granddaughter of a partisan resister, coffin maker, and chimney sweep. Her hand movements belonged to someone who knew how to fell trees and thatch roofs. We sat in the big leather armchairs and looked out through the French doors, where the trees swayed and the slantwise rain lashed at the terrace. We sipped our wine, listened to the wind chastising the metal chimes. As winter approached, the night air roiled up from the valley, crashing against the jagged lip of the town like detonating surf.

"Thank you for what you did today," she said. "On the call with *il grafologo*."

"I only said what I thought was true. It's possible, though, that I might be thrown out of the family."

"In my experience, widows are excellent at holding grudges."

"The Serafino women are gold medalists."

"What a remarkable woman your grandmother is."

I waited for the wind chimes to dim away. "Do you mind if I ask what happened in there for all those hours?"

Elisa stretched her hands into the firelight, gathering up a synopsis. "Well, she fell asleep for at least twenty minutes after we had tea, so that needs to be taken off the clock. Then she asked me to read the letter aloud to her. By the end, I was crying, but she just listened quietly. She's like a statue in a park, the way she sits there listening, as if nothing can surprise her."

"She's also half deaf," I said on a sip of wine. "It's the secret to her longevity. For at least a decade, she has only heard fifty percent of what the world delivers."

"You're funny," she said without laughing. "She told me about her hundredth-birthday party and all the guests she's invited. It sounds like quite the production."

"Donata might call it something else. How did she take the news of what happened to Aldo?"

Elisa brought her eyes back from the fireplace. "She said she was relieved to know that Aldo died with someone who loved him at his side. She said that it made her happy to picture my mother bringing him soups that she learned to make down here."

"I was expecting her to be angry. Maybe in shock."

"Well, after her nap and some goose livers, she also said that he was a selfish *bastardo egoista*."

"A mixed result, then."

Elisa got up to rearrange the fire with an iron poker. She rolled the bark side of a split log onto the winking coals and leaned another piece on top. When she was happy with the fire's configuration, she came back to her chair. "Your grandmother asked to see my mother."

"You said she's unwell."

"Yes, she's not been well for a long time. But I think your grandmother implied that unless my mother comes to Valetto the cottage dispute will never be settled, that her daughters will always stand against it."

"I think I can convince the widows to let you stay part of the year," I said.

She shook her head. "I know you are trying to do the decent thing, but it's the principle of the promise. My grandparents didn't save *part* of Aldo Serafino's life, after all."

This irked me, and I took a sip of wine to take the edge off my reaction. I wanted to tell her that the cottage was the place where I'd discovered my own intellect and easiness with solitude, that it was in this very room where I'd written much of my book, one of the few things that had given my life meaning after Clare's death. But it was clear that she was determined to make her claim and that she believed history and a deathbed promise trumped whatever emotional attachment I might have to the place. Looking into the glowing embers of the fireplace, it struck me that I was a historian who wanted to argue against the authority of his own discipline.

She said, "Your grandmother says that she has wanted to talk to Alessia for many years, that there are things she wants to tell her before she dies, that she missed the chance with her youngest daughter. She said she wants to make amends."

My mother barely spoke to Ida during her final years and had stopped returning the letters that came from Italy. "Make amends for what?"

"She wouldn't say, but tomorrow I'm going to drive north to see if I can convince my mother to make a trip down here. I'd like all this to be settled once and for all."

"Will she will come?"

"My mother doesn't like to think about the past unless it's to remember old recipes. She doesn't much like the present, for that matter. Half the time, she won't even answer her telephone. She's what you might call *unplugged*."

"But it sounded like she has fond memories of being here."

"When I was growing up, she always told me wonderful stories about the fruits and plants she gathered here, about cooking alongside your grandmother, but she refused to come with me to claim the cottage. She said she has no interest in reliving ancient history."

My mother had described her childhood in the villa as a series of trials and torments, from the cold stone floors to the winter morning fogs. Sea smoke, she called that particular fog, as if she'd survived a shipwreck. As she got older, she returned to Valetto less and less.

Elisa said, "Your grandmother also wants you to come north to see the town and the house where her husband died, and the grave where he is buried. As the historian, you are being assigned the task of documenting his death. You're supposed to bring back proof and take photos for the family album."

I ran my hands along my knees. My pant legs were still slightly damp. "I'm supposed to be working on a guest lecture about the social history of abandonment in Italy, starting with the Etruscans."

"It's not Etruscan, but you might be interested in our ancestral village up in the Ossola Valley. There are fewer than fifty people now. My mother still lives alone in the house where your grandfather died. The neighbors help her out. She has always refused to move to Milan to be closer to us, to her grandchildren." Elisa contemplated our reflections in the French doors. "Well, I suppose there is only one grandchild in Milan after Matteo went with his father to England."

The chimney flue took a gulp of smoky air.

"That must have been hard, to have him leave."

"He and his father are very good pals." She pulled herself out of her chair. "I should go check on our polenta con funghi. Perhaps you can refill our wine for dinner."

φ

Fifteen minutes later, while we ate our polenta at the kitchen counter and drank more wine, Elisa asked, "What was your wife like?" and I heard the air empty out of my lungs. "I'm sorry," she added, "your aunt Iris told me about your loss the day I arrived. I hope I'm not prying."

As with all Elisa Tomassi's questions, this one came earnestly and it seemed important not to deflect it. I held a sip of wine in my mouth and, after a moment, I said, "*Clare . . .*" as if the question had simply been to remember my dead wife's name. For half a minute it felt like trying to describe the sound of water, but then I tried to imagine Clare as someone you might meet on a train, or at a dinner party, and how you would recall the way she squinted when she didn't quite hear something and asked you to repeat it. Or you might remember that she put an ice cube in her sauvignon blanc and whispered *lowbrow* while doing it with hooligan glee. I wanted to give an objective, ordered account of Clare moving through the world, but then it came out headlong and in no particular order.

"She was tall, pale, had a wicked sense of humor. Every Friday night she made pizzas for Susan and me and made us dance in the living room. In bed at night, she used to paddle her feet back and forth to go to sleep and her feet were always cold, so she wore hiking socks to bed. It was this funny sound, all that wool rubbing together, that seemed so natural to me. In the middle of the night she would wake up in a sweat and have to take the socks off and she'd throw them across the room and it sounded like a bear roused from hibernation."

Elisa laughed at this, cradled her wineglass in one palm.

"She had an incredible memory, knew poems by Emily Dickinson and Elizabeth Bishop by heart, even though she'd only taken three English classes during her university days. She could remember notes she'd written in the margins of novels all throughout the house. She loved to argue and debate, but she did it carefully and with curiosity, always willing to be proven wrong. Apart from hand-tossed pizza, she was a terrible cook and was easily frazzled in the kitchen. She could poach an egg perfectly, that was about it, and she made her technique of adding white vinegar to the water and creating a little whirlpool for the egg to land in sound like particle physics. She held secret grudges, pretended not to. She wrote long letters and emails to her brothers in Maine, who wrote terse, ungenerous replies. Until she was banned from doing so, she performed terrible magic tricks at Susan's childhood birthday parties, and she played the guitar in the basement when she made candles. Joni Mitchell and Rickie Lee Jones covers . . . Every fall she had allergies, and she never laughed if she didn't think a joke or wisecrack was funny. She was ruthless that way, left you hanging in midair. Didn't want to insult your dignity by laughing at something that you both knew wasn't really funny. What else? She loved ginger-flavored candies and would run someone down to beat them to a discount clothes rack at an outlet mall." I shot out a laugh. "Her thumbs were double-jointed and she always got into bed an hour before me to read and think or listen to audiobooks. On our first date, at this terrible New Jersey Italian restaurant I took her to when I was in grad school and she was in law school, she said to me, 'Tell me something, Hugh Fisher, are you always so gently disheveled?' and she said it with a smile, as if it were a compliment, and I went ahead and kissed her, figuring she knew what she was getting into."

Elisa nodded into this detail, either agreeing with my wife's assessment of my appearance, or with the sentiment behind the story. "She sounds wonderful," she said softly.

"She was also fiercely independent," I added, in case I'd glossed over a crucial aspect of this woman she'd never meet. "There was a devoted group of bird-watchers and a hiking club and an annual pilgrimage with Susan to a women's folk festival while I stayed at home and graded papers."

After a long moment of silence, Elisa asked, "After she died, what was the first thing you forgot about her?"

No one had ever asked me about Clare in this way. "Her voice," I said. "The precise sound of it." I could remember certain qualities—her wry, throaty laughter, the way her singing was high and clear and folksy in the shower or the basement—but the sounds themselves, the tone and timbre, had all vanished. All this came to me as I stared down at my empty plate.

"How many years has it been?"

"Six."

I went to the stovetop and served myself a second helping. This violated some unspoken Italian rule about the guest and the chef, and I felt it bristle in the air between us. Had I always been a guest in this cottage? But I needed something to do with my hands, so I ate some more. "It's delicious," I said. I was experiencing a flaring vulnerability hangover, and I remembered this feeling from the early days of grief, when I dodged my colleagues after they'd stopped by my office to drop off a sympathy casserole. They always left a little dazed by what came out of my mouth. *Grief is a locked room*, I told one of them, *and I'll be trapped in here forever.* I never made eye contact with that particular historian again. Rallying, I asked Elisa about her children.

She took her time answering, staring up at the chestnut rafters to either collect her thoughts or wait for my ode to a dead wife to dissipate. Then she looked at me and said, "Marcella wants to be a journalist or a documentary film-maker, depending on the day. She wants to tell stories about the downtrodden and the oppressed, sees herself as a heroine in ripped jeans. She's very smart and kind, but there's a bit of hostility. I used to think it was just a phase, but it's been there since she was thirteen. When she's not out with her friends at some benefit concert or fundraiser, she's going to a hip-hop class or jogging around the neighborhood. She's very loyal to me, in her own way, though she can't abide any discussion of feelings. That is her idea of certain death."

"Susan is the opposite," I said. "She's big on feelings and insights, though she has an economist's way with words. When she asks why I'm walking through an abyss of loneliness it sounds like she's reading a nutrition label."

I waited several beats before asking Elisa about her son in England. My Clare monologue seemed to have earned me the right to this question.

She said, "As a boy, Matteo loved practical jokes and he was always falling off bicycles and roofs and playground equipment." She took a bit of polenta, chewed, considered, chewed again. "He's always been very good at accents and impressions, and at school he had a special talent for imper-sonating his teachers. He loved science and mathematics but thought history and languages were very boring. He played soccer at school and bocce with the old men in our neighbor-hood, who called him *piccolo maestro* because of his skill at the game. His bedroom was always a disaster area, full of dirty clothes and posters of motorcycles, and he kept a pet lizard under a heat lamp. As a kid, when it was someone's birthday, he could be very sweet. He would make something with his hands out of wood or put together a playlist."

"What was the best practical joke he ever played on anyone?"

"He made posters for psychic readings and put his sister's mobile phone number on them and pasted them all around the neighborhood. For weeks she got calls asking her to help find lost dogs or determine whether a husband was cheating."

"Kind of mean," I said, "but also kind of brilliant."

"Agreed."

"You said he went to live with his father in England?"

She ran a fingernail into a grout line of the tiled counter-top. "Matteo and I always butted heads. His dad never really parented him, so I was left to lay down the law. And let me tell you, it was a very permissive law because I worked such long hours at the restaurant. After the fire, when our marriage started to go downhill, it felt like Matteo took his father's side. He wants to be a chef, or so he thinks, so now he's dicing on-ions and peeling potatoes for Benjamin's new London gig."

"Do you talk to him regularly?"

She ignored this. "You know, he would have had a perfect impression of Signor Fumigalli. Where did your aunts find that Milanese peacock?"

"He used to work with Iris at the university. They were colleagues."

"Matteo would have perfected his Fumigalli impression within a few minutes and had us all in stiches."

I smiled at this image and put down my fork. Neither of us seemed interested in eating any longer. A dead wife and absent son had been conjured, a second bottle of wine had been opened, and my thoughts kept circling back to my own outpouring. Ever since I'd named Clare's voice as the first thing I'd forgotten, my mind had been rubbing it over, and I felt exhilarated by the possibility of understanding more about my own losses and eroding memories. What other half-buried things did I know about my own grief and wife that, if asked about directly, I could surrender? That for several years I kept Clare's mobile phone active because I didn't want anyone else to take her phone number. That during the time before I released the number, I sent her texts from work, only to come home and read them on the phone that was always charging by her side of the bed. These seemed too incriminating and neurotic to volunteer, but then something broke to the surface.

"I think Clare thought about leaving me once."

Elisa wiped a spot on the counter with her napkin. "What makes you think that?"

"Years ago, when I was going for tenure and Susan was maybe five or six, Clare picked her up from school one afternoon and drove to the Upper Peninsula of Michigan to go camping for a week. There was a note on the kitchen counter when I got home."

"Maybe she just wanted to be in the woods and hear the birds."

"No, I think it was more than that."

"Did you do something wrong?"

"I was gone a lot, doing research to finish my first book. And when I was home, I was distracted and easily annoyed. I'd sit in my study surrounded by a pile of books and papers.

I was convinced if I didn't get tenure my life would be ruined, that I'd end up working as a line cook in Ypsilanti."

"There is nothing wrong with being a line cook," Elisa said.

"I know, I just mean—" I cut myself off in case I said something else incriminating.

Elisa folded and unfolded her napkin into a square. Without a hint of accusation or judgment, she said, "Well, perhaps the camping trip was to send you a signal to get out of your head and stop ignoring your family." She glanced over at me, then back down at her napkin folding. "Did you ever ask her if she planned on leaving you?"

"I wanted to ask her about it before she died but it had come to feel irrelevant. You don't want to say to the dying person, so, I've been thinking about that time you disappeared for a week and went camping with our daughter. What was that about? Because maybe you already know what it was about, but if you ask, and she says I was going to leave you, then everything might be tainted."

"Why would it be tainted? She didn't leave you. She obviously decided to come back."

"Yes, but maybe it wasn't for me. Maybe it was for Susan."

"You can't think like that. Did you change after she came back?"

"Yes. We started having date nights again and I took Susan on outings every Sunday afternoon."

"Let me guess, to ghost towns in Michigan?"

"Very funny. We went to museums and movies and I taught her how to swim at the YMCA pool."

"Then it sounds like you redeemed yourself. As a father and a husband."

"That's a generous interpretation. If you ask Susan, my real calling was to become a widower. She likes to remind me that Clare's car is still in the driveway, unregistered, with the tires deflated."

Elisa asked, "Do your neighbors complain about the car?"

"There seems to be no statute of limitations on grief, so they resist calling the city to complain. Midwesterners will do a lot to avoid social discord. But I wish I could be more pragmatic with Clare's things. Susan has offered to help me sort through everything and take it to the Goodwill."

"What is Good Will?"

"A charity where you can take your old toasters and sweaters."

"One day you will wake up and be ready for Good Will."

Elisa took out her cigarettes from her purse and went to stand by the kitchen door. She opened it a crack, lit her cigarette, blew some smoke out into the night air. It had stopped raining and the wind had died down.

"You can smoke in here," I said. "My mother always did."

"It's a disgusting habit. Please don't encourage it."

"I've been wondering, why is your English so good?"

"That's kind of you to say. It's not perfect. I studied for years in school and always made friends with the exchange students. My ex-husband also liked to correct my mistakes."

"You mentioned he's Scottish."

"Yes. Before moving to Milan, Benjamin was head chef at a Glasgow hotel."

"He left Italy after the fire and the divorce?"

"It sounds quite melodramatic when you put them in the same sentence."

"Sorry."

"He stayed for a year, then got the job in London, and he

told me Matteo was coming with him the night before they left. Matteo couldn't even look me in the eyes."

She leaned against the doorframe, holding her cigarette at an angle. It felt like we'd arrived at the end of something, so I collected the dishes and took them over to the sink.

"Thank you for the delicious meal."

"Don't wash up," she said. "I'll do it later. Also, I would hardly call that a meal."

I turned the faucet on to take a feint at rinsing.

"Would you like to take a walk?" she asked, her voice half out the door.

I said nothing because it seemed like she already knew my answer. I reached for my jacket and grabbed the flashlight that had hung beside the refrigerator for decades, its batteries dutifully replaced by Milo every winter solstice.

φ

We passed through the terraced gardens silently, the hulking villa on the crest of the hill like some beleaguered warship floating through the night, a single cone of lamplight coming from Iris's apartment. Elisa shone the flashlight at the cobblestones as we climbed up toward the piazza, but as the clouds began to break apart, she switched it off so that we could see a silver-white whorl of starlight hanging above the valley. We stood quietly, her breath amplified by the ascent and all that wine and the fringed hood of her parka. We could faintly hear the river far below, and I could make out the silhouettes of the darkened, empty houses on the other side of the canyon.

"Why do you want the cottage so badly?" I asked.

She put her hands into her pockets, leaned back, stared

up at the sky. "I see the cottage as an offering to my family. It somehow makes what happened to my grandfather a little more bearable."

She continued to walk along the pathway and I fell in beside her.

She said, "Maybe it's more than that, I don't know. It just feels like the right thing." She stopped, turned to me. "Marcella says I'm running away from my own life."

"That's exactly what Susan says about me. How do twenty-somethings know so much?"

"Because they have no experience to get in the way of their theories."

"Well said."

"You could have taken a sabbatical in Florida or the Caribbean. Instead, you came back to spend time with four old women on a slab of tufa and give lectures about abandoned towns. What does that say about you?"

"It says everything about me. I hate the beach, for one thing. I didn't realize it when I asked for the sabbatical, but I also came back to Valetto looking for some trace of who I used to be. As a boy."

"What was he like, this boy?"

"Shy, earnest, kind, wildly curious."

"And he was happy here?"

"So happy. At least that's how I remember it. I'd leave my parents fighting in the suburbs of the Midwest and I'd come here to be with my crazy aunts and my fearless grandmother in a medieval villa. They treated me like a prince. I lived in the cottage by myself, ate mortadella sandwiches over the sink, spent my days reading and doing crosswords and exploring the valley and playing chess with old men in the piazza. Most afternoons, Milo sent me across the footbridge for magazines or gelato and to pick up groceries or prescriptions for my aunts. Every day there was a new mission. It was paradise. The happiest I've ever been."

"I bet you were a very sweet boy."

I felt myself flush in the darkness, not because I couldn't accept this simple compliment for the boy I'd been, but because I knew it to be true and felt a pinprick of panic that nothing of my younger self could be salvaged.

Sensing my reaction, Elisa said, "I also bet your aunts and grandmother spoiled you rotten."

"There's no denying it." I gently took the flashlight from her and aimed it up at the building façades that rose from both sides of the alley. "In a lot of ways, this is the place where I became a historian," I said, moving the light across the wet stone and stucco. "It was in these buildings that I first studied all the things people had left behind. Some of them were abandoned after the big earthquake in 1971, including my grandmother's restaurant. It's the one on the corner."

We took a few more steps and I shone the flashlight across the weathered sign above the boarded-up doorway. The painted letters of the name—*Il Ritorno*—had vanished years before, but there remained a faint, watermarked outline ingrained in the wood. Elisa craned up at the sign, and then peered in through one of the unboarded windows.

"I heard about the restaurant from my mother. Your grandmother put her to work in the kitchen after the war."

"I didn't realize."

"Yes, until she went back up north. Can we go inside?"

I remembered taking Clare and Susan inside the abandoned houses and the restaurant one summer. I'd made the mistake of building the interiors up to be catacombs of history, places where you could contemplate the tide head of elapsed and passing time, and it was immediately apparent that neither of them could see it. What they saw were blooms of blue-green algae ravaging plaster walls. The left-behind dinner plates and cutlery, the open green wine bottles, the medicine cabinet that still held a razor and two aspirin lined up on a shelf, these were all just items of wreckage for them. Clare began sneezing and Susan looked at me as if she'd found me in our garage engaged in a shameful hobby. We left in silence and never spoke of it again, but I remember holding it against them for years, that they failed to see how these rooms were not only my boyhood sanctuary but wormholes through time, places where you might inventory the hours and the minutes of other people's lives as precisely as a crime scene. Here was the glass someone drank from right before the earth shook and the ceiling collapsed. Here was the aspirin for the headache or the fever, and you couldn't help wondering why it had never been swallowed.

I led Elisa toward the back of the restaurant, into the kitchen through the unlocked door. As soon as we were inside, I had the sensation that we were divers picking our way through an underwater shipwreck. The ferrous, damp air burned the back of my throat, and I noticed Elisa putting her nose into the collar of her parka. But then she took the flashlight from me and started to inspect the kitchen with a kind of forensic glee.

"They were in the middle of plating the meals," she whispered.

Six china plates and two soup bowls sat on a stainless steel counter. Some of them were empty and sheathed in dust and plaster and some of them fluoresced with mold when the light made contact. A single plate still had a large bone on it, bleached and stripped clean from decades of work by mice and rats and ants. I'd always been surprised that a dog or a feral cat didn't find their way into the kitchen and carry it off. I was expecting Elisa to be repelled by all this. Instead, she leaned closer and shone the light just a few inches from the bone.

"Pork chops," she said brightly.

Then she turned to the stovetop, where there was a big blackened soup pot, two small saucepans, and a frying pan, their contents turned to indecipherable swaths of color and char.

"I can imagine your grandmother standing right here, plating the food," Elisa said. "If she's doing six meals at once, they were probably pretty busy."

"The restaurant was full the night of the earthquake. You can tell from the dining room."

"Show me."

We walked through a stone archway and ducked under a wooden beam angling down from the ceiling. A dozen tables were arranged around pillars and over by the windows that faced the street. Chairs and bottles of wine were toppled over but the place settings were remarkably intact—tarnished silverware, blackened cloth napkins, small plates stippled with mold where some of the guests had already taken their antipasti or primi piatti. The wineglasses had all turned opaque, some of them broken or on their sides, some of them upright and crystalized red. Elisa walked around the room while I guided her with the flashlight. At a table by the window, she pulled one of the cane chairs upright, sat on it, and placed a tattered napkin across her lap.

"I'll have the special," she said.

"You're very brave," I said.

"I can imagine them sitting here when it happens."

"And then they all start running for the door."

"They must have been terrified."

"I've never understood why no one ever came back inside. Why not clean up or salvage something? My grandmother says she never even came back for her knives."

"Because all of it was cursed," Elisa said matter-of-factly.

"And then some American boy comes along and decides these buildings are full of mystery."

"Yes, I can see you here. I admit it's not for everybody." She stood, patted down the pockets of her parka. "I think I need another cigarette to clear my head."

As we walked back toward the kitchen, Elisa noticed a tattered paper menu, the page mildewed with tiny black specks and blue-green starbursts. "Oh, my God. Can I take this with me?" she asked, holding it into the flashlight. "I want to see what they were serving."

I'd made it a rule to never remove anything from abandoned places, including the buildings in Valetto, but there was genuine awe washing across Elisa's face, so I told her to take the menu with her.

We walked back through the kitchen and she stopped at the stove for a second, moving one hand between the burners and the stainless steel counter. "The flow is perfect," she said. "The chef can take a small turn to the right to plate on the countertop and the waiters can come from the other side." She took a step toward the counter. "My mother would have stood here, a little to the right of your grandmother. No one is in anybody's way and the chef is at the center of everything. They knew exactly what they were doing."

She continued out the back door and lit a cigarette in the alleyway. It had started to rain again and we walked back down toward the cottage in a light drizzle, passing the darkened villa, neither of us speaking until we got to the front patio.

I said, "I better go find somewhere to bunk down at the villa. Iris's guest room might be off limits at the moment."

"If they've locked you out, there is a spare bedroom here," she said. After a few seconds, perhaps slightly embarrassed, she added, "Of course you know there is a spare bedroom."

"Thank you. I think it'll be okay."

"If you decide to come north with me tomorrow, I'm planning to leave at eight o'clock sharp. I will meet you on the other side, in the parking area beside the footbridge."

I told her I would think about it and let her know in the morning. We said good night and as I climbed up through the terraced gardens, I thought about the room up north where Aldo Serafino had written the letter and taken his final breath, about the possibility of a headstone in a cemetery, of witnessing his final resting place. A historian lives for such pinheads in the map of time, but there were also reasons not to go north with a woman I barely knew. For one thing, I'd lose momentum on my lecture and research. For another, whether I liked it or not, I'd be part of a delegation to lobby for her mother's return to Umbria, which would only strengthen her family's claim. Despite the fact that neither Elisa nor my aunts showed any interest in my scheme, I clung to my vision of spending summers of studious leisure in the stone cottage and that Elisa would live in it most of the year, rent free, before fleeing the hot and dry Umbrian summers for Milan or the Alps. But how would such an arrangement work, even if all parties could be persuaded? And what would she actually *do* in Valetto to make a living and then take the summers off?

All this conjecture evaporated when I came through the villa's front door and switched on a lamp. An envelope with my name on it, written in my grandmother's hooped cursive, stood propped on the hallstand. Inside was a notecard *From the desk of Ida Serafino*:

Dearest Hugh,

Your grandfather wrote that a man is a frail thing, not much more than a wire . . . And I don't think I can die in peace without knowing more of the where and how that particular wire unraveled. Would you be willing to find out on my behalf? I've asked Signora Tomassi to entreat her mother to return to Valetto and she's agreed to allow you to accompany her up north. Thank you in advance for your service.

Yours sincerely,
Ida Serafino

There was no denying such a request, it seemed to me, as I folded the note into my pocket and moved down the hallway, switching on lamps and auditioning rooms where I might sleep. Eventually, I settled on a divan amid the papery rummage of my grandfather's former study and fell asleep to the sound of the rain and the smell of old books. The woody edge of lignin as the pages of a book yellow has always been a special comfort to me, despite the fact that it's a visceral reminder of the past dissolving into thin air.

10

Early the next morning, I left a note for my grandmother, telling her that I'd go north as she asked and
do my best to document Aldo's final days. Then I
went to Iris's apartment to pack for the trip. When
I knocked gently on the door, Iris answered in a fleece robe
and Turkish slippers, a cappuccino in one hand. She looked
at my slept-in clothes and said, "I thought perhaps you'd
moved in with the northerner over at the cottage."

"I slept in the library. I didn't want to disturb you." I
waited to be invited in. "I also wasn't sure whether I was still
welcome in your apartment."

Still blocking the doorway, she said, "You're my youngest
sister's only child. You will always be welcome." She opened
the door wider and I stepped inside. From behind me, she
added, "Even if I think what you've done is foolish and will
someday deliver us all to ruin."

In the living room, her manila files had been arranged
across the floor and tagged with neon yellow and blue and
pink Post-it notes. "How is your Venetian missing-person
case going?"

"Dead ends and blind alleys." She threw an arm out to encompass the room, shuffled between the folders to sit at her desk. "It will be quiet here without Rinaldo's proceedings." I could hear the deflation in her voice.

"He's back in Milan?" I asked.

"He leaves this morning." She considered the vanishing geometry of her screen saver. For a week, her forensic zeal had found an outlet at the side of an old colleague, a man she respected, perhaps loved. Now she was returning to the drifting sands of her own investigations, to the bounced emails she sent to a dead San Francisco detective. "Do you want a cappuccino and some raisin toast?" she asked wearily.

"Thank you, but I don't have much time. I came to pack a few things."

"Where are you going?"

I briefly thought about telling her that I was traveling to give a lecture, but the truth seemed important. "Nonna asked if I could go with Elisa to the town up north where Aldo died. She also asked if Elisa could bring her mother back to Valetto."

Iris let her eyes linger on my scuffed Swiss boots before slowly coming up to my face, a very thin line of cappuccino foam across her top lip. Quietly, she said, "When was this decided?"

"Last night, when Elisa visited with Ida."

"I see. And you're going?"

"Yes, Elisa is waiting for me on the other side of the footbridge."

She plucked a tissue from a box on her desk and dabbed her lips. A smear of lipstick came with the milk foam and I realized I'd never seen her without makeup. I said, "I'll only be gone a few days. Hopefully Alessia will agree to come back and meet with Ida."

Iris dropped the tissue into a wire trash can under her desk. It was full of Post-it notes, tissues, red yarn, and orange peels. She gave out the sort of sigh Umbrian widows have been perfecting for millennia—a bellows at the base of a fire. "Your grandmother is turning one hundred and has no idea what she's asking of people half the time. She's invited people from Australia and England for her birthday party, old people who were born here and their grandchildren who have never set foot in this town. She sends invitations like she's a queen summoning her subjects back to her crumbling empire. She can be quite selfish, if we're speaking frankly."

I'd never heard my aunt say anything unkind about her mother. She roused her computer screen with a few clicks of the mouse, attempted to level out her voice. "No, I don't think you should go. In fact, I strongly advise against it." She made a few more mouse clicks to underscore her warning. "It will only stir up the past and all its pain. We are all too old for this now."

The antique clock on the wall behind her suggested it was a quarter to eight. I looked at my phone to verify, since not a single clock in the villa ever ran true or agreed with its ornate housemates. I knew Elisa wouldn't wait for me, and I didn't have time to delicately defuse my aunt's feelings, so I said, "I've left Nonna a note telling her that I'm going, and now Elisa is waiting for me across the bridge. I'm sorry, but I've decided to go."

Without waiting for her reaction, I went into the guest room and packed some clothes, my laptop, and my camera. When I came back into the living room, she reminded me of my mother: rigid-backed, engulfed by an unnamable, darkening mood. The suggestion of a tightly held rant that, if loosed, might shatter feelings and windows. I walked over to the desk and leaned down to kiss her on the cheek. She stiffened, her face unyielding. As I headed for the door, she said, "You really have no idea what you're doing to this family."

φ

Elisa stood beside a cherry-red, soft-top Jeep Wrangler, its tailgate open and its engine giving off a throaty diesel hum. It had roll bars, fog lights, a winch. "This was not the car I imagined you driving," I said. "Are we going on safari?"

"Meet Floria."

"From *Tosca*?"

She nodded, took my daypack and laptop bag, stashed them between some spare gasoline canisters, and closed the tailgate. As we climbed into the front seats, she said, "I named her after the prima donna who is handy with a knife." I must have looked momentarily nervous, because, as we pulled up past the footbridge, she added, "My dicing and julienne skills are widely admired."

And then she gunned the Jeep up the steep hill and sped us out along the winding two-lane roads that eventually led to the autostrada, the corridor that divides rural Italy with all its variegations and tiny hamlets from a national system of tollbooths and homogenous roadside commerce. North of Orvieto, there were noise walls built along neighborhoods and towns, screening out the local houses and lives, and every so often a red SOS call box by the side of the road. I told Elisa that I'd always found the autostrada depressing because it left the real Italy behind and only those who could afford its exorbitant tolls were making use of it. It was owned by the Benetton family, I said, and they'd done their best to make people pay for the autostrada's efficiency, as if they'd won a monopoly on straight lines throughout the country.

"That's precisely why I love it," she said. "There is no more haggling with narrow, curvy streets and truck drivers who think they own a particular backcountry road. You have paid to be in a private club. What could be better?"

Elisa favored the left lane, passing semis and buses and tourists in rental cars. I'd never driven in a soft-top Jeep before and I was surprised by how loud it was, how I felt as if the diesel engine and all-terrain tires were churning just inches below my vibrating seat. She asked me if I wanted to listen to some music and, before I could answer, directed me to a canvas tote bag full of CDs and had me riffle through it to locate her current mood. She cringed at Vasco Rossi and shook her head at a handwritten disc cover for *Matteo's mix tape for Mamma*. "It will be years before I can listen to that again," she said. "Keep going." Eventually, she settled on Puccini, followed by Van Morrison and Bob Dylan. She lit a cigarette as we passed out of Umbria, the windows cracked, singing flatly along to "Recondita armonia." *Tosca ha l'occhio nero!* Tosca has black eyes!

After some time, she said, "I studied the menu from your grandmother's restaurant and I realized that half of what I ate growing up was off that menu. The soufflet di pollo, the truffled pork loin on special occasions . . . it all comes from Ida."

"Did she show you the family bible of recipes?"

"Yes. Incredible. And I love the commentary, the recipes that are well suited to listless appetites and ladies with melancholy. We used to treat food as the most important kind of medicine." She drew on her cigarette. "The recipes made me sad as well."

"Why sad?"

"It was the food of my childhood, until I was about twelve and my brother was nine. My father went to work in South America for an oil company and never came back, and my mother had what you would call a nervous breakdown. She was very depressed, could barely get out of bed. All the meals and cooking stopped, and half the time I thought we were going to starve. She'd taught me how to forage, and I used to go out before school to find mushrooms and nettles and greens so that my brother could eat lunch."

I said, "That sounds terribly difficult." It was a phrase I remembered from my few grief counseling sessions and it sounded shallow and mechanical, even though I meant it. I thought about my own mother after my father left, the way she sat in the darkened living room with a negroni, pretending to be a widow, watching daytime television. I had this in common with Elisa, I thought, our abandoned mothers who, in turn, performed their own kinds of vanishing.

Elisa said, "I became the little woman of the house and took over the cooking. I'd set rabbit traps and go fishing for river trout and follow her recipes, which I now realize were mostly your grandmother's. She never wrote them down, so I'd go upstairs to her bedroom and wake her and ask her to tell me how to braise the rabbit or make a particular sauce. Then I'd bring her a little bowl of whatever we were eating. I don't know how we survived, to be honest. We never had any money in the house. If I hadn't gone to Milan on a scholarship, I might have married a woodcutter and had seven children."

"What happened to your brother?"

"He married a Swiss woman and lives on Lake Maggiore. He builds the most beautiful wooden boats."

"It sounds like he inherited your grandfather's woodworking skills," I said.

Elisa smiled over at me, grateful that I'd made the connection.

I said, "Did your mother ever recover?"

"No, not really. They took her to a mental hospital in Milan for a year and she came back to us like a ghost. The whole town looks after her now, makes sure she has food, brings her back to the house if they find her out wandering too late."

Elisa finished her cigarette and stubbed it out in the ashtray clipped to her door. She stared out at the road. "Sorry, I didn't mean to tell you my whole life story."

"Don't apologize. Now I understand why your mother couldn't come to Valetto."

"I tried to explain to your grandmother that she isn't well. But it's hard to say no to a woman who is nearly one hundred."

"They were friends," I said. "Our mothers."

"They were?"

"According to my aunt Rose, they were inseparable when your mother lived at the villa. They did everything together."

"I've never heard my mother mention your mother."

"And I never heard my mother say the name Alessia Parigi. In fact, she didn't even mention that the family took in refugee children during the war. She was like a book on a shelf that hadn't been opened in decades. In many ways, she was a stranger to me."

φ

On the outskirts of Florence, we passed through a series of tunnels, the other Italy flickering to life between concrete embankments—umber-stuccoed villas carved into hillsides, their long driveways lined with silver cypress and zealously trimmed hedges. We'd been on the road for a few hours, so I floated the idea of stopping in Florence, Bologna, or Milan for a nice meal and good coffee, but Elisa said she'd promised her mother that we would arrive in plenty of time for dinner. She said the bright side was that we would take the scenic route along Lago Maggiore to Cannobio and then head up into the mountains. I remembered a mention of the hills above Cannobio from my grandfather's letter, a labyrinth of switchbacks and stone bridges. "When did you speak to your mother?" I asked.

"Early this morning. She is usually up at four and waits until it's nearly light to go for her walk. I thought that if I called her while it was still dark she might actually pick up."

"Does she know I'm coming?"

"I said a friend was coming with me. That was all."

"How long is the drive?"

She looked at the clock on the dashboard. "It depends on how fast I go once we get away from the speed cameras. Another five hours."

"I'm happy to take a turn driving."

"Nobody else has ever driven Floria, not even my children or my ex-husband."

"Well, we better keep you caffeinated, then. We might also need to eat at some point."

"When we stop for petrol we can pick up sandwiches from an Autogrill or Chef Express."

"I can't believe that's the lunch of choice for a trained chef." I'd had visions of finding a venerable old taverna or *salumeria* for lunch.

She hummed along to Dylan's *Blood on the Tracks*. "If you look inside most chefs' refrigerators at home, they are quite barren. Mine usually has a wedge of cheese and some yogurt and mushrooms and chocolate. Marcella makes fun of me for it."

I read aloud from my phone. "'A cappuccino with low-quality milk . . . the only good thing is the kindness of the bartenders . . .'"

"Are you reading the online reviews?"

"Of course. This is a good one. 'What is gruesome is the disorganization and rudeness of the staff.' And here's another. 'Business lunch with pork sandwich, dirty toilets, and hallucinating prices.'"

Elisa let out a laugh. "Internet translations have made Italians sound like lunatics."

"Or like a nation with a head injury. Here's my favorite one: 'The collation leaves it to be desired and the girl was alone and in trouble to manage everything. Sandwich was inexplicable.'"

She grinned, touched her lower lip. "Please stop." She turned up the music and we continued for an hour without speaking. I read a few chapters from Barzini and she smoked another cigarette and sang along to the music in her flat, exuberant voice. I'd never encountered anyone so unabashed about their own tuneless singing. When she pulled into the parking lot for Chef Express, she said, "Please prepare for hallucinating prices and inexplicable sandwiches."

I followed her across the parking lot and into the tile-and-glass expanse of backlit sandwiches wrapped in plastic and arranged on shelves, into the wide aisles of chocolates and potato chips and stuffed animals. But there was also a deli case, where unwrapped sandwiches were laid out on wooden boards and dried meats hung overhead. Elisa took my elbow and guided me over to the deli case. In the same instant, we both looked up at the hanging hams and salamis and realized they were plastic replicas of meat, no doubt ordered from Chef Express corporate. A young woman appeared in a black apron and Elisa ordered for both of us, as if I were a tourist who couldn't be trusted to order the local specialty. She ordered a *panino francescano* for herself and a *panino allo speck di cinghale* for me, as well as two coffees. While the woman wrapped our sandwiches, Elisa told her that she admired the cantaloupe and lettuce garnishes that had been placed strategically around the sandwich boards. "*Abbastanza bello*," she said to the woman, quite beautiful, and I could hear in her voice that there wasn't a hint of sarcasm. The woman said she did her best to make the sandwiches look appetizing and asked if we wanted to sample any of the cured meats. Elisa said we'd be delighted and we proceeded to take razor-thin slices of prosciutto, speck, and salami in pieces of wax paper. As we left with our sandwiches and coffee, I suspected this was Elisa's way of moving through the world, effusive at the stray garnish and chatty with store clerks.

φ

Midafternoon, we finally got off the autostrada and drove along the western shore of Lake Maggiore, through little towns with restaurants already shuttered for the winter and geese wandering along the roadsides. The lake was virtually boatless, the ferries no longer running, the water the color of slate. I'd come to this area once before, with Clare, Susan, and my mother at Christmastime. Because the weather was dismal and the towns were more or less empty, my mother had booked a heavily discounted stay at a luxury hotel in Stresa, the iconic location where Hemingway had spent his leave as a convalescing ambulance driver in 1918. Although my mother had never read Hemingway, she made friends with the concierge and became an expert on the famous writer's stay at the hotel during our visit, telling us that *A Farewell to Arms* had its origins here. She told us about the dry martinis Ernest ordered at the bar, the billiards he played with an old count, the rowboats he took out on the lake. As we neared Stresa, I suddenly remembered sitting at lunch in the hotel dining room with my mother, Clare, and Susan, a very old pianist playing Frank Sinatra tunes to three tables of chagrined, out-of-season tourists, and my mother said she wanted to visit an old friend who lived in the area and asked if I could drive her the next morning. I agreed to drive her, and when my mother went to her room that night, Clare, Susan, and I all speculated about who she might be visiting. An old flame from her youth, perhaps, because the way she effused about Hemingway, this young dashing officer before he'd found his fame, this writer she had never read, it surely had to be rooted in something deeply personal and suddenly awakened. We took turns guessing the mystery lover's name—Alberto and Roderico were front-runners—and the kind of life he led. But then, in the morning, my mother said she wasn't feeling well and never brought up the idea of the visit again.

As we neared the white façade and ironwork balconies of the Grand Hotel des Iles Borromées, it occurred to me that my mother might have been planning to visit Alessia up in the Ossola Valley but had lost her nerve. It seemed unlikely that they had kept in touch after Alessia left Valetto, since my mother hadn't known the fate of her own father, but perhaps my mother remembered the name of the town where Alessia was from, before the family moved to Milan, and she planned to simply show up looking for her childhood friend more than half a century later. As we passed the hotel, I remembered that we'd had rooms facing the lake, that we could see Isola Bella from our balcony, the very place my grandfather had described in his deathbed letter, his memories of a paddling expedition in a canoe with a suitcase full of grenades and radio equipment.

φ

As we drove up from the lake, through the heavily wooded valley above Cannobio, my phone rang and I saw that it was the villa's number. All of my aunts had cell phones, albeit seldom used or charged, but there was also a landline in the first-floor hallway, between the library and the billiard room. And because I'd only ever received a few calls from this number, usually after a death in the family or another earthquake, I expected the worst, that perhaps my grandmother had died suddenly, just shy of turning one hundred. I told Elisa that I had to take the call, and I answered to the sound of a distraught Aunt Iris. "Tell me, have you arrived in the town where she lives?"

"No," I said, "but we're getting close."

The connection shuddered as we drove into a swath of

spotty cell coverage. For a full minute, every sentence was submerged and clipped. I said, "You're breaking up. I can try to call you back when we have better reception," but then we rounded a curve on a mountain switchback and came into a clearing over the valley. There was a clicking noise, before Iris dropped in with a clarity I've never forgotten: ". . . after three days, some partisans found them down in the chestnut grove in the valley, right near the river. Barefoot, dresses torn, nettles in their hair . . . arms and legs badly scratched . . . they refused to tell us what happened . . ."

"What about three days?" I asked.

Elisa turned down the music.

"What are we talking about here exactly?" I asked.

"About what happened to your mother and Alessia when they went missing. In the spring of 1944."

The Jeep's engine revved into another steep curve, the trees flashing by the roadside.

"They told us they'd wandered off, that a wild dog attacked them down in the valley. But I think we always knew that wasn't the truth." Iris breathed into the phone, sniffled. "They refused to speak of it after that first day, but your mother, she was never the same. And Alessia had night terrors. Her screams woke up the whole villa. All of it nearly killed your grandmother. The guilt, the worry . . . Silence kills us from the inside . . ."

I saw an image of my mother sedated and on a respirator during her final days in the hospital, writing notes to make sure I knew where to find things in her house when I prepared it for sale. Bank-account passwords, bills she hadn't paid, the location of her filing-cabinet key. There had been no outpouring or inventory of her past, no words of regret or sorrow, just some handwritten notes about personal finances and household maintenance. In one note, I remembered, she told me to clean the gutters and trim the front hedges in the spring before the open house. Thinking about her in that hospital room writing notes about passwords and gutters and hedges, I felt the blood drain out of my face. I cleared my throat and asked how two young girls could just vanish for three days.

Elisa slowed below the speed limit as the road flattened onto a plateau. A truck honked and gunned into the left lane to pass us.

"Aldo had already left and your grandmother was in Florence the day they disappeared, to meet with the Red Cross about the refugee children." Iris took a moment to sob away from the mouthpiece, then came back. "The girls weren't supposed to be outside, you see. Violet and I were put in charge of all the children, just until dinnertime, but we were in our mother's bedroom trying on her dresses and all the jewelry she kept hidden during the war. That was Violet's idea. She was the oldest. But I was old enough to know better, and I've never forgiven myself. Hugh, I really must go lie down. I wanted you to know before you got there, before you found out some other way."

The line clicked and went dead. We were driving so slowly now that the engine was a faint hum beneath my feet. Elisa pulled off onto the shoulder and asked me what had happened, and I tried to parse what I'd just heard into some kind of narrative shape. If Elisa didn't know our mothers had been friends, then she certainly didn't know about the two of them going missing for three days in the spring of 1944. She listened while I summoned the details, looking out into a copse of ash trees along the roadside. After a while, she said, "Maybe they just wandered too far into the valley.

They gathered mushrooms and edible plants and slept by the river." There was nothing in her tone to suggest she believed any of this. My mind kept circling back to two barefoot girls, not yet ten, and the eternity of three days.

φ

Elisa's ancestral village was built into a hillside, tucked up in the Vigezzo Valley, one of the seven Ossola valleys that branch off a central river plain in northern Piedmont. The village stood at the end of a winding, one-lane road. A few hundred houses, most of them empty, had all been built in the seventeenth and eighteenth centuries from local stone, their steeply gabled roofs made from slate, their chimneys improbably tall. We hadn't spoken of the phone call for half an hour and Elisa took refuge in recounting the town's history. While she talked about the village's decline, I wondered about its exodus, about those who left for jobs after the war. Compared to southern Italy, earthquakes and landslides are less common in much of the north, so the forces of abandonment are more likely to be social than seismic. As we drove up the hillside, the village above us, she told me that since chimney sweeping was the traditional trade, the residents had gone to great lengths to advertise their prowess and compete with their neighbors for the tallest chimney stack. "My grandfather went down his first chimney when he was ten years old. Boys were in high demand because they could fit down the narrow chutes."

We pulled along a field, where a very old woman in a yellow headscarf was leading a flock of sheep down to a fenced pasture. The woman looked up at us with an expression that I'd seen countless times in the remote and dwindling towns

I'd visited, a kind of stupefied wonder that a visitor had arrived in this outpost of oblivion. Elisa slowed the Jeep, lowered her window, and called out to her, the woman cupping one ear to capture the words above the plodding sheep. They called back and forth in dialect, most of it unintelligible to me, but it was clear they were talking about Elisa's mother. The woman waved us on and we drove up to a narrow, three-story house perched above the town, its walls covered in ochre stucco, its towering chimney billowing smoke. Rhododendron hedges and a low wall of stacked, lichened stones hemmed in its front yard.

Elisa pulled into the paved driveway. "The sheepherder, Camilla, says my mother has been out collecting but should be home by now."

"She still forages?"

"She collects junk, mostly. You'll see." She sat for a moment longer, both hands on the steering wheel, bracing herself. We grabbed our bags from the back of the Jeep and I followed her into the yard full of free-roaming chickens. Elisa pointed out her mother's sculptures made from the things she found along the roadside—bottle caps, pieces of broken glass, tangled strips of wire, sun-bleached animal bones. In the garden, hidden in tiny grottoes and rhododendron hollows, there were hanging mobiles of wire, bone, and glass.

"I have to warn you," Elisa said, "there will be a lot of clutter. It's part of her condition, an obsessive need to collect things and arrange them constantly. Also, I don't think we should tell her right away who you are. *Le nuove informazioni sono difficili per lei.*" New information is difficult for her.

I wanted to reassure her as we walked in single file along a retaining wall beside the house. In this permanent strip of shade, it smelled of moss and damp wood, and I could see the places where the stucco had flaked away from the house exterior, exposing jagged rents of white and pewter-colored stonework. We walked through an unlocked kitchen door, set down our bags, and Elisa began calling out to her mother. The kitchen had been given over to the dyeing of fabrics and smelled faintly of paint and glue. A bedsheet or a curtain lay in the sink, soaking in purple dye, and the open cupboards were lined with brushes and jam jars of buttons, pebbles, and nails. I'd been expecting squalor, the ramshackle atmosphere of a hoarder, but this was something entirely different. Things were ordered and arranged, but every cabinet door was open and not a single piece of furniture stood at a right angle. From somewhere above us came a woman's high trailing voice, telling us to climb the stairs.

We passed into a narrow hallway lined with shelves of canned food and Elisa pointed out that the cans were all arranged by the color of their labels. Then we were climbing up two flights of squeaking, wooden stairs, glimpsing rooms of Cubist furniture arrangement and slanting framed pictures on the walls. By the third floor, I was dizzy and out of breath, but now we were standing in a lofted bedroom with a broad balcony and a silver-haired woman sitting on a bed with a pair of scissors, surrounded by photographs and magazines. She was gluing strips of text and pictures to decoupage a wooden box. In her seventies, tall and thin, wrapped in a woolen shawl, her long hair tied back with a schoolgirl's navy velvet ribbon. Elisa walked over to the bed and kissed the top of her mother's head and Alessia wrapped her arms around her daughter's waist.

Elisa said, "*Ecco*, Mamma, this is Hugh Fisher from America. A history professor."

"*Molto piacere di conoscerti*," I said.

She peeked around Elisa's waist to take me in and for a moment appeared startled to have a stranger standing in her attic bedroom. She studied me for a few seconds before offering up a polite smile and looking away. "*Piacere di conoscerti, Professore.*" It's a pleasure to meet you, Professor. They cuddled and spoke in dialect-studded Italian for a few minutes—discussed whether I was a boyfriend, if we'd be spending the night, what we'd like to eat for dinner, and whether Elisa's American friend would enjoy a tour of the town. While they talked, I looked around the room and wondered if this had been the place where Aldo Serafino wrote his deathbed letter. I tried to imagine him tucked up under the eaves, with a view of the valley and the town's steep slate roofs and towering chimneys spread beyond the balcony, Alessia as a ten- or eleven-year-old girl carrying soup up the narrow, rickety stairs.

"Hugh, if it's all right, Mamma would like to show us off to her friends and give us a tour of the town. Would that be okay? We can also buy some supplies to make dinner."

In Italian, I said that sounded like an excellent plan, and Alessia said to her daughter, "He speaks very good Italian for an American."

φ

Alessia led us through the streets in a pair of rubber boots and a purple woolen poncho, pointing out frescoes and statues with her hand-carved walking stick. As we moved along, she rapped on windows, called up to balconies, hollered into a shop front, rousing old women and men from dimly lit interiors, from watching television or preparing their evening meals. Elisa knew all these people well, had no doubt grown up in their midst, but her mother insisted on calling her the famous chef from Milan who was just visiting for one or two nights. I could tell this pained Elisa a little.

In the village's only shop, we bought some vegetables, cream, cheese, flour, bread, and a bottle of red wine. Alessia put the groceries into a canvas tote she'd brought along, and I insisted on carrying it. We walked toward the church and Elisa said she planned to make us gnocchi and a roasted chicken, if her mother would allow her to slaughter one of her chickens. Alessia gave her a genuine look of anguish and shook her head in disbelief. "Every time you come here you want to butcher one of my hens. I won't allow it." For a full minute, nobody said anything, then Elisa told me quietly in English, "She eats nothing but eggs and canned beans."

The church was extravagant for a remote village parish. Vaulted frescoes, ornate columns wrapped in gold leaf, confessionals of carved mahogany. Beside the altar, the skeleton of a venerated saint under a dome of glass. Alessia kneeled in one of the wooden pews to pray for a few minutes and then we headed back out into the falling dusk, a layer of cold, alpine air descending over the valley. It felt like it might snow. I wanted to ask about the village cemetery where my grandfather might have been buried, but I knew Elisa was working through a plan for how to broach the topic of Aldo Serafino and Valetto with her mother. We walked up the hill and back to the house, the village drowsy with woodsmoke and lamplight.

While Elisa started dinner—gnocchi alla bava and vegetable soup—I was given the job of replenishing the fire in the living room. I carried in wood from a covered pile beside the house, listening as I passed the kitchen to the complex negotiations between mother and daughter. Elisa needed more space to cook but Alessia said she wouldn't be able to find anything if she went around changing everything. I added some wood to the dying fire and waited for it to take hold. The living room, like all the rooms in the house, was all angles. One wall was covered in tilted framed photographs of the family during the 1970s and '80s, judging by the outfits—first communions and birthdays and Christmas portraits—and I realized they'd been placed in chronological order, from left to right, Elisa's father suddenly erased from the images halfway through.

I called down the hallway to see if I could help with dinner preparations, but they politely declined and told me to please make myself comfortable in the living room, so I settled in to read Barzini by the fire. When I came into the kitchen half an hour later, Alessia and Elisa stood rolling out ropes of gnocchi and cutting them on the floured kitchen table. Alessia was giving her daughter, the famous chef from Milan, pointers about how to apply the right amount of pressure to the dough. Elisa told me to refill my wineglass, and I sat watching while they made the final preparations. We cleaned off the table and Elisa served us bread and bowls of soup, and then we used the same bowls for the gnocchi.

We made small talk while we ate. Whether or not it would snow, the road repairs they were completing farther down in the valley. Mother and daughter caught up on recent accomplishments, weddings, and childbirths across a network of cousins and grandchildren, discussed whether Marcella, Elisa's daughter, was going to become a journalist or a documentary filmmaker. Matteo, working for his father in London, was mentioned only in passing. Alessia asked me about America and I talked about the college where I taught history and my sabbatical. Then, somehow, I was telling them the story of being in Rome with Susan, of the gladiator standing between us and holding a plastic sword to my throat. I went to retrieve the Polaroid bookmark from *The Italians* as proof from the living room and handed it to Alessia, who agreed that I looked exactly like a stunned fish plucked from a lake. We all laughed gently at my expense and ate for a few moments without talking.

"Have you ever been to Rome?" I asked Alessia.

"I've never been farther south than Umbria," she said between mouthfuls. "My parents sent me down there during the war to get away from the air raids in Milan. The little crumbling town where they sent us was called Valetto."

I hadn't meant to guide the conversation into this cul-de-sac, but Elisa seemed almost relieved that I'd led us here. She wiped her mouth with a napkin, took a sip of wine. "Hugh knows all about Valetto, Mamma. His mother was born there and he spent some summers there as a boy."

"*Che coincidenza*," said Alessia, spooning through her gnocchi and blowing on it.

Elisa said, "Do you remember how I was going there to inquire about the stone cottage that was promised to us?"

Alessia shrugged.

"Well, that's where I met Hugh. He is the son of Hazel Serafino."

Alessia looked up from her bowl.

Elisa said, "I learned that you and Hazel were friends when you were at the villa."

"Ancient history," Alessia said quietly, returning to her gnocchi. "Are you making dessert? We will need something sweet after this."

"We said we'd just have cheese and dried figs."

"I never agreed to that," Alessia insisted. "I was hoping for a proper dessert."

Elisa took a sip of wine. "Hugh's aunts and his grand-mother still live in the villa," she said patiently. "Don't you want to know about them? I showed them all the letter from Aldo Serafino."

"I don't like to talk about that."

"About what, *exactly*?"

"*Le lettere ed i morti.*" Letters and the dead.

Elisa let some silent eating take hold before turning back to her mother. Softly, she said, "Yes, well, as it happens, Hazel Serafino died a few years ago."

Alessia gently rested her spoon against the rim of her bowl, folded her arms, blinked, thinned her lips. "Because we were both already old, I suspected she might have passed away, but I didn't want to believe it." Her gaze floated over to the windows above the sink, into the dark void between the house and the retaining wall. In a distracted, faraway voice, she said, "But then she stopped answering my letters."

It came to me that I hadn't seen any mirrors, clocks, or books in the house. Since I couldn't quite absorb the reper-cussions of what Alessia was saying, I continued eating and thought about the arrangement of the rooms. Evelyn Wood-row, my briefly retained therapist, had told me that my grief was not, in fact, a locked room with me trapped inside. She insisted that I had the key in my own pocket. But the locked room of grief had always remained vivid in my mind, and I pictured it now as a bedroom choked with slanting furniture and cockeyed picture frames. Even the sealed windows were askew. I suddenly understood that this room resembled Van Gogh's *Bedroom in Arles*, that the walls and the doors were violet-blue and the light at the window was citron-yellow, that it was a shadowless and timeless room of angles and distortions. When I looked up from my reverie, they were both staring at me.

"Hugh?" Elisa said plaintively.

"I'm sorry, was there a question?"

"Mamma asked how your mother died."

"She had complications with asthma and developed pneumonia. It came very suddenly. She was gone in just a few weeks." I rolled up my shirtsleeves, looked for something to do with my hands. "Sorry, I'm not sure I understand." I swallowed, something I do often when I speak Italian, as if I'm trying to purge English from the back of my throat. "You and my mother wrote letters to each other?"

"Yes," Alessia said, "until just a few years ago."

I cast my mind back to the house in Ypsilanti, Michigan, when I was growing up, saw myself standing at the mailbox after school and laying the bills and junk mail onto the kitchen table. We rarely got personal mail, but a few times a year there were birthday cards and letters from Italy, and in my memory they were all postmarked in Umbria. Wouldn't the boy who read espionage novels and spied on his Italian aunts in a medieval villa have noticed an aberrant postmark from Piedmont? Then I remembered that when I was packing up the house after my mother died I'd come across old bills from the local post office for a PO box. At the time, I'd assumed it had been part of my mother's part-time business selling Tupperware and Amway to other church ladies. It was how she supported us after my father left. But now I wondered if decades of this correspondence with Alessia had been sent to the post office box instead of the house. After Hazel's death, I was so distracted by my own grief for Clare that I wasn't able to finish sorting through my mother's personal effects, so I gave away all her furniture and put the rest of her things in my garage, including two metal filing cabinets that, I felt sure, contained these letters. I wanted to ask Alessia whether she sent her letters to a post office box in Ypsilanti, Michigan, but it seemed pedantic given that she was wiping tears from her eyes with a napkin.

Elisa seemed to know what I was thinking, because she tapped the edge of the table with her thumbnail and said, "But I never saw letters from America come to the house."

"That's because she sent them to the shop and they held them for me there," Alessia said.

"Why couldn't the letters come to the house?" asked Elisa.

"They were private. We started writing to each other when we were teenagers, after some years of silence. I don't remember how it started. My mother didn't like it when I spoke about my time down south during the war. After what happened to my father, it was too painful for her. I wanted something of my own from that time. No one knew about the letters for all those years." She turned to Elisa. "Not even your father. Not even you and your brother."

I saw an image of my summers in the archive, where I foolishly clung to the details of distant, everyday lives. An ambassador's fountain pen. Winston Churchill's handwritten lunch note, *½ lb. cold chicken*, written in fountain-pen cursive, comforted me, made me think a human lifetime could be understood, measured, chronicled. Meanwhile, I had known precisely nothing about my own mother's life. I could hear the sound of the fire faintly snapping in the living room. Insisting on logic and chronology, I said, "If you stayed in touch all that time, then my mother must have known what happened to her father up here." It wasn't clear whether this was a question or an accusation.

Alessia said, "*Lei lo sapeva.*" She knew.

"But she never told anyone in my family," I said.

Alessia moved her bowl a few inches away from her.

Elisa asked, "And she knew about the letter Aldo Serafino wrote when he was dying?"

"I never told her about the letter or the promise of the cottage."

"*Perché?*"

"Because I knew the cottage had been left to her."

"But your parents saved Aldo's life," Elisa said. "The Serafinos owed our family something for that."

"It isn't that simple." She rubbed the knuckles on one hand, unable to look at either of us. "I'm very tired and now I want to go to bed." Alessia slowly pushed her chair back and walked away from the table. We listened as she climbed the wooden stairs, pausing briefly on each landing.

"She will be better in the morning," Elisa said. "But I'm also very tired. I've made up my brother's old bedroom for you. It's the first one on the next floor."

Something had shifted between us, and I couldn't name what it was. She began carrying dishes to the sink and I insisted on doing the washing up. She found a metal drying rack and placed it beside the sink. "Good night," she said. "Sleep well. My mother will be up at four for her walk, but she's quiet as a ghost."

φ

I spent a sleepless night in the brother's childhood bedroom, surrounded by the props of his adolescence—posters of Ferraris and bikinied women, an A. C. Milan soccer pennant, a scale model of a navy destroyer. I lay in the lumpy single bed, under an Afghan of orange-and-brown chevrons, staring out the window at a sliver of moon. I texted with Susan, who has always been a night owl, but I didn't tell her about the day's revelations. I wrote that I was doing research in the foothills of the Alps and would be back in Valetto in a day or two. It struck me, after I'd sent that text, that I'd always kept things from my daughter under the guise of protecting her. In Michigan, after she first moved to England, I'd pretended to be emerging from grief when, in fact, I was still paying Clare's cell phone bill so that no one else could take her number. And I'd never told her—nor would I—about my suspicion that her mother had once made a feint at leaving me. Susan texted me the details of her easyJet flight to Rome for Ida's birthday, which was less than two weeks away, and wondered if she should take the train to Orvieto. I texted that I'd be happy to pick her up at the airport in Rome and reimburse her for the flight, which earned me: *unnecessary but if you like, thank you.*

φ

Because I didn't fall asleep until the small hours, I woke after eight and went in search of Elisa and her mother. They were drinking coffee in the kitchen, Alessia still bundled from her morning expedition, her bounty spread out on the table— pieces of quartz, shards of granite, a broken blue glass bottle, a fern frond.

"We wondered if you were ever getting up," Elisa said.

"It took me a long time to drift off."

Alessia asked me in Italian if I wanted some coffee and one of the pastries she'd bought at the shop. "Every morning, they deliver the *fetta biscottata* from a bakery on the lake," she said, "and I picked them up after my walk."

"That would be wonderful," I said, sitting down at the table.

"Mamma will show us your grandfather's grave today," Elisa said.

Alessia placed my pastry and coffee in front of me. "*Grazie*," I said, taking a sip. All I wanted to talk about was my mother and the three days that, apparently, had been erased from the transcript of her life.

Elisa must have seen this in me, because in English, she said, "All in time."

"I speak some English," Alessia said in Italian from the stovetop. "Ida Serafino taught me a little when I stayed at the villa."

After a silence, I asked, "Do you mind if I ask where Aldo Serafino died?"

Mother and daughter looked at each other, then Elisa said, "In Fredo's room."

"Your brother's?" Of course I'd slept in the room where my grandfather had died, looked out the same window at the alpine night.

"The good news," Elisa said brightly, "is that my mother assures me the mattress was replaced sometime in the 1970s."

We all laughed, a little uneasily.

"During the war," Alessia said, "after my parents moved back here from Milan, it was a spare room where partisans slept before they went up into the mountains. Then it was my brother's room, and then it was your grandfather's sickroom before he died. It is the closest bedroom to the kitchen."

"Do you remember him?" I asked.

Alessia stood arranging small milk-glass jars on a wooden spice rack. "At the villa, I would see him sometimes talking to men in the garden or on the terrace when we snuck upstairs. He read to us that first winter, down in the cellar. I remember . . . *The Adventures of Tom Sawyer*, in Italian . . ." She wiped each white glass spice jar with a wet cloth. "When he showed up here after the war he had a long beard and he was already sick. He'd been hiding up in the mountain hut for a long time. He didn't want to be a bother, so he tried to chop wood and help with the chores, but he was too sick. We had to carry him up the stairs one time. The window in the bedroom was always open because of his fever, and sometimes I'd find him weeping into his hands, or talking to himself. I remember one time he was looking out the window up at the mountains and he said something to me—" Alessia turned a few glass jars inside the spice rack.

"What?" I asked gently.

"'*Lassú ho seppellito la metá della mia brigata.*'" I buried half my brigade up there. "He told me that he made caskets for them when he could, the way my father had taught him, and that it made him sad that they weren't able to build a casket for my father. I'm sorry, maybe I am misremembering. My memory isn't always so good."

I said, "Thank you for sharing that." I was coming to understand that my grandfather had died a broken man. Felled by guilt and grief after living alone up in the mountains, his partisan friends buried nearby, the sepsis eventually taking him whole. How could Aldo Serafino have returned to his old life in Umbria, with its asparagus plots and frescoes, after all that? I took a sip of my coffee and asked Alessia, "Why didn't your mother ever send his letter about the cottage?"

Alessia turned to face me. "She was never going to accept charity from anyone. The Serafinos had taken me in during the war. As far as she was concerned, there was no debt owed. Also, she had no desire to move five hundred miles away to Umbria. It might as well have been the moon or Mars to her. Our people have been in this valley for seven generations."

Elisa said, "She may not have sent the actual paper, but the gift was made the moment he signed the letter."

Alessia slotted a glass jar into the rack. "*Non sai niente del passato.*" You know nothing of the past.

φ

At the cemetery, we walked along in the gently falling snow, along the graveled footpath beside the row of iron-gated crypts. Like the village church, the cemetery was extravagant for an outpost in the Alps. Some of the gravestones were decorated with artificial flowers and photographs or sketches of the dead, and many of them had tiny peaked roofs. I could see how these decorations might offer comfort to the living, but then Alessia explained that after about eighty years, the cemetery exhumed each grave, removed its headstone or marker, and placed the bones into an ossuary in the perimeter wall. "To recycle the plots," added Elisa, "so the cemetery doesn't fill up."

I hadn't been in a cemetery since my mother's funeral, and I remembered that Clare, who'd been cremated and scattered from a mountaintop in the Upper Peninsula of Michigan, had hated cemeteries. In Maine, her parents were in a big family plot that dated back to the eighteenth century, and her biggest fear, during those long white afternoons of morphine near the end, was that she'd somehow end up on that New England hillside with her small-town ancestors. She'd written out the instructions for her at-home memorial service with the precision of a wedding planner, right down to the Joni Mitchell tunes that should be played, the hand-made candles to be burned, the invite list, and the menu, but the scattering was mentioned almost as an afterthought, as if driving eight hours to the shores of Lake Superior in winter was a trivial affair. "If you keep me trapped in an urn, I'll haunt you both," she'd said. But that was exactly what we did for three months until the guilt got the better of us. It was Susan who'd put the urn on the breakfast table one Saturday morning and tossed me my car keys.

We came upon Aldo's snow-dusted grave in an older part of the cemetery. The headstones were humbler than the ones along the avenue of family tombs—mostly thin slabs of curved white marble—but they'd all been kept clean and free of the moss and lichen that seemed to grow everywhere in the alpine north. There was a stone planter of cyclamens in front of Aldo's headstone, and I wondered if Alessia had visited the grave for *il giorno dei Morti*. The inscription read:

ALDO SERAFINO
NATO IL 15. 3. 1901
MORTO IL 3. 9. 1947
INGEGNERE, PADRE, PATRIOTA.

Engineer, father, patriot. I'd expected his epitaph to have some of his poetic sensibility, or the suggestion of the partisan struggle to build a new republic. I asked Alessia if it would be all right if I took a photograph of the headstone for my grandmother and she consented with a slow nod. We stood in silence while Alessia tucked her chin and began a murmured prayer. I wanted to feel the gravity of seeing my grandfather's final resting place, or a sense of resolution, but instead I thought about how my mother had known of Aldo's death from her correspondence with Alessia and how she'd kept it to herself for more than half a century. As we walked back along the graveled footpath to leave, I pictured my mother's headstone back in Michigan, which she'd prepaid, along with funeral services, twenty years before her illness and death. For a plainspoken woman of few words, her headstone was remarkably voluble. It listed the bookend dates of her life, followed by a long, chiseled Italian epitaph—*Vivere nel cuore di chi resta significa non morire mai*. Living in the heart of those who remain means never dying.

φ

We returned to the house in the early afternoon and I lit a fire in the living room hearth. The cemetery had put Alessia in a mood, and she disappeared into her bedroom for several hours. Elisa made some hot chocolate and we sat by the fire drinking it, the snow whirling against the windowpanes. "You're easy to be around," she said after some time. "I never feel like I have to talk if I have nothing to say."

"I come from a long line of silence," I said, but then I thought this sounded like a deflection, so I added, "Yes, it feels very easy."

We both stared into the flames and I heard myself swallow. She took off her glasses, rubbed her eyes, put them back on. "And thank you for being so patient with my mother. If you try to saddle her all at once she will buck you off."

"She's fragile," I said. "There's no hurry."

"You are okay to stay another night? I plan to ask her at dinner if she will come back with us."

"That's fine," I said. "Though it's hard to imagine her coming."

"I know."

We watched the fire and the snow falling outside some more and eventually Elisa curled on the couch beside me, her head a few inches from my lap, and closed her eyes. I heard her breathing flutter as she fell asleep and I found myself wanting to take her glasses off, in case she should suddenly turn her head into the cushions. I reached for my Barzini and read half a chapter about the Sicilian Mafia, but my mind kept coming back to Elisa's slow exhalations. When you have gone years without intimacy, there is no human proximity or kindness that goes without notice. The woman selling you a movie ticket inadvertently grazes your hand, or the waitress touches your shoulder as she places the bill on the table, or the old man on the street gives you a grandfatherly look of approval, even a wry little salute, when he notices the fedora you've appropriated from his generation. In these moments you feel some recess of yourself flush to the surface and you understand, if only for a moment, why everyone in your life has been telling you to get a dog ever since your wife died. All this is to say that I found myself transfixed by Elisa's steady breathing beside me, not entirely sure whether I should leave the room because of the delicate and private nature of a midafternoon nap, or bury myself in that comforting sound.

I'd returned to skimming Barzini's pages when Alessia appeared in her dressing gown. It was barely five o'clock. She sat in the rose-print armchair by the fire, her long silver hair falling in front of her shoulders. She reached into the pocket of her dressing gown, produced a color photograph, and handed it to me. I tilted it into the lamplight. It must have been taken on a road trip sometime in the late nineties, my mother, Clare, Susan, and me standing in front of the monochromatic vastness of the Grand Canyon. Susan looked about nine or ten, and I'd recently gotten tenure, apparently, because I was trying to pull off a defiant Van Dyke beard.

I handed the photograph back to Alessia but she told me *tienilo*, keep it. Then, looking down at Elisa, she said to me, "My daughter asked if I would let you read your mother's letters, so you could find some peace. She said Hazel was a stranger to you, which makes me very sad. She wrote beautiful letters and I could always hear her when I read them, even though I hadn't seen her since we were girls and we never spoke on the telephone. If you like, I will show them to you." I didn't know how to reply, so I just silently followed after her as she got up and walked down the hallway. We climbed the stairs slowly together, rising up from the warmth of the lower floors to the drafty uppermost rooms. She led me into her lofted bedroom under the eaves and I saw that the entire floor was a slanting grid of addressed and post-marked envelopes, each one carefully slit open and placed at a skewed angle to its neighbors. She'd arranged them with the same off-kilter geometry that she'd applied elsewhere in the house, to soup cans, furniture, and picture frames.

"*Li ho sistemati per te*," she said, I arranged them for you. "The top left is the beginning, August 1951, when she was still at the villa, and the bottom right, beside the bed, is the last one she sent from Michigan. They are in the correct order, by the year."

She had cleared a little walkway in the middle of the letters and she used it now to get to her bed and retrieve the empty cardboard box that must have housed my mother's correspondence. She brought it back toward the doorway, where I stood transfixed.

"Are you all right?" she asked.

"There must be hundreds of them."

"I never read them again after the first time, but I always liked knowing they were safe. Who knows why we wrote for so long. I never saw her again, but we told each other everything. I will let you read them in peace." She turned on the overhead light and I heard her slowly descend the stairs.

I have always been intoxicated by the smell of paper as it ages. The hoarded past can smell like rancid almonds or rotting flowers, and sometimes it breathes in the atmosphere of the places where it's stored, the plastic or cardboard, but also the attic or basement. What I smelled emanating from all these foxed envelopes was damp wool and lichened slate and the resin of old larch beams, and I was already half-drunk with it before I opened the first letter.

11

There were 206 letters, all in Italian, from the time my mother was sixteen until she was in her late sixties. Most were a few pages long, single-sided and written to the margins on crepe-like airmail paper, but there were also ten-page missives on my father's monogrammed stationery from the 1970s, from before he left us. I translated obscure words and phrases on my phone, arranged the pages faceup, trying to take in the span of years. I stood in the middle of all that paper, exhilarated but also filling with a raking sadness.

Hazel's handwriting evolved across the letters, from the florid and swooping teenage cursive at the Umbrian villa to the tightly looped font of a woman at the end of her life in Ypsilanti, Michigan. But it was her voice behind the letter formations that belonged to someone I'd never met. Part of it was that my mother had rarely spoken Italian around me, and I'd received only a handful of letters from her, all in English, during my college and graduate school years. That voice had been stilted, wary, self-pitying, occasionally sentimental, whereas the voice of this correspondent was intimate, generous, and vulnerable. Here was a description of her shared apartment in Rome, after she'd first left Valetto—*the balcony is the size of a postage stamp, barely fitting the clay pot of gardenias that I bought with my first paycheck, but I stand here so happily every morning with my coffee, watching the city wakening*—and here was a breathless description of her early days with my father, after they'd met on a beach in Greece in the late 1950s—*when Jerry Fisher puts his camera to his face, his mouth drops open in astonishment, like a boy craning up at the stars.* She used the word *incantata* to describe her feelings—enchanted.

Her first winter in Michigan, pulverized by the cold and depressed at being so far from home, she wrote, *I feel the ice in my bones and it is hardening my moods. I forget what the color blue looks like. Umbria is another planet.* It was the news of my birth in 1965 that fell through me like a hammer, the unexpected tenderness of it. *Hugh Ignazio Fisher entered this world at 3:15 a.m. on March 2nd, weighing seven pounds, three ounces. My beloved bellows and bawls like a drunkard being murdered (colic) but when he sleeps in short bursts, I stop the clocks in the kitchen and the hallway so that I can adore him in total silence.*

I went to get some air out on the balcony, and as I looked over the high-chimneyed slate rooftops, it occurred to me that I'd never taken my mother's death as an occasion for grief. There was the tsunami of Clare's loss, and by comparison my mother's death, in her early seventies, barely made a wake. She'd always been a cipher to me, an empty room, but now, at the foothills of the Alps, I was overwhelmed by the idea that she'd kept herself alive and fully expressed in these private letters. Did I just not look hard enough for her in that half-lit house in Ypsilanti, or in the undecorated cottage above the ravines in Umbria?

I went back inside to the letters and searched for some mention of my mother and Alessia's going missing during the war. If the letters mentioned that time at all, they spoke of the two girls walking along the calanchi ridges of the valley, of going blackberrying with Ida at dusk, of the early days helping in the restaurant, but then, as she settled into her new life in the American suburbs in the autumn of 1966, when I was not yet one and as she braced herself for another winter, something broke through:

I saw him again and I never told you about it. My last summer in Valetto, before I took the job as a secretary in Rome. It was nearly ten years since they'd forced him out of the town but he was back visiting his son's family. I was walking through the piazza, right in front of the church, and he was sitting on a bench with his two small grandchildren, a girl and a boy, and they were all eating gelato. He dressed like an old man, in a cheap brown suit and a hat with a big brim, even though he didn't look old enough to have grandchildren. He looked up at me and touched the brim of his hat, said buona giornata signorina, and I didn't recognize him for a second. I said good day, smiled at the children, and then it was as if my body knew something my mind didn't. I felt a stone drop into my throat and my hands started to tremble. It was his voice and the angle of his shoulders and the black polished shoes with the laces in double knots. I kept walking but I could feel him watching me, feel the ferret wheel of his mind spinning.

When I got home to the villa I lay in bed sobbing and then I filled with the purest rage and I went back out with one of Milo's hunting knives, hours later, after it was dark. I was certain that I'd find him still sitting in the square, waiting for me to return with a knife. Of course he wasn't there. But the next day he came with his family to the restaurant for lunch and I was their waitress. The whole town still remembered that he was a fascist and informer during the war, that his family's farmacia was tainted with partisan blood, but my mother insisted we be civil, that years had passed and it wasn't his family's fault. She was as oblivious as ever.

He watched me carry the plates from the kitchen to the table, studied the way I poured the wine, gently reminded his young granddaughter of her manners when I was within earshot. I felt like a spider pinned to a felt pad when he looked at me. I had visions of breaking a wine bottle over his head, or holding a steak knife to his throat, but do you know what I did? I started crying again in the kitchen and I told my mother it was nothing, that I wasn't feeling well. For years, I wanted to tell you that I slit his throat or pushed him into a ravine, that I confronted him, told his toddler grandchildren what he'd done to us, but the truth is, Alessia, I fed the man a bowl of Paradise Soup flavored with the salt of my own tears.

I sat on the edge of Alessia's bed, read and reread the same passage, triangulating between English, Italian, and the stray cursive phrases that receded into the paper. I gave up on trying to hold the letter between my shaking fingertips and set it on the bedspread. One of my history majors was keeping an eye on my house while I was gone, picking up the mail and watering the plants once a week, and I imagined calling her and asking her to drive across town to my house. I would tell her to open the garage, take the small key from the top of the metal filing cabinet, and unlock the drawers. I'd ask her to look for handwritten letters in Italian, hundreds of them, probably all grouped together. If a person bothered to look, they would be easy to find. Once she'd located them, I would ask her to look at the dates and find one that was written toward the end of 1966. You're a forensic historian, I'd tell her, and now read me what it says. And I'd listen to her sound out the Italian and I'd translate it silently. Right there, I'd say, is the moment we stick the pin into the map of time.

But I didn't need to hear the response to this letter to know why it felt like I was waiting for something hard to dissolve in my stomach. There was only one pharmacy near Valetto, in the neighboring town of Bevona, and the Ruffo family had run it for generations. For as long as anyone could remember, the prescriptions and night creams and first aid supplies that made their way over the footbridge, the medicines that fought Serafino infections or the tonics that restored Serafino appetites, had all come from Farmacia Ruffo. During my boyhood summers in Valetto, when Silvio Ruffo, the disgraced fascist and pharmacist, returned from his Rome exile on occasional weekends, I had played chess with him in the square, had breathed his cigar smoke, and had listened to his litany of complaints about Italian politics while he fed stray cats from his coat pockets. He must have known who I was, the American nephew of the elder Serafino sisters, the son of Hazel Serafino, but I couldn't recall ever talking about my life in Michigan. Had my mother known that he sat among my chess opponents in the square? I'd come to Valetto alone for five consecutive summers, until I was thirteen, and didn't speak with my mother between June and August, and she never asked me about my time at the villa. It was Aunt Iris who kept an eye on me and paid for my plane tickets while my mother was busy either preparing to be abandoned by my father or pretending to be a widow after he left. She didn't start returning to Valetto for the summers until I was in high school, and then it became her haphazard tradition, every few years, until she stopped coming altogether sometime in her sixties.

It was dark outside and it had stopped snowing. I turned the letter facedown on the bed beside me. I didn't know what Silvio Ruffo had done to my mother or to Alessia, but I knew, from my mother's words, from her tone, that it was the kind of harm that cuts a human life in two, separates it into the *before* and *after*. I heard footsteps coming up the stairs—it was Elisa, bounding two steps at a time, refreshed from her nap. I suddenly noticed that the house was filling with the smell of cooking meat and onions. I looked at my watch and realized I'd been up here for several hours. A little breathless, Elisa found me sitting on the edge of her mother's bed, staring down at the back of the letter. She leaned against the doorframe, a dishtowel over one shoulder, her hair pulled into a tight ponytail. "I asked her to let you see your mother's letters, but I didn't realize it would be all this." She looked wary of entering the room. "Are you okay?"

"I'm not sure."

"Well, I'd like to hear about what you found. I'm making us some dinner if you feel like eating. Lamb shanks from the local butcher."

"Before we go—" I gestured to the facedown letter.

She walked into the narrow aisle between letters and sat on the edge of the bed beside me. The mattress was old and soft, so we tilted toward each other, and I could smell flour and rendered fat coming from the dishtowel on her shoulder. "Does it talk about the three days?"

When I said nothing, she picked up the letter and started to read, angling the handwriting into the light. She read the one-page letter several times, her lips moving, turning it over each time she got to the end, even though she knew that nothing had been written on the back. I expected that she might be blinking back tears when she turned to face me, but when her eyes dilated in the lamplight I saw anger forming like a bruise. "Do you know who it is?"

"Yes," I said.

"Is he still alive?"

"I don't know."

I tried to pinpoint the last time I'd seen Silvio Ruffo. It had been more than fifteen years ago, perhaps sometime in the nineties, when Clare, Susan, and I came to Valetto to stay with my mother in the stone cottage. Had my mother seen him again as an adult? She rarely left the cottage during her summer visits, preferring to garden in the mornings, before it got too hot, and to read her Agatha Christie novels and drink her negronis on the front patio or back terrace in the afternoons. I saw Clare, Susan, and me walking across the footbridge and up the hill into Bevona, stopping in at the pharmacy for aspirin or Dramamine for the flight home, and it occurred to me that my mother must have always come to Italy with her blood pressure and asthma prescriptions already filled, that I'd never known her to run out of her medicines during her three-month visits.

"Mamma must have known this was here," Elisa said, her voice jagged, "when she brought you up here."

"She told me she'd never read them again after the first time." Instinctively, I wanted to protect Alessia from whatever was unraveling beside me. Very reasonably, I said, "This letter was written almost fifty years ago."

"She remembers everything, like an elephant," Elisa said. "She's also an expert liar."

Elisa stood with the letter and headed for the door. I followed after her, trying to keep up as she raced down the narrow wooden staircase. For two days she'd been strategizing about her mother's memories and emotions, one tripwire move at a time, and I knew all that was over by the time we got to the bottom landing. She called out to her mother, trying to contain her anger, moving from room to room, but there was no answer. We found Alessia back in the living room, sitting under a lamp in her fireside armchair, staring into the flames, drinking a cup of warm lemon water in anticipation of dinnertime.

"Why didn't you answer when I called you?" Elisa scolded.

Alessia didn't move her eyes from the fireplace. Very slowly and calmly, she said, "I've always hated the way you yell from other rooms."

I stood in the doorway, suddenly faint with hunger and the afternoon's revelations.

In Italian, Alessia side-mouthed that her daughter had always been bossy and that she had an infamous temper. "We used to call her *la mangusta*," she said, the mongoose. "If she is angry enough, she will kill and eat a snake whole. Even the poisonous ones."

Elisa gave me an exasperated look. "Why don't you come in and sit down?"

I took a few slow, tentative steps into the living room and installed myself on the couch, crossed my legs, cocked my head to one side, tried to look as if the letter in Elisa's hand was a piece of sheet music and we were about to hear a recital.

Elisa leaned beside her mother's chair with the letter. Alessia didn't budge her hands or eyes from the fire. I thought: *If you don't look at or touch the past, it can't wreck you.*

Elisa said, "I have some questions about one of the letters, about something Hazel Serafino wrote to you in 1966."

"She was in America by then."

"Would you like me to read this one aloud?"

"I can think of nothing worse."

Elisa leaned into a sarcastic smile, took a step back from the armchair, brought the letter to her side. She walked over to the wall of picture frames, stared up at the slanting geometry of her childhood. When she finally spoke, I could hear her Italian thickening with dialect. She turned toward the fireplace so that she could direct her words at the back of Alessia's rose-print armchair. "*Eccole*, the old Italian women with their secrets, carrying them to the grave like a penance, *sì, sì,* I protect my family from all that I have endured, I suffer in silence so that you may prosper, my children . . . I am a protector, a beloved guardian . . ." She glanced down at the letter. "Actually, Mamma, you were not able to protect us from anything. After you were done having your nervous breakdown, sitting in that very chair after you came home from the hospital, Fredo and I were practically starving. I had to steal from the shop, or trap rabbits and forage for mushrooms so that we could eat. You ran away from us, into your own mind and moods, but whatever you suffered from we lived it, too. We endured the pity of every person in this *villaggio del cazzo*. Our father was in South America and our mother was in bed or staring into the fire or out walking and collecting her garbage, already a million miles away. Everything that has happened to you has also happened to us. I need you to understand that."

I stared at Alessia, her jaw faintly trembling. She took a sip of warm lemon water and said something that sounded like *pietra*, the Italian word for stone. Then she set the cup on the floor beside the armchair, ran her hands along the arms of the chair, continued to regard the fire as the only animate thing in the room.

Elisa came back to the fireplace, kneeled on the floor, placed the letter in her mother's lap. "I am begging you."

"I taught you to never beg."

"Will you just read the letter and tell me what it means?"

When Alessia finally moved her hands, it was to make the sign of the cross and reach into a pocket of her dressing gown for a pair of reading glasses. She perched the glasses on her nose and gently picked up the letter by the edges and unfolded it. As she read, I watched her face for tiny detonations of emotion. When she was done reading, she shook her head, shrugged, thinned her lips, set the letter on her lap. She looked around as if she couldn't understand how this drafty room and these cruel strangers had suddenly enveloped her. And then came the brittle sound of paper as she crumpled the letter and tossed it into the fire.

Elisa darted her hand into the fireplace to retrieve it, but the edges were already winking with blue-yellow flame. She dropped the burning letter onto the rug, picked up Alessia's teacup, and poured the rest of the lemon water on top. The doused edges feathered out and I glimpsed some smeared letters of blue ink. Alessia gripped both sides of the armchair to stand. "You brought that on yourself," she said without emotion. We both watched her as she slowly walked from the room, listened to her methodically climb the stairs.

Elisa was still kneeling on the floor and I wondered what would happen next. I imagined Alessia tossing the letters out into the snow from her bedroom's balcony, or bundling them back down here to burn them in the fireplace after we'd gone to bed. Without looking at me, Elisa said, "I think it's safe to say my mother won't be coming to Valetto to claim the cottage. Your aunts will be delighted."

"Maybe she'll be different in the morning," I said. "And if not, I can call my grandmother and tell her that Alessia can't come. The cottage is still mine to give."

"No," she said, getting to her feet, "it's not yours to give. In fact, it hasn't belonged to the Serafinos since 1947, since the day Aldo signed that letter."

"Nobody knew," I said softly.

Elisa glanced at the space beside me on the couch, where just a few hours ago she'd curled into a nap. "You've been kind to me and very patient with my mother. Help yourself to some dinner. Tomorrow, I can drive you to Milan, but do you mind taking the train back to Orvieto from there?"

"What about your things?"

"Perhaps you would be kind enough to ship them to me."

"Of course."

She walked out into the hallway and climbed the stairs. I refueled the fire with some more wood and sat for a while longer on the couch, staring at the crescent of lemon rind beside the ruined letter. I thought about the miracle of the archive, marveled that all of our words aren't unanimously read, charred, and extinguished by those who outlive us.

φ

After eating alone in the kitchen, I stood outside in the snow, talking to Milo on his cell phone. He was catching me up on the preparations for Ida's hundredth-birthday party at the villa, telling me that Donata had threatened to quit if they didn't hire a caterer, and so Iris, as treasurer of the household, had conceded to pay the Bonoglio family, who ran one of the lackluster restaurants in Bevona, to prepare and serve the food. Trying to segue into the burning past, into the reason for my call, I asked Milo if there was a final head count for who was coming.

"Somewhere between fifty and two hundred."

"Dear God." I watched my breath smoke in the alpine air.

"Your grandmother did not keep count of who she sent invitations to. Your aunts let her send them to whatever addresses she had in her little book."

"Aren't people RSVP-ing?"

"It was not a requirement of the invitation," Milo said affably. "I understand that there is an old couple coming from Melbourne, Australia, the Brocatos. They have not returned to Valetto since the 1960s, if you can imagine it. They called the villa to give their arrival details. I will be picking them up at the airport in Rome."

I could hear the sound of a knife being sharpened on whetstone and I pictured Milo in his workshop, his sanctuary of lumber, awls, and calipers. I pushed out a cloud of breath into the cold air. "Do you happen to know if Silvio Ruffo is still alive?"

Milo made a whistling calculation with his mouth. "Ruffo? I have not seen that old fascist bastard in many years. Probably dead. Yes, I would say almost certainly dead."

"Can you find out?"

An interval of sharpening. "It's possible to do this. Why do you ask?"

"Just curious," I said. "You mentioned him one night when we took the dogs for a walk and I hadn't thought of him in years. I used to play chess with him in the square."

"Did you win?"

"No, he beat me every time."

"That figures. He was always a cunning old hyena, even when he was not very old. As it happens, I have to go into town tomorrow. I will stop by the farmacia and ask his grandson."

I said good night to Milo and went back inside the house, where all the lights were out except in the kitchen. I used my cell phone to find my way up the stairs and into the brother's bedroom, the room, I now knew, where my grandfather had written the letter and taken his final breath. On the narrow bed, I texted Susan that I loved her and that I was excited to see her soon, and then I waited for sleep to descend, my mind fogging over with the harrowing puzzle of what had happened to my mother.

Sometime before dawn, I woke to the sound of a woman screaming. By the time I made it to the stairs, Elisa was already bounding one flight above me, apologizing for her mother's night terrors. When we made it to the top-floor bedroom, we could see Alessia sitting up in bed, the letters still arranged on the floor. Elisa asked from the doorway if she was all right and Alessia told her not to turn on the light. *"Era solo un brutto sogno,"* Alessia said, just a bad dream. Elisa went and sat beside her mother on the bed, her arm around her shoulder. I felt like I was intruding on something intimate and fragile, so I began for the stairwell. Then, from behind me, I heard Alessia say, "If you both sit quietly and promise not to talk, then I will tell you what I remember." I came back into the room and stepped between the letters toward the bed. Because the moon was full and the window-sills were edged in snow, the room had the glazed-blue and submarine quality of an ice cave.

· 12 ·

Here are the two barefoot girls in the chestnut grove, eight and nine, holding hands. My mother is the taller, older girl. Stones in the pockets of her torn dress, nettles in her hair. Alessia began her story with the ending, with being found in the valley instead of becoming lost, and then she worked her way backward to the afternoon that he arrived at the villa. It came in slivers and slurries, in narrative whorls. Until the very end of the story, she used the third person, spoke of *the girls* down in the valley.

The girls have been missing for three days and two nights when two partisans hear them singing in the grove. At first, the girls panic and run when the men walk among the ancient, gnarled chestnuts, but then the men begin to walk slowly away, telling them to follow the river and the clay footpath back toward Valetto. The girls follow all the way back to the villa, where Hazel's mother, certain that both girls are dead, is overcome with emotion. Beneath the ragged hems of their dresses, there are constellations of mosquito bites, and their arms and legs are badly scratched. Ida

Serafino tends their wounds and welts, makes up feather beds for the girls in her own bedroom, prepares them delicate broths that are known to help the listless, the stricken, and the convalescing. She brings them toys and puzzles and books, plays music, brings in the other children to perform impromptu puppet shows and charades, but no amount of enticement will produce the story of how the girls vanished for three days.

Hazel will speak only to Alessia, and Alessia won't speak at all. The girls develop a secret language of gestures and glances, never leaving each other's side, holding hands beneath the blankets at night. Distraught at the lingering silence, Ida Serafino summons the two partisans to the villa to see what they remember about finding the girls in the grove. Hazel and Alessia sit in the dining room while they listen to Ida talking to the men. One of the partisans, the local butcher, recalls that the girls were singing to each other as they walked along, something about a golden eagle that lays two eggs in her cliff-top nest, but when both chicks hatch, a few days apart, the bigger one kills the smaller sibling. This is the predatory bird's way, he says, though no one in living memory has seen a golden eagle in the valley.

φ

Now they are running barefoot across the piazza and through the town, thudding along the cobblestones. Hazel is in front, because she is older and faster and because this is the place where she was born. She leads Alessia through the alleyways and down the hill, passing alongside her family's villa, the lights snuffed for fear of air raids. Both girls can imagine its rooms and hallways in the dark, the three older Serafino sisters asleep in their beds and their mother down in the cellar with the smaller refugee children. They can imagine the embers still glowing in the fireplaces, the copper pots hanging in the kitchen, everything in its place, but something tells them to keep running, that they won't be safe until they're down in the valley.

They cut through the terraced gardens and wind along the hard-packed trails, the ridges of calanchi like white blades winking in the moonlight. It's a warm spring night and they can hear the eddying of the river along the bank. Hazel takes Alessia by the hand and leads her into the chestnut grove. Above their heads, they hear hundreds of bats chirping and flitting between the branches as they swoop for insects, but Hazel says they will be safe here until morning. They nestle at the base of a tree and use Alessia's yellow cardigan as a blanket, their knees drawn up, their heads touching. Alessia can hear Hazel's breathing and heartbeat as if they are her own.

In the darkness, Hazel tries to comfort her friend by whispering stories of the villa before the war, about the *capo d'anno* celebrations when the villa opened its doors for the annual dance, when everyone drank too much wine and grappa and all the town's children commandeered the rooftop terrace. They waited for her father to set off his famous homemade fireworks from the terraced garden—spinning arcs of blue and yellow starlight. My father is an engineer, Hazel reminds Alessia, so he knows how to make explosions without burning down the villa. Alessia nods, says she can almost see it, as they lie back and stare up through the chestnut branches.

Hours before dawn, they hear the sound of bootheels on river stones. *È l'aquila*, Alessia whispers, still half asleep, it's the eagle, but they both remember Ida's stories of wandering Germans and escaped prisoners and fascists looking for young men to join the militias. It could be any man in a pair of boots. Hazel puts her finger to her lips and they stand so she can hoist Alessia up into the branches of a chestnut tree. She climbs up after Alessia and they move into the higher limbs, waiting for the man to move along the riverbank or walk into the grove. They hear the sound of a struck match and smell its sulfurous afterburn. Through the branches and leaves, they can see him standing with a cigarette, shoes off, bare feet in the river. Eventually, the man dries his feet and puts his socks and boots back on and wanders farther downstream. They lean back against the chestnut bark and sleep until dawn in the crux of the tree.

φ

From the cellar, they can hear him moving in the rooms above. The floors are stone, but through the wooden door at the top of the stairs they sometimes hear him on the telephone, or when he puts the needle on the gramophone and walks through the house humming along to sad violin music. His voice is dry, thin, and flat, like a piece of flint, Alessia thinks, and she can't quite keep his voice and his face in her mind at the same time. When he showed up at the villa two days earlier, his eyes were small and darkly on the verge of tears. But then, during their first night in the cellar, when he opened the door and summoned them both upstairs, he said it the way people say their own names, without any surprise in it at all.

Now, in the late afternoon of the second day, they wait for his voice to uncoil from the top of the stairs. There is a boarded-up window that lets in a few slats of light, and they can see the day fading in the empty green wine bottles and the brown glass medicine jars lined up on a shelf. The cellar smells of chalk and wet stone but also something Alessia remembers from being sick, a bitter powder she can still taste on her tongue. The brown jars have labels on them, but she can't read the faded writing. Hazel has placed a dozen of the jars on the middle stairs, hoping they won't catch any of the light from the house above when the door is opened. She has taken a length of rope from an old tool chest and tied it between the two railings on the stairs, right above the brown bottles. She used two cow-hitch knots, the knot her father taught her for tying a donkey to a railing.

They wait for hours, carve their initials and the date into the stone wall with a nail, eat the rice and dried figs he left for them, drink the water from the ceramic jug. They whisper in the darkness, rehearse the steps of their escape, but Alessia feels Hazel shaking and wonders if they will be strong enough to run up the stairs once he trips and falls. They wait so long that they fall asleep sitting on the floor, their backs up against a workbench. When the door finally opens, they hear their names as if from the end of the long hallway. Alessia's eyes open. She feels Hazel grip her arm. Neither of them moves. The eagle says their names again, his voice dry and patient.

In the band of hallway light at the top of the stairs, Alessia can see his black polished shoes, the laces tied in double knots. Hazel puts her hand on Alessia's and rubs it, telling her not to move or speak with her fingers. Then, very slowly, one black shoe dips down onto the first step, then the other. He stands, waits, reaches into his pocket. They can hear the tiny rattle of a matchbox and both of them are sure he will see the bottles and the rope if he lights a match. In the few seconds before he strikes the box, Hazel stands up and moves through the darkness, and Alessia is certain that she's going to climb the stairs. But then there's the sound of breaking glass, of the remaining bottles on the shelf hitting the stone floor. The eagle's voice and the match strike up in the same moment so that he's yelling from inside the flickering light as he hurries down the stairs. The smashing glass has stopped and now they both crouch on either side of the stairs, just outside the match light, Hazel with a shovel in her hand. The black shoes come to rest one step above the bottles. He stands there holding the match out toward the cellar, telling them that all his neighbors have fled the town and no one will hear anything in the house. Alessia thinks he might turn and go back up the stairs, but then one shoe drops onto a brown bottle and the rope pulls taut around his leg, the match snuffed in the air as he tumbles.

They can't see whether he is at the bottom of the stairs or still partway down, but they clamber up toward the hallway light. A few steps up, Alessia feels his chalky cold hand around her bare foot, feels him pulling her back down, but then there's the sound of the shovel, of the wind being knocked out of him, and she feels her foot come free. They step over the rope and the bottles, take the last of the stairs until they're running down the long hallway toward the front door. As they burst onto the cobblestone streets, the church bells are ringing and Alessia makes herself count all nine tolls as they run through the darkness.

φ

We are playing hopscotch in front of the villa when he arrives on foot. Alessia briefly allowed herself to use *we*, and then *I*, as she recounted that first afternoon. The older girls, Violet and Iris, are trying on their mother's dresses and jewelry in their parents' bedroom because Ida is in Florence for the day and they have the run of the place. Hazel and I know we are not supposed to be in front of the villa, but ever since Aldo Serafino fled north on horseback a week ago the rules of the house have come undone. When we see the man walking toward us, Hazel says it's Signore Ruffo, the farmacista from the next town over. He is tall and skinny with a mustache. I think of the pharmacist in our neighborhood in Milan, see him dressed in a tie and white coat with his name embroidered over the pocket, climbing a wooden ladder to retrieve powders and pills from the upper shelves. The pharmacist walking toward us is wearing a blue shirt with the sleeves rolled up, and his dark eyes are sad, as if he's been crying. Alessia's head was on her pillow while she told us this, her eyes closed, Elisa stroking her hair.

When Signore Ruffo gets close to the chalk lines of the hopscotch game, he tries to smile a little and he tells us that his own daughter, Greta, likes to play this very same game with her friends. *"Hai mai giocato con mia figlia a scuola?"* he asks Hazel. Have you ever played with my daughter at school?

Hazel shakes her head. The schoolhouse has been closed for more than a year.

Ruffo watches me take my turn and asks, "Who is your friend, Hazel?"

"Alessia Parigi," Hazel says. "She's just visiting."

I keep hopping between the squares, not paying any attention to the man watching me.

"Ah, yes," Ruffo says, "one of your parents' wartime houseguests."

We both look up at the villa in the same moment. The

front door is open, and we can see the balustrade of the stairs and the light from a lamp in the hallway. I think about whether Hazel's sisters are wearing velvet frocks and pearl necklaces and whether it's almost time for dinner.

Silvio Ruffo puts one of his double-knotted shoes into the hopscotch court. "I wonder if you ladies would do me a kind favor. You see, as it happens, Greta has fallen ill, nothing serious, just a little bout of something, a small fever, but I promised my wife I would try to cheer her up. I have procured her favorite treats, a box of Golia licorice candy and some Swiss chocolate. I can't tell you what I had to trade in order to find these sweets, but I just want to make her smile again. I wonder if you would help me surprise her?"

We both look at each other. I haven't seen a Golia in more than a year.

"How would we do that?" I ask.

"She is lying in her bed right now, reading a book, and we could bring her these treats together. They are in a paper bag in my kitchen cupboard. There is plenty to share and it would cheer her up no end."

"It's almost our dinnertime," Hazel says.

"You will be back in fifteen minutes, I promise."

I look over at Hazel, who looks back up at the villa.

Hazel says, "I need to tell my sisters where we are going."

"You will be back in no time at all," says Signore Ruffo.

He smiles with his teeth for the first time and it brings back a memory of the pharmacy in Milan, the way I was allowed to take a caramel from a glass bowl if I waited patiently for my mother to finish her business.

"Where is your house?" Hazel asks.

"Right across from the church," he says.

Hazel puts the pieces of chalk in her dress pocket and

runs up the stairs of the villa. When she steps inside the front door, I can hear her call out to Iris and Violet and tell them that we are running up to the piazza for a little while to visit Greta Ruffo, who is sick in bed with a fever, and that we will be home for dinner. I can't hear if there's an answer, no matter how hard I try, but then Hazel is running back down the stairs.

We walk up the pathway from the terraced gardens and into the narrow alleyways. All the windows of the houses are shuttered and the piazza is empty. So many families have left the town in the past month, and the ones that remain don't leave their houses if they can help it. We walk past the church in silence, Signore Ruffo a few steps in front of us in his black polished shoes. He points to a house that's tall and skinny, just like him, and we follow him up the stone stairs. Inside the entranceway, there are hanging coats and umbrellas and walking canes. There is a wicker basket of fishing poles with a soccer ball wedged on top and I wonder if there is a brother. I see a small pink umbrella and think it must be Greta's, the sick girl we have come to visit. Signore Ruffo closes the door behind us and walks through the house and we follow behind him. The darkened rooms smell of medicine and wax and cinders.

In the kitchen, he lights the cast-iron stove and says he will make us all some hot chocolate before going to check on Greta upstairs. From the icebox he takes a bottle of milk and pours most of it into a saucepan to warm it up, begins to stir with a wooden spoon. I know from Signora Serafino that milk and drinking chocolate are things of the black market. The Serafinos' two milking cows have been stolen, one by the fascist militia and one by the local German command. I'm almost hypnotized by the spoon whirling through the pan, then by the sight of the grated chocolate snowing from above. He pours four teacups of hot chocolate and puts them onto saucers and arranges them on the table. "Let me go see if Greta is awake, but please don't wait to enjoy your *cioccolata calda*. Don't let it go cold!"

Before he is even on the stairs, we are blowing into our hot chocolates and grinning at each other. We both take a sip and the chocolate is slightly bitter and we both agree that he should have added some sugar. His wife would have known to do that, I tell Hazel, and I wonder if she is upstairs at Greta's bedside and if she is, why he didn't pour five cups of hot chocolate instead of four. He is gone for what seems like a long time and so we continue to drink the hot chocolate and try to guess which cupboard houses the Swiss chocolates and Golia candies. Hazel, feeling brazen, drains her teacup and begins to quietly open the cupboards, one by one, to see whose guess is right. There is no sign of the paper bag with the sweets, but the cupboards are full of foods that we've almost forgotten about—packaged pasta, bread, jams, tins of meat. Hazel keeps opening cupboard doors while I sip my hot chocolate slowly. I think about all of these foods sitting here in the dark and suddenly I decide I don't like the girl in the upstairs bedroom, fever or not. At the villa, we've lately been eating bean soup and bread made from chestnut flour.

Hazel yawns and comes back to sit at the table. The kitchen smells like scalded milk and the overhead light is burning my eyes. I can hear a dog barking somewhere outside. Hazel puts her head on her arms and I tell her that she can't take a nap at Signor Ruffo's kitchen table, but then I feel a big darkness spreading through my chest and swimming down my arms and legs. I can hear his footsteps echoing down the stairs. *Greta è pronta per noi?* Hazel asks sleepily, Is

Greta ready for us? but her voice is too soft to carry. I watch her eyes blink and flutter. I listen to his shoes on the kitchen tiles. He says that his wife, daughter, and son left a week ago for the tiny village where his in-laws live, a town in the north of Umbria that is still safe. I picture a town up in the mountains, like the village where my parents grew up in the Ossola Valley, the windows of the houses unshuttered, smoke pouring freely from the tall chimneys, the children walking to school holding hands. For a moment, before the room dims away, I imagine Greta walking to school with her pink umbrella.

φ

Alessia switched back to the third person as she made her way into the final room of her story.

Later on he is calling the girls up from the cellar in the darkness. It is the middle of the first night and he leads them down the long hallway into a study. When they are inside, he locks the door behind him and puts the key into his trouser pocket. Behind a big wooden desk an Italian flag hangs on the wall, but it has a golden eagle in the center—wings upturned, head to the right, beak slightly open as if it's about to shriek. There are two chairs in front of the desk and he tells the girls quietly to take off all their clothes and to stand on the chairs. He tells the girls that if they don't do as he asks, he will go back to the villa and kill everyone in their beds. Hazel is the first to stand naked on the chair and then Alessia, both of them shivering. He ties their hands behind their backs with waxed shoelaces and sits down behind the desk.

He shines a lamp up at them, studies their nakedness, asks them questions. He wants to know the last time they saw Aldo Serafino, how he left, whether escaped British prisoners have come to the villa. He wants to know who Hazel's mother went to see in Florence, whether they have a radio in the house, what is said about the war and the fascists at dinnertime. Hazel says nothing and Alessia looks up at the eagle on the flag and tells her friend about the birds that live in the mountains and valleys of the north. She begins to sing a song her grandmother taught her, about a golden eagle laying two eggs but when both chicks hatch, the bigger one kills the smaller one so that they won't have to share the nest. It's not a sad song the way her grandmother sings it because, in the end, she tells Hazel, only the biggest and strongest eagles will fly over the valley.

The farmacista gets up from his desk and leaves the room for a few minutes, locking the door behind him. When he comes back, he has a panting black dog on a leash and a ceramic bowl in his hand. He puts the bowl on his desk and from up on the chairs the girls can see that it has some kind of animal fat in it, maybe bacon grease. He tells the dog to sit and then he slowly begins to slather the girls' ankles and feet with the white fat. When he's done with their feet, he moves up their legs and thighs, onto their shaking bellies, around their chests and necks and back down their spines. The white fat has a slightly sweet smell and it feels like cold wax. When he's finished he calls the dog over, points to Hazel's chair, and snaps his greasy fingers.

The dog sniffs the air, growls, leaps, knocking her screaming off the chair. On the floor, the dog yips and barks into the flurry of Hazel's arms and legs. Alessia jumps down and tries to kick her chair onto the dog, but the farmacista grips the back of her neck and forces her onto the floor. He grabs the dog's leash and pulls the animal over to Alessia and then she is disappearing, her arms over her head, the sound of her voice muffled, as if through water.

Alessia caught her breath and sat up. I was sitting on the edge of the bed, looking out the windows at the sawtooth mountains backlit by dawn. I could hear Elisa gently weeping from behind me. "To get the dog off me," Alessia said quietly, "Hazel started to yell everything she knew. How Aldo Serafino left on horseback after dinner two Sundays ago, that her mother kept a radio in the kitchen under a floorboard, that two escaped British prisoners were hiding in the cave along the path behind the villa. The farmacista pulled the dog by the leash and took him back out into the yard beside the kitchen. When he returned he said he would boil some water on the stove so we could take a hot bath and clean up, that we were helping Italy return to the glory of ancient Rome. He looked up at the flag and said we could all dream of being great again, even an Anglo mutt like you, Hazel Serafino, and then he led us into the bathroom of cold white tile and we watched him pour the boiling water into the tub. He spent a long time getting the temperature just right, adding cold, adding hot. When we were both in the water, he told us that he would let us go in a few days if we continued to be good girls. But if you tell anyone what has happened here, he said, I will kill both your families, right down to your baby cousins and ancient grandmothers.

Alessia broke off, looked out the window at the dawning light. "And so we never told anyone. A few days after we were found in the valley, the bodies of the two British prisoners who were hiding in the cave were found mutilated in the piazza. All these years later, I sometimes still wake up in the middle of the night and I'm standing on that chair and I am certain that I can never step down from it."

Elisa rubbed her mother's back while they both stared off at the mountains in the distance. To give them some privacy, and to anchor my mind back in the present, I stood up from the bed and walked slowly into the aisle between the letters, counting the envelopes as I went, thinking about my mother licking and sealing each one. I couldn't imagine what it felt like for Alessia to tell this story for the first time to her daughter, and what it felt like for Elisa to hear it in my presence, so I found myself caught between wanting to be invisible and wanting to bear witness to what had been conjured. And then, a few feet from the door, the magnitude of what my mother had endured and kept from me, from her entire family, made me so light-headed that I had to put my hands on my knees and bend over to steady myself. It passed quickly, and I was relieved that Alessia and Elisa were still turned toward the blushing light behind the rim of the mountains. After a moment, they lay down together on the bed, holding hands, their heads on adjacent pillows, and I continued out into the hallway.

φ

We slept the day away, the windows blue with snow light. Elisa stayed in bed with her mother, and I retreated to the brother's bedroom, where I passed in and out of troubled dreams, moving between darkening sorrow and flickerings of outrage. My phone vibrated sometime in the white bowl of that afternoon and I ignored it, but fifteen minutes later I was listening to a long voice mail message from Milo. As it happened, the old fascist was still alive and living in a nursing home in Rome. His grandson at the pharmacy said he was ninety-six and frail but that his mind was still sharp. The message went on to itemize the overnight disasters on the birthday-party front, including a menu from the Bonoglios that called for black truffles in just about everything. "They have a brother-in-law, naturally, who is a known truffle hunter. Ciao!" As I put my phone on the nightstand, I felt my mind trying to get a foothold.

Of course he was still alive. Of course I'd played chess with my mother's tormentor. History is irony on the move, as Emil Cioran reminds us. It is also a flood of coincidences, overlaps, omens. Thomas Jefferson and John Adams dying just hours apart on the fiftieth anniversary of American independence; the brother of Lincoln's assassin saving the life of Lincoln's eldest son a year before the attack in the theater; the license plate on the car of Archduke Franz Ferdinand having the numerals for Armistice Day, the end of World War I; Hitler shadowing Napoleon in birth, ascent to power, invasion of Russia, and defeat by 129 years all the way through. These confluences had always struck me as belonging to a branch of history that was controlled by conspiracy theorists and fringe dwellers. Coincidence and irony, after all, suggest that a master conceit is at work, if only we could discern its calculus.

But as I lay in bed and stared up at the ceiling, I understood that countless weather vanes had directed me to this very moment. Elisa's arrival at the villa, Aldo's letter found in the attic, my boyhood summers in Italy, the day trip to Florence by Ida Serafino . . . If you went back far enough, you could blame my current feelings on the Marquis de Rays, the unscrupulous French nobleman who sent a few hundred Italians into the South Pacific in search of a phantom paradise in the nineteenth century, my maternal great-grandmother among them. We are all accidents of history and the cosmos, in the end, but I was nonetheless dumb-founded by the fact that I had played chess in the piazza with the man who had stolen my mother's girlhood. I didn't know if I would tell Alessia and Elisa that Silvio Ruffo was still alive, but I knew there was no way to unknow it, that once the past throbs in the veins of the present there is no more pretending to be a passenger reading idly on a train.

PART THREE

The next morning, Elisa drove me to the central train station in Milan. At dawn, we'd driven down through the valley and along the lake, Alessia in the front passenger seat and me in the back of the Jeep. She was going to spend a few weeks with her daughter and granddaughter because Elisa didn't want her staying alone in the house after the harrowing night we'd just shared. We'd dropped her off at the apartment in the Isola district, Elisa's daughter, Marcella, coming out to the street in sweatpants and slippers, barely awake and disgruntled as she helped her grandmother onto the sidewalk. "I will be back soon," Elisa said. "Make up Matteo's room for Nonna." Marcella had walnut-brown eyes and dark, cropped hair. Her nose and one eyebrow were pierced with tiny silver hoops. She asked in Italian who I was and it was Alessia who answered, standing with her canvas rucksack of clothes and her alpine walking stick. "Hugh Ignazio Fisher," she said, "a famous historian from America and the son of my lifelong friend, Hazel Serafino." When I got out to move into the front seat, Alessia kissed me on both cheeks and said *buon viaggio*.

Fifteen minutes later, Elisa and I pulled up across from Stazione Milano Centrale, a building finished under Mussolini and made to look like a monumental bathhouse of imperial Rome, its façade adorned with eagles, lions, bulls, and mythic winged horses. For a few minutes, we watched the strident commuters with backpacks and briefcases, the tourists with roller bags bustling across the paved square in front of the station. Part of me wanted to tell her about Silvio Ruffo, that he had survived into his nineties, because I'd been thinking about nothing else since Milo's voice mail. But I couldn't quite formulate the words or the reason for the telling. What could be done with the wreckage of the past? As a historian, I'd always believed that studying the past could reveal hidden meanings and patterns, that motifs lurked in the underbrush, but now I saw the neap tide of history washing up flotsam on an empty beach. When I pictured the two girls, our future mothers, standing on those chairs, it was like looking through the wrong end of a telescope. I was waiting for some kind of meaning or anger to come into focus.

Breaking the silence, I said, "I'm happy to send your things, but I don't have your address."

We'd been tentative and quiet with each other ever since hearing Alessia's story, so I felt a surge of relief when she looked over at me and smiled warmly. "That's kind of you. I'll text it, but there's no hurry. What's your phone number?"

I told her my cell phone number and she put it into her phone. Then she texted me: *grazie di tutto, mi mancherai.* Thank you for everything, I will miss you.

I looked down at my phone screen and texted that I would miss her as well. "Ciao," I said, opening my door, but then I felt her hand on my shirtsleeve. I turned back and she leaned over to embrace me across the gap between the seats, her chin grazing my left shoulder. *Car hugs are universally awkward*, she said into the side of my neck, my cheek in the warm net of her hair. When we pulled apart I found myself just inches from her copper-flecked eyes. She hesitated for a split second before leaning in to kiss me very gently on the lips.

"I have wondered whether I would do that," she said.

"Since when?"

"Since that first day in Valetto when you came up to the piazza."

This came as a surprise. Then again, I was usually the last to know about a woman's interest in me. One winter after Clare's death, Susan came home to visit and we walked around campus together, in and out of the history and social sciences building and the coffee shop where I read or graded papers in the afternoons, and she proceeded to list the women who were waiting for me to make a move, right down to a physical anthropologist and the history department secretary. I told her they were just being kind to a widower and she said my obliviousness was the perfect nectar for hummingbirds. It's economic, she said, you're signaling a shortage and that boosts demand and therefore wing-flutter.

Elisa sat back in her seat and put both her hands on the steering wheel. "I'm going to see if my mother will stay with us and see a psychologist. She's never spoken to anyone about what happened to her, not even when she was in the hospital in the 1970s. I know this one thing doesn't explain her life . . . or my childhood."

"No, but it certainly didn't help anything."

"Maybe it's too late, I don't know," she said.

"*Non è troppo tardi finché non è troppo tardi.*" It's not too late until it's too late.

"Thank you, Confucius."

"Sorry. I need more coffee."

"Promise me you'll buy it before you get on the train. There's a good place around the corner, on Via Settembrini."

"I will."

I opened my door, stepped onto the pavement, and went to retrieve my bags from behind the tailgate. When I saw the two gasoline canisters, I asked in Italian over the seats whether she'd ever had occasion to use them. "*Neanche una volta*," she said, not a single time. "They are empty and waiting for the moment when I am stranded on the roadside and I walk for miles to fill them up." I heard her laughing as I closed the tailgate.

φ

I took my espresso at the counter on Via Settembrini and walked across the square and into the darkened mouth of the station. I could feel Elisa's kiss still burning, the simplicity and tenderness of it, and I was grateful that there was nothing expected of me, that I wouldn't have to engineer a faltering advance or seduction. We would be great friends, I thought, writing thoughtful emails back and forth, perhaps scheduling occasional Skype calls. But then it came to me that my romantic life had been put away forever, its furniture wrapped in dustcovers. I saw a terrifying vision of me attending faculty potlucks until I retired, always bringing along the same seasonal casseroles and anecdotes about my trips to libraries and reading rooms, or to abandoned towns and villages. It shocked me to realize, as I stood in line to buy a train ticket, that it had been more than twenty-five years since I'd asked a woman out on a date.

Because the world often conspires to reflect your emotions or thoughts back at you, the clerk in the ticket office was not the usual gruff middle-aged man or blowsy matriarch but an attractive woman slightly younger than myself and with a cheerful grin. I could have bought my ticket at one of the self-service machines, but I'd had a bad experience in Venice years before and never used one again. As I got to the front of the line, I felt as if this interaction was now part of the morning's plan. Martina wore a name tag, a navy blazer, a red tie and matching pocket square. As I sat at her wood-veneered desk, she asked me whether I was visiting Italy and I told her that I was from Michigan and had just been up in the Alps. She complimented my Italian and said that most tourists didn't bother to learn. I wanted to tell her that I'd come to Italy many times, that my mother had been Italian, at least partly, but then she gestured to her computer screen as if it held a map of the country. "Now that the Alps are behind you," she said brightly, "where will you go next?"

There was a slight hesitation, but by the time I said *Roma*, it felt like I'd been pondering this detour all through the previous night and during the drive down from the mountains, the way I would call Farmacia Ruffo and ask the grandson for the address of the nursing home where his grandfather lived. I was headed to Rome on research and wanted to pay my former chess opponent a visit, bring him some chocolate and newspapers or magazines for old times' sake. I thanked Martina, took my ticket for the high-speed train, and began to walk toward the platform, letting the idea play out in my mind. I could still be back in Valetto by evening, spending just an hour at the nursing home before taking the train again.

Standing on the platform, googling the pharmacy phone number, I didn't delude myself that I would confront the man who'd tampered with my mother in her youth and balance the ledger. Neither did I believe, like Elisa, that this one event, this childhood cruelty, explained the rest of my mother's life. But I knew it had taken something unnamable from her and, consequently, something from me. If nothing else, I wanted Silvio Ruffo to know that his actions had flowed across the decades like a tidal bore coming upriver. And it wasn't until I called the number and heard the grandson on the phone, the way he cheerily asked about the Serafino widows and freely gave out the address, that I realized the Ruffos had forgotten the past entirely. They had erased it. And it was the carefree sound of his voice that shifted something in me. I blossomed briefly with an anger that felt ancient, formidable, and uniquely Italian. As I boarded my train, I carried it like a swollen fist at the center of my chest.

On the train, I passed the three hours by sleeping and passing in and out of ominous dreams. There were no chairs or girls in my dreams, but there was a chestnut grove knotted with vines and dappled in wild orchids. In the shallows between sleep and waking, I stared out the window at the whirring landscape, the drumbeat of my anger like a second pulse. At the station in Rome, I bought some magazines and a box of chocolates to suggest good faith, then I bought myself a cheese-and-salami sandwich and proceeded to eat it in the back of a taxi, a choice that marked me to the driver as a glutton and a philistine.

We drove in silence up into the hills of the Casalotti zone, outside the ring road, on the outskirts of the city. The taxi pulled through the gates of the Casa di Riposo and up a steep drive lined with pines and hedgerows. I paid my fare, grabbed my bags, and stood in front of a main building that resembled a renovated motel or budget conference center. The walls were pale brick, the doors and window frames white-glossed metal, and I could see plastic chairs and tables arranged on a paved patio. Beyond the sliding electric doors of the lobby, a front desk floated above a waxed and shining tiled expanse, and the man behind it was dressed like a concierge—sports coat and tie—instead of a nurse or attendant in scrubs. When I gave my name, said that I'd spoken to the grandson, and asked if I could see Silvio Ruffo, the desk clerk smiled and picked up a telephone. Into the mouthpiece, he asked if Signore Ruffo was awake and available for a visit, never mentioning my name, and then I was directed to the activity room.

I walked down a long corridor that smelled of lemon and bleach, the walls painted a dusty pink. Every now and then I could see an alcove where a few residents watched TV or dozed on red vinyl chairs and couches. There were artificial ferns and ficus plants in faux copper pots, as well as Van Gogh and Kandinsky prints on the walls, which seemed like strange choices—in their acute angles and rhomboids of color—for a place where dementia bloomed like mold. But since there were no locked doors or nursing checkpoints, I assumed the dementia patients were in another wing and that, true to the grandson's story, Silvio Ruffo still had his faculties. In the activity room, I asked a young woman in a white smock where I'd find Silvio Ruffo and she pointed to a man alone at one of the tables.

Silvio Ruffo sat in a mustard-colored cardigan—wiry, bone-shouldered, his hairless scalp the color and texture of parchment paper. I approached from an angle before moving into the light of the windows. His eyes, when they shifted to my face, were cloudy with cataracts.

"You might not remember me, Signore Ruffo," I said in Italian, "but we used to play chess together in Valetto when I was a boy."

He blinked, said nothing, reached behind both ears. It took me a moment to realize he was turning his hearing aids on or up. His eyes widened for an instant, as if the room's frequencies had flushed his vision clear. I stood staring at him, trying to comprehend his physical form as precisely as a botanist examines a new species of algae. His face was angled and geological, the bridge of his nose a white knuckle, his forehead a high ledge for liver spots. His flannel shirt was buttoned to the hilt, his neck so thin that there was a deep recess of shadow below his chin.

"I brought you something," I said, putting down my bags and placing the magazines and chocolates on the table. It was only now that I became aware of my choices in the railway station newsstand—a magazine on travel, one for amateur mechanics, and one about restoring old houses. These suddenly seemed like outlandish choices for a ninety-six-year-old man confined to a nursing home.

"*Come ti chiami?*" he asked softly.

"Hugh Fisher," I said.

"Do you still play chess?"

I said that I was out of practice. He picked up the magazine on house restoration, turned a few trembling pages. "*Prendi la scacchiera*," he said, pointing to the shelves along one wall with his chin. *Fetch the board.*

I wondered if I had the wherewithal to play chess, whether it would quell the anger I'd been nursing for hours. But I decided that, if nothing else, it would prolong our interaction and give me time to find an opening. When I came back with the folding wooden chessboard he was slicing open the plastic wrapper on the box of chocolates with a small pearl-handled pocketknife. His hands were shaking, and I wondered how such a knife could be allowed among the residents. The box was turned facedown and he sliced away from his body, directly into the narrow seam that ran the length of the lid. While I set up the board, he removed the plastic, turned the box over, and lifted the lid, revealing a grid of chocolate domes and cubes.

He studied the chocolates before putting one into his mouth and chewing slowly, his dentures clicking faintly. Looking at the board, he said, *I like to be on white*, and so I turned the board around. During our games in Valetto, he'd always let me take white to make the first move, perhaps deferring to my age, but now it seemed he was claiming that advantage for himself. I'd played chess regularly in college and grad school and only occasionally since becoming an academic, but I'd continued to read websites about the history of the game, about iconic tournaments and strategies. It was a welcome distraction from research and grading papers. So when he moved a white pawn to the middle of the board, I immediately knew that he was inviting me to undertake the Sicilian Defense, the very sequence he'd used to beat me routinely in the piazza all those years ago. I moved my black pawn to c5 and he moved his knight to f3. He reached for another chocolate and popped it shakily into his puckered mouth.

"You knew my mother's family," I said.

"Everyone knew everyone in Valetto."

I put a pawn on d6, protecting the first piece I'd moved

and blocking an attack from his white pawn. My bishop was blocked, but I was already thinking about the move that would flush it onto the board. I have always loved the fact that Italians developed a word—*fianchetto*—to describe the bishop's flanking advance on the long diagonal. "The Serafinos have been coming to your family's pharmacy for generations," I said.

"My father began the business," he said, "to help the people of the towns, including the people up on the rock."

He thrust his pawn onto d4 and I captured it with my pawn on c5. He could have, in that moment, used his queen to take my pawn, but that would have exposed him to an attack by my knight if I developed it, and he'd be forced to retreat his queen. Instead, he moved his knight to capture my pawn. Then I moved my knight to f6 and he countered by moving his knight to c3. I was now in a perfect position to play the Najdorf variation, a seemingly simple move that nonetheless blocked both white knights and also prevented his bishop from coming down to harass my king. This is a well-known sequence, but I was still surprised by the speed with which he recognized it and responded, moving his bishop to disrupt my plan. I was forced to move a pawn to defend my knight. "Your game hasn't changed a bit," I said.

"I've stayed true to my principles. *Festina lente*," he said, quoting Horace in Latin. Make haste slowly.

He looked at the board only right before he made each play, as if the move itself was an afterthought. I remembered this infuriating habit from the square, how he'd blow a nimbus of cigar smoke above our heads and stare into it, as if it were a cloud of conjecture through which he was divining his path to victory.

Within a few moves, our queens were in play, and the

game continued aggressively for fifteen minutes. He had control over the center of the board and clearly intended to pound away at my kingside. With his dispersed attention and the clip of the game, I could feel my anger loosening its grip. I tried to picture my mother standing on the chair, remembered her insistence when I was growing up that we could never own a dog. I would begin by asking him if it was true that he was a member of the fascist party and what he remembered about the spring of 1944. If he deflected or directed his milky gaze out the windows behind my head, I would describe the letters and tell him I knew what he'd done. But when I imagined the moment of confrontation, I found myself staring into my own smoky cloud of conjecture. Would I flip the chessboard over, threaten him with his pocketknife, roll up a magazine and snap it across the side of his foxed and ravaged head? All these possibilities seemed absurd as the game slackened into its inevitable middle. The aggressive play stalled out and there were long pauses between each move.

At one point, Silvio Ruffo meditated for a very long time over a particular sequence for one of his pawns whose capture was imminent. He had only two possible options that made sense, but he deliberated endlessly, and I wondered whether he was trying to whittle away my patience. Arms folded, head listing to one side, his attention on the hemisphere of space above the board. I could hear his ragged breathing above the ticking second hand of his gold watch. I could hear the television game show over in the corner, where three elderly women talked listlessly about which of the prizes was the most valuable.

After a full five minutes, Ruffo's head now slightly tucked, I asked whether he'd run out of ideas, and he didn't respond. His eyes were open and angled at the floor. I tapped my wooden queen on the board and crinkled the plastic wrapper from the chocolate box, but he stayed motionless. I sat there for a long time, eventually making eye contact with the woman in the white smock, who was now packing up jigsaw puzzles and watercolors on the other side of the room. She came over and looked at Ruffo, his head now resting on his chest. In Italian layered with a Baltic accent, she said he nodded off a lot with his eyes open and there was nothing to worry about. She told me that the best times to visit were in the mornings, just after breakfast. This was the same advice my grandmother's caregivers offered up. As she moved back to her tidying up I felt a resurgence of anger, not at Ruffo, but at myself for botching my chance to confront him. I would have to return with a better strategy, perhaps take him for a walk in the gardens after breakfast and lead him to a bench where I could un-scroll the map of the past.

I left the chessboard midgame and gathered up my bags. As I stood, I knocked one of the magazines onto the floor with my laptop bag, and when I bent down to pick it up I noticed his shoes. They weren't the polished black leather shoes that my mother had described in her letter but a pair of worn blue-and-white sneakers, banded by several inches of his pale and hairless shins. Then I noticed that his frayed shoelaces were double-knotted, and it was this detail that shot through me. I put the magazine back on the table and reached for his pearl-handled pocketknife. I folded it, slipped it into my pocket, and walked out of the activity room. On my way out, I asked the woman in the white smock to please tell Signore Ruffo that I would return to finish our game.

At the front desk, the concierge called me a taxi and I waited in front of the lobby, my fingers rubbing the pearl knife handle. I can't fully explain why this small theft felt so satisfying, why I stared at the knife on the train all the way back to Orvieto, why I took it out to show Milo when he came to pick me up at the station. I was a deep-sea diver emerging from the wreck of time, floating up to the surface with a candlestick or a fob watch lacy with rust. Here was proof of my submarine contact. "That's a pretty little knife," Milo said. "Where did you get it?" And as we wended our way toward Valetto in the autumn twilight I told him everything, about the phone call from Iris and the letters and the town up north and my encounter with Silvio Ruffo. He said nothing until the story was finished, and then he asked if I was going to tell the widows. When I didn't answer immediately, he outlined the reasons for keeping my grandmother in the dark, that such news might startle a *centenaria* to death. Folding the knife and putting it back into my pocket, I told him that the Serafinos had gorged themselves on silence for long enough.

I t wasn't until Milo and I were walking across the Valetto footbridge in the dark that the demands of the present came rushing back. My grandmother's hundredth-birthday party was in ten days, there were festering disputes with the caterers and a guest list of unknown size, and Donata had fallen into a blue funk. Milo itemized these obstacles in his usual meandering, offhanded way as we walked through the Etruscan archway and across the piazza in front of the church. A few feral cats were chasing each other in one of the narrow alleyways.

"Which house did the Ruffo family live in?" I asked.

He stopped halfway across the square to get his bearings. After a moment, he pointed to a wrought iron lamppost and the tall, narrow house behind it. "That one," he said. "They lived there and Ruffo walked over the bridge to the farmacia every morning. When they forced him out after the war, he and his wife and daughter left for Rome, but they let their teenage son stay behind with an uncle and he helped run the shop and they lived above it. Even after the son grew up to become a pharmacist, they continued to use the house for storage. I wouldn't be surprised if it's still full of bandages and expired cough syrups."

The house had been empty for decades, but I'd never gone inside it as a boy, since it was one of the few deserted houses kept locked. In the pale light of the lamppost, I imagined its interior, the long hallway and the study, the stone cellar with its brown glass jars lined up against a wall. What proof remained of my mother's ordeal?

When we came to the pathway above the villa, Milo asked if I needed firewood down at the cottage. Somehow, amid the day's tumult, I'd forgotten that I could return to the cottage, that all claims against it had been relinquished. It also occurred to me that Susan was arriving in three days to stay for a week, and so I asked Milo if I could borrow his Fiat to pick her up in Rome. I was hoping a two-hour car ride would give me a chance to tell Susan everything that had happened before she visited with the Serafino widows. As we cut through the terraced gardens, Milo explained that the car was indeed available for use but that the lower gears and reverse were something lifted from Dante's *Inferno* and that, if it was all the same to me, he would prefer to drive me to fetch my beloved daughter. He clapped me on the shoulder and said he would bring me some firewood. I told him it could wait until tomorrow, that I was going straight to bed.

"Will you tell them in the morning?" he asked. "If you like, I can ask *le signore* to meet you in the dining room, which is now in very good shape. I cleaned the fresco with antibiotics and spackled and repainted the north wall for the party, the one with the crack and rising damp." Excellent plan, I told him, let's say ten o'clock, and then I went inside the cottage.

Elisa's knives and espresso maker and measuring cups in the kitchen brought that morning's kiss back to me, a distant episode on the early tide of the longest day in history. She'd left some eggs and butter in the refrigerator, and I made myself an omelet before carrying my bags into the bedroom nearest the living room. This had always been my mother's room, and judging from the vase of wildflowers and the made-up bed, where Elisa had slept. I briefly thought about changing the sheets, but it felt comforting to lie back against the pillows that smelled of her.

I had no desire to read *The Italians* or check my emails, so I waited in the darkness for sleep to come. My mind drifted toward the gathering of my aunts and grandmother in the morning and I tried to find a toehold, a way to begin. With my history majors, it was sometimes the artifacts of the past that brought history alive for them, the physical proofs, and I always made a point of taking them into the archive to see the ticket stubs and fountain pens and bullet casings that had walk-on roles in major events. I thought about Silvio Ruffo's pocketknife, now on the nightstand, and how I might begin by setting the knife on the big wooden dining table. But then I was pondering how many things the knife had sliced into during its lifetime and realized the knife was a digression. It wasn't proof; it was a memento. The only way to begin was with everything I'd seen up north. I would bring up the photos of the cemetery on my laptop, and of the room where Aldo died and where I'd slept. Only then, once the evidence of Aldo's final years had been laid out, could I move to the story within the story—the concealed room that had been waiting within the walls of my family's history for almost seventy years.

φ

It was Aldo's headstone my grandmother wanted to linger on. I enlarged the image so that it filled my laptop screen and brought it over to her wheelchair. "Cyclamens," she said softly, pointing to the snow-dusted pot at his graveside. I zoomed in on the inscription to make it easier to read and she said that she hoped for something a little more effusive on her own headstone. She gestured for me to take the laptop over to her daughters, who were bundled against the drafty, cavernous room in thick wool cardigans and shawls, sitting on three different sides of the enormous table. They each took a turn inspecting the headstone, and then we repeated the process for the remaining signposts of Aldo Serafino's vanished years.

I could sense their satisfaction in seeing concrete details—roadsides he'd walked along, mountains he'd climbed, the room where he'd taken his final breath—but I could also feel their disappointment. It was Iris who said what perhaps they'd all been thinking: "He might have been brave to go north, but he was a coward not to return home to his family." So I told them what Alessia had shared with me, about Aldo's head in his hands, about his grief and guilt over burying his partisan friends and his erratic behavior near the end. I said, "He was not the man who left here on horseback in the spring of 1944." A heavy silence took hold of the room and I wondered if they would, in time, soften toward his memory. But when I saw my grandmother fold up her reading glasses, it felt as if she were folding up an entire era of her life and putting it away.

After a long while, Violet changed the subject by picking up the thread of the looming birthday party. She reminded her sisters and her mother that the caterers were coming that afternoon to finalize the menu and take a deposit.

"Will Donata be here?" Rose asked hopefully.

"She's skulking in bed, from what I can tell," said Violet. "But someone needs to stand up to these truffle hunters before they swindle us. Charging for bruschetta by the piece should land a person in jail, if you ask me."

I felt the room pulling away from me into the upswing of a discussion about antipasto price gouging. I closed my laptop with a slight snap. "Iris told me about my mother and Alessia going missing for three days in 1944."

In the long pause that followed, I could hear the electric-coil heaters ticking and the slouching dog's breath from under the table.

"It's never been a secret," Violet said eventually.

"Then you know what happened to them?" I asked.

"They ran off and were found wandering down in the valley," Violet said. "They were lost."

"There were more letters," I said, "up north. Between Alessia and my mother, more than fifty years of them. I found a mention of something and then we asked Alessia what it meant. She told Elisa and me about everything that happened to her and Hazel for those three days. It was absolutely terrifying, what they both endured. And deeply traumatic."

My grandmother's face turned ashen, her hands dropping beside her wheelchair.

Iris asked, "Alessia couldn't be persuaded to come?"

"No, they've given up on the cottage."

"Because we called their bluff," said Violet, reaching down to rub a sleeping Rocky IV.

"I don't think she could face coming back. Not after what happened to her down here," I said.

"There was a war on," said Violet, still bent to her dog, her voice half under the table. "That's what happened down here."

Very quietly, my grandmother said, "I always knew it was something terrible."

"I suspect we all knew," said Rose.

Iris folded her hands on the table and stared into the wood grain. "Will you tell us?" she asked me. "Because I think we all need to hear it."

And so I began to tell the story, not the way I'd heard it, in reverse, but the way it happened in life, from beginning to end, from Silvio Ruffo's black polished shoes stepping onto the chalk marks of the hopscotch game to the two girls standing naked on the chairs to the cellar escape and the chestnut grove. The fear they carried if they told anyone, the particular burdens of that silence. I told them about the escaped British prisoners dead and mutilated in the piazza after the interrogation, and about my mother having to serve the Ruffo family in the restaurant years later, and how it unhinged her. In the middle, I talked about my mother's depression and secrecy when I was growing up, after my father left her, the way she declared herself a widow and withdrew from the world. But all the while, I said, there were these fiercely intimate and private letters flowing back and forth across the Atlantic, delivered to a shop in the Alps and a post office box in suburban Michigan. It was as if Hazel and Alessia had made a pact and refused to break it. "In those letters," I said, "my mother had room to be herself, and it was someone I never knew. Maybe someone none of us knew." I looked around the room, watched as the four Serafino widows absorbed the cascade of information and made their own private connections. How would they see my mother differently knowing that she'd kept her own pain, as well as the fate of Aldo Serafino, a secret for so long?

It was only after I'd told them everything I learned up north that I recounted my visit to a nursing home on the outskirts of Rome. I put the pearl-handled pocketknife onto the table and then I picked it up again and clenched it in my hand. Up until now, they'd been too overwhelmed or stricken to cry, but somehow the sight of the pocketknife made them all weep. My aunts produced cotton handkerchiefs from cardigan pockets and beneath shawls. My grandmother pressed a crumpled tissue to one eye, then the other.

"Hazel knew about Aldo," my grandmother said flatly, as if it suddenly made sense to her. "For all those years."

"She punished us for what we let happen to her," said Violet. This came as statement of fact, without defensiveness or blame, and her voice was gentler than I'd ever heard it.

"We were in charge that day," said Iris, looking directly at Violet.

Violet glanced over at the empty fireplace and then briefly at her sister's face. "I was the oldest," she said gravely. "It was my idea to go up to Mother's bedroom."

"If anyone is going to burn themselves at the stake," said my grandmother, "I'll be at the front of the queue. If I hadn't gone to Florence that day, things would be different . . . If your father hadn't left us, things would be different. If the Germans hadn't come through the Brenner Pass, things would be different . . . But that's not life. In life, things are never different."

Rose, who hadn't spoken in over an hour, said, "I'm going to take a walk in the garden with Chester and pray for Hazel's memory. May she rest with God in eternal peace."

She crossed the room with her dog in tow, toward the bruised daylight pressing against the windowpanes. When she opened the front door, a wintry breeze blew in, smelling of damp limestone, and it seemed to rouse us all back to the present. My grandmother rang the little bell she kept in a leather sleeve on her wheelchair armrest and Nina came in to wheel her back to her apartment. "I need to rest before the caterers arrive," she said. As she backed away from the table, I told her that Susan would be arriving in a few days, that she was coming for the big celebration. "Marvelous," she said without emotion, and then it was Iris, Violet, and me sitting under the fresco that Milo had swabbed with antibiotics to kill off decades of bacteria.

φ

Over at the cottage, I cleaned, made up the other bedroom for Susan, and gathered up Elisa's kitchenware. I carefully packed two small boxes, one for the glass measuring cups, each encased in bubble wrap, and one for everything else. In the evening, Milo brought me some firewood and I heard that the meeting with the caterers had not gone well, that Donata refused to attend and that the restaurant owners would not accept a personal check, only a cash deposit, because they said the trust between the two families had been eroded. Like it was a crumbling hillside, Milo said, as he detailed his mad dash to the bank before it closed to withdraw the caterers' blood money from the Serafino household account.

As a distraction, I worked on my lecture. I wanted to conclude my talk with that idea that although Italy had more than twenty-five hundred towns that were abandoned or barely populated, there had been a handful of comebacks. In Bussana Vecchia, for example, hippies and artists had reclaimed the town starting in the late 1960s after it had been abandoned for more than a century following a massive earthquake. They moved into the vacant houses, filled in potholes, repaired roofs, and even found a way to restore electricity. Today, you could walk among the grottoes where artists sold handmade jewelry, paper, and leather goods. There was even a pay-what-you-want coffee shop run by a Dutch sculptor, and a tiny, improbable jazz and blues club set inside a stone cellar.

On the day Susan was due to fly into Rome, I spent the morning working on my laptop at the kitchen counter, and I'd just typed *Italy has always believed in her resurrections—in politics, religion, and history*, when I heard a knock on the door and found Iris standing on the stone porch. The November sunshine had returned and she was dressed as if for a late-autumn picnic, wearing an olive gabardine coat and a pair of sturdy walking shoes. She said she'd taken a stroll first thing and hoped she wasn't disturbing my work. I invited her in for some tea.

"It's been years since I've been inside the cottage," she said, taking off her coat. "May I look around?"

"Of course."

She went to survey the rooms while I waited for the water to boil. A few minutes later, she sat down at the kitchen counter and told me that I'd kept the place sparse.

"It's only been a few days since I was allowed to reenter," I reminded her.

"All the same," she said, "it needs some decoration. The villa attic is full of things that might brighten it up."

The villa attic was, in fact, the final resting place for a century of forgotten furniture, clothing, paintings, rugs, toys, and memorabilia. The one time I'd been up there with Milo, searching for Christmas decorations, we'd come upon a nest of baby mice inside a wooden chest of blankets.

"I like it bare," I said. "Helps me think." What I thought, but didn't say, was that it also preserved my mother's Spartan presence in the cottage. I poured us some tea and added the splash of milk and one sugar she liked. She stirred her tea and idled the conversation for a few minutes between sips, how she was looking forward to seeing Susan again and hearing all about Oxford, how Donata's depression couldn't have come at a worse time. Then, across the rim of her teacup, she said, "I miss her, you know. Your mother."

"Me, too," I said, though it was more complicated than that.

"I always wanted to be a better friend to her, but she was hard to get close to. She was very private, a bit withdrawn. *Riservata*. We went for walks when she visited. But we didn't see her for years after she first left for America with Jerry."

"Why didn't anyone ever come to visit us in Michigan?"

"We weren't invited, for one thing," she said.

I remembered phone calls from Italy twice a year, a procession of birthday and Christmas cards, a few airmail letters. When they all got word of my father's suicide, there were tender letters from my grandmother and Iris sent me a handwritten copy of Wallace Stevens's "Thirteen Ways of Looking at a Blackbird." I remembered she'd written it out in English and Italian, on two different sides of the same piece of parchment paper. I wondered, all these years later, what she'd meant the poem to signify, but I also remembered the line *It was evening all afternoon*, because it somehow captured the mood in our house after my father left, the sense that we lived in a state of permanent twilight.

"How did she sound in those letters to Alessia?" Iris asked.

I recalled that in one letter, dated in the late 1950s, she'd written the phrase *you are my only blood* to Alessia. Even now, I wanted to shield my aunts and my grandmother from the devotion my mother had reserved for Alessia. So I said, "She could write things to Alessia that she could never say to the rest of us."

"She was always so distant." She took another sip of tea, swallowed it contemplatively. "I suppose it started that afternoon Violet and I went up to Mother's bedroom to try on her clothes and jewelry. We could have done more to protect her."

"You were teenagers," I said.

Iris turned the rings on her left hand, lining up the center stones in a way that reminded me of someone entering the combination to a safe. She said, "I was talking to Rinaldo on the telephone about our situation."

I watched the steam rising from my cup, trying not to react. "Which situation is that?"

"That your mother's kidnapper is still alive and living free as a bird in a Roman nursing home."

The word *kidnapper* suggested this had become another manila folder on Iris's living room floor, and I felt myself flush at the thought of her telling Rinaldo about my mother's ordeal. I said nothing, but it came to me that now Rinaldo Fumigalli knew that Silvio Ruffo was still alive, but Elisa and her mother did not. By telling the Serafino widows everything I knew, I'd unearthed a pocket of history and couldn't control where or how it was shared.

"Sadly," Iris said, "as Rinaldo reminded me, there is a statute of limitations for a crime such as this."

"The man is also ninety-six," I said. "That's another limitation."

"Yes, he's surely near the end," she said, tracing a C with one fingertip along the edge of the teacup handle. "Better if we handle this informally. As a family."

"You sound like a mafioso."

"They don't have a monopoly on ironing out the wrinkles in family laundry."

"Like I told you all the other morning, I plan to go back to the nursing home to confront him."

"What, so he can drift off in the middle of another chess game?" She drained her teacup, set it onto the china saucer with a clink. "What if instead of you returning to the nursing home, we invite him here?"

"What, just invite him over for dinner?"

"No, no," she said, "to the birthday party."

"For starters, it looks like he can barely make it down a hallway."

"We can get him a wheelchair if we have to. I have thought it through: we issue a special invitation to the whole family, handwritten by Ida, and tell the Ruffos that so many of the old families are coming back to Valetto for a reunion, that it will be their chance to see the place where their patriarch was born one last time. We must make it clear that Silvio Ruffo has been invited as a special guest by the centenarian herself." Her eyes were ablaze. This had been ticking over in her mind for days. While I'd been rubbing the pearl-handled knife in my pocket, she'd been polishing this hypothetical chestnut in her mind.

I said, "Then what?"

"I would take another cup of tea, by the way."

I was glad to have an excuse to turn away from her. I took the kettle from the stovetop to fill it in the sink while she talked.

"We confront him. Together, as a family," she said.

"During the birthday party? With all those people around?" I put the kettle back on the stove.

"It could happen after the birthday celebration. Maybe we invite him into the study or the billiard room, where we are all assembled. We confront him with his family and lay out the evidence of his wrongdoings. Since it's Ida's celebration, she should be the one to decide how it will take place, but it needs to be a strategic and communal ambush. In sociology, we call it a degradation ceremony. Garfinkel came up with the term in 1956, if I'm not mistaken, and he said moral indignation and shame are the two primary ingredients. We shall have plenty of both."

I watched the blue gas flame below the kettle and wondered if this scheme had been imagined in the clear light of day. Iris had thought out the logistics and the conceptual framing of what would take place, but I couldn't help thinking of Rose's story of finding a dead husband's shoes drying in Iris's oven. Stalling for time, I said, "It sounds messy," though in truth it was considerably more thought-out than my idea of returning alone to the nursing home.

When I turned to face my aunt, she said, "You know, we never decided as a family to keep those three days she went missing a secret. And I don't think your mother woke up one day determined to never tell us what happened to our father. Life chips away at us."

She sounded wise and reflective, but I wasn't sure I could trust it. I thought about a professor emeritus at my college returning for a faculty meeting one semester, the way he delivered a touching monologue about the end of history. It wasn't until after he'd left the meeting that the department chair, another old-timer, revealed that the professor had attended the meeting by mistake but that he didn't have the heart to tell him. Two decades earlier, the man had retired from anthropology, not history.

I poured the boiling water into the teapot of fresh leaves and we waited for it to steep.

"For most of my life," Iris said, "I've carried this guilt and shame. I knew something terrible had happened to Hazel, but I didn't know exactly what. No matter what you say, I was partly to blame and old enough to know better. I'd just like a chance to be there when we all look into his eyes. Will you please let me have that?"

"What about the others?" I asked.

"They all agree this is the right way to make peace with the past. Even Violet."

"You've all discussed it?"

"You're not the only one who can call a meeting of the Serafino widows."

She reached into her purse and produced an envelope with my grandmother's spidery, hooped cursive, made out to *Silvio Ruffo e famiglia*. When I didn't take the envelope from her, she propped it against the pepper grinder on the counter. I turned back to watch the steam rising from the teapot spout, letting the idea take form.

15

That afternoon, Milo and I sat outside the pharmacy in the idling Fiat. We were on our way to Rome to pick up Susan, but I'd agreed to hand-deliver the invitation to Roberto Ruffo, the grandson of the fascist and Bevona's current pharmacist. Because Milo was worried the car wouldn't restart, he left it running, as if for a heist, while we went inside—Milo insisted on helping me deliver the note, so he could provide support in case my emotions got the better of me.

It was a Saturday, a little before two. The morning shoppers routinely picked over the stores on weekends, usually back at home by lunchtime, so we found the pharmacy mostly empty. Roberto Ruffo—fifties, balding, mustached, wearing a white coat and tie—leaned over the counter to consult with an elderly woman in a wool scarf. They were discussing the pros and cons of various antifungal ointments. When the woman had settled on her purchase, we made our way to the counter and into the pharmacist's cheerful regard. He recognized Milo, and I reminded him that we'd spoken on the phone a few days earlier. "Gentlemen," he said, spreading his hands, "tell me, who will win the match be-tween Perugia and Paganese tomorrow?"

I didn't follow Italian soccer and was glad to be with Milo, who said that naturally Perugia would win after their victory the previous weekend, and that they had found some momentum. For a minute or so, the two local men conjec-tured about the shape of the season while I took in the pharmacy—the sleek modern shelving under halogen spot-lights, the geometric carpet, the spotless glass display cases, and the green neon cross above the consultation window. The only concession to the pharmacy's long history was a framed photograph of the original shop with its canvas aw-ning and gaslight sconces. With his perimeter check of the third-tier-football season complete, Roberto turned his at-tention to me and thanked me for visiting his grandfather in the nursing home. My hands were in my pockets and it felt oddly thrilling to rub one fingernail against the pearl-handled knife while I smiled affably up at the pharmacist.

"What can I help you with?" Roberto asked us.

I must have hesitated for too long, because Milo took the lead. "In fact," Milo said, "we have come to extend an invita-tion from the entire Serafino family."

Milo waited for me to hand the envelope to the pharmacist.

"Please open it," Milo said.

"After I told Ida about my visit to the nursing home, my grandmother thought Silvio Ruffo might enjoy a chance to return to Valetto, to the place where he was born. A lot of the old families will be coming back for the celebration."

Roberto opened the envelope and unfolded the invitation.

"It was penned," Milo said, "by *la centenaria* herself."

Roberto delivered a professional-grade smile. "*Molto,*

molto gentile," he said. "One hundred years is a true accomplishment. Brava!" He carefully folded the invitation back into its envelope, his tone becoming hushed and confidential, as if he were offering us counsel on a new, untested prescription. "*Allora*, I cannot be certain if he can attend, due to the incapacities of old age and his fickle moods. My grandfather can be hard to predict. But, rest assured, gentlemen, I will show him the invitation next time I visit. I try to go down at least one Sunday a month and take him to mass and confession."

I saw a flash of Silvio Ruffo on his arthritic knees in a confessional and wondered what he offered up to God.

Milo said, "Naturally, we can accommodate any of Signore Ruffo's needs. For example, if he has trouble walking, I am planning to have a means of transport to carry the old and infirm across the footbridge and through the town."

He used the phrase *un mezzo di trasporto*, a means of transport, and I wondered if this was an improvisation and what such a thing might look like. Would Milo use his moped to take the elderly former residents across the bridge one at a time? Sensing that we hadn't done enough to communicate the importance of the invitation, Milo added that it would mean a lot to Ida Serafino *personalmente* to have all the Ruffos present at her celebration. He said, "We will also have a donkey procession and Lorenzo Conti's famous homemade nocino." The bell ringer's green walnut liqueur was famous in Valetto for its ability to strip paint and dignity. The fact that Milo was talking up Conti, a man he despised, was proof that we had entered the realm of theater.

Roberto glanced up at the entrance to the store, perhaps hoping for a customer.

"When is your next visit to your grandfather?" Milo asked.

"Maybe next Sunday," Roberto said, "since tomorrow I will be watching Perugia slay the Paganese." He winked at us, smiled.

Gravely, Milo said, "The party is next Saturday." He gestured to the envelope. "We're very sorry for the lateness of the invitation."

Roberto picked up the envelope again. "*Mi scuso*, I didn't realize the date."

"The thing is," Milo said in a judicial tone, "the caterers must have their *exact and final* numbers very soon."

This was a particularly deft move on Milo's part, to appeal to a fellow Italian's sense of bureaucratic due process. Caterers needing their final numbers might as well have been a papal decree. We watched as Roberto looked at his wristwatch before reaching for the cordless telephone that hung on the wall next to the cash register. "Gentlemen, why don't I call the nursing home right now and see if my grandfather would like to attend? He may be napping, but let's see."

He punched in the number and asked the front desk if Silvio Ruffo was available, said that his grandson was calling. In the long, agonizing delay, I imagined a disgruntled Ruffo coming to the phone, hearing of the Serafino invitation, and accusing me of stealing his pocketknife. Eventually, Roberto started to speak again. "Ciao, Nonno. What did they feed you for lunch?"

. . .

"Again?"

. . .

"No, they can absolutely do better than that."

. . .

"Any good movies on television?"

. . .

"*Sì, sì*, I like westerns as well. John Wayne is a very nice actor. Listen, I am standing here in the pharmacy with Milo Scorza and Hugh Fisher from the villa in Valetto. They have invited our entire family to the birthday celebration of Ida Serafino. If you can believe it, she is turning one hundred next Saturday."

. . .

"I know, truly ancient." Roberto smiled knowingly at us. "If we come down to pick you up, would you like to attend? They have invited you as a special guest."

. . .

"Don't worry about that, Nonno. I suppose I will have the junior pharmacist hold down the shop."

. . .

"Yes, there will be food. And also nocino and a donkey procession." Roberto put the phone to his chest and looked at us. "My grandfather wants to know if there will be a donkey race?"

Milo said, "No, no, there are no races anymore. Just a procession with the old family flags."

Roberto relayed this information into the mouthpiece. I studied the pharmaceutical calendar on the wall beside the phone, moved my eyes between the red-circled dates of the season's football games.

Roberto said, "*Molto bene*, Nonno, we will make the arrangements with the Casa di Riposo. Ciao!" Roberto put the phone back on the wall and looked at us as if he'd just negotiated a peace treaty. "He will come," he said brightly. "Please tell the caterers to include seven hungry Ruffos at your grandmother's celebration. I know the others will come as well."

"*Favoloso*," I said cheerfully. "The more Ruffos the better."

We shook hands with the pharmacist and returned to the idling Fiat. After Milo finessed the gearshift into first and we pulled onto the narrow street, I said, "And for best actor in a leading role, the award goes to Milo Scorza."

Milo grinned at me. "Yes, I accept this award, on behalf of my entire family." The engine whinnied and he shifted into second. "I must admit, telling him that the caterers needed their exact and final numbers was *un colpo di genio*." A stroke of genius.

φ

In two hours we were at the airport, Milo circling the terminal because he refused to pay for parking, while I waited at the baggage claim assigned to Susan's flight. In a series of texts, as Susan made her way from the gate, she asked why in the world she would ever check a bag, especially for an easyJet flight from London. I texted that she had a good point, and that I would never make such a horrific blunder again. She told me to stay where I was and appeared fifteen minutes later—honey-brown hair in a braid, day pack over one shoulder, Guatemalan-print laptop case under one arm, stainless steel water canteen in hand, noise-canceling headphones around her neck. As she came toward me, I felt a surge of affection. I hadn't told her anything about the entanglements over the cottage, despite getting the first email from Iris about the "squatter" right before we'd met up in Rome a few weeks earlier. I realized there was a good chance that Milo would refer to recent complications on the car ride home, so as I hugged Susan I decided I should deliver a few headlines of my own.

"You look well," she said, taking me in.

"It's only been a few weeks since I saw you."

"Almost three," she said. "I'm starving, by the way. Can we grab something?"

"Milo is circling for us, but let's grab you a sandwich for the road."

"Why is he driving us?"

"He won't let anyone else drive the Fiat."

"That seems both very Milo and very Italian," she said.

I texted Milo that we were en route and we went in search of food. Susan let me take her laptop satchel but insisted on keeping her backpack. She'd been vegetarian since the age of twelve, so we had to go to three different places before we found a sandwich on whole wheat bread with fresh mozzarella, tomato, and basil. She let me pay for the sandwich and she unwrapped it immediately to take a bite as we headed for the exit.

"So," I said, "a lot has happened here and I should have told you about it."

A blue-eyed admonishment above her sandwich. "You always hide things," she said.

"It's been a complicated time. And the whole thing is going to sound like an Italian soap opera."

"I'm excited already."

I said, "I'll tell you the whole story in the car, but I wanted to give you some advance warning, in case Milo brings it up."

As we walked along the curb, we could see the iridescent-turquoise Fiat at the end of a line of waiting cars, Milo's arm out the window. When we got close, Milo sprang onto the sidewalk in his shop coat and holstered cell phone, embracing Susan heartily and insisting on stowing her backpack in the cramped trunk, along with the handsaws and wrenches and coils of rope. We all got into the car, Susan in front, me in the back, the radio crackling with nostalgia and soccer scores. The sun was already setting as we pulled onto the A12 and drove along the coast before turning inland. Susan had learned Italian during summer trips to Umbria and on a semester abroad in Florence, and so we all settled into a stretch of small talk in Italian—the unseasonably warm weather, her Christmas vacation plans, Milo's preparations for the birthday party. After finishing her sandwich, she leaned between the two front seats and said, "So, I hear there's been a situation at the villa? Who wants to fill me in?"

Since the Fiat didn't have a rearview mirror, Milo had to glance over his shoulder to see my reaction. I gave him a nod and he seemed to relish the chance to summarize the turmoil of the past few weeks. In the fading light, and for the better part of an hour, he meandered through the revelations and investigations, starting with Elisa Tomassi's arrival at the villa with Aldo Serafino's letter and ending with my trip up north. Occasionally, Susan or I had to untangle him from a knot of exasperating detail or diversion—the vehicle Rinaldo Fumigalli drove, the brand of antibiotics he used to clean the fresco, what he could remember eating as a boy during the war—but eventually we got him to the Alps. He stopped speaking abruptly and it was clear that I should be the one to walk Susan into the final room of the story. By that time, we were approaching Lake Bolsena, a volcanic lake where the Etruscans held out against the Romans for centuries. "They were eight and nine," I began, "and your grandmother was the older girl . . ."

φ

Because Donata was still depressed and avoiding the villa, there was no communal dinner planned for that night. I made Susan some pasta at the cottage before sending her into the custody of her elderly relatives. She was expected to visit with each of them in turn, beginning with my grandmother. Standing in front of the hallway mirror, she braced herself for a night of interminable chitchat and questioning. She took out her braid, brushed her hair, applied some lip balm with a pinky. "They're all going to ask why I don't wear makeup and whether I have a boyfriend," she said, looking at herself. She looked down at the two taped boxes on the hallstand—the name *Signora Elisa Tomassi* written in marker on each box, but without an address—and she asked me what was inside. "Elisa Tomassi is a chef," I said, "so she brought some utensils and whatnot with her. I said I would send them back to her. That reminds me, I need to text her for the address."

From the hallway, Susan said, "You text each other? You're in possession of an actual woman's mobile telephone number?" She stood grinning against the doorframe.

"Have fun with the widows."

She blew me a kiss and then she was out the door. I reached for my phone and texted Elisa that I hoped things were going well with her mother and that I needed her address for the packages. I waited for her return message but then, after a minute, she was calling my phone.

"I hate texting," she said without introduction, "so I thought I would just tell you my address. *Come stai?*"

"I'm okay," I said. "I moved back into the cottage and Susan just arrived. She's staying for the birthday party."

"You must be pleased."

"She's gone to visit the widows. How are things with your mother?"

"She has agreed to see a psychologist, at least for now. She had her first session yesterday."

"How did it go?"

"When she came out of the office, she said the woman was very nosy. I take that as a good sign. I quit smoking again, by the way."

"Good for you."

"It's been thirty-six hours and my apartment has never been so clean. What's going on there?"

"Chaos with the birthday party planning."

"You only turn one hundred once, so you must get it right."

"It's next Saturday, and they're still fighting with the caterers and trying to work out how many people are coming. Donata has also gone out on strike."

Elisa let out a short, bright laugh. "Sorry, I shouldn't be laughing."

"It's like we're all living in an absurdist stage play," I said, walking into the living room. From outside, I could hear the wind moving through the trees and the slow gonging of the metal chimes. In the French doors, I saw my reflection ghosting back at me in the darkened windowpanes. "There's something I didn't tell you when I was up north. I only found out the day before we left." Until the words came out, I hadn't realized that I'd been waiting for and dreading this phone call. I'd wanted to tell her after the nursing home visit, but it had left me feeling as if I'd run aground, as if I'd failed both of us and our mothers. When Elisa said nothing, I was certain that I was about to ruin everything between us.

"He's still alive," I said. "Silvio Ruffo."

She must have stepped out onto a balcony or terrace, because I heard a sliding door open and close, followed by the ambient tide of traffic. "And how do we know this?" she asked quietly.

"His grandson still runs the family pharmacy in the nearby town. I had Milo find out. Ruffo lives in a nursing home in Rome."

"*Ma esattamente quanti anni ha quello stronzo?*" And how old exactly is that asshole?

"Ninety-six," I said, "and I went to see him. To confront him about what he'd done all those years ago."

After five seconds of silence, she said, "I can't believe I'm just hearing this."

"I wasn't sure if it was the right thing to tell you and your mother."

"I didn't realize you got to make that decision for us."

"I'm sorry," I said.

We waited, leaning into the undulations of Milanese traffic.

"What happened?" she asked. "At the nursing home."

I resisted my impulse to omit the chess game and the fact that I'd shown up with chocolates and magazines, albeit as a foil, and I told her about both. I told her almost everything, right down to the Kandinskys in the hallway. What I didn't tell her about was the pearl-handled knife, which was still in my pocket. "He fell asleep," I said. "In the middle of the chess game."

"So you never got to denounce him?"

The verb *denounce* belonged to public hearings and trials, to a people with a history of turning against traitors in their midst. I silently auditioned *denunciare* in my mouth. "That's right," I said. "I planned to go back, but then Iris came up with a scheme to invite him to my grandmother's birthday celebration so that we could all denounce him as a family. It looks like he's going to come."

A truck foghorned through the squall of Milanese traffic right as she said, "Are you fucking kidding me?"

"No, I'm not."

She took a sharp inhalation, drawing on a phantom cigarette. "Do the Serafinos have anything else better to do than play espionage with other people's history?"

"This is our history, too," I said calmly.

"Okay, *professore*, but let me tell you . . . there is only one person alive who lived through this terror, and that is my mother, correct? Everyone else was a spectator. Playing billiards or dress-ups at the villa. You're all still treating her like she's a little refugee girl living down in your cellar."

"That seems a little unfair."

"I will decide what is best for her." I could hear her footsteps as she moved across concrete or paving stones. "I just can't understand why you didn't tell me when you first found out."

I turned away from my reflection in the French doors, heading for the bedroom where Elisa's wildflowers were beginning to wilt by the bed. I apologized again. After a long pause, Elisa said that she needed to go make dinner.

"What about your address?" I asked.

"I will text it to you," she said.

Just before the line clicked out, I heard the sound of the door sliding behind her. The text with her address never came. I lay back on the bed, sensing that I'd let something important slip beyond my grasp. I remembered Milo saying to me on my arrival *You must swim on a tide of great sadness* and I felt it now, an old and familiar sorrow welling up at the edges of my thoughts. Determined to bring myself back to something purposeful, I reached for my laptop to work on my guest lecture, but instead found myself typing a letter to my dead mother:

> I remember that we lived in a house of closed doors and drawn curtains. You always told me it was to save on heating and cooling costs, but it never made sense to me. In the winters, I'd come home from school and have to open and close three doors before I finally found you in the living room, dressed in black, sitting in the blue pall of the television. My entire childhood unfolded in this twilight, it seems to me now. It was always early evening in our house, regardless of the season and time of day, the living room smelling of the kerosene heater and your cigarettes, one window and curtain cracked an inch to let in a slit of Michigan air and siphon off some of the fug and sadness. You told me what was for dinner when I came home and directed me to the snack in the kitchen—always a Glad-wrapped plate of perfectly sliced apples and carrots, sometimes with folds of crepe-thin prosciutto and sometimes with a dollop of peanut butter. If I was driven to the company of books, maps, and stamps, it was in the span of a thousand dusks, when you sat marooned in the living room, the light fading from the windows, until I finally came back to turn on the lamps.
>
> We ate at the kitchen table the way strangers eat

together on a cruise ship. We were polite and careful
with each other, did our best to dredge something of
interest from the day's banalities. No one ever spoke of
the oceanic void all around us. I don't think you could
have named a single friend I had between elementary
school and high school. I made a point of never inviting
them over, for fear that they would discover that you
weren't yet a widow, just a divorcée in black, or that we
lived under an oppressive cloud of a sorrow I could never
name. When my father went and took his own life—
that was the way you phrased it—I was almost glad that
now we had a reason to live the way we did.

Knowing what I know now, I don't pretend to have
found the name of the sadness that pervaded all the
rooms of that house. We can rewind history until we
find a wire coil or a linchpin or a forking path, but it's
always a game of hypotheticals. There's a perfectly good
chance that you were destined to be sad, angry, and
reclusive even if you'd had an idyllic childhood. But
what kills me, Hazel—the dead seem to demand first
names—is that you kept yourself alive on paper, your
spirit somehow embalmed, in all those letters you wrote
to Alessia. Meanwhile, you hoarded yourself from the
world and from me. I had to open and close three doors
just to find you sitting like a monument in the twilight.
What you were trying to keep at bay all those years
was, of course, already in the house. And I wonder,
sometimes, whether I breathed it in, that nameless sense
of being left behind . . .

16

Over the coming days, Susan and I were drafted into service for the party preparations. In the piazza, we hung silk flags that represented Valetto's oldest families, including the Serafino coat of arms—a red rooster crowing below a yellow starburst. Along the railings of the footbridge, we tied wreaths for the donkey procession—intertwined olive branches and dried lavender stalks bundled with scarlet ribbons. The wreaths were my grandmother's idea, each one hand-fashioned by Rose. We set up wooden benches around the perimeter of the piazza and helped Milo haul a hundred folding chairs into the dining room. The guest list was still a moving target, but Milo insisted that he'd kept a tally of likely attendees and that one hundred would be the high end. It was the official number given to the caterers and it took on the gravity of newly passed legislation.

By Tuesday, some of the former residents began arriving from far-flung places—Melbourne, Vancouver, Brooklyn. They were all staying at the same two hotels in Bevona, where Milo had negotiated a discounted bulk rate. They made forays into the town to view the current situation—the new fissures and seismic erasures—and to enter the houses their families had abandoned decades earlier. Most of these houses, if they were still standing, didn't have title deeds or official documentation from the municipality; they had simply been handed down through the same bloodline until they eventually stood vacant.

Inside the villa itself, a small army of teenagers—all of them friends and cousins of my grandmother's nursing aides—had been enlisted to clean and clear clutter. In the *sala grande*, the old billiard room, and the library, slipcovers were removed, cherrywood-and-crushed-velvet furniture was vacuumed and polished, and stacks of papers and memorabilia were boxed up and moved into the attic or the cellar. In the dining room, all of the furniture was removed so the terra-cotta floors could be scrubbed and waxed. Milo employed some day laborers to rake and bag the rotting leaves that were strewn across the grounds, and he oversaw their work with his cell phone in one hand and a machete in the other, stopping occasionally to lop off a tree or shrub branch that offended the gods of symmetry. He hauled in pea gravel for the walkways, freshened the ponds, strung tiny lightbulbs between the silver cypress trees. My grandmother watched all this unfold, secretly delighted but insisting that too much fuss was being made. As the dining room began to fill with rental tables and chairs, she insisted on handwriting place cards for the people she knew would be coming.

There was no mention yet of how we would confront Silvio Ruffo, whether it would happen in the throes of the party, while people ate their *formaggi e frutta*, or whether it would happen in a room set aside for the denunciation. Iris, who'd been deputized by Milo to oversee the flower ordering and delivery, said that she would share the plan once it was finalized. But when Rinaldo Fumigalli arrived on Tuesday evening, following Iris up the stairs to her guest room with his kidskin valise, I suspected that she was waiting for his counsel. I imagined them up in Iris's apartment with a scale model of the villa, moving tiny plastic partygoers between rooms according to a master plan for ensnaring Ruffo. When Susan asked Iris one morning whether it was possible that the old man had become a different person in his golden years, my aunt looked at her over the glass vase she'd just polished. She said, "*Il lupo perde il pelo ma non il vizio.*" The wolf loses his hair but not his vice.

By Wednesday morning, the villa looked as if it had been rented out for a destination wedding. In the mineral sheen after a light rain, the newly graveled walkways and the freshly trimmed and raked gardens gave the villa an aura of curated neglect, as if its leanings, cracks, and disfigurements were a charming sort of patina. The windows had been cleaned with newspapers and vinegar, and they became opalescent with the November clouds. I had never seen the villa and the grounds looking so beautiful, and I couldn't help feeling that we were preparing for the end of an era.

φ

When Elisa called on Wednesday afternoon, I was eating lunch with Susan in the cottage. We'd spent the morning helping Milo bring supplies across the footbridge. He'd traded in his moped with its carrier on the back for a borrowed donkey and cart that were to be part of the birthday procession. We'd unloaded crates of wine, the bottles bought from a local vineyard and wrapped in sheets of thick white paper, in direct violation of the verbal contract that all wine would be supplied by the caterers and charged by the pour. When Susan saw Elisa Tomassi's name flash across my phone screen, she opened her laptop and said that it was fine if I wanted to take it. I stepped out onto the terrace.

"Thank you for answering my call," Elisa said.

"I wasn't sure how we left things."

"I think I overreacted. I felt like you'd been keeping things from me."

"I never intended to."

"I know. *Perdonami.*" After some seconds, she said, "Listen, I've convinced my mother to come back to Valetto."

I looked back through the kitchen windows, where Susan was eating a salad in front of her laptop. I'd already reclaimed the cottage, moved myself into my mother's bedroom, the room where I'd slept beside Clare on all of our trips over the years. My daughter had taken over the room where I'd slept as a boy, where I'd read poetry and learned to be in my own company, the bed pushed up against the window. This was the house where I first became a traveler, a loner, a historian.

"For a visit?" I asked tentatively.

"For the party."

"Oh."

"Her psychologist disagrees, but I think it will be good for her to be part of the denunciation. To have some closure, as you Americans say. I've also invited, well, demanded actually, that Marcella come, because I think it's important that she knows our family history."

I was holding the phone six inches away, as if the extra distance might modulate what I heard in her voice. When I brought the phone back to my ear, she was asking if I was still there.

"Yes, I'm still here," I said.

"If we are invited to the party," she said, "we would like to come. I plan to drive us down this afternoon. We would be there late evening."

I still couldn't formulate a response.

"We can stay in the town across the bridge," she said, bristling, "in one of the hotels."

After a long pause, I said, "You're welcome to stay with us here in the cottage. We can make room." I couldn't connect my courteous, stiff tone with the jagged emotions roiling through me.

"Listen, Hugh," she said, "if you are afraid that the northern clan of barbarians are going to take the cottage, you can set your mind at ease. We have moved on from that. We will stay for a few days and then come back to Milan. I think it will be nice for your grandmother to see my mother again."

"Yes, it will mean a lot to her," I said quietly.

I looked up at the villa, at the three arched windows that overlooked the terraced gardens from my grandmother's bedroom.

She said, "I think there's something that gets in the way between us. I feel it."

"What's that?"

"Don't pretend you don't know."

"I'm not pretending."

"You're afraid."

"Of what?"

"Of your life coming apart at the seams. But in fact that already happened, a long time ago."

I said nothing. The thought of Elisa, Alessia, and Marcella staying in the cottage with Susan and me seemed unfathomable, like a blueprint for an impossible skyscraper or cantilevered bridge. And it wasn't just the domestic simulation that I felt pressing down on me, it was the memory of the kiss in the front seat of the red Jeep Wrangler, named after Floria Tosca, and the pomegranate smell of Elisa's hair. That kiss had been delivered to me like a telegram from a life I'd packed and sent away. Perfect in its brevity, this kiss came unencumbered, but now there was the threat of other telegrams from the turbulent underworld of human emotion, and that I might be asked to send one of my own messages in reply. I counted to five, the way the strip-mall life coach had taught me, and blew some air out between my lips. "Please don't stop at Chef Express on the way down here," I said. "Your family deserves better."

I heard her smile into the phone. "My mother would never allow it. We will pack sandwiches and apricot juice and peanuts in the shell."

"I'll make us some dinner for when you get here."

"Please don't go to any trouble," she said. "It will be late."

"Just text me when you get here and I'll come help you across the footbridge."

After I hung up and went inside, I told Susan about the impending arrival. Because she is clear-eyed, pragmatic, and economic-minded, I expected her to ask where everyone would sleep, how five adults would divide up a two-bedroom cottage. Instead, she looked up from her laptop and said she'd go up to the villa to bring down extra bedding.

"Don't tell the widows," I said. "I'm going to let it be a surprise."

"Devious," she said. "It's the right course of action. Good for their aging neural networks." She got up and went to the kitchen door, but then she turned back to face me. "It's going to be okay," she said, "no matter what happens."

"Do I look nervous?" I asked.

"Absolutely terrified," she said, closing the door behind her.

φ

Almost seventy years earlier, Alessia had been shuttled south through the night with the other refugee children, wrapped in a wool blanket and led across the footbridge by a Milanese nurse. Now she picked her way slowly toward Valetto with her alpine walking stick, one hand on the railing tied with wreaths. Although the bridge is just wide enough for four people to walk abreast, Elisa, Marcella, and I trailed behind her with the few bags they'd brought with them. The night was threaded with fog, the riverine breath of the valley pungent as smoke. Because we couldn't see the rocky escarpment that supports the bridge's piers, or the slopes of calanchi beyond that pitch down to the valley floor, I had the sensation that we were suspended within a cloud. Then, halfway across the bridge, there was a clearing in the fog, and in that little dell of open air the Valetto rooftops and the campanile of the church came into view. Alessia stared up at the silhouette of the town and made the sign of the cross. The word *pilgrimage* came to mind.

On the other side, we mounted the stone ramp, passed under the Etruscan archway, and walked into the piazza. Alessia craned up at the bell tower and made a visual inventory of the houses along the periphery. Wordlessly, she pointed her stick at the narrow stone house that still belonged to the Ruffo family, as if she were marking it for our future reference, and then we continued into the narrow passageway that led to the defunct restaurant. She stopped for a moment under the nearly erased sign and whispered back to Elisa that this was where she had first learned to cook.

This quiet reverie continued all the way down to the villa gardens. We stood for several minutes amid the recently pruned evergreen espaliers, looking up at the villa's hulking façade, a few stairwell and hallway windows flushed with lamplight. When we made it down to the cottage, Susan stood waiting to greet us in the kitchen. After all that quietude, our voices sounded booming and ungainly in the cramped, tiled kitchen. There were introductions and questions about the drive down south. There were offers of cookies and tea and hot chocolate, the prospect of a fire in the living room. We moved between Italian and English and some universal, halting language of gestures between weary travelers and their hosts. Elisa said that they were grateful for our offers but that they were all exhausted. Not missing a beat, Susan explained the sleeping arrangements with the tone of a pilot announcing a transatlantic flight route. Her Italian was soft and lilting but also decisive. Nothing was up for discussion. She and I were sleeping on the couches in the living room, Elisa and Marcella would take the bedroom nearest the kitchen, and Alessia would take the bedroom at the back, next to the bathroom. When she had finished her instructions, Alessia took the back of Susan's hand and kissed it, whispering *molto gentile, molto gentile*, and I watched my daughter brimming under an older woman's affections, something I hadn't seen in years.

φ

In the morning, everyone agreed that I should go and announce the arrival of the Tomassi-Parigi family to my grandmother, to give her some warning before they descended on the villa. So I headed up to the villa fifteen minutes before Susan planned to walk them over. I found Ida sitting at a narrow writing desk, dressed in a navy blazer and a green silk scarf. She was sorting through a pile of letters under a brass lamp. Nina, the caregiver on duty, told me that a flood of letters and phone calls had been arriving at the villa for the past two days, all of them from people confirming their attendance at Saturday's centennial birthday celebration. My grandmother looked up at me absentmindedly.

"How many?" I asked her.

She considered the lemon-and-lime budgerigars flitting between their perches in the domed cage. "At least eighty more than we told the caterers."

This moment, now that it was here, seemed inevitable. My aunts had put my ninety-nine-year-old grandmother in charge of her own guest list, without any parameters or assistance. What did they expect? Milo had been too distracted with his own repairs and preparations to intervene, and the unmitigated terror of the growing guest list had sent Donata into a deep depression. She had tried to warn them, tried to insist on a cap. For a second, I mistook the expression on my grandmother's face for torment, but then she said that they would simply divide the portions in half, that it wouldn't be the worst thing if people didn't gorge themselves. This was, of course, a very un-Italian thing to say. The cultural expectation was that the hosts would fete their guests with wine and food until nothing more could be consumed. If the Serafinos skimped on portion sizes, the scandal would be known within two days for a hundred miles. It would prove, once and for all, that these elderly women had never been real Italians to begin with, that Anglo-Saxon blood—miserly and stoic—had always been the main branch of the Serafino river. From the grave expression on Nina's face, she clearly knew her status in the world hinged on whether the birthday guests would be poured half or full glasses of wine.

"Do my aunts know?" I asked, coming over to the desk.

They both shook their heads at me.

"Would you tell them for me?" my grandmother asked.

I sat down on the bench at the end of my grandmother's canopied bed. Old age was a pedestal from which you importuned your relatives and friends. I said that I'd talk to the aunts and Milo and that we would need to tell the caterers as soon as possible. "We'll also need to order more tables, chairs, silverware, china, and flowers."

"Violet says the Bonoglios are trying to bankrupt us," my grandmother said.

"Let me handle it," I said, instantly regretting the assurance in my voice. The Tomassi-Parigi family, led by my daughter, would be arriving any minute. "Alessia Parigi is here," I said. "She's returned."

My grandmother took off her reading glasses and held them under the brass lamp, reflecting two discs of quaking light onto her blazer lapels. She opened her mouth to speak, closed it again.

I said, "Susan is going to bring them up in just a few minutes. Alessia, Elisa, and Elisa's daughter, Marcella. They've all come for a few days."

"For my party?" Her astonished voice belonged to an eight-year-old girl.

From across the room, without looking up from the pill organizer she was loading, Nina muttered, "*Perfetto, altra tre bocche da sfamare.*" Perfect, another three mouths to feed.

Ida waved a dismissive hand and said, "We'll need fennel

tea, and Coca-Colas for the girls. And pâté on crisp breads if it's not too early for livers."

It was not yet nine o'clock in the morning.

I said, "They are also here to confront the old pharmacist."

Ida set her glasses down. "Just in the nick of time. Rehearsals start tomorrow morning."

"*Rehearsals?*"

"Iris wants to walk us through the denunciation. I told her that I wanted a proper celebration first, before we confront him, so it will have to come after we have cake."

I pictured Iris and Rinaldo plotting guest movements up in her apartment. For half a day, on the train to Rome, walking down the corridors of the nursing home, I'd felt something akin to rage. I'd carried it for a handful of hours, righteously, on my mother's behalf. Now the unfolding events came at me through the scrim of other people's emotions and decisions, blunting the anger to a weary kind of exasperation. Silvio Ruffo's pocketknife was still in my pocket. Every morning I placed it there along with some loose change that I always carried and never spent.

This thought summoned Susan and three generations of the Tomassi-Parigis to my grandmother's doorway. Susan gestured to the lamplit interior, and it was Marcella who stepped inside first, wearing a pair of frayed jeans, unsure of where to stand or look. She introduced herself, eyes down, and moved up against the stone mantelpiece, allowing her mother and grandmother to take the center of the room. As they entered, my grandmother used the writing desk to pull herself to her feet, Nina cursing under her breath and hurrying to her side. Ida hobbled toward the Moroccan ottoman and the leather recliner and planted herself here, a few feet short of her guests. Alessia came toward her. In one hand she held her alpine walking stick, in the other, a wire mobile strung with shards of glass and polished stones.

The two women studied each other while the rest of us looked on and the budgies flurried and chirped. Alessia handed the mobile to my grandmother, who thanked her and held it up to the light of the windows, before asking Nina if she would hang it above the birdcage. While Nina busied herself with finding a hook in the drawers over by the hotplate, my grandmother patted the ottoman and Alessia sat down in front of her. "*Perdonami,*" Ida said. "I don't have a gift for you. I had so little warning."

It seemed important to witness this moment while also trying to give these two women some measure of privacy. I noticed Elisa studying the framed photographs on the mantelpiece, her eyes settling on the Christmas portrait of me, Susan, and Clare, taken ten years earlier, in the faux winter of a Michigan mall portrait studio. Marcella and Susan stared up at the glass-fronted display case of vintage novels and cookbooks, at the family bible of recipes on the wooden stand, united in their desire to look away from this collision of the past with the present. My grandmother offered me, Alessia, and Elisa fennel tea and offered our daughters Coca-Colas, a brand Susan had boycotted for over a decade but which she now accepted from Nina. The pâté and crisp breads were seemingly forgotten. We all sipped our drinks from the edges of the room while the reunion at the ottoman got underway. Because there was no way to hold seventy years in a single sentence or thought, they began by cataloging births and deaths, by naming grandchildren and their accomplishments.

After ten minutes or so, my grandmother spread her hands over the mottled leather armrests of her recliner. She said, "I'm deeply ashamed for what happened to you here when you were in our care. In *my* care . . ."

"*Non avresti potuto saperlo.*" You couldn't have known.

"I could have done more to protect you and Hazel." She pulled a tissue from a sleeve, blotted one eye. "At the time, I was intent on helping the war effort. Aldo had just left . . . well, you know all this." She put her hands in her lap, worrying the tissue with her fingertips. "I do not ask for your forgiveness—I have no right—but I offer you my sorrow, for whatever it's worth. On Saturday, I will be standing with you when we denounce him."

I couldn't tell whether my grandmother had forgotten Silvio Ruffo's name or couldn't bring herself to say it. In the medicine cabinet of her bathroom, there were plastic bottles of blood pressure and cholesterol pills wrapped in *Farmacia Ruffo* labels.

Alessia said nothing, but as she looked down into the arabesque of the carpet I could see something welling up inside her. She held her walking stick beside the ottoman like a flagpole, turning it slowly in her hand. After a moment of contemplation, she said, "I would like to go down into the valley today. I have fond memories of us foraging for the restaurant after the war was over."

"It was just the two of us, wasn't it? Hazel wouldn't go down there. I never knew why."

I remembered my mother avoiding the valley on her visits.

"Is the Fiorentina still there?" Alessia asked.

"The old pear tree?" Ida said. "Who knows? I haven't been down there in twenty years."

From the hallway came the sound of tapping on terracotta, and then all three of my aunts' dogs appeared in the doorway a few seconds before their owners. My grandmother called across the room, "This is Alessia Parigi, one of the children who stayed with us during the war," as if any of this were in doubt. She took hold of Alessia's hand and held it up as proof. My aunts entered the room, took turns saying hello, but only Iris came over to the ottoman. "I am Iris Serafino and we are all very glad that you came," she said. "You are always welcome here."

"I remember you, Iris," Alessia said. "You used to draw maps that showed where everything was buried in the gardens."

"Yes, I remember now," said Ida, looking at her daughter. "You were the family cartographer."

I saw Iris as a teenager, plotting the exact location of the hams, tinned apricots, and flour that had been buried strategically throughout the gardens. She'd been forensically minded even then.

The ten of us stood huddled and shifting around Ida's bedroom. My grandmother, suddenly emboldened and impatient with the silence, looked at her daughters and said, "I rather cowardly asked Hugh to tell you that eighty more people are coming to the party than we thought. At least eighty. You've all heard the phone ringing and seen the mail being delivered. Well, that's the truth of it." She folded her arms and leaned back in her recliner, closing her eyes for a few seconds. It struck me that she'd chosen this moment to confess because an abundance of witnesses would minimize the fallout. This tactic seemed to work, because Violet said that she would tell Milo, who was the only one still on speaking terms with the caterers.

From over at the mantel, Elisa said she would be happy to speak with the caterers on the family's behalf. "I have been a professional chef for more than twenty years," she said, "and we catered many weddings in the early days of the restaurant, when we could barely make ends meet. I know these people, their ratios and margins."

The aunts looked at her as if she'd just volunteered to negotiate with a serial killer. Susan gave an approving nod, and Marcella said that she would accompany her mother to negotiate, a hint of Milanese swagger in her voice.

"We are the ones who have made this bed," said Iris, "and now we must lie in it. This is a family matter."

My grandmother turned her head to let her words drift back toward the mantelpiece. "Miss Tomassi, if you are willing to speak with the caterers we would all be deeply grateful. Now that's settled, I feel as if I ought to rest." She looked at Alessia. "Will you come back to visit me this afternoon after you've gone into the valley? I'd like to know what you find down there."

Alessia patted Ida's hand, offered up a little smile, and gripped her walking stick to stand. As she left the room, we all followed after her, one by one, as if forming a procession.

17

While Elisa and Marcella walked into Bevona to speak with the Bonoglio family about the catering order, Milo led Alessia, Susan, and me into the valley along the winding, chalky pathways. Since Milo knew the valley better than anyone, he insisted on being our guide. He walked slowly beside Alessia, stopping every ten minutes or so to offer her water from a wineskin bag. In his pressed jeans and postman-blue shop coat, he narrated the decline of the valley as we walked along, how the chestnut stands that were once divided among families had become overgrown, how the ancient olive groves were now gnarled and unpruned, how the sediment and farm runoff in the river had killed off the salamanders and crayfish.

We walked along the green, silty river, the pale sunlight spangling through the bare tree branches. Alessia pointed to the chestnut grove with her walking stick and we assembled under the leafless crowns, the ash-colored trunks knobbed and deeply furrowed. Milo told us about the chestnut festivals of his youth, and how, in the summertime, a cloud of chestnut pollen overwhelmed the valley and brought old women out onto their stoops to complain of the sickly floral *tormenta*. Alessia pointed to one of the trees and said this was where she and Hazel had spent the night all those years ago. Susan rested her hand on Alessia's shoulder while I craned up into the arthritic limbs of the old tree, imagining the two girls sleeping against its rough bark.

Alessia said she wanted to see if the Fiorentina pear tree was still alive, and we continued back along the river. She couldn't remember where it was, but Milo directed us to a wooded area where figs and plums grew feral in the summertime. "Pears need full sun," Alessia told us, "so if it is still alive it would be in a clearing." We tramped through the gold-and-mulberry leaves, looking for an opening in the bare crowns.

"Your grandmother and I," Alessia said to me, "came down here to pick the fruit in the late summer. She said that a Serafino ancestor had planted a great orchard two hundred years earlier but that only a single tree remained. We filled a pail with speckled-green Fiorentinas. She told me they were in Renaissance paintings, these pears, and we made cakes with them for the restaurant. I remember they tasted slightly bitter and very crisp . . ."

We continued to walk through the damp leaves, Milo scouting in front, holding branches aside for Alessia. After an hour of circling, Milo suggested we turn back, that in all likelihood the tree had been overrun by the stands of oak and nettle. Reluctantly, Alessia agreed, and we headed toward the river in silence. But then, a few hundred yards from the riverbank, Alessia stopped in a deeply rutted bowl of earth. A smaller tree stood encircled by towering oaks and ashes, its dark branches scaled white with lichen. "That is her," said

Alessia, coming close enough to put one hand against the bark. The pear tree may have been technically still alive, but it was growing listless and stooped in the shade of taller trees. Alessia walked around the tree, assessing it from all angles, craning up at the branches. Susan asked if she wanted her to take a photo of the tree with her phone, so that they could show it to Ida, but Alessia shook her head. "No, no," she said. "La signora will not want to see it like this."

On the way back to the villa, as Alessia gathered some wild mushrooms that were pinning up through the leaf cover, I thought back to the first meal Elisa had made me—polenta con funghi—with mushrooms she'd foraged in the valley. It was the same night she asked me about Clare and listened with careful attention to my stream of memories and associations. As we slowly ascended to Valetto's pedestal, it occurred to me that ever since that outpouring—for the first time in years—Clare hadn't presided over every gap and silence between my thoughts.

φ

Milo took Alessia with her mushrooms to the villa for another visit with Ida, and I returned to the cottage with Susan. Through the French doors of the living room, we saw Elisa on the flagstone terrace holding a glass of wine, a cigarette in her mouth, squatting in front of the chiminea to feed it firewood with her spare hand. Marcella sat on one of the leather couches with her own glass of wine, watching her mother as if she were framed and illuminated by a colossal television screen. Marcella told us that the meeting with the caterers had not gone well. After a pause, she supplied the word *disastro*.

"What did they say about the additional guests?" I asked.

She pointed to the terrace with her chin. "*Chiedi a lei.*" Ask her.

When I closed the French doors behind me, Elisa looked up from her squat in front of the chiminea. I told her that her mother had found the Fiorentina pear tree down in the valley, but she didn't seem to hear me.

"I have taken up smoking again," she said, "just in the last hour."

"I understand it didn't go so well with the caterers."

"They are worse than I thought. Imbeciles, canteen cooks, not worthy of sharpening a knife or peeling an apple . . . The husband, who calls himself a chef, lectured me on the nature of Umbrian cuisine, as if I were a fucking schoolgirl. I told him there was no such thing as Umbrian cuisine, that every hill town and village made its recipes according to its own customs and history. That Umbria is the marriage of the north and the south, that her food is the fruit of this marriage." She came out of her squat on a big smoky exhalation. "You should have seen the look on his face after my dissertation on Umbrian food." She stood with one hand on her hip, looking into the chiminea.

"What did they say about the additional head count?"

"Yes, indeed, they took particular issue with that."

"How so?"

"They will not adjust the number unless you pay a surcharge up front."

"And what is that?"

"For each additional guest above one hundred persons, you will be charged double."

"That doesn't sound like standard practice."

She looked at me, nudged her glasses onto the bridge of

her nose, shook her head. "Sometime I would like to see you lose your temper. You don't have to throw a chair or smash a glass or anything too dramatic, just maybe raise your voice or suddenly be lost for words. Look up at the heavens in exasperation. Shake a fist. *What would it take?*"

Watching the smoke funnel out of the chiminea, I said, "They say I have trouble getting in touch with my emotions."

"And who are *they*?"

"The therapist I saw briefly, my daughter, my dead wife. Probably everyone who has ever known me."

She shrugged, dusted some ash from her corduroy pants.

"So what happened?" I asked.

She regarded the mouth of the chiminea, where a new piece of oak began to kindle and spit. "I told them to go fuck themselves. That I could cook for two hundred people in my sleep and that they should go back to shoveling sheep shit like their ancestors before them." She went to take a slug of wine but stopped, her glass halfway to her mouth. "Marcella had to take me outside for some fresh air, and then I sent her back inside to apologize on my behalf, to tell them that her mother wasn't right in the head and to ask if, at the very least, we could take possession of the food and wine they bought with the Serafino cash deposit."

Through the French doors I could see our daughters watching us, Marcella apparently providing closed captions for her own version of *Il Disastro*.

"The party is in two days," I said unhelpfully. There was an unbroken line of dread connecting the back of my throat to the pit of my stomach.

"They have agreed to our picking up the food and wine they have purchased," she said, "though I am not permitted on the restaurant premises. It's possible they have put a contract out on my head, that a carpenter turned assassin in some ghost village is loading his *pistola* right now."

I let her exaggerations go unchallenged, watched a chasm of blue sky open out above the valley. Mostly to myself, I said, "I didn't think things could get any worse."

"Worse than *what*?" she said, leaning down to put another piece of oak into the chiminea. She was overfeeding the fire, building an inferno. She said something into the flames, which, in Italian, sounded like "Were you going to let those Bonoglio sheepherders rape your ancestral purse?" When she stood back up she looked at me. "*Ecco*," she said, one hand passing down her front, "now you have an award-winning Milanese chef who will be in charge of all the food. What could be better?"

To get away from her unflinching eyes, I stepped over to the edge of the terrace. "It's very kind of you, but we can't ask you to take that on."

"You are not asking me. It was my idea."

"But why?"

"Other chefs have underestimated me my whole career, starting with that big Milanese oaf who ignored me for a year when I was a university student. Call it a chance to put the Bonoglios of the world in their place. And besides, it will make my mother happy to finally see me in action. You know she never once came to the restaurant in Milan? I'll be cooking in honor of your mother as well."

I was touched by this idea, but I said, "It's an enormous gift to our whole family. But I just don't understand how you can do it all."

"We will recruit my mother, our daughters, waiters from the other town, your grandmother's nursing aides, their friends and cousins . . . I can do the cooking and prep with six to eight people in a pinch, but I will need a small army to serve it. We will only plate the primi and secondi piatti but the antipasto we will serve from a buffet table, maybe even the dessert . . ."

When I didn't turn around, she came over to stand beside me as I looked down at the bend of the copper-green river. I said, "You should probably know that my aunt Iris and Rinaldo Fumigalli have developed a plan to denounce Silvio Ruffo at the party. They want to share the plan with everyone tomorrow morning." I stopped short of saying *dress rehearsal.*

"*Incredibile!*" she said. "The Milanese peacock has returned?"

"He has."

"How gracious of them to share a plan to confront my own mother's attacker."

"We can tell him to keep out of it," I said. "I'm happy to do it."

Elisa drew on her cigarette, held the smoke in deliberation. "No, no, let's see what they have concocted first. To be honest, I can't be sure my mother will go through with it. Every time I bring it up she goes quiet or leaves the room. Nonetheless, this old mongrel will be held to account."

Neither of us said anything as we stared off at the tree line on the other side of the valley. Then Elisa bent down to stub out her cigarette on the flagstone and said, "Well, I had better go work on the denunciation menu."

φ

When we all gathered in the villa the next morning, it appeared to be for a lecture, not a rehearsal. We were summoned to the library, the box canyon of towering and laddered bookshelves that had been de-cluttered by Nina and her teenage crew. My grandfather's hulking desk had been excavated from under decades of *National Geographic*s, papers, and family photo albums. Iris stood behind the desk with a whiteboard she'd surely had Milo lug down the stairs from her apartment, a marker in one hand and some handwritten notes in the other. Professorial in her wool-knit suit and pearl necklace, she gave the impression that we were about to receive a lecture on the sociology of deviant behavior or the rise of nationalism.

Elisa sat with a notepad in her lap. She'd been up most of the night working on her menu, a shopping list, and a detailed inventory of prep tasks, and she'd insisted that she would tell the Serafino family of the new catering plan herself. When Nina wheeled my grandmother across the library floor, Ida took stock of the room, from the unencumbered desk to the dusted silk taffeta lampshades, and reached back to pat Nina's hand before pointing to the open space beside Alessia and Elisa. To no one in particular, Ida said, "I can't get over what they've done to this room! Isn't it marvelous?" Then, turning to Elisa, she asked, "Miss Tomassi, how did it go with the caterers?"

"We have a plan," Elisa said quietly. "I will share it at the end."

Milo, who'd trailed in after my grandmother and knew the neighboring town's affairs like his own skin and thoughts, gave me a providential nod, as if to signal he knew that the Serafino and Bonoglio families would henceforth and forever be engaged in a blood feud, *una faida*, and that he could be counted on in battle. But when Donata emerged from the hallway a few seconds later—pale, hobbled, wearing a fawn-colored overcoat she clutched by the lapels—I realized he'd been signaling his wife's halting resurrection.

Iris cleared her throat and we all turned to the whiteboard, where she'd written down the schedule for Saturday—from the 11:00 a.m. gathering of guests to the 3:30 p.m. denunciation. She said, "What unites all denunciations is the act of citizens accusing someone of wrongdoing and standing against them. In our case, we're making a public accusation." She glanced down at her notes before looking over at Alessia, who was arranging a small constellation of pebbles and glass shards on a low coffee table. "It seems to me," she continued, "that we are also creating a public record of moral failure. And not just for what Silvio Ruffo did. The failure also belongs to our family and the town. Valetto could have done more to stand against its only fascist committee member. The residents were worried that without a pharmacist they would suffer, and so they turned a blind eye, not forcing Ruffo out until more than a year after the war had ended. Naturalmente," she said, "the failure is also very personal. On the day that my sister and Alessia were led from the villa, I was trying on my mother's clothes and jewelry instead of carrying out my responsibilities to care for my sister and her friend. This has been, for me, a lifelong regret, even before I knew the full circumstances of their disappearance."

I saw a flash of Iris lecturing in Rome and Milan, how she'd succeeded in the masculine, class-obsessed realm of 1950s Italian academe despite her gender and mix of Umbrian and English pedigree.

"What I envision," Iris continued, "with my mother's gracious permission, will take place during the toasts, when current and former residents are invited to raise a glass to Ida and offer their reflections or memories. Near the very end—and it's important the full birthday celebration has run its course—we will invite Alessia to speak of her time with the Serafino family. This is when she will confront her assailant."

The word *assailant* was a reminder of the forensic online forums where my aunt spent her days. When Alessia didn't look up from her stones and glass, Elisa put her arm around her mother's shoulder and leaned in to whisper something in her ear. They conferred quietly for a few moments, before Elisa said, "My mother does not know if she will have the strength."

"Of course," said Iris very gently. "We have a contingency plan for this."

"And what is that?" Elisa asked.

"If Alessia cannot confront Silvio Ruffo, then the Serafino family will do it on her behalf."

"No, grazie," said Elisa. "I will do that if she is unable."

"And me," I said from under a silk lampshade. "On behalf of our mothers."

"Very well," said Iris, turning to face Ida. "And, Mother, you are sure this is the way you would like your celebration to end? It's not too late to find a different way. We could invite him to the villa the next day with his family."

Ida considered the Gothic window at the far end of the library, a design not local to the region, but which a Serafino forebear must have insisted on having to rarefy their view of the valley. We could see ribbons of cloud scudding in over the hills. "No," she said. "It has to be in front of the people who still remember those times."

We didn't discuss what Alessia would say to Silvio Ruffo almost seventy years after her interrogation, or what would happen if he denied everything. Instead, we watched as Donata, who'd been staring into the carpet the whole time, asked when the caterers would be delivering the rest of the food.

Iris, sensing that her time was up, stepped away from the whiteboard and held the marker out to Elisa, who suddenly had no choice but to stand in front of us all and confess what had transpired. She took her notes and walked toward the front, taking the marker from my aunt. Standing before us in an oversized purple sweater, her hair pulled into a chignon, she said, "*La famiglia Bonoglio non si occuperà del cibo per la festa di compleanno*." The Bonoglio family will not be catering the birthday celebration. Donata whispered *Madre di Cristo*, Mother of Christ, my grandmother said *Oh dear*, and Violet burst out with *porca miseria!*, which usually translates as *dammit* but was more likely in her mouth to hold a literal warning of what was to come—*pork poverty!*

"When I met with them," Elisa continued, "to tell them of the additional guests, they insisted on doubling the cost for each new person. I said this was unacceptable and an argument ensued." She pushed her sweater sleeves up to the elbows and I caught a glimpse of the tiny Greek-letter tattoo on her wrist. "So, with your blessing, I will be taking over the catering," she said. "The Bonoglios have agreed to hand over any items they purchased with your deposit, minus any labor costs so far."

"We'll be lucky to get a sack of rice," said Violet. "And, what, now we overpay you instead of the Bonoglios?"

"I will not accept payment for my services," said Elisa with stinging formality. "Though we will need to pay some of the helpers."

"This is unbelievably kind of you," said my grandmother. "Can it be done?"

"It can be done," said Elisa.

"Will you share your plan, signora?" asked Milo. Beside him, Donata was holding her face in her hands.

Elisa turned to the whiteboard and wrote *Preparare, Cucinare, Servire*. "I have divided each part into a list of steps and the number of people I will need in each team."

"Are we playing football?" asked Violet.

Rose, always the diplomat, looked at her sister and put one finger to her lips.

"Actually, this *will* be a team sport. The biggest team," Elisa said, "is the servers." She looked at Nina, who'd been texting on her phone the entire time. "Signorina, your friends who helped clean the villa, do they want to earn some extra money?"

Nina flushed when she noticed the whole room looking at her. "I can bring five or so."

"*Eccellente*," said Elisa. "Have them come this afternoon to help finish setting up the dining room and the sala grande with the extra chairs and tables." She turned to Milo. "Signor Scorza, do you know any of the waiters and waitresses in the neighboring town?"

"*Certo*," he said, "I know most of them."

"If you spoke to them, do you think we could get eight to come work the party?"

"It depends on price," he said matter-of-factly.

"If the Serafinos agree, we will pay them fifty percent more than what they earn in their restaurants, for six hours. But no one who works in the Bonoglio restaurant. Spies and *sabotatori* are not welcome here."

Milo glanced over at the aunts, who said nothing, and then at Ida, who nodded. "I will do it," he said.

Elisa at the whiteboard again: "That leaves the cooking team." She took up a piece of tattered paper from under her notepad, and as she held it up, I realized it was the grimy menu she'd taken from the abandoned restaurant weeks earlier. "I would like to serve a menu that is a combination of the old and the new, of local Umbrian dishes, but also the recipes that were once served in Il Ritorno."

My grandmother leaned forward in her wheelchair. "May I see it?"

Elisa brought the menu over and set it on the low table in front of Ida and Alessia. They took turns trying to read the names of the dishes through the ash and grime.

"Some of these meals came from my grandmother's book of recipes," said Ida.

"But this is the summer menu," said Alessia, turning the menu over.

"We will adapt it for the season," said Elisa. "For the cooking team, I will need at least six persons."

"You can count me as a half," said Ida. "I can't roll dough anymore because of the arthritis but I can chop rather slowly."

"I will also help," said Alessia.

"*Anch'io*," said Donata from the other side of the room, her face now out of her hands. "I will take the umbrichelli. It has always been my specialty, and we will be judged by its quality." Umbrichelli was the local pasta, a spaghetti-like strand that was thicker and chewier and said to have been made by the Umbro tribes who settled the nearby hills. Milo regarded his wife for a long moment before patting the back of her hand.

"All three sisters will also help with the cooking," said Iris, not bothering to consult Violet or Rose. "Just tell us what we need to do."

"We want to help," said Susan from the side of the room.

Elisa smiled at the daughters. "You ladies will oversee the

dining room setup. I will be like a stern butler in an old British castle, measuring the cutlery and glass placement with a ruler. I will draw up a list of all the jobs."

"And what about me and Milo?" I asked.

"I am already texting with some of the waiters I know," said Milo, looking down at his phone.

Elisa began to write the menu on the whiteboard. "You two will also have the most important job of all."

"And what's that?" I asked.

"Going to rescue our provisions from the talons of the Bonoglios. Once I know what we have, I can finish my shopping list for the town markets and supermarkets. There is one more job left," said Elisa, turning to Rinaldo in the front row. He sat beside Iris in a cashmere argyle sweater vest and tie, quietly leafing through a book on medieval palazzos in a cone of lamplight. He looked up and smiled, pinned into acquiescence. "*Come posso essere di servizio?*" How may I be of service?

Elisa savored the moment, adjusting her eyeglasses to better see his face. "We will need someone in the front entrance hall, to take coats and greet guests as they arrive."

Iris bristled on Rinaldo's behalf, opened her mouth, perhaps preparing to say that a distinguished professor emeritus could not be asked to stoop to such menial depths. To his credit, Rinaldo raised his perfectly manicured hand to ward off Iris's objections. "I would be delighted," he said benevolently, though I doubt any of us believed it.

φ

Milo and I drove up to the Bonoglio trattoria, which was tucked into a side street of Bevona. Although it's normal to find trattorias in Italian alleyways—restaurants often command the main streets—the Trattoria al Forno di Bonoglio looked as if it had been hand-selected for banishment in the narrowest and darkest back lane in all of Umbria. Since the Fiat would have blocked traffic in the cramped alleyway, a kitchen hand came outside to direct us along a serpentine route to the loading dock in the rear. Milo had emptied out and cleaned the Fiat's trunk and back seats, and he left the car idling while we loaded crates of produce, sacks of flour and grain, and a few cases of wine—all under the cauterizing supervision of the aproned Bonoglios. On my last trip into the kitchen, I glimpsed the dining room: a mural of pack mules slouching along a mountain road, faded tablecloths, heavy wooden-framed chairs in dire need of recaning. Perhaps the Serafinos' catering order was supposed to fund a modest renovation.

After we unloaded the supplies at the footbridge for Nina's cousins to ferry across, Elisa joined us for a shopping expedition that took us into the surrounding market towns. We trailed behind her, carrying her selections in sacks or wrapped in newspaper, watched as she haggled with butchers and cheesemongers, flattered greengrocers into by-the-box discounts. The Fiat's trunk was loaded with produce and herbs and wheels of cheese, with entire legs of ham and whole salamis. Thankfully, the fresh meat she'd ordered from a farm outside of Orvieto would be delivered to the footbridge the next morning. The back seat was stacked with boxes of greenhouse melons and tomatoes, one of Elisa's few concessions to buying outside the season. Elisa wedged herself between the boxes to cradle them from potholes and Milo's abrupt accelerations and turns.

In the villa's kitchen, Elisa worked the old women as if

they were all fifty years younger. The full menu was written out on Iris's whiteboard—from aperitivi to digestivi and the five courses in between—along with each prep task and its owner. My grandmother was in charge of prepping the chicken livers for the *crostini di fegatini di pollo*, removing the gallbladders from the livers over a metal bowl. Alessia mashed a vat of nettles, destined for a creamy bruschetta spread, while the aunts peeled potatoes and kneaded bread dough. Donata sat at a stainless steel counter dusted with flour, rolling lines of pasta for the umbrichelli. As the only full-blooded Umbrian, she kept a watchful eye over the other preparations, ready to speak up if local traditions were violated. Only Elisa was allowed to handle the vintage cherry-red Volano meat slicer—which had been in the family since Aldo's days—razor-slicing pound upon pound of charcuterie for the antipasto.

After I was more or less banished from the kitchen, I went to see how the other preparations were coming along. In the dining room, I found Susan and Marcella setting the tables with Nina and her crew of locals, mostly teenage girls in Converse sneakers and carefully stressed jeans. I looked on as Susan inspected each wineglass, holding it up to the windows before placing it strategically on a table or giving it a polish with a cloth napkin. It was clear to me that she'd delegated the tasks around the room—the napkin-folding station, the flower-arrangement station, the silverware polishing, the decoration hanging, the place-card setting. It was an economist's fantasy of the division of labor.

Nina and Susan had also excavated some memorabilia from my grandmother's apartment. Arranged on the walls of the dining room were photographs and objects that charted the course of my grandmother's century—her framed birth certificate, images of her Australian girlhood, scenes of her as a governess in Rome, pushing a perambulator through a cypress-and-pine parkland; the early days with Aldo at the villa and the trail of daughters in baby bonnets that followed; scenes of her standing in a white apron in the restaurant kitchen. Like a shrine to our culinary ancestors, *The Zanetti Book of the Table* had been relocated to one corner on its wooden Victorian Bible stand.

I continued outside and found Milo in his workshop, where he was retrofitting an old donkey cart with shocks to give it more suspension for the comfort of the elderly and infirm. "How will they get up the stairs at the end of the footbridge?" I asked. "For this," he replied, "we will carry them up." I wasn't sure who *we* referred to. I guessed that the average age of the waiters Milo had commandeered was sixty-five. "We should have hired porters," I said, half jokingly, to which Milo confirmed that Nina's brothers and cousins all liked to lift weights at the local gym. That settled, we decided to take the widows' dogs for a walk as an excuse to confirm that the piazza and the footbridge were ready for tomorrow's donkey procession. We fetched the dogs and wound up through the alleyways into the main square, where Susan and I had hung silk flags days earlier. The flags of the oldest Valetto families, their coats of arms, swayed lazily from window ledges and balconies, the perimeter of the piazza lined with wooden benches.

Just as the church bells began tolling, we noticed two men standing in front of the Ruffo house—one of them stoop-shouldered and frail, wearing a wool cap and clutching a walking stick, the other middle-aged and rummaging through his pockets. As we came closer, I saw that it was Roberto and Silvio Ruffo. The anger I'd nursed on my train ride to Rome, on the visit to the nursing home, suddenly bloomed back like a migraine. There were tiny pinpricks in my peripheral vision and I could feel the blood draining out of my hands. I shoved my hands into my pockets to find the pocketknife's cool pearl handle. Milo said *Mio dio*, good God, very quietly, but he was already guiding the dogs toward the men, who'd turned to look our way.

"Gentlemen!" Roberto said, directing a big smile at the dogs, "we are all very excited for the big festa tomorrow. Of course, there is also another game slated for Perugia and I have high hopes of victory, so I may be ducking outside here and there to catch the scores. You remember my grandfather, Signore Ruffo."

The old man scrutinized us as if through a tunnel. Roberto reminded his grandfather that I had come to visit him in the Casa di Riposo and that the gentleman beside me was Milo Scorza, the tuttofare for the Serafino widows. We all shook hands. Silvio Ruffo's palm felt like cold wax. He leaned tenderly down to pet behind Volpino's ears, the dog craning up to lick his thin, veined wrist. When he came back up, he settled his gaze on me and said, "We did not finish our chess game. It passed without a victory." In the November light, his eyes were the color of oysters.

"We need a rematch," I said.

"*Finalmente*," said Roberto, pulling a key on a small metal fob from his pocket, "the house is mostly for storage now, but I was going to take my grandfather inside for a tour of memory lane."

"I have not been inside the house in more than fifty years," Ruffo said wearily.

"*Buona giornata*," said Roberto, taking his grandfather by the elbow.

We watched as Roberto helped his grandfather climb the stone stairs to the front door and slipped the key inside the padlock. As the Ruffos stepped inside, I could make out a hallway vanishing into gray-green depths.

18

A gas-blue November day. My grandmother rode sidesaddle on the back of a donkey, its mane braided with ribbons and dried flowers. Milo held the reins and led her slowly across the footbridge, at the head of the procession, two hundred or so people trailing behind in their wedding and church clothes, bearing gifts; two donkeys hauled carts in the rear, one with those too feeble to walk, and one with a band of local musicians playing drums, mandolins, and accordions. During its glory days, the town had hosted an annual donkey race, with jockeys in silk jerseys competing from nearby farms and towns. Now, the donkeys had to be rented from an *agriturismo* in the valley, where tourists slept in overpriced yurts and were led along the river and told stories of Etruscans saving their tears in ceramic jars. Ida Serafino, in her dove-gray turtleneck dress and black stockings, rode on the back of a jenny named Pomona, the Roman goddess of fruit trees, gardens, and orchards.

It wasn't clear who had conceived of the birthday procession—or was it a parade?—but it unfolded like some time-honored Umbrian tradition. Reunited friends reminisced and held hands, grandmothers carried babies, old men in dun-colored suits chided each other for still being alive. A group of Augustinian nuns, from the pilgrimage town that Rose visited every year, walked along in their black habits and orthopedic shoes. At the end of the footbridge, the carts were unhitched so that the donkeys could climb the gentle incline of the wide stone stairs. Nina's cousins and the veteran waiters, solemn as pallbearers, carried half a dozen elderly former residents, some in wheelchairs, up into the piazza. Silvio Ruffo, dressed in a moth-colored suit and homburg, refused to ride on a donkey or be borne aloft. Instead, he used his cane to pick his way into the piazza.

The parish priest waited in front of the church to give Ida Serafino her birthday blessing, dabbing holy water onto her forehead as a bookend to her baptism a century earlier, on another continent, and then she was helped back into her saddle and paraded like some ancient, hilltop bride around the square, waving and smiling at the marveling witnesses to her tenure on the planet. Then, representatives from each of the other old Valetto families led their own rented and festooned donkeys around the square to great applause. Milo's sons, Nico and Antonio, both in their fifties, led a donkey draped in the family flag—an anvil, a reared horse, a lemon tree. The Ruffo coat of arms, borne along by Roberto Ruffo, consisted of a cypress, a snake, and a lodestar.

After the procession, we all fanned out into the narrow alleyways and headed down to the terraced villa gardens, where guests could set their gifts on a long trestle table and antipasti and aperitivi waited among the espaliers. Although it was unseasonably warm for November, Milo had placed a dozen propane patio heaters at regular intervals, and the guests clustered around them in small groups, nursing flutes of prosecco and small plates of crostini and bruschetta smeared with nettle cream and herbs. The musicians flanked the guests, playing regional folk songs, the singer recalling lost loves and ruined harvests and wolves in mountainside lairs. I wanted to believe that the band had walked up from the valley, but the truth was that Iris had found them online, a group of Rome-based web developers who played chamber and folkloric music in their spare time. I watched as Alessia nodded along to the music, a glass of unsipped prosecco in hand, while Susan and Marcella stood protectively on either side, occasionally fetching her a canapé.

After half an hour in the gardens, the guests were invited into the villa itself, Rinaldo in the entrance hallway to help with the removal of their coats, hats, and shawls. He'd arranged a series of coatracks and long benches along the walls, each of them numbered to help the guests find their garments after the party. In his heavy tweed jacket and paisley foulard, he was all banter and pleasantries, a Victorian butler at a country estate. Another spread of antipasto—draperies of paper-thin charcuterie—had been laid out on the enormous mahogany table along one side of the dining room, but the guests were more interested in wandering the ground floor of the villa, an elderly Serafino sister or the centenaria herself as tour guide. Nobody suspected the decades of neglect that had unfolded in these now bright, taffeta-lamped rooms, the fireplaces roaring with burning chestnut and oak, the mantels adorned with flowers, the crushed-velvet sofas dusted and perfumed. In the billiard room, the men ruminated on games of skill and chance, on British imports, on dead relatives who'd made furniture or pianos. The billiard table was set up as if for some perfect, hypothetical game, the lintless green baize drawing admirers like a dazzling lakeside meadow.

Before long, the charcuterie and prosecco merged into Montefalco Sagrantino wine and il primo, the guests somehow instinctively knowing when to take their seats. It wasn't clear whether my grandmother's seating arrangements—all those place cards in swooping calligraphy—were an act of willful calculation or oversight. Former estranged neighbors were forced to find their adjacent place settings, while divisions of class, politics, and faith were ignored at many of the tables. Atheists were seated next to the devout, conservatives next to liberals. I found myself wedged between a Venetian dentist whose father had been born in Valetto and an Umbrian farmhand. Susan sat across from me, next to an Augustinian nun who, between birdlike sips of prosecco, interrogated my daughter about the mechanics of social media, a Dantean realm that was strictly forbidden at the convent in Perugia where she'd lived for two decades.

The Serafino widows, released from the kitchen, had all been spread out, each of them taking up the role of table hostess. Iris and Violet sat with their adult children and grandchildren, who'd come in from Rome and Naples, and Rose sat with the other nuns from Perugia and her hairdresser from Bevona. As the guest of honor, Ida sat at the front of the room with Nina, Alessia, and some distant Australian Serafino relatives. All of the Ruffos sat at the same table, with a Brooklynite thrown in for good measure. And as a nod to the impending denunciation, Ida had asked for the stuffed head and shoulders of a wild boar to be brought up from the cellar and hung—glass-eyed, tusked, black-snouted—directly above Silvio Ruffo's place setting.

Elisa, Donata, and Nina's cousins stayed in the kitchen, sending the bow-tied waiters out with the first course—umbrichelli in a sauce of black truffles and anchovies, dusted with local pecorino. Still coming to terms with the awkward seating arrangements, the guests were forced to switch topics and offer up an assessment of the venerable local pasta. Milo, who kept moving between rooms to restock the fireplaces, listened to their favorable assessments from the hearthstone beside the small stage set up for the musicians. Everyone seemed to agree that while anchovies were not native to landlocked Umbria, the sauce was *deliziosa* and the pasta was perfectly correct, a victory for Donata, who'd spent a full day hand-rolling every strand.

When the second course and side dishes came out—a choice of wild boar stew sprinkled with gremolata or pomegranate guinea fowl, both served with broad beans, chicory, and baked polenta—I watched Silvio Ruffo eating under the boar's head. From scanning the place cards, I noticed that Greta Ruffo, whose fictional fever had lured my mother from the villa in 1944, sat with her husband quietly, barely talking to the rest of the family. She was in her seventies, a fashionable woman in a pantsuit and scarf, with high cheekbones and dyed auburn hair. She didn't seem to acknowledge the three generations of pharmacists—brother, father, nephew—on the other side of the table, and I wondered what she knew of her father's history. Her brother was big-jowled and slow-blinking, wearing an Armani blazer and polo shirt. He and his cheerful middle-aged son, Roberto, sat on either side of Silvio Ruffo.

With dessert and the toasts approaching, my emotions felt washed out and obscure. My mind drifted to my basement in Michigan, to my bookshelves and email inbox, to the guest lecture on abandonment I should have finished by now. It was Susan's voice that brought me back to a table of dinner guests looking at me.

"Dad," she said from the other side, "Sister Baldoni asked if you knew about the Roman settlement of Carsulae."

The nun smiled at me, her cheeks flushed by prosecco.

The Venetian dentist looked up from the guinea fowl he was dissecting with surgical gusto and said, "It was destroyed by an earthquake in the first century B.C., if I remember correctly."

"Yes," I countered, feeling a little upstaged, "and then deserted."

The sister looked at me blankly, so I repeated this in Italiah. She asked whether I'd visited the ruins of Carsulae on my *tour della desolazione* and I realized Susan had been giving her an overview of my research and my recent book without my noticing. I shook my head.

The nun pointed at me sternly across her plate with her knife. "You and your daughter *must* come to our little town and see the ruins and the fourteenth-century frescoes. Come visit when your aunty Rose is called to her next pilgrimage."

I wasn't sure I was ready to see Rose on her knees before the patron saint of impossible causes. The Umbrian farmhand confessed that he'd never been to Perugia proper, even though it was less than a hundred kilometers away. The talk at our table continued in this cautious manner for the better part of an hour. Conversations about Umbrian towns and fava bean festivals and the varying weather across the valleys, mountains, and lakes. I could hear a similar drift of talk at the nearby tables, but at a few tables the sound was mostly of clinking silverware below the accordion and mandolin of the band. I decided to make a sortie to my grandmother's table, to see how she and Alessia were holding up.

"The food is magnificent," said Ida, as I leaned beside her chair. She gestured with her chin at the Ruffo table, where the old pharmacist was spooning chunks of polenta into his wild boar stew. "Even the old devil is eating with abandon. For a man of his age and build, he has quite the appetite."

"I know," I said. "I've been watching him eat."

Alessia sat beside my grandmother. She'd been served the guinea fowl, which stood untouched beside her pasta bowl. From across the table, the husband and wife from Melbourne smiled at us in appreciation of the food, oblivious to our conversation.

"You know," Ida said confidentially, "in *The Zanetti Book of the Table* there is a recipe for *folaghe in umido* . . . for stewed coot . . . and it's the only meal that my mother said was banned in her household when she was growing up." She took a breath, looked back at the Ruffo table. "It was a cursed meal, said to kill anyone who cooked or ate it. The coot is this funny little migratory bird and a terribly good swimmer. Travels by night in huge flocks. Sometime in the nineteenth century, fishermen came from all over Italy to hunt these birds from boats on Lake Massaciuccoli . . . near Pisa . . . and my great-grandfather was among them. They brought down six thousand coots in one day and my ancestor was shot and killed in the tremendous shower of all that lead." She brought her attention back to her plate and half-eaten meal. "We should have asked Elisa to serve Silvio Ruffo a bowl of stewed coot while everyone else got the boar or the fowl."

Through a gap in the tables, I could make out *The Zanetti Book of the Table* over in the corner, splayed open on its Victorian Bible stand, and I wondered if it contained other cursed recipes, or annotations on how to poison a despised dinner guest with a sliver of death cap mushroom in a bowl of hare stew.

"Almost there," said Ida, patting Alessia's hand. "Once the desserts come out, Iris will address the guests."

Alessia didn't lift her eyes from her water glass, and I returned to my table, where I caught a dwindling conversation between the dentist and the nun about the intricate embalming practices used to preserve the bodies of the saints. Susan sent me a text that I read under the table:

```
You missed the unabridged history of the
mummification of the saints! Everything
good over at grandma's table?
```

I texted her back:

```
Tutto bene! I should go check in with Elisa
```

The kitchen was full of waiters delivering empty plates to Nina's dishwashing cousins. I found Elisa off to one side, bent over a dessert cart, decorating a cake with the precision of someone defusing a bomb. Her hair pulled back, she was wearing one of my grandmother's old monogrammed white chef coats, the sleeves dusted in cocoa powder. As an ode to the last Fiorentina pear tree growing in the valley, Elisa had put a pear and chestnut cake on the menu for dessert, but she'd also made a surprise birthday cake for Ida—a tower of chocolate layered with mascarpone cream filling and topped with Baci hazelnut chocolates from Perugia. She'd given me a sneak preview of it earlier in the day. "Do you think your grandmother will like it?" Elisa asked as I stood by the cart.

"She'll be speechless. We can never repay you for this."

"It is a gift," she said, placing a Baci on the top layer, "so no repayment is required."

"The food is superb, all of it. Thank you so much for everything. Really."

"It was a team sport, right down to the chicken livers your grandmother prepped."

"You know," I said, "I'm guessing you're not great at accepting compliments or gratitude."

She looked up at me, smiled, straightened, wiped one hand down her chef coat. "That's fair, sorry. You're welcome. I'm just nervous for what comes next. How is it going out there?"

I gave her the state of play in the dining room, right down to her mother's untouched guinea fowl, Silvio Ruffo's appetite, and the mummification discussion at my own table.

"We better get to the cake and speeches then," she said. "Since I couldn't fit a hundred candles on the cake, I had to improvise." She'd found a candle in the form of a C, and she placed it onto the top layer and took out a lighter from her chef's coat. "When I push the cart into the dining room," she said, "you will need to start singing 'Happy Birthday' to get everyone going."

When I came back into the dining room singing *tanti auguri a te* the nearby tables joined in, and soon the whole room cheered and sang as Elisa pushed the chocolate cake toward my grandmother's table. Ida was predictably touched, holding Alessia's hand on one side and Elisa's hand on the other while she blew out the burning C with a fitful breath. The band riffed a few celebratory tunes and then the waiters brought out the other desserts, the coffee, grappa, and nocino, while expats and Umbrians continued to shout *buon compleanno!* from the sidelines. Then Iris walked to the stage and took the microphone from the singer, and the band went in search of their dessert.

In her wool day frock and pearls, a tiny balloon of grappa

in hand, Iris thanked the guests for coming from near and far and asked for a round of applause for our illustrious chef, Elisa Tomassi. I stood up from my chair to clap and soon the whole room joined me in a standing ovation. Across the tables, I made eye contact with Violet, and when she gave me a little wave and mouthed *brava!* I realized that she'd finally softened toward Elisa. How could the devotion of the menu and cooking go unnoticed, from the ode to Ida's restaurant to the hand-decorated chocolate tower? Over at the dessert cart, Elisa waved to the applauding crowd and proceeded to slice into the uppermost terrace of her cake.

When the guests sat down again, Iris addressed them from the stage: "A lot can happen in one hundred years. In the case of my mother's century, I am talking about the invention of antibiotics, television, the jet airplane, the personal computer, the submarine, the bikini, the internet . . . not necessarily in that order. I would be here all afternoon if I continued."

A wave of gentle laughter lapped among the tables.

"We have gathered here to celebrate the life and times of Ida Serafino, born Ida Maria Zanetti, in Leichhardt, a suburb of Sydney, Australia, one hundred years ago today. As you can tell from the photographs around the room, Ida was a rare beauty. It's easy to see why my father, the late Aldo Serafino, was leveled by her on a trip to Rome in 1927. At the time, Ida was working as a maid and helper to a governess for a friend of her mother's family. In fact, Ida is as lovely today as she was back then. For her three surviving daughters, we have the privilege of living in her gracious presence each and every day. So, I'd like to raise a glass to a century of Ida walking among us. May her remaining years be peaceful and filled with joy!"

Iris raised her glass and the guests cheered *salute!*

"As a way to celebrate my mother's life," she continued, "we thought we would invite her friends and family to offer up remembrances of Ida during her many years in Valetto, or even just to recall the history of this place where she has lived for so long. *Allora*, so, who would like to begin?"

What followed were warmhearted speeches from former residents and relatives. An elderly Umbrian woman recalled coming to the villa as a young girl with her mother, that every winter Ida Serafino opened up her house to the surrounding farmers and their families. The rooms smelled of roasting chestnuts, the woman said, and Aldo Serafino would teach the farmers how to play billiards with the official British rules, and she would hear the *pock pock* of the colliding wooden balls while Ida found clothes for the children that her own daughters no longer needed. A cousin from Australia, roughly my age, talked about her late mother's affection for Ida, even though they had only seen each other a few times in their adult lives, about the way Ida's Christmas letter each year was accompanied by a palmful of fennel seeds and a handwritten recipe copied from the family gastronomic album. A blunt-faced man, whose childhood home had fallen into the valley in the 1970s, remembered the festivities in the square, the bonfires and the enormous cauldrons stirred with paddles and filled with red wine and floating oranges, the Good Friday processions when the crucifix was taken from the church and the residents played the Romans in pursuit of the Savior.

Unexpectedly, Milo took the stage with a small glass of nocino and told the story of working for his father at the villa, that he had known Ida Serafino since he was a newborn, that she had attended his christening and overseen the house where he'd found his life's purpose. "You have been the lamp burning at the end of the hallway for as long as I can remember, signora," he said. His speech was oddly touching, and I briefly forgot all about the denunciation and contemplated a remembrance of my own—the times Ida read me Ovid aloud on the terrace, the Cokes she'd given me in the bookish jumble of her bedroom. Violet and Rose had agreed not to give speeches, that Iris, professor and accomplished public presenter, would speak on behalf of the Serafino sisters, and so after half an hour, it appeared that the speeches were winding down and that Alessia could make her way to the stage. I glanced over at my grandmother's table, where Ida, still moved by Milo's speech, dabbed both eyes with a crumpled tissue. Beside her, Alessia sat crosshatching the frosting on her cake slice with the tines of a fork.

As the guests returned to their own tableside banter, to the business of pouring coffee or sipping a digestivo or eating dessert, something happened that we didn't anticipate: Silvio Ruffo pushed back his chair, stood slowly, and began to hobble toward the stage with his cane. It couldn't have been more than thirty feet he needed to travel, but I remember the sensation that time was dilating, that he'd been moving across the terra-cotta tiles for eternity. The clinking of silverware welled up from the corners of the room, where the waiters were busing the last of the dinner plates, and above the diners' heads I could see Elisa watching Ruffo's advance, arms folded, her head cocked incredulously to one side. When he finally made it to the stage, he gripped the microphone with one hand, brought it a few inches from his mouth, and shot a pneumatic sigh through the PA system. His suit coat was unbuttoned, his trousers hitched with suspenders almost up to his sternum, a stem of dried lavender in the buttonhole of his lapel.

"*Signore e signori*, my name is Silvio Ruffo and I am ninety-six years old." He took little sips of air, coated the room with his amplified, wheezing breath. He reached behind each ear to calibrate his hearing aids, first one, then the other. "I was born here, in the town that has been slowly dying for centuries, in one of the houses that is still standing. It's been there, right across from the church, since 1756. Not quite as old or fancy as the villa we now stand in. My father started the pharmacy across the bridge and I took it over and then my son and now my grandson runs it. We have always been simple, hardworking people. We have cured Valetto's headaches and fevers and eased her gases for a long time."

Pockets of generalized, polite laughter. Alessia still refused to look up from her cake plate. I saw my grandmother place a consoling hand on her back.

"What I remember about this town is the same thing I remember about Italy. That she was once a solid thing built with the toil of honest hands, with dignity and fervor, but that she let her springtime bloom go to seed. We have all lost the eternal flowering of our youth."

He took a breath, gazed up at the ceiling fresco, made a little sonic dent with his chin against the microphone.

"Today, this place, like most of the country, is filled with false and sentimental ideas about who we really are. The truth is that we've been ruined by communists and the Mafia and British imperialists, and it's been that way since the last war. Italy died, if you ask me, on April 28, 1945."

This was the date Benito Mussolini was executed. This recollection hovered for a moment before it shot through the room with such force that people nearly dropped their dessert forks. For the first part of Silvio Ruffo's speech, the guests had deferred to this ancient, ravaged head behind the microphone, to the omniscient, gauzy regard, but now they groaned, folded napkins, and let them drop on top of cake plates. A few couples got up and walked from the dining room into the brightly lit hallway. Elisa crossed the room to be with her mother while Roberto Ruffo stood from his table, buttoned his sports coat, and started for the stage to prevent further embarrassment to the family name.

"*Roma è eterna*," Silvio Ruffo enunciated into the microphone. "All men die, but ideals alone can live forever. The Italy that I believed in, *la patria*, with her ginestra flowers and piney woods and golden orange groves, with her laurels and true people united by a common cause . . . she can never truly die. Everything I did here, for the true cause, so that ancient Rome could flourish again in our blood and bones, came from the righteous chambers of my own heart and mind . . ."

I remember intercepting Roberto Ruffo as he made his way to the stage and the startled look in his eyes when I told him, in Italian, to take his fascist mongrel of a grandfather back to his seat. When he bristled, I stepped up onto the lip of the stage and forced the microphone from Silvio Ruffo's varicose grip. I stood close enough that I could smell the grappa on the old man's breath, see the cheese crumbs on his lapels, but he regarded me as if at a rheumy distance, blinking slowly, patiently, as if he'd conceded a pawn in the dwindling twilight of a chess match. From the side of his mouth came *Non puoi fermare la storia*. You cannot stop history. And then he turned back to his audience, telling them that uniform Christian thought and action was the very thing that we had all lost, and so I grabbed him by the elbow and began to forcibly remove him from the stage. Roberto Ruffo yelled at me to unhand his grandfather and then, somehow, Milo and his two sons materialized at the foot of the stage. In the commotion,

Milo implored me to please release Signore Ruffo, that they would escort the two gentlemen back to their seats.

"*Per favore, Hugh, lascialo andare.*" Please, Hugh, let him go.

I turned to see that I was now holding a very old man who weighed less than a hundred pounds by the back of his spindly neck. I could feel the tremolo of his pulse against my fingertips and the dry parchment of his skin. I could see the whites of his watery eyes as he kept me walled in his peripheral vision. Pushing some air between my lips, I let my hand go slack at his neck and brought my fingers to my sides. Milo continued to triage Roberto's rant while one of the Scorza sons extended an arm to help the elder Ruffo, who used his cane to step off the stage. We all watched and listened as the contrail of Ruffo indignation faded across the room and the family delegates reclaimed their seats.

I stood alone on the stage. For a moment, it looked as if three generations of Ruffo pharmacists might gather their things and retreat in protest, so I brought the microphone to my mouth and said, "My name is Hugh Fisher. I stand here today as the son of the late Hazel Serafino, the youngest of Ida's daughters. You must excuse my actions, but Silvio Ruffo has done grave harm to my family, to my mother."

The room guttered into silence as the Ruffos settled in their places. In fives and tens, one table at a time, all two hundred guests turned their attention toward me. The dead were being invoked, ancestral lines were being named. The waiters stopped clearing dinner plates and stood motionless in this newly charged atmosphere.

"My mother was nine years old in the spring of 1944, when Silvio Ruffo, as the town's only member of the fascist party, abducted her and Alessia Parigi from the villa and cruelly interrogated them. Alessia was one of the refugees from the north that my grandmother took in during the war. My mother has passed away, but I believe she never fully recovered from this ordeal, that it stunted her. Perhaps not just because of the interrogation itself, but because of what happened afterward, because of the deaths of innocent men. She blamed herself."

I looked out at the tables and waited for the next thing to come out of my mouth. I expected my throat to be burning with rage, to feel my heart hammering in my chest and ears, but I felt oddly calm and unhurried. Whatever adrenalized flood had led me to grab the old fascist by the neck had ebbed away. I was self-possessed, making an inventory of the room—the shoes pointing my way under the tablecloths, the poised coffee cups, the burning chestnut logs snapping in the hearth. I pointed toward my grandmother's table. "Alessia Parigi is still alive and sitting here with my grandmother."

Alessia sat with her eyes down, Elisa and my grandmother holding her hands.

"Silvio Ruffo kept the girls locked in the cellar of his house for three days before they escaped. This is all documented in letters from my mother and in the testimony I've heard from Alessia Parigi. Today, we, the Serafino family, denounce the actions of this man and we demand a public apology."

In Italian, my denunciation was all staccato consonants and enunciated vowels. I could feel it ripple through my jaw and throat—*Oggi noi, la famiglia Serafino, denunciamo le azioni di quest'uomo e chiediamo una scusa pubblicha*...I moved the microphone into my other hand and took a breath, just as Roberto Ruffo waved a big arm in the air, loosened his tie, and delivered a soccer stadium roar that boomed under the frescoed ceiling—*Che carico di stronzate!* What a load of bullshit! He surveyed his family at the table, looked indignantly at his father and grandfather, O-mouthed and appalled. "This American bastard knows nothing about this town. He insults us like we are fucking dogs!"

Greta Ruffo sat very still, her face ashen, her husband's hand in hers. A few tables away, Nina was helping my grandmother from her seat and they were negotiating whether or not to use the wheelchair. Then I saw Elisa guiding Alessia by the elbow into the curving aisles between the tables. The four women started slowly toward me, and I watched as my aunts, one by one, fell in behind them, slow and dignified in their day frocks. Before long, all nine of us were crowded onto the tiny stage, Alessia small and frail beside me. Elisa took the microphone from me and very slowly handed it to her mother, who held it like a burning candle. When she bent her elbow to bring it closer to her mouth, I wondered if she'd ever heard her own amplified voice.

When it finally came, her voice was small but definitive. She didn't look at the crowd, but at some private point through the windows at the back of the room. "*È vero,*" she said, recoiling for a second against the reverb. "It is true that on May 16, 1944, when I was eight years old and Hazel Serafino was nine, Silvio Ruffo came down to the villa and asked us to visit his sick daughter, Greta. He told us that if we came to his house, we could share the treats that he'd bought for her."

Alessia stood very still and straight, an invisible wire connecting her spine to the ceiling. "When we got to the house, we fell asleep with something he put into the hot chocolate and we woke up in the cellar. It was not until the third day that we could escape."

Roberto Ruffo yelled *Queste sono tutte bugie!* These are all lies!

Elisa leaned into the side of her mother's head and whispered something. Alessia took the microphone in both hands and floated it a few more inches from her mouth. She clenched her eyes shut, opened them, found her visual ballast at the back of the room again.

"He led us into his study and made us take off our clothes and stand on two chairs. He rubbed animal fat onto our bodies and let his dog scratch and growl and nip at us until we told him what we knew. It felt to me like we stood on those chairs for a very long time, but in truth I don't remember how long . . . He told us that he would kill our families unless we told him when and how Aldo Serafino had left the villa, whether the family was hiding British prisoners of war. We told him about the two escaped prisoners hiding in the cave below the villa gardens, and a few days later their bodies were found mutilated in the piazza."

By the time she lowered the microphone to her side, Roberto Ruffo had stopped yelling. Distantly, almost imploringly, he said, "*Queste cose non sono vere. La signora sta ricordando male. Succede.*" These things are not true. The lady is misremembering. It happens. Then he looked at his father beside him, and then at his grandfather on the other side. The old fascist regarded the space above the table, the way he did during a chess match, then shook his head very slowly and resolutely. He folded his arms and set his jaw in defiance. "See," said Roberto Ruffo, widening his attention back to the transfixed room. "None of this can be true."

Alessia shifted her weight from foot to foot and made eye contact with the members of the Ruffo table for the first time. "In the wall of the cellar," she said simply, "we scratched our initials and the date with a nail. Perhaps it is still there beneath the house."

All two hundred guests, who'd been leveled by this rupture of the celebratory peace, allowed themselves to now discuss the allegations at hand. Many had been forced to sit with strangers and old adversaries, and so the deliberations were cautious, almost formal, a roomful of conference attendees discussing some hypothetical moral failure. But then a few former residents old enough to have roiling memories of the war spoke up, their voices trembling and overwrought. They affirmed Silvio Ruffo's connection to the fascist party, that he was widely known as an informer to the Germans, and that they'd kept him alive because of the pharmacy. "We turned a blind eye after the war," said a hard-bitten man from Spoleto. "As long as he moved away. In hindsight, we should have shot him out in the woods or hung him from the bell tower."

The Augustinian nun at my table, flushed to the earlobes with prosecco, tales of saintly plunder, and a public denunciation, stood abruptly in her black habit and orthopedic shoes and suggested that we investigate the allegations by going to see if the initials were still inscribed in the cellar wall. The other nuns from her convent levied a wary glance at her from their tables, but the idea was already galvanizing the room. Aunt Iris, stirred by this forensic turn of events, called out from the stage—*An excellent idea, Sister!*

Roberto Ruffo got up from his chair and addressed the nun across a few dozen heads: "Let's say the initials are there, Sister. How do we know the girls didn't play sometime with Greta down in the cellar?"

Roberto Ruffo and the nun stood staring at each other over the sea of cake plates and emptied grappa glasses.

I heard a woman's voice and it took me a moment to realize that it didn't belong to the nun, that it belonged to Greta Ruffo. She remained seated, clutching her husband's hand.

"Could you repeat that, signora?" asked the nun.

"I wasn't friends with Hazel Serafino or any of the children at the villa. They never came to my house when I was in school. At the end of April 1944, my brother and my mother and I all went up into the mountains to stay with my mother's parents. My father stayed behind to watch over the house."

Roberto Ruffo began to pat down his trouser pockets. "We have stored pharmacy supplies in the house for many years and I have the key right here. We have nothing to hide. Please, anyone, come see for yourselves!" He said it with such bravado that I suspect he couldn't imagine more than a few morbid guests taking him up on his offer.

But something unnamable was pressing down on the room. We had opened up a fissure in the town's history and stood staring into its seismic depths. The guests remained silent for a long time, unsure of where to look or what to do with their hands, making small calibrations of wristwatches, necklaces, and water glasses, caught between Italy's ironclad sense of decorum and her centuries-old infatuation with spectacle. Even if most of the room knew that these allegations were true, I didn't expect many would want to bear them witness.

The Augustinian nun went to the front of the room, took Alessia by the hand, and led her out into the entrance hallway. In twos and threes, and then fives and tens, the rest of us followed, funneling back out into the sunny Umbrian afternoon, our centennial birthday procession flowing in reverse, up through the terraced gardens and back into the alleyways, the Ruffos pulled magnetically through the crowd, Roberto Ruffo still in flummoxed denial, Greta still holding her husband's hand, the fascist grandfather trailing slowly in the rear with his cane. I walked somewhere in the middle of the crowd, pushing my grandmother along in her wheelchair.

We all assembled outside the Ruffo house, amid the silken flags and wooden benches in the piazza. The accused stood twenty feet away, facing the stone steps, and the guests flanked him on either side, behind some invisible cordon. Roberto Ruffo climbed the stairs, unlocked the door, and switched on the hallway light. Alessia trailed behind the nun, picking her way up the stairs with her alpine walking stick, followed by Elisa and my aunts, then Susan and Marcella. My grandmother insisted on coming inside, so Nina, Milo, and I helped her out of her wheelchair and very slowly up the stairs, one at a time, and then down the long hallway. We passed rooms filled with boxes and slipcovered furniture, rooms choked with the smells of old newspapers, bandages, and topical ointments. The door to the cellar had to be jostled into submission, and the stairwell lightbulb had burned out long ago, but with a few cell phone lights we all ventured down slowly, Nina and Milo bracing Ida's forearms for support, and me in front to block a potential fall.

With the nun at her side, Alessia took her bearings at the bottom of the stairs and led us to the now empty shelves against the stone wall. She took hold of Elisa's phone and began to scan the wall with a spray of digital light. Even now, Roberto Ruffo prattled in denial, apologizing for the state of things, telling us how the cellar hadn't been used in many years and that he suspected, actually felt quite certain, that rats had taken up residence. "In the winter," he said, "they seek shelter and can squeeze through the tiniest chinks in the stonework . . ." Alessia moved around the space with the light, picking out pockmarks and divots, the fingertips of one hand splayed against the wall as if to read Braille. Eventually, she lit up six inches of etched stone:

H.V.S. + A.C.P.

MAGGIO 1944

We all studied the spot. Alessia said, "Hazel Veta Serafino e Alessia Carmen Parigi," and Roberto Ruffo, who'd finally stopped speaking, stepped forward, craning into this tiny LED universe. He traced one fingertip along the curvature of the letters and it seemed important to him that we see him deliberating, nodding, deciphering. Then he reached inside his trouser pocket, pulled out his own phone, and adjusted it to turn on the flash before capturing the illuminated square. He looked down at the photo on his screen, studied the transcript of the proof, then looked back at the wall to compare it with the proof itself. He made a small clicking noise with his mouth, shone his phone at his feet, and lit his own methodical ascent up the stairwell and into the hallway. We could hear his footsteps above us as he walked down the hallway toward the front door. Milo and I helped my grandmother back up the stairs, while Elisa and Marcella helped Alessia. We emerged in front of the birthday guests, disoriented, our eyes adjusting to the daylight. My grandmother, exhausted, sat back in her wheelchair and Nina placed a blanket over her lap. Silvio Ruffo had turned away and now stood with his cane, looking into the air above the valley through an aperture of space between two houses.

Roberto Ruffo stood inside the conferring semicircle of his family, showing them the picture on his phone, beginning with his father, then Greta and her husband, then the rest. He walked over to his grandfather and held the phone out in front of the old man's face, but Silvio Ruffo shook his head and looked down at his feet. Frustrated, Roberto turned away to find that the crowd had formed a long line behind him, orderly as a bank queue, and they were waiting for the excavated proof to be passed around. He obliged and the phone moved along at a clip, beneath nods and sighs and grave shakes of the head. When it came full circle, Roberto put the phone in his trouser pocket and folded his arms. After a moment, I realized that all two hundred of us were staring at the back of Silvio Ruffo's bald head as he gazed out onto the valley. It was unclear what would happen next. We were a people tethered to history but loosed from protocol.

From the stone steps, Iris cleared her throat to get everyone's attention and said, "If nothing else, we demand an apology. A public acknowledgment of the pain and suffering this man has caused our families. Some gesture of remorse."

A murmur moved through us and settled into communal agreement, but Silvio Ruffo refused to acknowledge the voice from the stairs or the crowd behind him. He walked slowly across the square with his cane and lowered himself onto the church steps. As he sat, a few inches of his hairless, papery shins appeared above his black dress socks. It's hard to say what he could have done in the unraveling minutes to appease us. Begged for forgiveness, wept into his moth-colored suit sleeve, prayed to Santa Maria Goretti, the patron saint of forgiveness? Frustrated by his position across the square, some of the guests began making sorties and delegations over to the church steps, entreating and threatening the old man on behalf of the Serafino and Tomassi-Parigi families, appealing to his sense of decency, to the Ruffo family name. It had the atmosphere of some ancient morality play, a stylized public reckoning.

There were deliberations about strategy among men who played bocce together, speeches of recrimination from war veterans, reframings of history by widows who swore they would never step foot inside the Farmacia Ruffo again. Silvio Ruffo ignored all of these appeals, and when a widow took it upon herself to slap his face in outrage, none of the Ruffos intervened on his behalf. They stayed in their semicircle at the periphery of the square.

When I finally walked over to stand directly in front of Silvio Ruffo, I asked him calmly to apologize and accept responsibility for what he'd done. I could see pinpricks of red blushing to the surface on the cheek where the widow had slapped him. He looked up at me from the wide church steps, blinking slowly, his mouth slightly open as if in thirst, and then he reached behind both ears and switched off his hearing aids. In an instant, I could see the sonic world drain away from his oyster-colored gaze. And it was from inside that fortress of silence or half-sound that he continued to stare up at me, holding me in place for several seconds. Then something shifted, and he reached for his cane to pivot himself up off the steps, and he moved into a gap between two houses, out toward the perimeter path above the valley.

The crowd implored the Ruffo family to take charge of the situation, to convince their elder to return and ask for forgiveness, but the family looked on helplessly. Some yelling and sobbing ensued, and it was Sister Antonio, the Augustinian nun, who discovered, all at once, that it was coming from a dozen children who were standing in our midst. Our communal reckoning with the past was already traumatizing the present and the future. The nun announced that this was

no spectacle for children, and their parents, slightly stupefied and ashamed, began to hold the younger ones close and
then usher their charges back to the villa to collect coats and
shawls and children's backpacks.

"Before you all leave," Iris said from the stone steps, "Silvio Ruffo needs to be taken from this place, and he can never
return. When he dies, he cannot be buried in the Valetto
cemetery. We must all understand this, even the children."

It had the ring of textbook sociology or anthropology, of
something lifted from a study of degradation rituals. We
were sending him into exile. The Ruffo family seemed to
grasp this banishment immediately, as if an ancient code of
conduct lingered in their veins. In the Ruffos' ragtag Umbrian lineage—peasant forefathers, Roman confederates, in-
vaders and defenders of the isthmus—some had surely been
outcast along the way. When they buttoned their coats and
cinched their scarves against the cooling afternoon, we all
understood that they had brought their belongings with them
from the villa, that regardless of the outcome they had known
there would be no return to the Serafino hearth. Roberto
Ruffo looked up at Alessia on the stone stairs of the house,
made the sign of the cross, kissed his fingertips. He said, "Signora, on behalf of the Ruffo family, I am deeply sorry for the
actions of my grandfather. It is a stain on our family name
that cannot be erased. May God grant you peace." When
they walked away, it was toward the Etruscan archway
and the footbridge and not in the direction of their disgraced
patriarch. The front door of the Ruffo house stood open, a
single lightbulb still burning from the depths of the hallway.

19

The denunciation had blown through the villa like the tramontana, the Umbrian winter wind that sometimes hurls itself out of the valley to loosen roof tiles and down trees. In the aftermath, we moved through the rooms in a silent daze. During the epic cleanup—the dishwashing, the stacking of rental chairs and tables, the bundling of table linens into laundry baskets—nobody spoke of what had transpired. My grandmother retired at her usual time with a pot of fennel tea, at the threshold to her second century, and Marcella and Susan led Alessia back down to the cottage before it was fully dark. My aunts vanished, one by one, into their apartments, Iris with her hand on Rinaldo Fumigalli's tweed elbow. As I walked between rooms, looking for stray wineglasses and appetizer plates, I kept coming upon Milo, now in his shop coat, sweeping ash from the hearthstones. We were cautious and wordless with each other. What was left to say on the matter of a spring night in 1944, or about a man who had refused to make amends for his misdeeds? History does not offer us closure. It offers us the inscrutability of the present. It offers us a river of paper, or a digital ocean whorled by so much flotsam.

Drifting back into the kitchen, I watched as Elisa stood alone, disassembling the vintage Volano meat slicer to clean it. As she bent over to peer into its inner workings, I asked her if there was anything left for me to do and she said that this was the last of the cleanup. I told her that I wanted to go down into the valley and throw the pocketknife I'd stolen from Silvio Ruffo into the river. That maybe this would give me some sense of completion. She wiped the disc blade with a bleach-soaked cloth, not looking up, as if she'd known about the pocketknife all along.

"Give me ten minutes and I will come with you," she said. "Unless you want to be alone."

"I'd like you to come," I said.

And so we picked our way down the chalk-white pathways into the valley after dark, stood by the river as it flowed, dark and silty, at our feet. Before I tossed the knife into the river, she took a moment to study it, opened the blade and ran her thumb across its edge.

"He kept it sharp," she said, handing it back to me.

I tossed it out toward the middle of the river and we listened to its tiny *plunk*. I wanted that sound to mean something, to be satisfying, but the sound and the gesture struck me almost immediately as hollow. I tried to imagine the knife washing downstream, that it might be found by a farmer or fisherman who would use it on an apple or a piece of bait, without any thought of its history, but all I could conjure was the knife buried in clay and silt.

"Did it matter?" I asked. "What we did?"

"It mattered," she said, looking into the moonlight scaling the water. "We shamed him in front of everyone. We shone some light down into the cellar of that house. That meant something to my mother, I think, though I doubt she will ever speak of it again. After we walked back to the villa from the piazza, she told me that she wants to go home to the mountains and doesn't want to see the psychologist in Milan again."

"My mother thought therapy was a kind of sorcery."

"I want to believe that in her mind, she has finally stepped off that chair. That she feels some kind of healing. Will you let me believe that?"

"I will let us both believe it."

We stood for a few moments, listening to the wind and the river, before climbing back up to the town. The idea of sleep seemed impossible, so we walked up through the terraced gardens, past the cottage, and back toward the piazza. Before I knew it, we were walking along the perimeter path along the edge of the volcanic pedestal, out toward the spot where a bronze plaque commemorates the vanished house of the medieval Franciscan saint, the wrought iron staircase that spirals into midair above the valley. I hadn't been back to the Saint's Staircase since I was a boy, not since that morning I climbed down to find a figure rearing up at me through the fog. Despite knowing it had been a trick of light and perspective—a shaft of raking sunlight pinning my silhouette onto a vaporous cloud—the sense of dread I'd felt on the stairs had stayed with me, off and on, for years. It returned during blackouts and storms, during in-flight turbulence, and on those white afternoons when Clare was dying by the hour in the bedroom we shared. And it had come for me—I realized now—when I sat reading my mother's lost letters under a slate roof in the foothills of the Alps.

So when I saw Silvio Ruffo sitting on a low wall by the

gated entrance to the stairs, the thickening in my throat was immediately familiar. Hours after his denunciation, unclaimed by his family, he sat with a few purring stray cats at his feet, feeding them scraps of salami and prosciutto from his pockets. As this surreal vision settled over me, my mind gravitated to the idea of him putting sliced meat into his pockets during the antipasto course of the birthday party and that he'd been carrying it ever since. In all likelihood, his pockets were full of charcuterie during all phases of the denunciation. When Elisa saw him I felt her whole body tense beside me. She took my wrist to pull me up a dozen feet away.

I'd be lying if I said I didn't feel a moment of pity for the old man, wondering how he'd get back to the nursing home, whether his disgraced children planned to leave him out here all night. My brain went to logistics, to the impossibility of bringing him back to the villa or walking him across the footbridge. So I pulled out my cell phone and dialed the local carabinieri headquarters in Bevona, told the disgruntled officer that a ninety-six-year-old man had been abandoned in Valetto and he needed to be collected by the Ruffo family. I told the officer that the grandfather was by the Saint's Staircase and that he should go knock on the apartment door above the Ruffo pharmacy. Elisa stood silently beside me, mesmerized by the sight of Silvio Ruffo tearing a ribbon of prosciutto and hand-feeding it to a tabby with a kinked tail.

Maybe his hearing aids were back on, maybe he heard everything I'd said into my phone, but he didn't let on by turning in our direction. Instead, after a long silence, he pinched his trousers above his bony knees, used his cane to leverage himself into a standing position, and shuffled over toward the spiral staircase. There was a padlocked iron gate and a danger sign in front of the staircase, but like most deterrents against falling off the rim of Valetto, it was far from foolproof. If you were determined to get onto the stairwell, all you had to do was step over a foot-high stone ledge farther down the pathway and then circle back on a narrow strip of gravel and dirt. And that's exactly what Silvio Ruffo did, with a fair amount of effort, planting his backside on the ledge, then lifting his legs one at a time to swing them over, then reclaiming his cane on the other side.

When he got to the top of the stairwell, he gripped the iron railing, used his cane to anchor himself to the step below, and began his halting descent. To navigate the corkscrew bend, he had to adjust his hips and upper body in tiny increments. All this is to say that we had a full minute or so to stop him or call out his name. I heard Elisa wonder in Italian what he was doing, but we both knew what he was doing. I remember that when he paused on the bottom step he finally craned up at us through the spiraled iron railings, his chin lifted, his body taut with defiance. I've revisited that moment countless times in the years since, trying to understand the hollowed-out expression on his face, or why I experienced a moment of magical thinking, certain that it was his figure that had startled me on the stairwell as a boy—a premonition in the fog. Looking up at us, he had the wild and imperious stare of an injured bird of prey, a lame goshawk unhooded and appalled by the loss of his empire. He turned away, took a breath that lifted his shoulders, extended the tip of his cane into midair, and stepped into the blue void of the valley. We heard the updraft billow through his suit like the snap of a spinnaker. Then we heard the muffled impact of him hitting the cliffs a hundred feet below.

We waited for the carabinieri to arrive with a Ruffo

delegation, but when they came an hour later, it was only Roberto with them, his hair tousled, wearing sweatpants and slippers. It was striking that only the grandson had come, and I wondered whether the son or the daughter guessed what had taken place. The carabinieri asked us detailed questions about what we'd witnessed and why we didn't intervene. *Eravamo sotto shock*, Elisa said, We were in shock, though we both knew that didn't quite cover it. Then there were phone calls and radio dispatches, a helicopter was roused from some distant outpost, and we all waited into the dawn hours for the body to be airlifted and taken to a nearby morgue. One of the carabinieri took notes about the birthday celebration, about our grievances against the old man and the denunciation, and we were told that they might have further questions and that we'd be asked to make official statements at the local headquarters. Roberto Ruffo explained to the carabinieri that his grandfather had been Umbria's oldest living fascist, and that *ha fatto molto male qui*, he did great harm here.

"And did you come for your grandfather after this denunciation?"

Roberto said, "We returned to look for him after the party, but he'd already vanished. I walked all through the town, calling his name, but he was hard of hearing."

There was something perfunctory about the way he said it, and I wondered if the young officer believed a word of it as he wrote it down.

"*Allora, di chi é la colpa?*" asked the officer, shrugging. Then who is to blame?

He wasn't necessarily looking for an answer, but I said, *Storia*, History, and I was serious, but also enjoyed watching him add it to his mental list of suspects. The sun had come up, warming the air with pinesap and turning the chalk-white ridges on the western side of the valley the color of saffron. I took Elisa by the elbow and we started back for the villa.

φ

It was only in the retelling that Elisa and I grappled with our silence at the stairwell. After breakfast, we assembled Alessia, the widows, our children, Milo, Donata, and Rinaldo, to describe Silvio Ruffo's final moments. We all sat in the library, nursing cups of tea and coffee. At first, there was palpable relief that Silvio Ruffo had been loosed from the world, but then there was a discussion about whether or not we'd collectively sent him to his grave and whether Elisa and I should have stopped him.

"It felt like watching a big wave about to crash on the shore," Elisa said. "It didn't seem like we could stop it."

I described the way he sat with the stray cats, feeding them scraps of salami, the look on his face right before he stepped off the bottom step.

"We might have opened the doorway," my grandmother said from her wheelchair, "but he is the one who stepped through it. And what you're describing has nothing to do with remorse."

"*Esattamente*," Elisa said. "But there was also something dignified and ceremonial about it, like he was making an offering. Was it to us? I don't know."

"*Non era un'offerta*," said Alessia from the corner. It was no offering. She'd brought in a small spool of wire and sat wrapping some pieces of quartz for one of her creations. "*Stava riprendendo il controllo*." He was taking back control. "He wanted to be the one to decide how this story ends."

We all watched as she continued to wrap stones with wire, and we must have all decided that it was right for Alessia to have the last word on the subject. When he was buried in a shepherd's cemetery up in the Umbrian mountains a few days later, there was no obituary in the local newspaper, just his name and the dates that bookended his life.

20

Susan was due to fly out of Rome two nights after the birthday celebration, and I'd forgotten to arrange a ride with Milo. I hadn't had much of a chance to talk to Susan during the preparations for the party or in its aftermath, and so the thought of sustaining a three-way conversation with Milo as our chauffeur felt exhausting. When I told Elisa about my predicament, she insisted that I borrow her Jeep to take Susan to the airport. It wasn't lost on either of us that I was the first person she'd ever loaned Floria to, and the keys came with a detailed set of instructions and cautions, about the heater and the car's tendency—never her intention—to speed on the autostrada. She asked me to text her when I was leaving the airport. I thanked her several times, took Susan for a final lap of the villa to say her good-byes, and then we were crossing the footbridge in the falling dark.

As we wended down from the Umbrian hills in the Jeep, Susan said, "I'll come back for Christmas."

"I'd like that."

"Will the Parigi-Tomassi family be here?"

"Why would they be here?"

"No reason."

"What?"

She looked at her reflection in the darkened passenger window. "She seems good for you."

"What does that mean?"

"It means I haven't seen you look at anyone, let alone a woman, the way you look at her. Not since Mom died. Every time Elisa Tomassi walked into a room you stopped slouching. Marcella and I agree that something has probably already happened."

"I forgot about these millennial conspiracy theories."

She took a sip of water from her metal canteen, and I wanted to tell her that these days they provide water on international flights.

In the luminous green pall of the dashboard, she said, "Well, has it?"

I let the silence become almost unbearable. Then I said, matter-of-factly, "She kissed me in Milan, when she was dropping me off at the train station."

Susan laughed a little breathily. "*She* kissed *you*. Goodness, I hope she didn't force herself on you. Did you kiss her back?"

"This might cross some kind of boundary. These are personal matters."

"I love you and I want to know what's going on in your life."

"I don't ask you about your encounters."

"*Encounters*. Dad, seriously? Sometimes I don't even know how you landed in this quadrant of the twenty-first century. You are welcome to ask about my encounters, I assure you, but, to cut to the chase, there haven't been any since my first term at Oxford, when I slept with a boy from the Midlands with a sweet accent and a remarkable stutter. So, did you kiss her back?"

"Yes, I kissed her back."

"And?"

"Well, it was in a moment when we were saying goodbye, so I think that distorts things. She thought she'd never see me again."

"She's into you, Papa, trust me. Marcella agrees."

I threw out a scoffing sound and, despite the Umbrian chill, adjusted the heat down a notch. I couldn't pinpoint when Susan had appropriated the word *Papa* in moments of well-intentioned condescension, but it always made me bristle, like she'd grown up on a farm in Amish country instead of knowing the name *Foucault* by the age of twelve. She used the *Papa* invocation rarely, but it struck me now as her own kind of well-honed chess move—a flanking fianchetto advance. I studied the road and the dashboard gauges as if they were oracles.

"She does the same thing you do. Stares at you like you're the only thing in the room."

"You should be writing romance novels," I said.

"They'd all end badly." She turned the heat back up to its previous position. "So what happens next?"

I shrugged, re-gripped the steering wheel at 10 and 2, checked my speed. Italy is full of speed cameras whose locations are designed for unwitting tourists. Over the years, I've received half a dozen fines in the mail, delayed by months and forwarded by a peevish rental car company with a letter in blustery Italian legalese. "What time is your flight again?" I asked.

"Don't change the subject," she said. "When I come back

for Christmas, I will be very disappointed if you tell me that you didn't make a second move. A straight woman might kiss a man once, but she's certainly not going to repeat it without some kind of overture from you."

I moved into the slower lane so that I could better defend whatever I was about to say or deny next. "Is there economic data to support this theory?"

"If we're being economic and pragmatic about it, there's absolutely no reason for any of this to happen. You've both procreated and she's past childbearing age, so the planet and the gene pool don't have any skin in the game. There's no utility in it, but there's data that suggests happier people spend more freely, so, by that reasoning, some nano-portion of GDP hinges on your next move."

This made me laugh with sudden delight. "I can't wait until you're a professor and some hapless student wanders into your office hours. They won't know what hit them."

φ

At the airport, despite Susan's protests, I insisted on parking and walking her into the terminal. With her backpack, Guatemalan-fabric laptop satchel, the now emptied canteen, and the noise-canceling headphones around her neck, it was hard to say whether she was taking a two-hour flight back to England or heading into the tropics. She looked like an ornithologist about to start fieldwork in South America or the Congo. I asked her if she needed money and she squinted at me like a road sign coming into focus. "You're always trying to give me money," she said, "which is sweet but also slightly annoying and unnecessary. They give me a stipend, and it's plenty, and I make extra from tutoring."

I kissed her on the cheek, said I love you, and she pulled me into a tight embrace.

"I'm proud of you for standing up for Grandma," she said into my left ear. "Mom would have been proud as well."

This shot through me so quickly that I was forced to wipe away tears over her right shoulder.

"That's my signature move," she said as we came apart, grinning but also a little teary. "Make Dad cry before I get on a plane."

"You're excellent at it," I said, biting my bottom lip and searching through my pockets for my handkerchief. "The other one is asking Dad if he's ever going to stop moping after his dead wife while standing in the nosebleeds at the Colosseum. I think you've also done it in restaurants and once, if memory serves, at a neighborhood garage sale."

"Timing and location are everything in a good emotional ambush," she said. "Incidentally, you may be the last man on the planet still using a handkerchief. They're kind of gross."

"I see others out there. They're popular among retired men of a certain age," I said, laughing, enjoying this chiding ritual that always took the edge off our goodbyes.

"I'll text you when I land," she said.

"Please do."

I watched her stand in line for security until she turned around and waved me off.

φ

As instructed, I texted Elisa that I was leaving the airport in Rome. She immediately responded with *e com'é La Floria?* I texted that Floria was running like a dream, and that I intended to make serious headway into her CD collection on the drive back to Valetto. She directed me to a Milanese band from the 1970s called Aktuala, an eclectic mix of Arabian, African, and Indian influences, and I found myself pushing toward the Umbrian hills in a downpour of November rain, with exotic music filling the interior. Behind the steering wheel, I felt weightless and my mind began to drift. I saw myself in outline, or as viewed from above, the headlights picking through the trees, the road vanishing in my wake; heard the mystical twang of a sitar through a cracked window as if I were listening to a stranger's life swiftly passing by. This brash car and this enigmatic music were briefly my own. I tried to conjure my guest lecture on abandonment, to mentally run through what I'd written so far, but I found myself instead imagining all the ways by which I might make an *overture*—that was the word Susan had used, which, it struck me now, also meant an orchestral piece at the beginning of an opera.

For the past six years, during my commutes, in basement archives, or while waiting in line at the supermarket or to board a flight, the cascade of my thoughts had always flowed toward Clare, to the catalog of my memories with her. As I over-revved the Jeep into a tight turn, I couldn't remember the last time I'd lingered on her sitting at the dinner table to tell me about her day or singing down in the basement amid the smell of melting candle wax. I saw a line of trees up ahead, all banded in white, where no doubt other motorists had met their end on dark, rainy nights, and as I braked an enormous clenching sensation buckled through me.

Like many middle-aged men, I have thought every now and again about what a heart attack or stroke might feel like, and I wondered for a second if this burning sensation was just that. I pulled to the side of the road, turned the music off, the rain lashing against the soft-top roof, and I took a few balloon breaths. I suddenly remembered my father turning the radio off whenever he got lost on our Sunday drives—in those tessellated, submarine memories from before he left us—and I wondered if I was the sort of man who would turn off the radio so that he could die without static or distraction on an Italian roadside. I waited for the next big sensation to pummel me, and when nothing came I wanted to believe that I'd reached the bottom of something. Here was a door swinging open, an anchor pulling free. *There is no bottom*, Evelyn Woodrow had told me in her chiropractic museum turned therapy room, *just moments and hours of forgetting*. I suspected this to be true, but sitting by the roadside, listening to the metronome of the windshield wipers, I felt both fearful of forgetting my previous life and exhilarated by the idea of a leveling out.

I reached for my phone and pressed *(ICE) Clare* in my favorites. Fifty percent of my *In Case of Emergency* contacts, it occurred to me, were dead, but now the number was ringing, a number that had been released into the digital commons several years ago. It was after midnight in Umbria and after 6 p.m. in Michigan, in the hemisphere of the 734 area code, but none of this occurred to me as I sat in the lashing rain listening to the ringing tone. When a man's voice answered—*Consolidated Plumbing, this is Charles*—I listened incredulously.

Hello?

Sorry, I might have dialed the wrong number.

Were you after a plumber?

This number, I said, used to belong to my wife.

That right? I got it a couple years back on a new carrier. Old one had dead zones everywhere.

She died. Back in Michigan six years ago.

Aw, jeez, I'm sorry to hear that, buddy.

She always liked the number because it was easy to remember.

Yeah, it's real nice. The three sevens stick in people's heads.

Sorry to bother you. I must have accidentally dialed the number.

It's not a problem. Death is a hard thing. I lost a younger sister a few years back. Miss her terribly.

Sorry for your loss.

Yeah, thanks. Well, listen, if you ever need a master plumber, we do excellent work.

Actually, now that I think of it, I've had some issues with an intermittent leak in the basement.

You and half of Michigan.

We both laughed.

All right, I'll keep your number.

Sounds good. You have a great day.

You as well.

It's hard to say why this two-minute phone call with a stranger shifted my mood, why the idea of Clare's number passing to Charles the plumber, whom I might someday hire to diagnose a slow leak in my basement, filled me with a kind of peaceful resolve. I added *Charles, the plumber using Clare's number* into my contacts, and continued to drive. When I stopped to fill Elisa's tank with premium unleaded outside of Orvieto, I checked my college email account on my phone and saw a history department invitation to a holiday potluck, and it was the thought of these potlucks and my annual rotation of casseroles—sweet potato, chicken tamale, turkey potpie—that settled the matter: I would invite Elisa out for dinner. I texted her that I was twenty minutes away

and filling her tank with the most expensive unleaded gasoline that money could buy. La Floria deserves nothing less, I
texted. She texted me back to say that she would meet me at
the footbridge to pack a few things. I texted: ?

```
Marcella wants to finish an assignment at
the library in Milan. And Mamma is
homesick for the Alps. So we will leave
first thing tomorrow morning.
```

As this change of plans fell through me, I resisted the
urge to call and plead with her to stay another night. Instead,
as the rain eased, I drove the final stretch of road without
music, trying to imagine what the empty cottage and life
without the entanglements of the past month would look
and feel like. When I pulled the Jeep alongside the foot of
the bridge to park, Elisa was waiting with a flashlight, looking up at me as she directed me into a spot with the beam of
light, as if I were taxiing a 747 into a gate. I opened my door
and got out, saw that she'd brought a suitcase and a tote bag
over the bridge.

"Signore," she said, "I will need to inspect the vehicle
before you return the keys."

"Of course."

I stood next to her as we walked around the car. She
smelled of woodsmoke and pomegranates. She shone the
flashlight over the wheels and doors and hood. "Everything
seems to be in order," she said, running a finger along the
paintwork. "No new scratches or dents."

"I'm relieved." I placed the keys in her palm.

"How did you like Aktuala?"

"Trancelike," I said.

"Yes, probably not great for late-night driving."

"I enjoyed it."

She opened the tailgate.

I said, "I wish you weren't all leaving tomorrow."

"Marcella and Mamma are getting fidgety."

"I understand."

I picked up the suitcase and handed it to her. She wedged it beside the spare gasoline canisters. From behind her, I said, "Because I was going to invite you out for dinner."

"How nice," she said, her voice muffled from inside the car. "I'm sorry we won't be here for that."

"No, I meant just the two of us."

She closed the tailgate, turned to face me, smiled graciously. The flashlight was still on and aimed at my feet. "Perhaps some other time."

"You know that the offer to share the cottage is still on the table. You can come back any time. I will be here until the spring, but there's plenty of room for you, or all of you."

"That's very kind."

"I'll sleep on the couch or up at the villa if you all come. And if it's just you, you could have the bigger room," I said, looking away, "and I can take the bedroom in the back."

"No, I wouldn't like that arrangement," she said.

"Or the other way around. Whichever you prefer."

She moved the beam of the flashlight up from my feet, blanching my knees. "In fact, my preference would be that we share the same bedroom."

My instinct was to mumble something indecipherable. There existed a parallel universe where my hands were in my pockets and I snuffed out the moment with a nervous chuckle or a change of subject. Instead, in this universe, on this particular night in Umbria, I forced myself to move out of the shining circle around my legs and step toward her. Her face was in darkness, beyond the rim of light, and when I leaned in to kiss her I heard an exasperated, disembodied voice utter *finalmente*, and then I heard the sound of the flashlight clicking on and off, as if she were sending Morse code behind my back and out into the valley.

We walked over the footbridge and through the town holding hands, talking in the onrush of something new. She said she would still be leaving tomorrow but that perhaps she would come back for another visit, once her mother and daughter were settled back into their routines. As part of my research, I'd been planning to visit an abandoned town up near the Swiss border and knew I'd be passing through Milan just before Christmas. As we came into the terraced gardens, I asked if I could visit her on the way back. We looked up at the villa—a hulking cruise ship on the brow of the hill—just in time to see the last lamp being switched off.

Back at the cottage, we kissed quietly good night in the kitchen and then again in the darkened hallway before we went to our separate sleeping quarters. In my exhilaration, I made a fire and texted Susan so that she'd know about my overture.

> I made the move and it went well. You were right. I think she likes me.

A few minutes later, when a return text came in, I realized that I'd accidentally texted Clare's old number and that Charles the plumber had responded:

> Great news! Keep us in mind for that mysterious basement leak.

This made me laugh out loud, and when I texted the mishap to Susan, she responded an hour later from a taxi on her way back to her college at Oxford—

> Michigan's master plumbers also want this
> to happen!!!

From the couch, I watched the fire kindle and take hold and eventually begin to roar.

φ

In the month before I went north, the villa settled into a new routine. After her umbrichelli triumph, Donata started cooking again, and several nights a week we all dressed for dinner and sat at the big table under the fresco, including my grandmother in her wheelchair. Milo made his rousing chestnut-and-oak fires in the hearth and we spoke more about the present and the future than the past. The villa's revitalized condition sparked discussions of other improvements that could be made, from replacing some banisters to wallpapering the entrance hall to re-shingling a section of roof. "The Serafino villa has always been a bet against time," my grandmother said one evening. "In the end, we can't possibly win, but we must keep increasing the odds." During these dinnertime conversations, I noticed that Iris and Violet had softened toward each other in small but noticeable ways—with occasional moments of eye contact or agreement, with the stray offer to refill a wine or water glass. The claims and regrets of the past may not have been fully settled, but they no longer hobbled every moment between them.

In late December, I drove a rental car north toward the Austrian and Swiss borders, where a lakeside town had been abandoned in the 1960s. A power company building a hydroelectric plant had received permission to blast an area in the mountains to join two alpine lakes into one, thereby flooding the town permanently. After the evacuation of the townspeople and subsequent deluge, the only structure in the town that wasn't underwater was the bell tower of the medieval church that had been deconsecrated before the flood. An old woman who'd been born in the town had taken refuge in the bell tower and refused to come down. To take a stand against the power company and its actions, she rang the church bell in protest, almost without pause, for three days while journalists and locals looked on. I'd seen newspaper photographs that depicted the president of the power company pleading with the old woman from the bow of a dinghy. Eventually, she agreed to leave, but only on the condition that the church tower and its bronze bell remain intact.

And so I came upon the frozen lake on a remarkably still day in January, the dogtooth rim of the Alps jagged against a winter-blue sky. I'd discovered online that the lake froze solid and that it was safe to walk on, but I was cautious edging out from the icy lakeshore. From a distance, the bell tower resembled an obelisk jutting from the middle of a field of ice and snow, its Gothic portals and the bronze bell coming into relief as I got closer. Walking across the snow-dusted ice, the grinding of my footsteps amplified by all that alpine air, I could see pockets of thinner ice below, places where the opacity ran to turquoise, the way the shallows of a Nordic sound or a fjord or inlet can look tropical in certain light. And as I stared into these lighter blue depths, I thought about the ruins below, about the houses and chimneys of the town.

Craning up at the stone campanile, I realized that there was a long rope attached to the side, connected to the bronze bell above, and that this must have been part of the old woman's legacy, the protester who'd refused to abandon the place where she was born. My instinct at museums, cemeteries, and other kinds of hallowed ground is to be as still and silent as possible, not so much out of earnest respect but from fear that I will overwhelm the moment with the wrong sentiment, word, or phrase. I studied the rope, wondered who came out here in the winter to replace it over the years, trekking across the ice with an extension ladder when the rope grew frayed and brittle.

I stood for a long time craning up at the bell tower. Eventually, I took the rope, wrapped it around one gloved hand, and lowered myself into a squat. When I pulled, I couldn't see the bell from the base of the tower, but I heard a wooden groaning from up above, followed by the swivel of the headstock, and then the bell began to ring. It took a few pulls before I got my momentum going, but soon the bronze tolling filled the envelope of thin air above the frozen lake, echoing off the mountains and curving back at me as if I were standing under a dome of glass. I closed my eyes and felt the sound moving through the ice, imagined it ringing through all those empty rooms beneath my feet.

φ

Acknowledgments

I'm thankful for the 2018 NEA Literature Fellowship that allowed me to travel to Italy and explore abandoned and semi-abandoned towns and villages. Although Valetto is a fictional town in Umbria, it draws some of its history, culture, and geology from the real town of Civita di Bagnoregio in Lazio. Special thanks to Nancy Josephson and Stephen Day of the Civita Institute for helping me gain access to the town and its history, and to Tony Costa-Heywood, who has lived in Civita since the 1960s and was generous enough to share his memories and experiences with me. Nancy Josephson was also an attentive early reader, as were Michael Parker and Karen Olsson—thank you! Gratitude to Malena Villegas, who brought her Italian translation skills to the page during copyedits. I'm so thankful for my incredible editors—Jenna Johnson at FSG and Jane Palfreyman at Allen & Unwin—and for my trusted agents, Emily Forland and Gaby Naher. Your continued guidance and belief in my work mean so much to me.

As someone who grew up with three sisters, I was first inspired to write about a "sistership" when I read this line in W. G. Sebald's *The Rings of Saturn*: "Frederick was born in Lowestoft in 1906 (far too late, as he once observed to me) and grew up there amidst the care and attention of his three sisters Violet, Iris and Rose." As a nod to this inspiration, I decided to use the same names for three of the invented Serafino sisters.

I'm indebted to a large number of books and articles as part of my research, especially:

Pellegrino Artusi, trans. Murtha Baca and Stephen Sartarelli, *Science in the Kitchen and the Art of Eating Well* (1891; repr., University of Toronto Press, 2003).

Luigi Barzini, *The Italians* (1964; repr., Touchstone, 1996).

Italo Calvino, trans. Archibald Colquhoun and Martin McLaughlin, *The Path to the Spiders' Nests* (1947, rev. 1964; trans. of rev. ed., Ecco, 2000).

Iris Origo, *War in Val D'Orcia: An Italian War Diary, 1943–1944* (New York Review Books Classics, 2018).

John Seabrook, "Renaissance Pears," *The New Yorker*, September 5, 2005.

Maria de Blasio Wilhelm, *The Other Italy: The Italian Resistance in World War II* (Norton, 1988).

Alec Wilkinson, "The Serial-Killer Detector," *The New Yorker*, November 20, 2017.

Finally, a profound thank-you to my wife, Emily, for her tireless patience, love, and support, and to my two daughters, Mikaila and Gemma, who are inseparable sisters in their own right.